THE HAUNTING OF QUENBY MANSION

J.S DONOVAN

Copyright 2019 All rights reserved worldwide. No part of this document may be reproduced or transmitted in any form, by any means without prior written permission, except for brief excerpts in reviews or analysis.

Created with Vellum

1

LAST WILL AND TESTAMENT

It was dark, and the moon was full. Georgia bugs chirped in the humid air. A breeze rattled the leaves of fat Southern oaks. At the end of the brick road, ominously named The Path, stood the momentous Antebellum relic. Seventeen rooms, 2.5 stories high, and a survivor from a bygone era, the Quenby House was rich with history and had a set of colonnades on both the first and second floor. Spotted with little white flowers, vines and ivy climbed the mansion's chipped white paint and around the tall glass windows. More roses and thorns bloomed around its base.

In the night, silhouettes of neglected cabins and a struggling cotton field were visible beyond the massive building.

A dim glow leaked from one of the mansion's upper windows.

Apart from the flame dancing on a candlewick, the study was dark with tall bookshelves, chairs with cracked leather cushions, and a number of wilted flowers that decorated the windowsills and tabletops. There were other antiquities too, but none were a concern to Maxwell Quenby.

Hunched over his great grandfather's desk, Maxwell, a forty-eight-year-old man with sunken cheeks, a patchy beard, and red-rimmed eyes, heard movement in the long halls of his Antebellum-era home. In the candlelight, sweat glistened on his creased forehead and greasy black/gray hair. He hadn't bathed in days, and though the study was spacious, his natural odor seemed to hang in a cloud over his head. His calloused hand scribbled feverishly on the page before him.

It was the most important note of his life.

The first and last thing he'd say to the daughter he never knew.

Since the widow Cecilia and her lover Abel Quenby I completed the plantation decades prior to the civil war, every important document was signed on this heavy wooden desk. From the purchase of the first slave in July of 1843 to the final cotton sale in March of 1875, the deep scratches and ink stains on the desk's wooden surface ran as deep as the family's blood.

Muffled voices leaked through the walls.

Maxwell twisted back at the sound. *They found a way into the corridor.* His nearly black, beady eyes returned to the page. His vision blurred from his lack of sleep. A bead of sweat raced down his nose. Moving his lips, Maxwell read his draft. It was garbage. He balled up the page and tossed it back to the mountain of crumpled paper.

He pulled another sheet of paper from the pile and let his pen go to work. His hair tumbled down over his tired eyes. He should've cut it ages ago, but time escaped him. Time always seemed to escape him.

The doorknob to his study jiggled violently.

Maxwell's heart throbbed in his chest. His breath quickened.

The next draft of the letter dragged. He crumpled it up and threw it with the rest.

Light seeped through the bottom of the door.

More indistinguishable voices. They got closer.

Last time, Maxwell promised himself and made the note brief. It wasn't loving. It wasn't rude. It wasn't perfect, but it was what it needed to be. Maxwell forwent that perfectionist's voice and folded the letter with his trembling hands.

The door rattled on it hinges. The lock wouldn't hold much longer.

Maxwell slid the letter into a red envelope. His tongue traced the envelope's lip, and he sealed it tight.

Wood cracked behind him as something heavy slammed into the door.

Maxwell scribbled the day and time he wished the letter to be opened. If all else failed, the delivery must be precise.

Crack!

He set the letter aside and pulled open his drawer. His trembling hand withdrew a dusty snub nose revolver. Candlelight bounced over the tight frame. He checked the cylinder. Six rounds. He prayed to God it would be enough.

With a crash, the door swung open.

In the threshold, the figures looked like shadows, but Maxwell knew they were so much more. His finger squeezed the trigger desperately. The gun misfired. Maxwell leapt from his chair, knocking it over. The figures charged him. Their hands grabbed at him and tore the weapon from his grasp. He reached desperately for something to grab onto, but his efforts failed him. He was yanked from the study, screaming the only name that came to mind: his daughter's.

2

EVELYN

Detroit had its own pulse and noise. Sirens, shouting, and the bays of unseen dogs were the natural sounds of the manmade habitat. Iron clouds blanketed the stars, though even on a clear night, the city's glow would hide them.

With shifty eyes, Evelyn Carr watched the multi-story tenement from the opposite sidewalk. Her hair was blonde and her body slender. The pockets of her belted, black, double-breasted raincoat warmed her hands. Through the coat's lining, she felt the extendable baton concealed under the jacket.

An ambulance screamed down the damp road, splashing water on the curbside and on the toes of Evelyn's black heelless ankle boots.

Standing between the glow of two hooked streetlights, Evelyn withdrew the picture of the girl a final time. Twenty-two years old, raven black hair, and floral tattoos up her arms, upper chest, and neck, Molly was a college dropout, a societal failure, and another shadow in a city of faces. No one cared that she had been missing for seventy-two hours except her high school friend Alice, a good Christian girl, and the burnt-out thirty-three-year-old private investigator Evelyn Carr.

Evelyn refolded the picture and tucked it away. Looking both ways, she crossed the street. A granite-faced man smoking a cigarette on the tenement steps glared at her as a wisp of smoke seeped from his busted lip. His hard look was one Evelyn was used to. Just like most places, she wasn't welcome here.

Evelyn pushed through the double doors. The sound reverberated through the entrance hall followed by her boots clacking on the scuffed tile floor. She reached the elevator without passing another soul. It hummed and rumbled as it climbed the building, finally spitting Evelyn out on the seventh floor. The ceiling light flickered in the hallway that ended at room 712. Muffled heavy metal music thumbed through the closed door. Evelyn hammered her fist on its face and took a step back. Harsh bass and wicked guitar riffs replied.

She knocked again, much harder this time.

The doorknob jiggled, and a moment later, Evelyn faced a skinny man wearing only tight jeans unbuttoned above the zipper. Though not muscular, the pasty-skinned twenty-something year old had a toned body painted with skulls, naked ladies, and other decadent tattoos. A happy trail climbed from his beltline and to his innie belly button. His jet-black hair was combed to the side of his roguish face. Casually, he rested his forearm in the frame of the door. His dark eyes licked Evelyn from head to toe. The foggy haze lingering in the dimly-lit apartment behind him drifted over her.

"I'm here for Molly," Evelyn stated.

The shirtless punk smirked. "You her mom or something?"

Evelyn ignored the comment. "Tell her to come out here."

"She fine where she is."

Evelyn shook her head slightly. "No."

"What is that supposed to mean?"

Evelyn pushed past him. Their shoulders knocked together, and the unsuspecting boy stumbled back.

"Hey!" the punk shouted.

Evelyn stepped into the apartment den reeking with the stench of all sorts of herbal substances. Poster of various metal bands and scantily clad woman were tacked to the wall. Old food and used heroin needles sat on the glass coffee table in plain view.

The punk yelled at her again. Evelyn guessed he was commanding her to leave, but the overwhelming music drowned out his words. There were empty beer bottles in the kitchen sink and pizza on the stove, but no sign of Molly. Wasting little time, Evelyn bustled down the hall that became further mystified by thick smoke. From behind, a hand grabbed Evelyn's forearm. She turned back to the punk. He screamed over the speakers. "I will call the police!"

Evelyn stared at him with a cold face. "Really?" she asked sarcastically, bouncing her eyes to the drugs before yanking herself from his grasp. The punk stood dumbfounded as Evelyn reached the bedroom door and shoved it open.

The room was painted crimson like blood, with cheap red candles glowing on the dresser. It was like a scene out of some low-budget vampire movie. At the edge of the bed, Molly rested her head on the shoulder of another shirtless punk. She held a burnt spoon in one hand and a lighter in the other. Both of the twenty-something year olds sat up in alarm at Evelyn's approach.

The punk behind Evelyn spoke up, "She just walked in, man. I don't know what to do."

"Molly," Evelyn said, revealing her P.I. license. "You're coming with me." She grabbed the girl's wrist.

"Ow!" the girl shouted as she was pulled from the bed. "What are you doing?" she said with angst.

The punk on the bed rose to his feet in defiance. "Hey, let her go!"

Evelyn gave him a look that caused him to sit back down. He mumbled a few unpleasant words. Molly's wrist in hand, Evelyn twisted back to the shirtless punk who greeted her at the door. With her free hand, she withdrew the baton from under her coat and extended it with the flick of a wrist.

The punk's eyes widened.

"Excuse me," Evelyn said, feeling his tension. The ball of the baton pushed up the man's chin. He raised both hands and stepped aside.

"Jared?" Molly called as she was led out of the room, expecting the punk to do something.

The punk didn't move.

Taking Molly with her, Evelyn hustled out of the apartment and back to the elevator. When the door closed and the rumbly descent began, Molly wrenched free of Evelyn's grip. The goth girl rubbed her sore wrist. "You a cop or something?"

Molly's lack of resistance spoke volumes. There was hope that she'd be saved after all.

"Alice sent me to find you." Evelyn watched the digital floor numbers tick down. "She was worried that you relapsed."

"Alice?" Molly scoffed, but then averted her gaze.

Evelyn put away her baton. "When this door opens, I'm going to my office to meet with your friend. You can come with me or stay in the elevator."

"You didn't give me much of a choice back at the apartment," the girl mumbled.

"I thought you could use some persuasion, but I can't hold your wrist forever."

The elevator dinged. Evelyn stepped out without looking back. The girl's fate was her own. The elevator door closed. Quiet footsteps followed behind Evelyn. In silence, the two women walked the sidewalk together.

Black hair tossed by the wind, Molly crossed her arms over her chest. Goose bumps speckled her pale skin. "What are you? A private investigator?"

Evelyn stepped in a puddle. "Something like that."

"Are you allowed to be dragging people around?"

Evelyn didn't reply.

Two blocks down, they reached the parking meter and dingy minivan. Corrosive spots and peeled paint revealed the metal of the hood.

"You're taking me in *that*?" Molly complained. "Will it even run?"

"I didn't take you as a woman of class," Evelyn climbed into the driver seat, not waiting to see the girl's reaction. Reluctant, Molly took shotgun. They drove on damp streets and by skyscrapers spotted with glowing windows. The Tuesday night crowd gathered in long lines outside of nightclubs. Hobos and other street crawlers huddled under awnings that still dripped from the evening rain forty-five minutes ago. Cop cars zipped by, rushing to the scene of a crime.

Evelyn turned the car through an alleyway beside a cheap buffet restaurant. A gruff chef with an apron stained with greasy fingerprints tossed a bag of trash into the growing mound outside his back door. A skeletal cat ran out from behind it.

Evelyn parked her van in the small lot behind the adjacent office building: an old brick structure that had been standing for nearly a century.

"Do my parents know that I was..." Molly's voice trailed.

Evelyn turned the key in the ignition. The car sputtered off. "It was Alice that reached out to me. I've heard nothing from your parents."

"Figures," Molly replied. She covered her eyes with her palms. "Ugh. I'm so high right now."

The comment didn't surprise Evelyn. She turned to the girl. "Ready to go up there?"

"No," Molly replied. "I mean, I don't know. All my stuff is still at the guys' apartment."

"I'll pick it up in the morning," Evelyn replied.

Molly met eyes with her. "Why?"

Evelyn didn't have an answer. After locking the car, they hiked up the metal stairs at the back of the brick building. Evelyn sifted through her key fob and tried the lock. She had to jiggle it a few times before it opened. The room was little more than a metal desk and few chairs. Rusty street light oozed through the window blinds faded from exposure to the elements. Cinnamon caches placed through the room gave it a lively smell.

Dressed in a floral-patterned blouse, nice jeans, and spotless white tennis shoes, Alice stood by the desk and chewed her nail. She was a cute girl with a bob cut and an air of naiveté.

"Molly!" She squealed and hugged her tattooed friend. Molly didn't reciprocate the warm embrace.

"How did you know where I was?" Molly asked.

"I didn't," Alice replied. "She found you."

They both turned to Evelyn silhouetted in the doorway. Evelyn could've explained how she used the location finder from Molly's social media pictures to lead her to the various nightclubs, bribed the bouncers, reached out to club regulars, jotted down descriptions of the men, found one of their angry exes, got the punk's address, and waited until they had settled in their flat before making her move. Instead of saying all that, Evelyn smiled with pursed lips.

"Stay with me tonight," Alice said, taking Molly's hands in her own. "We'll take you back to rehab tomorrow."

"I got out last week," Molly replied. "I can't go back like this."

"This is the best time to go back," Alice replied. "Before you backslide any worse."

Molly grunted. "I'm not backsliding. I was only having fun."

"That fun almost killed you last time, and if not for Mrs. Carr, it may have killed you this time," Alice said. "Did you even know those guy's names?"

Molly didn't reply.

"Oh," Alice perked up. She pulled a white bank envelope from her back pocket and handed it to Evelyn. "I almost forgot this."

Evelyn took it and opened the tab. She counted a few fifty dollars bills inside. "That's very generous of you." Evelyn reexamined the money. *I really need to raise my fee.*

The two girls said their goodbyes and exited. Evelyn closed and locked the door behind them. She removed a cash box from her desk and studied the contents within. It was never a good month when she could see the bottom of the box. The last few months were bad. It wasn't a matter of how hard she worked or how good she was. Her livelihood depended on the client and how much they were willing to pay for her services. It sucked, but that was the reality of her business. Evelyn finished locking up the office and headed upstairs to her rented apartment.

The familiar sour stench of wood polish splashed Evelyn as she entered. After all these years, it was a surprise the chemical hadn't killed her sense of smell. Her husband Terrence stood amidst curled wood shavings littering the floor beneath the kitchen table. His large hand brushed a stained rag across the body of a freshly carved violin. A half-dozen violas and fiddles dangled from a taut metal wire connected to two walls. A wide wooden tool rack was nailed to the adjacent wall. It held chisels, clamps, wire cutters, strings, and other luthier tools.

"Hey," Terrence said without looking back.

"Hey," Evelyn replied and pressed her body against his back. She wrapped her arms around his chest, snuggling herself ever closer to the love of her life. "Hungry?"

"I have rice on the stove and the crock pot going." Terrence put down the rag. He turned to Evelyn, keeping his stained palms on the table's rim. Terrence stood over six feet. He had dark skin and a little chin beard he took pride in. As a blues and country lover, his shirt always had some sort of instrument pattern decorating them. Tonight, it was little guitars--the first instrument he learned to build--that were the size of polka dots. "How was it today?"

"Long," Evelyn replied. "You?"

"Made a sale," Terrence said with a smile.

Evelyn didn't want to remind him that bills come early tomorrow morning.

They enjoyed their meal in relative quiet. Conversation hadn't been either one of their strong suits. Both of them worked odd hours, and even though they thought about having a child, the timing and cost never seemed right. After they finished clearing their plates, they took a shower together. Water cascaded down the deep grooves on Evelyn's back. The scars reminded her of the "accident" all those years ago. She thought the crash would be the end. Instead, she met Terrence. The man who had saved her life. They were very different people. Evelyn bent the rules. Terrence was by the books. Evelyn folded to the back of most crowds. Terrence liked to be front and center. Pessimist: Evelyn.

Optimist: Terrence. Evelyn could go on and on with their differences, but it was their commitment and love that kept them strong.

The sun came up too early. Evelyn untangled herself from her strong husband. She flipped on the kitchen lights and made an omelet filled with red peppers, diced ham, and shredded cheese. She glanced at the cluttered dining room table that had slowly become Terrence's workshop over the last few years.

Evelyn slouched on the couch and put her plate on a cheap collapsible table. She sifted through the bills and rubbed her brow. It would be another close month. How many more of those would she have left before the close calls caught up with her? As she sealed away paid bills, she found a letter addressed to her by an attorney named Duncan Peters. Evelyn stared at it for a moment. The name didn't ring any bells. She opened it and pulled out the document.

The letter began, *"I write to you in regard to your father's estate..."* Evelyn paused. Rays of the morning sun climbed across the carpet floor and her pale cheek. She re-read the sentence and stopped at the word "father."

She had no memories of the man, or her mother. Evelyn was an ugly baby. A little pink screamer no one wanted. Her youth was a blur of orphanages, where she was too "unruly" to get adopted. At eighteen and with no parents, she was on her own.

Until she met Terrence.

Evelyn continued reading the letter. Its contents were vague about the inheritance and who her father was. It seemed more like an invitation than a legal document. Evelyn gave the lawyer a call.

"I'm sorry, but I'm under specific obligation not to discuss the contents of the will over the phone," Duncan Peters said.

"You expect me to drive two hours with no information about my father or his will?"

"If you wish to collect your inheritance, you will need to arrive in person. That was the deceased's final wish. I must adhere to it."

After the call ended, Evelyn let the couch swallow her up.

"What was that about?" Terrence said, standing in the hallway in his boxer briefs, toothbrush in his mouth.

"My father," Evelyn said, almost disbelieving.

Terrence stopped mid-brush. He stepped back to the bathroom, took out his toothbrush from his mouth, and spat in the sink. "Babe, that's great."

"I suppose," Evelyn put the letter aside. "It seems fitting that the only contact I'll have with the man is reading his will."

Terrence folded onto the couch next to her. "I'm sorry, but hey, maybe you'll finally get a chance to find out who he is."

Evelyn rested her head on his shoulder. A stir of emotions swirled inside. She didn't know if she should weep or rejoice. Why leave her the inheritance when he never once reached out to her? Was the letter a mistake?

Evelyn made a trip to the punks' house to clear her head. They opened the door slightly. "You know why I'm here," Evelyn said.

The punk slammed the door in her face. Evelyn kept her hands in her coat pockets until the door reopened and the bundle of Molly's clothes was thrown haphazardly into the apartment's hallway. Evelyn made the trip to the rehab center and dropped off Molly's stuff. The girl said some kind words and ended with the conversation by saying "I hate this city."

Of that, Evelyn agreed.

Terrence and Evelyn made the trek to the lawyer's office. The room had been painted a drab gray and displayed several paintings of large ships and beautiful mountain vistas. Duncan Peters was a heavy-set man with a droopy face, graying brown hair, and rimless glasses. He sat with fingers locked on the table. Terrence and Evelyn sat opposite of him in cushioned chairs designed to make the process easier. Evelyn found them uncomfortably soft.

Peters gave them both a pitying smile. "I'm sorry for your loss, Mrs. Carr."

"I didn't know him, but thank you," Evelyn replied.

"Let's begin," Peters lifted the weathered red letter from the top of his desk and cleared his throat. He read the handwritten print on its front. "To Notary Duncan Peters. Whether or not my body is found, deliver this letter to daughter Evelyn ten years after I'm presumed dead. Only on the tenth of March."

Evelyn leaned forward. *March 10th was the day I was put up for adoption.* "Ten years?"

"Yes," Peters said stoically. "I've had this letter in my possession since that time."

"Shouldn't you have told me about this?" Evelyn asked.

"I was left clear instructions not to," Peters replied. "Shall I proceed?"

Under the table, Terrence squeezed Evelyn's hand. Evelyn nodded.

Peters ran the sword-shaped letter opener across the envelope. He removed a single sheet of paper from within. "To Evelyn, my daughter. My heir. I failed you in life. I will not make excuses or justify my actions. That time is dead and gone. I will leave you with the only thing I have to give: my estate. Enclosed within this note is the key to our family home. May it give you more peace than it did me. Your father, Max."

Silence hung in the room for a moment.

"Is that all?" Evelyn asked.

Peters nodded and handed her the old gray key. "The address as well. 1 Quenby Avenue, Adders, Georgia."

"Adders? Never heard of it," Terrence said.

"Most people haven't," Peters said. "It's hardly a blip on the map."

"You lived there?" Terrence asked.

"I got out as soon as I could," Peters said, leaving no room for further questioning.

Evelyn took the key. It was heavy and spotted with rust. She locked eyes with Peters. "In his will, he said that if he is presumed dead. What does that mean?"

"Maxwell vanished from his home ten years ago. All of his possessions were accounted for. However, the body was never recovered."

"What happened to him?" Terrence asked.

Peters shrugged. "The police have been asking that question for many years."

On the drive back, Evelyn pinched the key between her finger and thumb and spun it slowly before her eyes.

"I didn't expect that. I wonder what happened to your father?" Terrence kept his eye on the road as he turned right.

Evelyn had about as many answers as Terrence. None. "If he was alive, someone would've known. But it's been ten years... and he wrote a will."

They drove farther up the road. Terrence smiled. "I wonder how big the estate is?"

Evelyn tucked away the key. "I don't know. Either way, we can try to flip it."

"It's your family home," Terrence said, as if Evelyn didn't know.

"It's in Georgia. What are we going to do with a house in Georgia?" Evelyn asked rhetorically. "I've never been south of Tennessee."

"I say we check it out," Terrence said, smiling. "It could be an adventure."

"Who's paying for it?" Evelyn replied, harsher than she had anticipated. Maybe the ordeal was doing a number on her after all.

"We have a little in savings," Terrence replied. "I thought you'd want to know more about your heritage?"

"I do, but... the timing's wrong," Evelyn replied. She studied the key again. *The timing's always wrong.* Her investigative instinct pulled at her like an itch she couldn't scratch. She knew practically nothing about her father and even less about her mother. "Ah, hell, let's do it. I could use a vacation."

"Now you're talking," Terrence said with childish glee.

They took a stack of money from the lock box and packed up the minivan with a month's worth of supplies and Terrence's luthier tools. If they were traveling that far down, they needed to clean the place and get it ready to put back on the market. Evelyn didn't know if she'd make it back down to Georgia again.

It was a long drive down south. Evelyn and Terrence spent most of it on highways that descended into woodland areas. Terrence woke her up when they passed the state sign. *Welcome to Georgia: the state of adventure.*

Following the GPS, they reached Adders without a hitch. Established in 1837. Estimated population: seven thousand. Once they got to town, Evelyn had to rely on a map to find Quenby Avenue. They drove through the small downtown area made up of farmer's markets, old brick and wood buildings, and rubbernecking locals. Beyond the town were sprawling cow pastures and horse farms.

The rusty minivan turned into a street flanked by pastures outlined by wooden fences similar to what one would see surrounding a civil war reenactment sight. Clusters of sprawling old trees spotted the outcropping. Evelyn lowered the window and allowed herself to take in the breeze. Unlike the city, the air was fresh, cool, and seemed to revitalize the soul.

Evelyn watched black and white spotted cows blur by. Her mind wondered as it did when she was a child. Were her parents rich or poor, happy or sad, nice or cruel? She stopped asking questions in her teens when she realize no one would adopt her. Back then, she was the ugly kid with long limbs, pepperoni face, and a bad attitude. The last part was an act. Evelyn didn't want to be adopted. She wanted to wait for her real father to return. After high school, Evelyn got a woman's body and well-structured, beautiful, but intimidating face. It didn't make her very approachable, and the reality set in that she'd be alone. *Focus on the house,* Evelyn reminded herself. If it was worth something, it could be the big break she needed to start her family.

They continued down a single lane road. Terrence pulled to the side of the street, allowing a big truck with a dead buck tacked down in the bed to pass by. The tobacco-chewing locals gave them curt nods and kept on.

"We aren't in Detroit anymore," Terrence said.

"What gave it away?" Evelyn said with a small smile.

Terrence playfully squeezed her knee. "There's that smile I've been missing."

"Keep your eyes on the road, buster," Evelyn said.

They drove by an old, two-story farm house. "You sure we're going the right way?"

Evelyn studied the map. "This is Quenby. It should only be a matter of finding the address."

A small road came into view. A white wooden sign was staked in the ground beside it. "The Path," the engraved blue text read. Below was the number 1. Terrence turned in, driving between rows of ancient, mossy-covered oaks that curled over the road.

"Look at this place," Terrence said with wonder.

Evelyn straightened her posture, awed by the beauty that she almost didn't notice the massive three-story plantation house at the road's end. Green vines with little white flowers climbed its walls and colonnades. Untamed bushes and weeds sprouted from its base. It looked like it came right out of *Gone with the Wind*.

"This can't be it," Evelyn said. The white paint was chipped but well-kept. The windows were dusty but intact. Acres of farmland sprawled out behind it along with a half-dozen wooden cabins and a vast cotton field.

"Is that what I think it is?" Terrence asked as he parked.

"It looks like it. Come on," Evelyn climbed out of the van. The spring Georgia air was soothing. Plump white clouds surfed across the indigo sky. Weeds grew between the cracks of the red brick road. The large shadow of the house cast over them as they approached. The set of colonnades on the first and second floor gave the building a look of unparalleled grandeur that captured the Georgian ideals of symmetry and order. Evelyn and Terrence stopped before the massive house.

"There's no way," Terrence said and chuckled. "There's no freaking way!"

Evelyn smiled at him. "Race you to the door."

They bolted between the pillars, laughing until they stopped at the door. Evelyn fished out the key. Taking a deep breath, Evelyn slid the key into the lock and twisted.

Click.

The door opened with a rickety groan. The mansion smelled of dust and old books.

"This is your father's house?" Terrence asked and rubbed both hands up his shaved head. "Holy crap."

They stepped into the large foyer big enough to host forty people. Clouds and angels were painted on a vast mural on the domed ceiling. Two sets of symmetrical stairs bowed up to a balcony with a hand-carved railing. Paintings in gold leaf frames decorated the walls boasting images of the mansion, the pastures, and the cotton fields in their prime. The floor had a thin red carpet over hardwood. It was dirty and dusty, but nothing important had been damaged.

"I'll get this out in the open," Evelyn said. "If we learn that my parents were a bunch of slave-owning bigots, you can't divorce me."

"Deal." Terrence craned his head back to one of the paintings on the wall. "I'm no art dealer, but that--if it's original--is worth at least four grand."

Evelyn wasn't the crying type, but today seemed the exception. "Terrence..." She wrapped her arms around her husband and turned her gaze to the painted angels on the ceiling. They had sly smiles, rosy cheeks, and long golden trumpets. Their soft eyes seemed to follow Evelyn as she moved. Age gave the mural the texture of cracked dirt.

Terrence finished speaking for Evelyn. "We're standing in a gold mine."

There were flame-shaped bulbs on the massive, multi-tier silver chandeliers overhead. Evelyn flipped the light switch. No luck. That wasn't unsurprising since the last resident hadn't paid the bills in a decade. Evelyn would be relying on fans and open windows to cool her. Even if she did have access to air conditioning, cooling this house for a day would cost more than her monthly rent.

Terrence and Evelyn grabbed some flashlights from the car and explored the halls. They were decorated with portraits of various men through the last two centuries. Their faces were stern and handsome with similar noses and jawlines, though some were inclined to plumpness and their eye colors were all a little different. Evelyn shined the light over each face, looking for a similarity between her and the men she assumed were her ancestors. The last portrait was from the 1930s, but the years descended down the hall ending at the oldest painting. It was a woman with long, braided blonde hair, alluring blue eyes, and small nose. Terrence looked at her and then Evelyn. "Yep. There's the one."

They continued the tour through the house, finding rooms where modern life clashed with the Antebellum era. They found stock investment books from the nineties, modern lamps, and updated plumbing in a few bathrooms. By the time they finished the tour, hours had passed. The house had seventeen rooms. These included three bathrooms. One needed new floors. Another appeared to be never used and had leaves filling the tub from an open window. The final bathroom was usable, but they'd need to get the water running before risking it. There were five bedrooms that were in various states of disrepair. All had different sized beds, wallpaper, and furnishings. Her father must've lived out the master bedroom because that was well-kept with a king-sized bed covered with an awning, a massive wardrobe, coat closet, two seater table, and more. The rest of the rooms included a study, billiard room, a bedroom containing objects like arcade machines and pool tables, two living rooms, a lounge, an art room, kitchen, and walk-in pantry. Finally, there was the basement that was a maze of clutter. There was an area in the center of the dark, sprawling, and dusty basement that had a couch, a TV, and two shotguns sitting upright on the cushion. There were a few boxes of shotgun shells that wore a coat of dust and were sealed.

"Oh," Terrence said and picked one up. He examined it. "It's loaded."

"Try not to blow a hole in the wall," Evelyn said, half-joking.

Terrence flipped on the safety and handed it to Evelyn. She was surprised by the weight and readjusted her posture to get a better grip on it. Terrence retrieved the other gun. "Let's see if these work."

"I don't know if we should be messing with them," Evelyn said.

"Everything here is yours, Evelyn," Terrence reminded her. "We can do whatever we want."

Evelyn rolled the gun in her palms. She smiled at her husband. "See if we can find some old cans."

"Now we're talking," Terrence replied and rushed up the stairs. Gun in hand, Evelyn followed soon after. *This house has got everyone acting spontaneous.*

They headed out the back and walked through the garden. It was lively, with all sorts of roses and other colorful flowers. There were a number of stone statues set up across the other grown brick path. Terrence would mimic their poses to get Evelyn to laugh. It worked. It was a good day to be alive.

They saw the cotton field to their left and the cabins nearby. There was also a stone building with a cotton gin and extra storage. Terrence found a nice spot on the rolling green plain spotted with oaks older than the plantation and roots so firm that they'd never be removed. Terrence set up a stand from scrap wood in one cabin and lined a few cans on top of it. He was a good shot. Evelyn was better. They were a little nervous someone would call the cops, but this wasn't a big city. Shooting a gun in the backyard was a rite of passage.

By the time they finished, it was sundown. Evelyn put the guns back downstairs and noticed a black spot on the ceiling. Terrence and Evelyn went upstairs and tried to find the room that had a leak. It seemed like it was beyond the hallway with the paintings, but there was no room behind that wall.

Terrence's stomach growled. They decided to head out.

On their way to dinner, Evelyn reached out to the local power company. The worker was a kind man with a Southern twang.

"Please, call me Jimmy."

It was dark when they rolled into town. "My husband and I recently moved into the plantation on Quenby."

"Maxwell's place. I know it."

"You knew my father?"

"I sure did. My family knew most of the Quenbys. They always paid for electricity years in advance. It ain't the smartest business decision in my opinion, but it kept us loyal to them."

"What can you tell me about Maxwell?"

"He was a reclusive man. Kind, though. Sad he went out the way he did."

They pulled into a mom-and-pop restaurant parking lot. "What do you mean?"

"Folks say he had enough. Went out to the woods one day and killed himself. No evidence of that, but it makes the most sense. I wish I knew more."

"Well, Jimmy, I'm his daughter. You think you can spot me a month's worth of power, just until my husband and I decide what to do with the house?"

"Daughter? I thought... never mind. I'll take care of you. Tonight hopefully. For Maxwell's sake."

"Thank you, Jimmy. You're really going above and beyond."

"I wouldn't treat a Quenby any other way."

Evelyn said her goodbyes and hung up, noticing that Terrence was staring at her with his handsome dark eyes.

"You get a lot done when you're nice." Terrence smiled.

"There's a time for war and a time for peace," Evelyn replied.

That night, they enjoyed some Southern deep-fried food,

mashed potatoes, and green beans. Terrence nodded along with a Southern blues band playing in the corner and joked about buying a cowboy hat. After they finished eating, he purchased a seventy-dollar white cowboy hat from the shop next door.

"Howdy, partner," he said when they climbed into the van.

"I don't mean to ruin your hootenanny, but shouldn't we be saving our money?" Evelyn said as they drove to the plantation for their first night.

"Eve, baby, it's all good. We own a mansion. We should live like it."

"That's what I call flawed logic," Evelyn replied.

"Come on now, girl," Terrence said in his best redneck accent. It was comically bad.

Evelyn laughed. "Fine. You can keep the hat. Only because it makes you look like a sexy cowboy."

"They call me the Black Stallion."

Evelyn couldn't remember the last time she laughed so hard. Terrence chuckled too, but it was clear he thought the name was much cooler than it was.

As the car rumbled down the red brick road flanked by symmetrical trees, light streamed from the mansion's upstairs windows.

"That was quick," Evelyn said, eyeing the house cautiously.

"I thought things moved as slow as molasses in the south," Terrence said and parked the car. "I guess they must've really liked your father."

"I guess." They stepped out on the circular brick driveway next to a stable house fit for a carriage and an accompanying hitching post. The grass around the brick was unruly and sprinkled with wild flowers just like the vines that climbed the dirty white walls. They pushed through the groaning double doors and flipped the switch. After flickering once or twice, the chandelier and various stained-glass covered lamps glowed with light and gave the house an elegant glow. By the dimmed shading, the chandelier's creator was going after the illusion of natural candlelight.

Evelyn tried out the sink. Water gushed from the faucet. It was dirty and brown for a few seconds and then became clear like crystal.

"This Jimmy guy, he's something else," Terrence said.

"I'm going to call him. Make sure he knows how grateful we are."

Evelyn left a voicemail and traveled upstairs to where the light streamed through the window. She couldn't find its source. *Odd.*

It was way past dark and Evelyn was tired. She climbed into the bathtub and washed her scarred body. The water was hot and steamy, filling the room in fog. How many elegant ladies had bathed in this tub? Evelyn felt giddy to think herself as one of them.

Suddenly, the faucet stopped and the power cut out. Evelyn soaked in hot water, with the room completely shrouded in darkness.

"Terrence?" Evelyn called out, letting water slosh out the side of the tub. She stood and felt her way to a towel. Wrapping it around herself, she tiptoed into the hall, careful not to slip.

"Terrence? Are you there?"

The hall light switch didn't work, either. The house was a black void. Evelyn felt her way to an oil lamp stand she'd seen earlier in the day, shook it to see if it still had oil, and then lit it up with the match set next to it. Being able to see about six feet in front of her, she navigated to the bedroom and pushed open the door. Terrence wasn't there.

"Terrence?" Her call echoed through the house.

"Down here!"

"Where are you!" Evelyn shouted back, heart pounding.

Using the lamplight, she carefully trekked through the creaking halls, by the odd vases and sculptures, and down to the foyer. She looked around, spotting the open basement door.

"Baby? Are you down there?" Evelyn said into the abyss before her.

No reply.

Carefully, she inched downstairs. Her light shined over the shotguns on the bed. She heard something through the adjacent red brick wall. It was a faint scratching noise.

Evelyn put her ear against the cold brick.

Scratch.

Scratch.

Scratch.

There was something behind the wall much bigger than a rat.

3

COOL DOWN

It sounded like someone was clawing on the other side of the wall. Evelyn couldn't bring herself to stop listening. The clawing was mesmerizing. Calming. Evelyn felt the scratching getting closer, like it was burrowing through the wall and toward her.

"Evelyn!" Terrence yelled from upstairs.

The lights flickered back on. The power returned to the house.

The scratching noise silenced. Evelyn pulled away from the brick wall. Her head was throbbing. She took inventory of herself. She still held the lamp. She was still wet from her bath. Hurrying upstairs and away from the long shadows of the basement clutter, Evelyn blew out the lamp and rested it on a nearby vase stand.

Terrence, dressed in his briefs and white t-shirt, looked back and forth through the hall until he spotted Evelyn.

"What were you doing down there?" Terrence asked

"Looking for you," Evelyn replied, holding her towel in place with her free hand.

"I went searching for the breaker box," Terrence admitted.

"I guess you found it," Evelyn replied, glancing at the lightbulbs illuminating the hall and foyer beyond.

"Yeah," Terrence replied "Still, we should get an inspector in here tomorrow. I don't want to be living in a house with faulty electricity. Even for a month."

"I heard something down on the other side of the basement," Evelyn confessed.

"What was it?"

"I don't know it. An animal maybe. It's hard to describe."

Evelyn led Terrence back down to the wall in the basement where she heard the noise. "Here?"

With pursed lips, Evelyn nodded.

Terrence knocked on the brick. "It feels solid." He put his ear against it. "Weird. I don't hear anything."

Always a little superstitious, Evelyn decided to give the basement a wide berth for the remainder of her visit. She reminded herself that she was an adult and should not be scared of such things. Nonetheless, she jogged up the stairs upon leaving the basement. She got dressed into her fitted but comfortable pajamas. As she put on her top, she studied her scars in the bedroom mirror. The deep etchings curved around her ribs just beneath her breast. She could shut her eyes and see the hazy fog lights of the semi-truck blasting toward her. The truck's horn blared like death's toll.

"You shouldn't be alive," the EMT said when they pulled her from the car that was crushed like a soda can. Terrence, a handsome stranger who stumbled upon the wreckage and called the ambulance, smiled genuinely at Evelyn as the EMTs took her away.

Evelyn curled in next to Terrence on the massive king-sized bed. She didn't know how old it was, but the mattress was more comfortable than anything she'd ever slept on. Terrence's snores slowly filled the silent house. Wind rattled the windows. Every time she closed her eyes, she could hear the soft scratching in her ear canal. Before Evelyn knew it, morning birds sang outside the window.

She twisted out of bed and opened the blinds to the acres of rolling land. It was all hers now. From a dingy P.I. office to living like Vivien Leigh, Evelyn could barely make sense of it all. With a house this big, it made Evelyn wonder why her father put her up for adoption. Surely he could've hired a nanny.

She took a morning run down the red brick road. The air here was clean and crisp, something that was foreign to Evelyn in the big city. If not for the years of wear and tear, the house would've been perfect.

Evelyn jogged under the shadows of the large oaks that ran parallel to the private road. She could imagine planters nurturing small seeds in the surrounding ground nearly two centuries ago. Now, the trees were mammoths. Evelyn reached Quenby Avenue and took a breather. *A street named after my ancestors, now that's a story to tell,* Evelyn thought with a smile. She didn't realize how badly she needed a vacation until now. No more cases. No more stresses. Only a big private house, at the end of a private street, where she was completely free.

On her way back, Evelyn thought about Terrence and how he might be feeling. With the cabins and cotton field in the back, Evelyn wondered if that made him uneasy. Terrence was of African-American descent but from the north. Most of his family were musicians, entertainers, and later factory workers. Like Evelyn, Terrence never had much money growing up. That was probably why both of them didn't fret scraping by every now and then. As Evelyn jogged back to the monumental three-story house, she wondered if she'd be spoiled by the extra space. At the moment, she was still inclined to sell the mansion for boocoo bucks and get a nice house in Birmington, outside of Detroit.

At Terrence's behest, the inspector made the drive over. He was a Georgia boy through and through with meaty muscles, scraggly beard, and a bent bill ball cap. Evelyn and Terrence traded looks, trying not to judge a book by its cover but hoping for a studious-looking person to inspect their electricity.

Stepping out of his white van, Inspector Hanson made a whistling noise at the sight of the mansion. "This is what we call a Twinkie."

"A what?" Evelyn asked, unsure if she heard him correctly.

"Like the treat," Hanson replied. "Clean on the outside. Messy on the outside. See, houses like this were never built for the twentieth century or any century beyond their own."

"Well, you could at least see the place before making an accusation," Evelyn replied. To rewire the house would be very costly.

They walked under the massive colonnades and into the foyer. Hands in his pockets, Hanson stared up at the mural. "Tell me what your issue is."

"Last night the power went out," Terrence explained. "I was able to restart the breaker, but we want to make sure the electricity is sound before we run into any more issues. Evelyn can state that I'm much better with instruments than electric stuff."

Hanson cracked an unassuming smile. They hiked down to the basement. Hanson flashed his small flashlight over the wiring on the ceiling. He mumbled a little bit and continued touring through the house until he found an outlet.

"Let's see," he said, and unscrewed the outlet casing. Crouching low, he flashed his light through into the hole in the wall. He did this at a few more locations before finally turning back to Terrence and Evelyn.

"Y'all got quite the house. The electric setup here. It's not just functional, it's neat. That's a rare thing for many houses," Hanson said.

"Can you tell us when it was last upgraded?"

Hanson thought for a moment. "Just looking by the wiring and set-up technique, possibly in the last twenty or twenty-five years."

Terrence wrapped his arm around Evelyn, pulling her closer to his side. "Maybe your father redid it."

"Seems logical," Evelyn said.

The inspector stayed for a few more hours, checking out the foundation, plumbing, and the rest of the house's essentials. "It's old, but as solid as any house. I'll say this, y'all found yourself a treasure. Touch up the paint, replace a few tiles, and clean up the clutter and this house could be ready to be put on the market."

Terrence paid him in cash, and they waved goodbye from the exterior second-floor balcony. They pulled up old metal chairs and scooted in front of the railing. They could see the tall oaks and red brick road that branched into Quenby Avenue. At one point, horses and carriages walked this path. Some were guests to parties, others transported servants. Evelyn found it cool to think about.

"It seems like a dream, don't it?" Terrence leaned back and rested his feet on the railing. "I mean this place, it's gorgeous."

"Once we get it cleaned up, we can start looking for a realtor," Evelyn said.

"Is that what you want?"

"I thought it's what we both wanted."

"Sure, but when are we ever going to live in a place like this?" Terrence asked. "I mean how many of these houses are still around and habitable? I could clear out the shed and set up my workshop. Blue grass is a big deal here. I'm sure it won't take long to get established. You can get an office in town, that way work and home don't get mixed together."

Evelyn sighed. "It is dreamy, I'll give you that, but… I don't know. How are the two of us going to take care of a place this big? If we sell, we can get a nice cozy home that's roomy but not overbearing. Do we really need a mansion to be happy?"

Terrence squeezed her hand. "As long as I'm with you, I'll be happy. But to live in a mansion--isn't that what people work hard for? One just fell in our laps. I can see it now, little Terrence and little Evelyn running through the front yard. Our own private chef in the kitchen. Cold beers under the starry night. Shotgun shooting. Horseback riding. County fried steak."

Evelyn smiled at her husband's positivity. "Let's not get ahead of ourselves. My father didn't leave us any money. He only left us the property. We're still dirt poor."

"I prefer the term financially challenged. We sell half the stuff in that basement, and that will change. 'Sides, aren't you interested in learning more about your father?"

Evelyn felt that. "He's dead, Terrence. I track living people." She got up. "We can make a decision after we clean the place up."

Evelyn put on some old stained clothes and got to work. She grabbed her dust mop, broom, and box of trash bags and started in the bathrooms, knowing they would be the worst. Getting the leaves out of the bathtub, scrubbing away the mold with a sponge, and running the water until all of the dark gunk was out of the faucet, she realized that the cleaning would take much longer than she thought. She grabbed her tablet from the master bedroom and took pictures of the rooms. Using a picture-taking app to draw colorful circles of various damages of the room, she was able to take inventory of every nook that needed cleaning and tile that needed to be replaced.

Terrence headed outside to see what needed to be rebuilt or repainted. It didn't look like all of the paint was original, so another few touch-ups shouldn't hurt the resale value.

As Evelyn traveled between two upstairs rooms, she got a sudden chill. Her skin crawled like she was blanketed with baby spiders. Slowly, carefully, she followed the cold breeze to a closed door down the hall. It was a room she'd yet to explore. She gave the knob a twist. It didn't budge. She felt the breeze escaping through the cracks, pushing her away.

Evelyn put her shoulder into the door. It slung open into… a nursery. It wasn't what Evelyn expected to find. The wall paint was pink and chipped. The bed was tiny and broken in on itself. The mattress had no blanket and was stained. Toys and dolls from a bygone era littered the floor. They were posed in odd ways. A doll faced the corner of the room. Another had both of its arms folded behind its back. Set off to the table was a massive dollhouse, reminiscent of the plantation where Evelyn stood. There were a number of hand-sewn dolls positioned through the miniature replica. However, the tiny replica of the nursery appeared to empty.

Evelyn approached the open window at the end of the room. Did Terrence open it, had it been open since they moved in? Using the tips of her fingers, Evelyn dropped the window like a guillotine. She stared at the cotton field beyond. It was acres of weeds and cotton plants that tangled into one another like a rat's nest. In the center of the field was a massive scorch mark.

Evelyn set aside her cleaning supplies and headed outside. A number of blackbirds cawed at Evelyn from the tops of cabins. Terrence smiled at her from atop his ladder as he sprayed down a hornet's nest.

The cotton field was just far away from the house that it

made it an unpleasant journey. Evelyn stepped through the tangle of weeds and thorns, catching a few in her elbow. *Why was there a scorch mark? No one had any reason to start a fire here.* The question buzzed inside of Evelyn's head as she pulled a thorn from her arm. A teardrop of blood trickled down her forearm as she stepped onto the burnt earth. Lying in the center of blackened dirt and weeds was a doll of a little girl. It had no legs and was made of fabric. The eyes had been carved out, leaving beneath plooms of dirty cotton on the sockets. Its dress was white and red plaid, reminiscent of the Antebellum era.

Suddenly, the world tilted. Evelyn became lightheaded. Something about the doll was familiar. It was like the key to an old memory that Evelyn couldn't quite recall. She scooped it up and returned to the nursery. The black birds watched her with cocked heads. Doll in hand, Evelyn approached the dollhouse. It fit into the nursery, completing the set. Evelyn took a step back. She couldn't shake the feeling of familiarity.

Evelyn and Terrence reconvened and made a trip to the grocery store. They stocked up for the month, knowing that the house required more than just a basic cleaning. Walls needed painting, faucets needed to be replaced, and a number of rat infestations were found throughout the basement and first floor. Evelyn and Terrence made a plan to take it a day at a time. "To mitigate stress," Terrence explained. They weren't in a rush, but if Evelyn knew anything about time, it's that it caught up to you when you least expected it.

That night, they cuddled under the covers and sighed simultaneously.

"I took care of most of the wasps," Terrence said.

"Good," Evelyn replied. "I can't stand it when you get stung."

"Hey, I only cried for a few hours last time," Terrence joked.

They chuckled and lay back.

"There's something about this place, Terrence," Evelyn said, her hands behind her head as she lay flat on the bed.

"Yeah, I feel it too," Terrence replied. "It's too good to be true. Heh, if my pops could see me now, lying in a plantation master's bed with his sultry daughter--"

"Sultry?" Evelyn interrupted with a cocked brow.

"Hey, let me finish. My pops would be proud of me for sticking it to the man. He was all about that, working in a union factory and all."

"And you?" Evelyn snuggled up next to her husband.

"I'm just looking for a good time." Terrence kissed Evelyn on the forehead. "Come on. Let's get some rest. Big day tomorrow."

Evelyn closed her eyes. She dreamed of the scorch mark in the cotton field, of smoke in her lungs, of fire licking her skin. She felt herself sweat. First normally and then blood. The crimson droplets snaked down her burning, thorn-pierced skin. Just out of view, shadowy figures watched her.

"Evelyn," one said, his voice deep and almost demonic.

Evelyn's body was scalding hot now. She needed to cool off. The flames rose. The pain started to become real and the smoke palpable.

"Evelyn!"

She thrashed against her will. Her dream was incomplete. She didn't know if she was on a stake or on the ground. All she knew was fire and the silhouettes watching her from beyond the waving flames.

"Wake up!" The demonic voice became Terrence's.

Suddenly, there was no more fire. She stood in blackness. Freezing-cold blackness. Her body kept swaying back and forth. Her eyes shot open.

Evelyn stared at white shelves. It took her a second to realize she was looking inside the open refrigerator. The contents were thawing around her bare feet. The liquids were swirling between her toes in a concoction of milk, orange juice, and beer. It stank. Her body was goose-skinned. With wide eyes, Terrence stood behind her. His hand was on her shoulder, shaking her awake. "Are you okay?"

Evelyn stepped away from the fridge and nearly collapsed. Terrence caught her. Evelyn's legs felt like jelly.

Terrence steadied her and shut the refrigerator door. "What were you doing out here?"

4

NEIGHBORS

"I don't know," Evelyn replied. Her head throbbed and her body trembled. She didn't realize it until now, but she was naked.

Throughout the multi-colored puddle, Evelyn felt various cool liquids swim between her toes and plop on the floor like a leaky faucet. Fog had tumbled from the open refrigerator and rolled across the wood floor. An eerie light shined over her snow-white skin, as if the large appliance was a portal to some otherworldly plane.

Terrence helped Evelyn steady herself. She could sense his fear and confusion. The feeling hitchhiked onto Evelyn. She clung to him, her fingers clenching the loose fabric of his shirt. He rubbed his hand down the scars of her back. "Were you sleepwalking?"

"I never sleepwalk."

"Not even as a kid?"

"Terrence," Evelyn looked him in the eye. "I'm telling the truth."

They had been a couple for three years and married for two. Terrence should know better than anyone. Surrendering his shirt to Evelyn, Terrence led his wife back to the bathroom to take a shower in the bathtub. She washed away the gunk from yesterday's groceries and strung her fingers through the blonde hair on her scalp. She sniffled and sneezed so hard that it hurt her chest. How long had she been standing out there to catch a cold, she wondered as she watched the water spiral down the drain between her feet. After she got dressed, Evelyn joined Terrence back in the kitchen. Groggy and mumbling to himself, he soaked up the liquid concoction with a hand towel. Evelyn squatted next to him, picking up lunchmeats and empty beer bottles.

"You get some sleep," Terrence said. "Please."

"I'm sorry-- I don't know what came over me."

"It's not your fault," Terrence said, but his tired inflection said otherwise. "Go on, I'll clean this up."

Not in the mood to argue and feeling a wave of fatigue, Evelyn returned to the bedroom and covered herself. Outside, the moonlight bled through the windows, gales howled in the night, and owls screeched. *It's stress. It must be stress.* Evelyn tried to make sense of the situation as she stared at the droopy canopy over the bed. Still, stress was part and parcel in her everyday life. This vacation was probably the best thing that had happened to her in years.

Evelyn didn't sleep that night. Maybe it was fear she'd sleepwalk again. Maybe it was the scratching sound that dug deep into her ear canal.

The sky turned from indigo to crimson to gold and then to blue. Evelyn forced herself out of bed. Shuffling could be heard in some nearby room. Terrence cleaning, most likely. After all, Evelyn saw him get up before sunrise. Feeling his gaze on her, Evelyn had closed her eyes and pretended to be asleep. She knew it was childish, but she couldn't escape the shame from last night.

She felt her stomach rumble and realized that there was, unsurprisingly, nothing in the refrigerator.

Evelyn walked outside to the balcony to clear her head. Green meadows, tall oaks, and red brick road. Birds fluttered on the blue cloudless sky. She closed her eyes and let the morning wash over her. Evelyn took a deep breath and exhaled all her worries. It didn't work. She decided to take a walk.

The backyard was breathtaking. Dozens of flowers of different shapes and colors tumbled out of raised garden beds and sprawled across the ankle-high grass. Fat-bodied bees sucked on nectar while beetles chewed the lush green leaves. Leafy vines climbed the back wall of the mansion, masking most of the chipped white paint. Evelyn stepped out into the back lawn. She could see the rows of cabins, six in all, three on one side and three on the other. A skinny dirt path snaked in between them and to the cotton field and cotton press that was a wall-less wooden structure with a pyramid roof and a massive wooden screw that ran into a box where the cotton was fed. The arms jutting out from the side of the structure were designed to hitch donkeys.

Evelyn walked the dirt trail, wondering what sort of people her ancestors were. They had slaves certainly, not more than ten by the looks of it, but were the masters cruel or just? Did they free the slaves after the civil war or lie to keep them like some plantation owners did? Adders was closer to Augusta in the center part of the state. If Evelyn remembered correctly from her college history classes, Major General William T. Sherman swept down to Atlanta and set the city ablaze along with many other plantations and cities. That was a hundred and forty-five miles west of here. Quenby seemed to have avoided the fires. Still, what did her family do after they lost? Were they broken like much of the Confederacy or stronger than before? Evelyn had no answers.

She found latches outside of the cabin doors, to lock the slaves in at night, Evelyn assumed. The wood door pulled out toward Evelyn but got stuck halfway on the dirt path. Evelyn sucked in her belly and slid through the crack. The cabin had a floor of packed dirt and featherbed mattress that was disintegrating. Fleas and other winged bugs crawled across the natty covers and feathers. They buzzed away at Evelyn's approach. There was a small wooden chest tucked against one wall, a wooden chamber pot on the other, and a small barred window too small for a child to fit through. Evelyn closed her eyes, seeing a family of three curled up in the sorry excuse of the bed. A mother and father huddling with their child in the middle of a cold night. They were covered in fleas and coughing.

Was this my origin? Evelyn shivered at the thought.

Slam!

A strong breeze slammed the door shut, causing Evelyn to jump. She walked over to the entrance and tried pushing the door open. It didn't budge. The latch had closed her in.

"Terrence!" Evelyn shouted and put her weight into the door. "Terrence, can you hear me?"

No reply.

"Perfect," Evelyn mumbled with an angry scowl.

She pulled out her cell phone. One bar of service. Of course. She dialed him and listened to the ringing until the call dropped.

"Just wonderful. Absolutely wonderful," Evelyn paced and slammed her shoulder into the door. It rattled the latch, but it didn't open. A shadow moved by the window. Evelyn twisted back to see... no one.

"Terrence. Is that you?" Evelyn asked, feeling for her

extendable baton but realizing that she left it in the bedside drawer. "Can you hear me? Hello?"

Evelyn tried the door again. Her efforts were futile. Not the type to wait around, she slammed her shoulder into the door again and again and again, building frustration and anger with every painful hit. Finally, the nail in the latch wiggled loose and Evelyn got the door open a foot. Taking a breath, she squeezed through the gap and back outside. Her shoulder pulsed in pain. A few loose bangs tumbled on her face. She brushed the strands away and massaged her bruised arm.

She saw a large diesel truck rumbling down the red brick path and pulling up to the front of the mansion. A man and woman got out and stood outside the front door. Evelyn looked around for Terrence. He wasn't outside. Evelyn walked around the side of the house and greeted the strangers. Middle-aged and graying, the man was tall and lengthy with a hooked nose and boil-ridden face. The woman was a similar build with a similar nose. They were twins, but the woman had a lazy eye.

"Can I help you?" Evelyn asked as she approached.

"You live here?" the man asked, taking off his cap and holding it against his belly. He wore a polo and slacks. The woman had a jean skirt and button-up shirt. His legs and arms looked like twigs jutting from the clothing.

"Yeah, this is my place now," Evelyn replied. "It was my father's house. Did you know him? Maxwell Quenby."

The twin exchanged looks.

"No," they said simultaneously.

Awkwardness hovered for a moment.

"Say," the man started. "You got any water?"

"I'm sure we do," Evelyn said. "Tap water, if that's alright."

"That'll do," the woman replied.

Evelyn entered and closed the door behind her. She

rubbed her throbbing shoulder. *What do these people want?* She trekked through the large foyer, through the hall of portraits, and into the massive kitchen once tended to by a handful of servants. She turned the faucet knobs added in the late fifties. Evelyn knew this because of the research she'd been conducting since she moved in. She grabbed two dusty glasses from the cupboard and washed them out before filling them with water.

She heard a door open in the foyer.

"Hey, Terrence, we have guests at the front door. I think they're neighbors or something!" Evelyn yelled through the house.

Glasses in hand, Evelyn returned to the foyer to see the two siblings inside. The man was halfway up one of the two curved staircases while the woman snapped photos of the various paintings with a small camera.

"Uh, what are you doing in here?" Evelyn asked, feeling the hairs on her neck rise.

The twins turned to her at the same time.

"Taking pictures," the woman replied.

"I can see that. Why?" Evelyn said.

The woman shrugged off the question.

"Don't go harassing my sister," the man said.

"No one's harassing anyone," Evelyn said as calmly as she could. "But, I never invited you inside."

The twins traded a look like Evelyn was crazy. They went back to doing what they were doing, whatever that was.

"Excuse me," Evelyn set the glasses aside. "I want you to tell me why you think it's okay to come into my house without my permission."

"It's not your house," the man said casually as he continued walking up the red-carpeted stairs.

Evelyn felt her blood pressure rise in a mix of fear and frustration. Before Evelyn could reply, the woman snapped a picture of her face. The strobe blinded Evelyn for a moment, prompting her to blink away the flash.

"No more pictures," Evelyn commanded.

The woman took one of her twin hiking up the second-story inner balcony.

"Hey, stop that," Evelyn ordered.

More photos.

Walking speedily, Evelyn grabbed the camera by the lens and ripped it from the woman's hands. The woman staggered back, horrified and with teary eyes. From the railing, her twin glared at Evelyn with hawk-like eyes.

"Get out of my house," Evelyn said, unsure what to do with the camera now that she had it.

In a feat of rage, the male twin stomped down the stairs. Evelyn took a step back while the twins joined each other in front of Evelyn. With nearly identical eyes, they glared at Evelyn.

"Leave," Evelyn commanded.

"Not till we get the camera back," the male said.

Evelyn smiled angrily. She opened the camera settings and clicked FORMAT. All the pictures were erased in an instant. "All yours," she replied.

The woman's face went red as cherry. "Do you have any idea what was on that?"

"I don't care," Evelyn replied. "Out."

The back door opened. Footsteps traveled through the downstairs hall. The double doors between the double curved staircase opened and Terrence entered the room, sweaty and sticky from yard work.

Neither the twins nor Evelyn turned to him.

"What's up?" he asked the crowd.

"Is this your wife?" the male asked him.

Terrence nodded slowly, still trying to comprehend what was happening.

"She deleted my sister's photos. We demand compensation."

Evelyn boiled and turned to Terrence. "They were taking pictures of our house, Terrence. I never invited them inside."

Terrence stepped closer, palms out in a nonthreatening manner. "Everyone needs to calm down."

"No one's doing anything until we are compensated for our damages," the male said.

"You're not getting anything," Evelyn replied.

"Clearly there was a misunderstanding," Terrence said and fished out his wallet. "Will a twenty make you feel better?"

The twins scoffed.

Evelyn turned to her husband. She wanted to scream, *What are you thinking?*

Terrence picked up the hint quickly. He pulled out the twenty and handed it to the woman. "Twenty is all you're getting. Now please excuse yourself from our property or we'll call the police."

The woman quickly pocketed the money.

The man studied Evelyn for a moment and then Terrence, as if committing their faces to memory. He grabbed his sister by the arm and hurried out the front door. Terrence quickly locked the door. Evelyn pushed aside the curtains and looked out the window. She watched the pickup grumble to life and screech down the brick path, leaving behind two nasty black tire marks on the red brick.

Wide-eyed, Terrence shook his head. "Weird people."

Without a word and with gnashed teeth, Evelyn started toward the bedroom.

"Where are you going?" Terrence asked with genuine concern.

Evelyn turned back to him. "Why did you give them money? You know they're going to come back, right? That's the type of people they are. The more we give them, the harder they're going to press."

"Hey, I'm not the bad guy here," Terrence said.

"Save it," Evelyn replied and hiked upstairs.

"Evelyn, I'm sorry!" Terrence shouted as she got farther up the stairs.

Evelyn headed into the bathroom and washed off her face. Purple circles curved under her blue eyes. She was feeling her two nights without sleep. If she could only get rid of that scratching noise in her head. After taking a moment to collect herself, Evelyn walked back to the balcony railing. Terrence was no longer in the foyer. He must've gone outside to keep on working.

Evelyn checked out of the window to make sure the truck hadn't returned and then started down on the right-side hall that didn't have portraits like the hallway adjacent. Frankly, the hall was quite drab with peeled paint and a rickety floor. It was like Maxwell never walked this way to this side of the house. Now that she thought it about, Evelyn could piece together her father's daily path by which rooms were up-to-date and which had fallen into disrepair. The kitchen, portrait hall, foyer, master bedroom, and master bathroom seemed to be the most well-maintained. The study followed, and then the bedroom full of arcade machines, trinkets, and other hoarded items.

Still feeling her heart racing, Evelyn sniffled. She used her phone to snap pictures of the hall's wall. Grabbing the van's keys from the countertop, she drove into town. She arrived at the paint shop and picked up proper supplies and a few cans of different shades of paint. She needed them for other rooms and decided to kill three birds with one stone. She arrived back at the mansion to see Terrence out beside the house and trimming weeds. He smiled sadly at her as the van rolled to a stop. When he saw the paint cans, roller, and brushes, he threw aside the hedge trimmers and rushed to Evelyn's aid.

"Thanks," Evelyn said, and handed him a paint can.

"Of course." Terrence followed her to the dingy hallway. "Have you decided what shade you're going to paint it?" he asked, obviously trying to put the fight behind them.

Evelyn admired his effort even if she couldn't let go of her irritation. "I guess I'll match the original." She stared at the off-white shading. Other rooms had a baby blue or light khaki tint. That or patterned wallpaper.

"Can I lend you a hand?" Terrence asked.

"I got it," Evelyn replied. "Keep it up with the back yard. You're doing a good job."

Terrence nodded to himself and slipped away from the hall, cracking the door to the foyer behind him.

Evelyn set out the plastic sheeting on the hardwood floor and popped the top of the paint can. She pulled out her stepladder, got the roller lathered up, and got started on the fresh coat. Somewhere deep in the basement, she heard a faint scratching. She forced herself to ignore it and kept on painting. It grew louder, like fingernails picking at her brain.

She closed her eyes, trying to ignore it. *You're just tired. You're only stressed.* The scratching grew louder. Evelyn clenched her eyes tighter. The noise subsided. She reopened her eyes and stumbled back, falling from the stepping stool and landing on her bottom on the hardwood floor.

Painted over the old drab coat of paint was a mural the length of the wall, displaying the cotton field, the black scorch mark at its center, a man with a featureless white mask, and a little girl standing amidst the thorny crops. The details were immaculate. Two black smudges like black holes were the eyes on the man's featureless white mask. The little girl had a yellow dress with a belt around her petite waist.

Her hair was sandy blonde like Evelyn's. Her expression was neutral.

Slowly, Evelyn examined her own palms. They were crusty and dry with different shades of paint. She cursed under her breath and noticed the diminished paint cans nearby. One of them was tipped over and running white away across the plastic sheeting and into the gaps between the floorboards.

Evelyn got to her feet, keeping her wrists curled and her hands from smearing paint on anything. She rushed to the kitchen and washed away the paint. Dry chips clung to the bottom of the sink. She looked out the window, noticing it was nearly sunset. Her heart raced, and she realized that her fear kept her blinking and her mouth dry. She trembled lightly and, without drying off her hands, she walked out the front door.

Dirty and sweaty, Terrence was making quick work of the tall weeds and bushes around the front of the mansion. Wiping his brow, he squinted at Evelyn standing on the covered porch. After a second, he noticed her ghostly expression and rushed up the stairs.

"What happened?"

Evelyn parted her lips, but no words came out. She led them through the foyer and into the freshly painted wall. Terrence's eyes bounced from the spilled paint to the mural dripping down the wall.

He turned to his wife before going back to the impressive piece of art. "You painted that?"

"I… I don't know," Evelyn whispered. "I don't remember."

Terrence rubbed his hand up his bald head and studied the mural that leaked on the plastic sheeting. The little girl and masked man were turning into runny blobs of color before their eyes.

"Do you want to go to the hospital?" Terrence asked.

Evelyn thought about it for a moment. "Yeah. Yes." She nodded.

"Let me get changed," Terrence said and kissed her on the forehead.

Evelyn stared at the cotton field, the little girl, and the masked figure that made her skin crawl.

Terrence returned downstairs wearing a shirt covered with miniscule violins. He brought Evelyn a nice shirt. She changed out of her paint-stained garb, and they climbed into the van.

She looked out the Georgia meadows and flatlands, chewing her fingernail. The ride was silent. Terrence fidgeting proved that he had questions, but he didn't voice them. Good, as Evelyn had no answers. An hour later, and they arrived at the hospital one town over. Adders didn't have one of their own. The doctor took the last-minute call and allowed them both to enter. He was a tall man with hollow cheeks, blue eyes so light they were almost silver, and thin white hair. His smile was small, secretive in a way, and his glasses were circular with a gold rim.

He shined a small light over Evelyn's pupils. "Have you ever experienced blackouts before?"

"No," Evelyn said, staying as brave as she could. "I've never painted anything in my life either."

"Has your diet or sleep schedule changed in the last few weeks?"

"Neither have been particularly ideal for the last few years. Worse lately, though. No sleep the last two nights," Evelyn admitted.

The skeletal doctor nodded to himself. "Does your family have a history of blackouts?"

"I don't know," Evelyn said. "I'm an orphan. My father passed away recently. I don't know anything about my mother."

"I'm going to prescribe you some medication," the doctor said after a moment of studying her. "It's still undergoing tests, but I believe it will nip the problem in the bud."

Terrence squeezed Evelyn's hand.

"Okay. I'll take it," Evelyn replied.

"Get lots of rest too," the doctor warned. "Blackouts are sometimes caused by sleep deprivation. Painting while in such a state is highly uncommon, however."

Evelyn took the signed prescription paper for a medication with a name she could hardly pronounce. As she stood, the doctor cleared his throat. "Oh, one last question."

Evelyn lowered herself back on the bed. Terrence awaited the doctor's words.

Tube ceiling lights reflecting in his glasses, the doctor's silver eyes met Evelyn's. "You're Quenby's girl, right?"

Evelyn nodded. "You knew my father?"

"In passing," the doctor said. "He stuck to himself. Many people stayed away from him."

"Why?" Evelyn asked, her interested piqued.

"He's a Quenby. None of your family has been liked in a very long time. Now, go home and rest," the doctor said, leaving no room for further questions.

Evelyn persisted anyway. "You've got to give me more than that."

"I'm not an Adders local. There's not much I can say." Off Evelyn's look, the man said, "Maxwell visited me a few times. Mostly for antidepressants. If there was ever a closed book, it was him."

Unable to get any more information out of him, Terrence and Evelyn went to the pharmacy and then headed back to the mansion. It was dark then and Evelyn felt wired. Terrence offered to clean up the paint and plastic sheeting.

"What about the mural?" Evelyn asked.

"I don't see why we should get rid of it at the moment," Terrence replied. "Paint's expensive, you know."

"Yeah, you're right. Keep it," Evelyn said, feeling uneasy even thinking about what she drew. After showering and putting on her nightclothes, she got a glass of water and drank one of the huge sleeping pills. She climbed into the bed and drifted quickly to sleep.

She didn't hear any scratching that night and could scarcely dream. All would've been well that evening if she didn't wake up in a cow pasture fifteen miles from her home.

5

RAW

The first emotion Evelyn felt when she awoke was fear. Quickly, she pushed her palms against the cold, hard earth and rose from the tall grass. In the night, the cattle pasture seemed like an endless sea of dark green waves. The grass on top of them bent their will to the wind. The icy gales caressed Evelyn's skin like death's cold touch. Evelyn twisted about where she stood, trying to make sense of where she was and how she got here. She had a million questions and no answers.

Sleeping cows spotted the field. In the far distance, the silhouettes of fence posts could be seen jutting from the earth. Evelyn looked at her dirty and wrinkled pajamas. Dirt caked in her blonde hair and under her fingernails. She felt her pockets. No cell phone. No wallet. No car keys. *Did I walk here?* Evelyn wondered. By the soreness of her calves, thighs, and bare feet, it felt like she had run a marathon.

Evelyn overcame the initial shock of the situation the only way she knew how: not thinking about it and focusing on what was in front of her.

"Get home, I just have to find my way home," she

mumbled to herself. Her small voice seemed like the only noise in this dark night. Under the blanket of stars, Evelyn hiked to the fence. Dirt and rocks bit into the bottom of her heels throughout her trek. She reached the metal mesh of the fence and forced herself over. Hugging herself, she kept forward in search of a road. Her teeth chattered. The stress made her heart hurt.

It took a while to find the street. It was a single-line asphalt road stretching forever between the Georgia fields. There were no road lights or telephone booths. Evelyn craned her head to the stars, trying to make sense of what direction she was going. Astronomy wasn't her strong suit. She picked a direction at random and started walking.

The farther Evelyn traveled, the colder the night seemed. Insects chirped out of sight. Something scurried in a nearby bush. Evelyn kept shifting her eyes. Georgia and the south in general was still a foreign place to her. She didn't know what dangers or what beasts lurked in the darkness. Part of her was glad she didn't know, for sometimes the truth was scarier than fiction.

As much as Evelyn tried to keep a clear mind, fears and anxieties poisoned her thoughts. The mural, the blackouts, and the scratching in the basement made her chest tighten. Was she stressed out, or was she losing her mind? Was this hereditary? Did mental illness course through the veins of her father or mother? How would she ever know? Maybe it was a stress thing. Was she too young to have a mid-life crisis at the age of thirty-three? Evelyn had no qualms admitting that she wasn't the most stable person, but she'd never experienced anything quite like this before, and that terrified her. For the first time since she arrived Georgia, she missed her apartment and dingy office in Detroit.

Lights showed in the distance. Evelyn held her dirty hand in front of her eyes to keep from being blinded as the vehicle hastily approached. She waved her other hand. The truck rumbled to a stop beside her.

"Looks like you could use a ride," the hook-nosed man from the driver seat said. Evelyn felt the hairs on the back of her neck rise, realizing that he was one of the twins that came to her house the day before.

"Don't you look at me like that," the man hissed. "You should be happy I even pulled over."

Evelyn turned back to the road. She still didn't know if she was even walking the right way.

"What are you doing out this late?" Evelyn asked.

The man looked her up and down. "I could ask you the same thing. Does anyone know you're out here?"

His question made Evelyn squirm. "My husband," she lied.

The man smirked. "I'm sure he does. Well? Are you coming along or are you walking?"

"Will you take me back home?" Evelyn asked.

The man looked at her with a neutral face. "No. I'm going to blow your brains out across my dashboard."

Evelyn's eyes went wide.

"That was a joke," the man clarified and looked at the road. "Last call. You in or out?"

Biting her lip nervously, Evelyn walked around the back of the truck and hopped into the passenger side. She had no means of defending herself. Her hair rose when she looked at the man in profile. His eyes were buggy, his jaw was sharp, and his hair was clearly cut and silky smooth. He wore a blue and white two-tone polo, khakis, and slip-on shoes. Apart from his twangy accent, the man didn't fit the Southern look. Still, he sped down the roads like someone familiar with the land.

"I don't forgive you for deleting my sister's photos," the man said.

"What did you think would happen?" Evelyn retorted.

The man's face became stern. "Remember who's driving this truck."

"Why did you come to my house anyway?" Evelyn asked.

"Something there belongs to me," The man said.

"What?"

The man didn't reply.

"Whatever it was, you had ten years to get it back," Evelyn replied.

"You think I was going to break in?" the man said, taking offense. "I'm not some two-bit criminal."

Evelyn stopped herself from reminding him there was little difference between breaking in when no one was home and walking inside her house uninvited.

They drove a little farther. In the dark, Evelyn couldn't tell if the roads were familiar or not. She looked at the glowing digital clock on the dashboard. 4:05 a.m. She cringed, thinking about how much sleep she was losing. Even worse, on where she had spent the last six hours if she'd been sleepwalking.

"I never got your name," Evelyn broke the silence.

"I'm not going to fall for that," the man said.

He turned onto Quenby Avenue and rolled to a stop at the beginning of the red brick path to Evelyn's mansion. "Is this far enough or are you going to call the cops?" the man asked sarcastically.

Evelyn ignored the snide comment. "Thanks for the ride," she said and opened up the door.

"I suggest you be careful out here this late at night," the man said. "Not everyone's nice to strangers intruding on their pastures."

Evelyn twisted back to him. "Those were *your* cattle fields?"

"Who did you think owned them?" the man asked rhetorically. "Now, get out of my truck. I don't want to see you nosing around my property again."

Evelyn hopped out and slammed the door behind her. Burning rubber, the truck roared down the street, hitting sixty miles per hour in a thirty-five.

With sore feet, Evelyn limped down the cool brick path to the plantation house. No light shone from it. The sprawling branches that flanked either side of the road and made a canopy overhead waved at her. Evelyn passed under the white colonnades and tried the front door. It was unlocked. That made her feel uneasy. Like all noise in a quiet house, even opening the door felt extremely loud. No lights were on. It didn't look like Terrence was awake. Good. She climbed into the shower and put on a fresh change of clothes before climbing into bed with her snoring husband. It felt good to rest her legs, but she couldn't keep her eyes closed.

The sun came up much faster than she would've liked. Sleepily, Terrence rolled over to face her and scratched his cheek. Keeping his eyes closed, he whispered, "Sleep well?"

"Yeah," Evelyn lied, not wanting to tell him that the medication failed and that she took a ride with their creepy neighbor.

"Good," Terrence said with a small smile.

"I was thinking that we can hire some locals to clean this place while we go back home," Evelyn said.

Terrence opened his eyes. "Why would we do that?"

Because this place terrifies me. "It feels like the right time."

Elbow planted firmly on his pillow, Terrence rested his head on his knuckles. "Baby, we still got mountains of work to do here before we're ready to sell. If we do sell. The view, the space, the idea of my own private workshop… this place is growing on me, Eve."

"I'd rather just have the money," Evelyn admitted.

Terrence gawked at her a moment. "It's… look, let's agree

not to make a decision until we get the place cleaned completely up. If you're still not comfortable, then we'll sell. Deal?"

Evelyn was too tired to argue. "Sure. Deal."

Terrence kissed her on the forehead. "Thanks. I'll make you some breakfast."

Evelyn watched him leave the room and then fell feebly back to her pillow. She stared at the bed canopy and sighed. When Evelyn finally forced herself up, she ate her breakfast quickly and, with a half can of paint, returned to the hall with the mural. She looked at the faces of the little girl and masked man that leaked down the wall in multicolored tears for a final time and used the paint-dipped roller to create a white stripe down their vestiges. A half an hour later, and it was like Evelyn had never painted the mural.

Picking up her painting supplies, she went to the next room and got started. After she finished touching up the downstairs rooms, she started taking inventory of the furniture. She snapped photos of every room before she got started, thinking it would be a neat selling point to see the before and after of the house. Outside the window, Terrence kept on with the yard work. He piled bushels of weeds and trimmed branches in a few tall stacks next to where he pruned bushes and flowers.

Evelyn stepped into the lounge. It was a wide room with velvet red furnishings, a large bookshelf, carpeted floors, fluffy curtains, and a fireplace with hand-carved wooden finishes. A four by four foot painting of the house hung above the desk. It displayed a horse and buggy parked out on the brick path with a number of well-dressed patrons waving from the second-story balcony while others were in mid-strut to the front door with their lady in hand. There was a sense of family and community. Evelyn looked at the painting with longing and then estimated its worth.

She started by adjusting the chairs and candlesticks into their proper locations. As she dusted, her mind went back to the cattle field and what would prompt her to go to such a place. Evelyn vacuumed the floor and fluffed the pillows. She checked the wallpaper, finding small tears on its surface but nothing that would diminish its value. Evelyn shut the door behind her, not planning on returning until the first open house. She tackled the cleaning process like her private investigative work: systematic and with the least amount of backtracking as possible.

The guest bedroom marked Evelyn's next stop. It was equipped and ready to settle in, dust notwithstanding. Evelyn approached the dresser's drawers that had been left open for who knew how many years. She studied the old clothes within. The shirts and pants were reminiscent of the seventies. They appeared to be owned by a female. *Were these my mother's or my aunt's?* Evelyn sifted through them in search of some clue to the owner's identity. Nothing. She made a pile on the bed and a mental note to wash them later. When the room was cleaned, she headed out into the laundry room in search of a hamper.

When she returned to the bedroom, all of the dresser's drawers were open again.

Evelyn eyed the room cautiously before stepping inside. She slowly pushed the drawers back into the dresser, watching the wheel track within to see if it was slipping. It was not. In actuality, the drawers would stick inside the dresser. She reminded herself that she needed sleep and tossed the pile of laundry into the washer. As the machine rumbled, Evelyn turned about the large basement. Her eyes went to the wall where she heard the scratching noise on their first night in Adders. The more she looked at it, the more claustrophobic the basement felt.

She headed outside for the first time since she got out of

bed. The breeze was nice and the sky was blue. Terrence listened to blues playing from an old music player. The sound was slightly muddled but the soul was still there.

"Like my new toy?" he asked as he yanked a deep root from the ground.

Evelyn looked at the old music player. "Where did you find it?"

"In one of the storerooms. I found a record player as well. One of the good ones." Terrence said with a wide grin.

"Do you mind if I join you?" Evelyn said, squinting next to him.

Terrence yanked up another weed. A clump of dirt hung on the dangling root. "I don't want you getting any blisters."

"Oh please," Evelyn chuckled.

Smiling, Terrence gave her a hand spade.

They started on the brick road, stopping for a moment to study the skid marks left by the twins a day prior.

Getting down on their hands and knees, they began pulling patches of grass growing between the cracked bricks. "I was thinking that we should see the town some night. I hear they have great live music."

"That'll be fun," Evelyn said with a little less enthusiasm than she had hoped. Terrence noticed.

"Can I bribe you with a deep-fried country-style funnel cake?"

"Do you want to give me a heart attack?" Evelyn jokingly replied.

Terrence leaned in close. "I want to go on a date with you, that's what I want."

Evelyn scooted away. "I'd rather focus on the house right now. We can go out after we're all done."

"That's probably the smart way of doing it," Terrence said, trying not to sound disappointed.

His phone rang. Trying not to get the phone dirty,

Terrence held the device gingerly and answered. "Terrence Carr speaking… Leo, how's it hanging?... Oh yeah, I know that feeling," Terrence chuckled and got up.

He muted the phone against his shoulder and whispered to Evelyn. "It's the blues musician from the restaurant we went to the other night."

Evelyn gestured for him to take his call. Terrence put the phone back up to his ear and returned inside.

Alone, Evelyn kept on working. The afternoon sun baked down on her. The air became humid and buggy as the day went on.

Dressed in a nice blue button up and slacks, Terrence hustled out the front door. Still on the ground, Evelyn brushed a strand of hair away from her eye and gave him her attention.

"We must've made an impression. The guy wants me to make him a guitar. I'm going to head over to his place and hash out the details," Terrence said. "It will only take a few hours."

"You don't need my permission," Evelyn replied.

"Thanks, baby," Terrence replied with a smile. "I would kiss you, but you're all dirty and sweaty."

"Oh, you're such a romantic," Evelyn teased.

Terrence rushed over to her and planted a wet one on Evelyn's lips. "There," he said in accomplishment and unlocked the rusty bucket minivan. "Relax for the rest of the day. I can't have my beautiful wife working in this heat."

"Enjoy yourself," Evelyn said and rose from the brick pathway. From inside the minivan, Terrence waved her goodbye and putted down the road. When he was gone, Evelyn returned to de-weeding the bricks. She was able to knock it out much quicker than she thought she would. After filling up a glass of water in the sink, Evelyn thought about the next project that would get her mind off her abnormal sleeping habits.

Not wanting to do work inside the house, Evelyn headed to the toolshed. The door was loose on its hinges, and Evelyn thought it would be a good time to learn some new skills. Finding a few old nails and a hammer within the shed, Evelyn got to hammering the door properly on its hinges. It didn't take too long before she stubbed her thumb. It swelled and throbbed, and her fingernail turned black. Walking off the pain and regretting that she didn't listen to Terrence's words, Evelyn caught a glimpse of someone standing out in the cotton field.

She pulled her thumb out of her mouth and called out, "Hey!"

The figure took off into a sprint in the opposite direction. Keeping the hammer with her, Evelyn took off after them. She brushed against the untamed cotton crops as she gained on the stranger. The person moved too quick for Evelyn to catch a good look. *What are you doing?* Evelyn asked herself as she ran. *Call the cops.* Yet, her P.I. instincts kept her tailing after the stranger.

She slowed to a stop on the black scorch mark dead center of the field. Her pulse quickened and her breathing staggered.

Standing amidst the cotton plants was a blonde little girl and a tall man in black wearing a white mask with button-size slits cut over the eyes. The world spun under Evelyn's feet. She tried to steady herself but could find nothing nearby to prevent her from falling. So, she fell.

By the time her bottom hit the packed dirt, the figures vanished, and a wave of tiredness hit Evelyn suddenly. Her head cramped. *I need sleep,* she told herself. Abandoning the work on the shed, Evelyn returned inside via the back door. She noticed something was amiss when she entered the foyer. All of the priceless paintings were scattered across the carpeted floor, the chairs and sideboards were turned on their heads, and flower vases were in shattered heaps.

Evelyn froze, wondering if whoever did this was still in her house.

She dialed Terrence.

"Pick up. Pick up," Evelyn muttered, afraid to go any farther into the house.

"Hey--"

"Terrence, listen."

"-- You've reached the voicemail of..."

Evelyn hung up and tried again.

Voicemail.

The floor above her creaked. Someone was walking around up there.

In her line of work, Evelyn had been to some shady places and encountered an assortment of suspicious individuals, but none had ever been in her home before. The threat felt real, tangible, something that she wasn't used to.

Something smashed upstairs.

The smart thing would've been to get out of house, but the knife in the kitchen called Evelyn's name. No part of her wanted to go up the curved foyer stairs, but letting someone destroy her father's things wasn't something Evelyn was going to allow. With the knife's cold hilt in hand, she conquered the first step.

SMASH! Something else broke.

Evelyn conquered the next step. She kept her fear hidden behind her stone-like expression. The steps groaned under her shoes. Her clothes stuck to her from the cold sweat dosing her body.

More movement. It was something big.

Evelyn had the element of surprise on her side.

Then, her phone rang. The noise echoed through the house.

The movement upstairs instantly ceased.

Stopping halfway up the stairs, Evelyn pulled out her screaming phone and answered, keeping her eyes on the balcony above her.

"Hey, it's me," Terrence said. Laughter sounded on his end of the line.

"Terrence," Evelyn whispered, "There's someone in our house."

There was a pause on Terrence's end.

"Call the cops. I'm on my way home now. Wait outside."

"Okay. Okay. Hurry," Evelyn stepped down from the steps and fled out the front door.

Keeping the knife with her, she faced the plantation. Her eyes bounced between the upstairs windows in search of moment. None. Her phone must've scared the intruder. She dialed 911.

In six minutes, a squad car came screaming down the road. A burly officer with short gelled gray hair stepped out. His face was square and flat with two different colored eyes: one green and one brown.

"Michaels," he introduced himself and stared up the house with a small confident smile on his hard face. "I'm here to help you. What can you tell me?"

"I last heard them upstairs," Evelyn explained. "I didn't see them. I believe there's only one, but there could be more."

Officer Michaels nodded to himself. "Wait here."

Before Evelyn could reply, the officer was pushing through the front door.

Evelyn awaited his return. She sucked on her swollen and bruised thumb. Minutes went on like hours. Michaels was nowhere to be seen.

Five minutes passed.

Ten minutes.

Fifteen minutes.

Evelyn heard the radio crackle inside the police cruiser. *"Michaels. This is Dispatch. Over."*

Evelyn stared at the vehicle. Its blue and red lights reflected in her blue eyes.

"Report in, Michaels. Over."

The front door of the mansion opened. Officer Michaels stepped out. His face was neutral and unreadable.

Evelyn awaited his response. "Well?"

The officer snapped out of his daze. "It's clear. There's no one there."

"You're sure?" Evelyn asked.

"See for yourself."

Evelyn walked into the house and down the hall.

"Anything missing?" Michaels asked.

Evelyn looked over the clutter. It made it hard for her to take inventory over everything. "It doesn't look like it."

She searched upstairs. Chairs were tipped on their sides, windows were open, and bedsheets were pulled from their mattresses. The vandalism seemed random and reckless. Evelyn walked through the master bedroom and bathrooms. "It looks like all of it is here," Evelyn told the officer as they marched down the stairs. She picked up a painting and hung it back on the wall. Thankfully, it was not damaged.

They headed into the basement. It was the only part of the house untouched by the rampage. That's what Evelyn thought at first until she noticed that both shotguns and all the shells were missing.

"Whoever was here stole our weapons," Evelyn told Michaels.

"Is there anyone you'd suspect?" the officer asked her.

"I've not communicated with too many people since I got here. The only ones that come to mind are these twins in their thirties. I never got their names. They stopped by yesterday. I never got their names."

Michaels jotted down a few notes as they returned to the foyer. "I'll see if I can't find them. Call if there's any more issues. Even if something feels wrong. We'll be here as fast as we can."

"Thank you." They returned outside as Terrence arrived.

He hustled out of the minivan and gave Evelyn a hug. "I got here as fast as I could. Tell me what happened."

"Someone broke in," Evelyn explained. "They took our guns and trashed the place."

"Are we safe, Officer?" Terrence asked.

"We'll be ready to answer your call at a moment's notice," Michaels promised. "I'll look into those twins and see if I can't find anything."

Holding hands, Evelyn and Terrence watched the police cruiser drive away.

"I can't believe this happened," Terrence said. "I'm sorry for leaving you here alone."

"It's not your fault," Evelyn replied. "Let's get this cleaned up. I want to make sure nothing's damaged."

The vandalism was not as costly as they thought. Most objects were just tossed across the room, not stomped or smashed. A few vases were shattered, but nothing irreplaceable suffered heavy damage. Evelyn tried looking at that as a positive, but it was still hard to get over the initial shock that someone broke into her home.

"You think we should get a hotel?" Evelyn asked as they put drawers back into a dresser.

"Leave all our stuff here? No way." Terrence replied.

"They have weapons, Terrence."

"I'm not going to let them do any more harm." Terrence said sternly. "This house is our only chance to live big in this world. I'm not leaving."

Evelyn gawked at him for a moment. He kept on working, but his motions were jerky and motivated by anger.

That night, they double-checked all the locks and kept a baseball bat under the bed. Neither one of them spoke or slept for a long while.

Evelyn's sleep deprivation finally caught up to her well past 1 a.m. She closed her eyes for what seemed like an instant and then woke up three hours later. Terrence wasn't beside her.

Groggy, she sat up and called her husband's name. She tried the light switch. It flickered, but the lights didn't turn on. Grabbing the oil lamp and matches, she walked out of the room. "Terrence. Answer me."

No reply.

Evelyn heard a scratching noise seeping out of the basement.

Her heart raced. The hairs on her neck stood. She turned the glass knob. The basement door creaked open. She took it one step at a time. "Terrence?"

She held the lamp high, illuminating the vast basement and blanket-covered objects within. The scratching noise got louder. *Was she dreaming*? She pinched herself. This was real. She saw someone standing by the far brick wall. Evelyn stopped. The person's back was turned to her. Their fingers scratched the coarse brick. The skin on the fingertips was raw and bloody.

"Terrence," Evelyn said quietly. She stepped closer. "What are you doing?"

Something inside told her to run away.

She put her hand on her husband. He didn't react to her touch, just kept on clawing until tears of blood snaked down the wall's coarse surface.

6

THE KEY

Terrence's eyes were shut. Drool trickled down his lip. His fingers kept raking across the wall. Scratch. Scratch. Scratch. Evelyn shook him. He didn't stop clawing.

"Terrence. Terrence. Wake up." After a moment of hesitation, she slapped her husband across the face with as much strength as she could muster.

Terrence didn't react. A red handprint formed on his cheek.

Evelyn felt the world spin. She grabbed her husband and pulled him away from the wall. Terrence's arms desperately reached out to keep on clawing, but the moment they were a few feet away, both his arms fell limply to his sides. Evelyn stared at him. She put her hands on his cheeks and turned his face to her own. He was still asleep.

Evelyn looked around the basement for something to stop his peeled fingertips from bleeding. She pulled a white sheet from atop a pagoda lampshade, shook out a cloud of dust, and swaddled Terrence's fingers with the cloth. She tied both of his hands together, unsure if her pacifist husband would turn violent. Grabbing his wrists, she led him up the rickety stairs. He shambled behind her. Using the oil candle to navigate the massive mansion, Evelyn guided Terrence through the large foyer and up the curving staircase.

Evelyn narrowly missed a shard of glass she failed to clean after the break-in. Every few steps, Evelyn forced herself to look at her sleeping husband. The wrappings around his fingertips were staining maroon. Breathing heavily, Evelyn reached the interior balcony: a place where the Quenby greats would watch over dozens of patrons attending an evening dance. She walked through the long hallway, flanked on both sides by closed doors, and then into the master bedroom.

Terrence tore his wrist from Evelyn's grasp and toppled face first on the king-sized bed. Evelyn stared at him with bloodshot eyes. He began snoring. Tense, Evelyn sat in a nearby chair and watched her husband sleep until the oil lamp flickered out.

Terrence called her name.

Evelyn jolted awake. The oil lamp fell at her feet and spilled across the hardwood. Feeling the sun beating down on her back, Evelyn got to her feet and wiped her drooling mouth with the top of her hand.

Terrence sat at the edge of the bed. With a horrified expression, he bounced his gaze between her and the maroon-stained rags on his fingers. "What happened?" he said with a hoarse voice.

"You were sleepwalking," Evelyn told him, joining him by the bed.

He raised up his rag-bound hands. "How…"

"You hurt yourself," Evelyn said, unable to bring herself to tell him about the specific cause of his injuries.

"And my face?" he asked, grimacing.

Evelyn smiled tiredly. "I slapped you."

Terrence looked at her, dumbfounded.

"Come on, let me get those bindings off of you," Evelyn said and untied the knot. Terrence winced when his hands were free. He went into the bathroom and washed his fingers in the sink, sucking air as the water touched his tender and broken skin.

Hands dripping, he returned to the bedroom. "Do we have any Band-Aids?"

"There might be some in the minivan. Inside the first-aid kit."

Terrence groaned and headed for the door. "This doesn't make sense. I've never had a blackout in my life." He cursed under his breath and left Evelyn's sight. Her beaten-down reflection looked back at her in the makeup table's mirror.

She went outside. Her husband's body was halfway out of the van. He grumbled to himself as he sifted through the contents under the seats. Defeated, he pulled himself from the vehicle and faced Evelyn. "I can't find it. I'm going to make a store run."

"Do you want me to drive?" Evelyn asked.

Terrence shook his head. "No. Get some sleep. I need to clear my head anyway."

He walked around the front of the vehicle and climbed inside. The minivan sputtered to life and disappeared down the road. Once Evelyn knew it was gone, she hunched over and felt her chest tighten. She controlled her breathing. In and out. In and out. It seemed to help the panic and confusion that was flooding over her. *Was there something in the water? Are we both sick?* Evelyn straightened her posture and inhaled as deeply as she could. Part of her knew that wasn't the answer. There was something wrong with this house. She needed to find out what.

The power had returned at some point during the night. It reset all the clocks, causing them to flicker at 12:00. Evelyn pushed open the basement door and gazed into the abyss below. She flipped the light switch, watching the large room flood with light. Slowly, carefully, she descended a single step at a time. It seemed much smaller in the daytime, and the shadows didn't stretch as far. Most of the articles within were odds and ends pieces of furniture stored for a later day. The couches were moth-eaten and the leather chair cushions were cracked. The small lounging area where Evelyn discovered the shotguns seemed to be the only place that had been used in the last decade. The couch there was stained. A box TV sat on its stand. A sheet of dust clouded its black glass face. Evelyn approached the brick wall. The few droplets of her husband's blood hardened on the ridged surface.

Why here? Why this place? she wondered. She traced her finger across the surface. There was nothing intricate about the brick. Nothing unique. Was there something behind it? Evelyn pressed her ear against the wall and listened. No sound. It was rock solid. Still pushed against the wall, she knocked on different points of the brick. No sound. No hollowness. *Was the clawing random*? Maybe, but this was the same place Evelyn had first heard the scratching sound that seemed to cling to her psyche like a parasite. As she turned back to the basement, she caught a glimpse of the black spot on the ceiling. It was a stain of sorts, possibly from an old leaking pipe.

She headed upstairs and into the portrait hall. She glanced up at the nameless man immortalized by paint. Many of them had stern faces and intense eyes, much like Evelyn, though none were blonde except the intriguing and beautiful woman that began the Quenby line. Terrence and her had been through this hall before, looking into the origins of the black stain but finding nothing. The wall behind the paintings had a hollow quality. There was something back there, but Evelyn had no idea how to access it without taking a sledgehammer to the wall. Something told her that wouldn't help the resale value.

She slid up the corner of one of the paintings in search of a breach in the wood that she could glance through. A few paintings later and without results, Evelyn stopped before the portrait of a chunky man dressed in a caramel-colored tailored suit standing next a cotton gin. She checked behind it and found something she never expected: a keyhole.

Evelyn peered through it but could only see blackness. She pulled herself away. What did this have to do with the blackouts, the scratching, the scorched cotton fields, the masked man and the little girl in the mural, and her father's demise? Evelyn didn't know. This could mean nothing, but she wouldn't know until she found the key unless… she rushed back to the master bedroom and tore apart her travel bag. She grabbed her lock-picking tool that she used in her P.I. business and the key her father left her.

She tried the key first. No luck. It wouldn't even fit into the tiny hole. She fished out the lock-picking tools and gave them a try. They met resistance partway through. Something was stuck in the keyhole. Evelyn shined a flashlight within, making out what seemed like part of a key that had snapped off. She searched her husband's tools, finding some glue. She slathered it on the back of her lock-picking tool and jammed it inside the keyhole. After a minute, she jiggled the lock pick out. The tip of the key that was once lodged there was now glued to the lock-picking tool's end. Evelyn peered through the keyhole. There was a room back there, but it was too dark to make out details. She tried unlocking it with her lock-picking tools again. However, the intricacy of the lock made it impossible. *What was he trying to hide back here?* Evelyn wondered.

She searched the floor of the hallway, the ring posts in the kitchen, the drawers in the master bedroom, and the desk in the study before returning to the portrait empty-handed. She stroked her chin. Searching every nook and cranny of the house would take weeks. She thought back to her private investigative work. Every missing person leaves a trail intentionally or unintentionally. It was inevitable. Secret keys were a different matter entirely. The owner would intentionally leave a trail, but one only he could follow. Evelyn knew nothing about her father, so digging into his past would not help her here. She had to rely on her own experiences and ask herself the fundamental question that began with "If I were trying to BLANK, how would I do it?"

Evelyn started with the obvious: leave a subtle reminder in the surroundings. The door was hidden behind family portraits, did that matter? Evelyn didn't know their names or their gravestones, so seeking the dead wasn't practical, plus that would be too obvious. Evelyn would want to hide the answer in plain sight, but not so plain that one searching would guess at first. Evelyn looked for subtle clues. She gazed at the portrait with the rotund man and the cotton gin behind him. It must've been painted when the cotton gin was still new. Evelyn studied the other portraits. None of them had buildings in their background, so why would this man choose to put one in his portrait's background? Evelyn snapped a picture of it with her phone and went outside. She walked through the tall grass and toward the cotton gin house. It was a wooden two-story structure by the cotton press. Its wood was dark, nearly black and gray. The first floor looked like a car garage with multiple ports where workers would pile cotton. Evelyn hiked to an outdoor ramp that connected the ground to the second-story door. She pushed open the old wooden door and stepped inside the building. Dust, hay, and a sparse amount of cotton littered the groaning floor planks. Some were broken and others were thin and weak. At its center was a crude cotton gin. The device was made entirely of metal, with an opening on top to feed the cotton and an area in the back to receive it once it had been funneled through. Evelyn withdrew her phone and studied the picture. At the time the portrait was drawn, the cotton gin was outside. She approached the metal tool and spotted something within its metal teeth. Nearby, stuck in the metal, was a key that had been lodged inside.

Evelyn saw that the tip of it had been broken off. *This is the one.*

She reached her hand inside and pinched the key with her fingers. She felt a sharp tug, and suddenly her arm was being pulled into the gin. Before she could realize what was happening, the metal teeth within were flaying her hand and wrist, sucking her deeper into the machine. Evelyn gasped, unable to scream from shock, and attempted to tug her hand free. It only went deeper. With her free hand, she grabbed her captured wrist and pulled with all her might. The metal teeth bent for a moment and then snapped as her hand was yanked out. Evelyn fell on her bottom and gawked at her hand, expecting to see tattered flesh and bone. Her hand was perfectly fine and held the broken key.

Evelyn closed her eyes. *I'm losing my mind.*

Key in hand, she returned inside, washed her face, and returned to the portrait hall. She took the piece of key glued to the lock-picking tool and glued it to the rest of the key. After it set, she gave the keyhole a try. A tall and skinny three-feet wide portion of the wall opened. Evelyn stepped back and peered into a tight corridor. Dust flakes danced. The walls and floor were unpainted wood. *I guess my father had secrets.* She stepped inside and walked through the hall that ended at a door. The door wasn't fully closed. The hinges were warped. The wood around the doorknob was splintered. The lock was broken.

Like every door in the old mansion, it groaned as Evelyn

pushed it open. Inside was an office about a quarter of the size of the other office, but dense with objects. There were piles of old books spilling out of a dusty bookcase, a desk covered with documents, an old globe, a rusty bed frame and lived-in mattress, and dirty plates, cups, and silverware. There was a scattered pile of balled paper that rested on the floor. It looked like rats took a bite out of it.

Evelyn knelt down and picked up one of the balled pieces of paper.

It read, *"To my beloved, in a less cruel world, we could've been together. It was never my desire to send you away, but sometimes sacrifices must be made for your safety and for mine. I write to you with my final breath. Come home. Take what is yours and do with it as you please. You are free of the burden of this town and family. Enjoy it, Evelyn, and know that I will always love you. Sincerely, Maxwell, your father. P.S. by the time you read this, I'll be ten years gone. I know you do not understand nor will you, but know this is better for us all. Wounds will be healed. Life will be stable."*

Evelyn read the note again before swiftly unballing another paper wad. *"I am in great danger, which is why this must be brief. I surrender my estate and everything I own to Evelyn Quenby, my daughter. Burn this house or sell it. Nothing good will come from this place. -- Maxwell."*

Evelyn picked up another. *"Evelyn, there's so much I wish I could've told you. There's so many things I wish I could've seen. From your first step, to prom night, to your wedding, I would've loved to be there for all of it. I imagine you grew up to be beautiful and smart, like your mother. Though I'm ashamed that I never got to see you personally. Enclosed in this letter is my will..."*

Eyes watering, Evelyn read another and another and another, learning about her father's love for her, his guilt, and this ominous danger that prevented him from telling her more. Evelyn felt her heart twist and a conflicting stir of emotions tear at her insides. If Maxwell loved her so much, why surrender her to the foster system? Why not reach out? Evelyn's frustration grew the more she read. Every draft of his letters was vague and filled with regret. She flattened them out on the old mahogany desk. Part of her wanted to burn them. The other part of her wanted to hug them close to her chest and cry.

Sniffling, she thought back to the danger Maxwell mentioned. *It sounds like he was murdered.* Evelyn shivered at the thought. If so, no one knew. A body was never found. By the smashed door into this private study, it may well have happened where Evelyn stood. An overwhelming sense of dread filled her. She wanted to run as far as she could from the room. Suddenly, she noticed something nailed on the desk panel. Cautiously, she approached. Her mouth dried. She turned the photograph towards her. It was sepia tone and showed a little girl, between seven and ten years old, with sandy blonde hair, freckles, and a wide smile. Evelyn recognized her from the cotton field and from the mural she drew.

Evelyn took a step back and covered her mouth. She looked around the dusty room cluttered with clothes, odd philosophical books, and a number of rolled papers. The walls seemed to close in on her. The old, rusty bed made her mind go to dark places. She thought about the scorch marks in the cotton field. The child's toy she'd found. What was the connection?

Evelyn felt like she was going to faint. She bolted out of the room and back into the hall of portraits. The front door opened.

"I'm home," Terrence shouted.

Evelyn shut the secret door panel behind her and put the painting back in place. She pocketed the key, composed herself, and walked out into the foyer to meet him. She knew her face was still stark white, but she did well to hide it.

None of this made sense, and bringing Terrence into the fold would be a distraction she couldn't afford. Like in Detroit, Evelyn would work her cases alone unless she needed help.

Terrence had Band-Aids around each of his fingers. He held a large camera bag in his hand.

"You were gone for a long time," Evelyn said, followed by asking, "What's that?"

Terrence unzipped the bag and pulled out the massive video camera. "I rented this for a few days to monitor our sleeping habits. I hope that's not an issue."

"No," Evelyn said. "I think it's smart."

Terrence smiled at her. "Good. I'll set it up." He bounced up the steps.

Evelyn looked outside the window. The sun was falling. Her mind went in circles, thinking about the blonde girl. Today was full enough already. She'd look first thing in the morning when she was better rested.

Terrence and Evelyn heated up some soup and ate in the vast dining room fit for twenty patrons. They didn't say much. Both were lost in thought. Between the break-in and blackouts, Evelyn could see the toll on Terrence's face. There was a tension in the air, fearful of what the night would bring.

After dinner, they went to bed. Evelyn felt odd having the dark camera lens watching her as they slept. Both of them doubled down on the doctor's recommended medication and drifted to sleep.

Evelyn dreamed of fire licking her skin.

She awoke before the sun came up and took a shower. When she got out, Terrence was awake. He had the video camera on his lap and was reviewing the footage on the small screen. Evelyn scooted in close to him. Terrence's Band-Aid-wrapped finger pressed the play button. They fast-forwarded through the first hour of tossing and turning, and then they both got out of bed with closed eyes. They walked out of the room.

Evelyn and Terrence traded worried looks.

They continued to fast-forward the footage until they watched themselves return to the frame an hour ago. Sleep-walking, both Evelyn and Terrence carried the missing shotguns. They stowed the weapons under the bed and returned to their sleeping positions. Terrence pressed pause. Evelyn stood up from the edge of the bed and peered under. A moment later, she returned with two shotguns.

"What did we do last night?" Terrence asked.

Evelyn knew she wasn't going to like the answer.

7

GUNNER

Evelyn checked the cartridge of the shotgun. One shot had been fired. The second gun told the same story.

Evelyn and Terrence sat in quiet for a moment, overwhelmed by the mansion's silence. Outside, trees swayed calmly in the wind. The unmowed grass spotted with dandelions, weeds, and other wildflowers bent as if bowing to the high sun.

Without a word, Terrence grabbed one of the guns and unloaded the shells within. By the time he finished, ammo was spilling from his palm onto the painted white floor. He trembled slightly and started on the next gun, getting frustrated when one of the bullets jammed in the chamber. Evelyn put her hand on his thigh to calm him. Terrence tensed up.

"I don't know what the hell we did last night," Terrence said with a trembling voice. "But I'm not going to take any chances."

"We need to stay levelheaded," Evelyn said.

Terrence shook his head, ignoring her words. "I'm getting

rid of these guns."

Before Evelyn could say a word, her husband was choking a shotgun in each hand and his pajama pockets were packed with ammo. Evelyn followed his march out the door. They walked out into the expansive backyard and far beyond the cotton field. Morning dew wetted their feet in their open toe slippers. Evelyn chewed her nails as she walked. Her other hand clenched a shovel. Terrence never asked her to pick it up, but Evelyn took the initiative. Sleepwalking with a high-powered weapon was not something she'd ever want to do again. Terrence dug a shallow hole, wrapped the weapons, and tossed them in. While Evelyn kicked the dirt over the shotguns, Terrence buried the ammo half an acre away, swaddling them in a towel before placing them in the hole.

After throwing their dirty clothes into the wash and showering, they put on their day clothes, sat on the walnut-colored sofa with green and gold floral upholstery in the living room, booted up their portable Wi-Fi hotspot, and opened their laptops. For a good hour, they browsed the local news in search of murders or gun crimes committed the night before. She found articles regarding an upcoming farmers market special and other small local events. There was nothing about murder or shots heard in the night. Evelyn didn't count her blessings. The day was still young.

"Maybe we'll never know what happened," Terrence said, his dark eyes glued on the computer screen. "Maybe it's for the better."

Evelyn nodded. In most cases, she'd want to know all the gritty details, but something about what happened last night made her stomach churn. She was hoping she'd have some recollection, but that hadn't happened for the other blackouts, and she knew that it wouldn't happen for this one.

"Life goes on," Terrence said, talking to himself more than Evelyn. "We move on. No need to talk about it. We'll get some medication, clean the house, and hit the road back to Detroit. Simple."

"We can't go back," Evelyn said, watching the news anchor with unblinking eyes.

Terrence turned to her with his lips slightly parted.

"If we committed a crime, and I pray to God we didn't, fleeing is the last thing we want to do."

"Just yesterday, you were the one who wanted to leave." Terrence turned her words against her.

"That was before the shotguns. Now let's delete the footage from last night and finish our month here, and then we get the hell out of this house and don't look back." Evelyn thought that her words were a little extreme, but ninety-five percent of the time, someone got arrested for a crime because they acted hastily. Whether they did anything nefarious last night or not, she needed to play it safe. Only for a few more weeks.

Hair pulled back into a ponytail and wearing a white zipped-up track jacket, Evelyn went on a morning run through the property. With blackouts, the break-in, the revelation that her father may have been murdered, Evelyn needed something constant in her life right now. The pain shooting up her calves with every swift step and the sweat on her brow were her salvation at the moment. Acres away, Evelyn could still see the monumental Quenby House. Its tall white walls, Greek-style pillars, and blanket of flower-spattered vines nearly stole her breath every time she took a second to look at the artifact. A blessing and curse, that house. A heart-stopping beauty built on the back of slaves.

Drenched, Evelyn began her journey back. She hadn't traveled far in terms of the scale of the property. She guessed they had between 20 and 25 acres total. A large portion of that was the cotton field, and another portion was for hay and livestock, of which there was none.

She returned inside and used a cloth in the large kitchen to dry her face. Resting her bottom against the countertop, she looked at the wooden kitchen island, the pantry the size of a small bedroom, and a small door leading to the meat freezer. Like the basement, the walk-in icebox was an extension added a century after the mansion's inception. Overall, the kitchen looked like it could fit five chefs and servers.

Following the sound of tools scraping wood, Evelyn stepped into the one of the empty spare bedrooms Terrence had converted into his office. Thought usually slow and precise, Terrence worked furiously on the guitar frame with the wood shaver. Dripping with perspiration, he turned his gaze up to Evelyn. His shirt with different instruments was unbuttoned partly down the chest, and the sleeves had been rolled up past his elbows. The laptop was open nearby, still displaying generic news articles.

"Whenever you're ready, let's visit Dr. Waxen," Evelyn said and walked away.

Terrence refreshed the browser page and went back to working on his newest guitar.

An hour and forty-five minutes later, and they were back at the hospital. Skeletal and silver-eyed, Dr. Waxen welcomed them into his office. He sat behind his imposing desk. On the wall, diplomas and certificates hung over his gray head. Skinny fingers locked on the desk's top, he bounced his drooping but lively eyes between them.

Evelyn slid the pill bottle across the desk. "It didn't work."

"You're still experiencing blackouts?" Dr. Waxen asked with his soft voice.

"We're still sleepwalking," Terrence injected and presented his Band-Aid-wrapped fingertips. "And we're hurting ourselves while we do it."

"Huh," Waxen said with acute fascination. "How about you, Mrs. Carr? Any unexplained phenomena?"

Too many to count. "I believe I'm hallucinating. I find things I thought I moved back in their original location. I'll see things I know aren't real. I'm not crazy," Evelyn thought she should clarify. "I think there's something in the water or maybe a gas leak in the house."

Terrence shifted in his chair. "The home inspector would've told us that, and when were you planning on telling me about all that stuff?"

"I thought it was sleep deprivation," Evelyn replied. "I didn't want to worry you with it."

"Well, I'm worried now," Terrence huffed.

Doctor Waxen cleared his throat. "The medication I prescribed you is the strongest I have. I can up the dosage and see if that helps, but I must say that the side effects are less than favorable."

"What are we talking about?" Evelyn asked.

"Nausea, headaches, cramps, drowsiness. Some find themselves steering the toilet seat every now and then. In summation, it's not a fun time, but you'll sleep like babies."

"Screaming and crying at 3 a.m.?" Terrence said to lighten the mood.

Waxen stared at him with hollow eyes. "Soundly."

Evelyn traded looks with Terrence. "We'll take it."

"I would suggest you stay somewhere other than your home for the next few days. Stress plays a large role in these types of situations," Dr. Waxen said as he wrote them another prescription and had a coughing fit. Evelyn and Terrence traded looks.

With most of their clothes still packed in their suitcases, Evelyn and Terrence found the Sunnyside Motel on the outskirts of town. It was a cute place, single story, and owned by a nice elderly couple with friendly smiles. At 44 dollars a night, the price couldn't be beat. The room was as "quaint" as the owners described, with a queen-sized bed, 20-inch TV, outdated microwave, and mini fridge. Evelyn knew she wasn't going to be storing much food in there. It appeared she'd be enjoying the continental breakfast for the next few days. Though neither one of them said it, their massive room in the Quenby House was miles better. Evelyn didn't like that revelation, knowing that adapting back to her low-income Detroit lifestyle would not be easy.

Sitting at one of two chairs on the circular table, Terrence checked his wad of cash and rubbed his creased brow. "We need to start selling stuff."

"I agree," Evelyn said, plopping down at the corner of the bed. "The break-in did a number on us. The paintings survived, thankfully, but a lot of the vases broke and the furniture that got pushed over is chipped."

"It's a good thing we're getting a few days away from the house. It keeps us humble."

"Half glass full?" Evelyn smiled tiredly.

Terrence returned the grin. "Always."

The light-heartedness helped push the horror of last night from Evelyn's mind, but only for the moment. The stress returned. She opened the small spiral-bound notebook she kept in the inner pocket of her black double-breasted raincoat. Chewing on the end of the eraserless pencil, she thought of the best way to clean up the plantation. They needed landscapers and to research what was actually worth money. After all that was finished, they'd need someone trustworthy to put an estimate on the house and property. It would be smart to search Maxwell's desk for any documents regarding the house's history. Evelyn guessed that would be a big selling point if the person could look past the ideas of slavery. Terrence seemed to be doing a good job of it, or at least a good job at not expressing his concerns to Evelyn. They never took the time to broach the topic seriously, and Evelyn was happy for that.

They spent the next three days at the Quenby House, cleaning, organizing, and getting the landscapers to start on the yard surrounding the house. Wearing green polos and driving a green van, they hustled out and worked swiftly at mowing and pruning the bushes. When the leader approached Evelyn in regards to the vines growing on the mansion, she replied. "Leave them. I think they're pretty." The workers were quick but not cheap. Thankfully, Terrence lucked out with the tractor owner. It was a friend of the musician from the bar, and he offered to cut the hay for free as long as he could keep the bales. Wearing his white cowboy hat, Terrence signed off on that and subtly directed the man to avoid part of the patch of grass behind the cotton field. Terrence didn't need to explain the reasoning to Evelyn. No one needed to know about the guns they buried.

During the evenings, Evelyn and Terrence set up the video camera and took the medication. When they woke up, they felt like they were experiencing the worst hangover ever. The dimmest light blinded them, their limbs felt weak, and their heads throbbed. As Dr. Waxen had promised, there were no blackouts and no sleepwalking. They checked the news. Still no word on any sort of gun crime committed. Terrence thought they might dodge a bullet. Evelyn was still holding her breath.

With all the activity, the Quenby House lost its signature silence. The tractor hummed in the distance, lawn mowers rumbled, and yard workers shouted instructions to one another. Evelyn snapped pictures of every antique she could find and felt convicted when she compared them to similar items on the Internet. Though she didn't know her father or her family, it felt like she was guilty of some sin by selling the family relics.

When no one was watching, Evelyn slipped into the portrait hall, turned the key, and snuck into her father's secret study. She clenched the little circular knobs on the desk drawer and pulled it out. Sharp ink pens and unorganized old documents lay within. Evelyn removed a black and white photo of a family of three standing out in front of the mansion and a 1960s Duesenberg car. There was a massive crease down the middle of the picture where someone had folded it many times. It showed a nicely dressed middle-aged couple with black hair and dark circles under their eyes standing behind a boy of seven wearing a sweater vest and slacks. Like his parents, his hair was dark, his eyes were underlined with black, and he didn't smile.

Evelyn turned over the photo. In cursive, a message said, *"The Quenbys. John, Alice, and little Maxwell. Spring 1966."* Though they were her grandparents, all Evelyn could think was that this was a big house for a small amount of people. She rested it on the stack of unfinished wills and removed the other documents. There were sales records for cotton and livestock, plummeting in price and quantity since the end of the civil war. By the looks of it, the Quenbys couldn't maintain the place after slavery was abolished. Their final cotton sale was in 1875. The closer she got to the bottom of the stack of documents, the more brittle and stained the pages became. Evelyn was surprised that the paper had survived as long as it did. With a gentle touch, she removed the original land deed dating back to July of 1824. The mansion was completed in 1832 and the first slave was purchased in 1843. When Evelyn searched the town of Adders on her phone, she realized that the Quenby property was older than the town itself.

With surviving receipts from every cotton auction, it was a wonder how this place hadn't been converted into a historical landmark. *That's why Maxwell must've wanted to keep this gem hidden.* Evelyn assumed. *The locals say he kept to himself.* Continuing her procrastination streak instead of cleaning, she shifted through the other documents. Money was funding the plantation from some unknown source. Evelyn wondered what it could be without the sales of cotton to support them.

As she sifted through legal and sales papers dating back one hundred and fifty years, Evelyn caught glimpses of the picture of the little blonde girl nailed onto the desk's backboard. She felt dread crushing her and pulled the photo from the nail. She looked into the little girl's eyes. For a moment, it was like the little girl was looking back. Evelyn shuddered and put the photograph face down. *Focus on the sale,* Evelyn reminded herself, yet like an itch she couldn't scratch, her mind went back to the girl.

The fourth night at the Sunnyside, Evelyn and Terrence scooted close together on the bed, with only illumination from the TV to light the small room. It felt like their Detroit home. The medication began to kick in, and Terrence rushed out of bed and into the bathroom. He dry-heaved for a little bit before returning to bed. Neither one of them had vomited as Dr. Waxen had said, but they'd gotten close.

They fell asleep a little bit before ten o'clock. Evelyn dreamed of Quenby House backed by the hot sun. One moment, she was standing before the massive house and next she was running from it. Suddenly, someone or something grabbed her by the neck of her shirt and dragged her down the hall. She realized that she wasn't her adult-self but a child. Her small hands reached desperately for something to grab onto while she was being taken, but there was no hope. She was dragged across the yard. Her screams were muted by a dry rag. Her legs and arms thrashed as she was pulled through the tall grass and into the cotton field. She was picked up and thrown down. Her little body thumped on the hard earth and the wind left her lungs. She smelled lighter fluid and gasoline, heard laughter, and was doused with liquid. It dripped through her blonde locks.

Evelyn thought she'd wake up from the nightmare when she saw the match produce a flame. A shadowy figure flicked at her and flames burst across her body. She screamed as loud as she could but out here, no one could hear her. Her flesh melted and her little heart raced. She thought she'd be dead by now, but the flames only grew hotter until all she knew was fire and agony.

Evelyn jolted awake, drenched in a cold sweat. Her heart sank when she looked at the cow pasture around her. Millions of stars speckled the sky. Cold air cut right through her pajamas.

Terrence sat cross-legged behind her. His eyes were closed and he was rocking back and forth, mumbling to himself. Evelyn pushed on his shoulder. "Terrence. Get up. Terrence."

Her husband's eyes shot open. He stared at Evelyn with a horrified expression, and then twisted around to study the field of rolling grass behind them.

"What--where?" Terrence tried to stand, but his knees buckled and he fell down to his shins.

Evelyn put her hands on his cheeks and turned his scrunched-up handsome face to her. "Shh. I know where we are."

"Wha... how?" Terrence said.

"Trust me," Evelyn replied. "Come on. We need to move."

Evelyn helped Terrence up. Her leg wobbled beneath her. A throbbing headache rattled her brain and she started seeing double. The drug hadn't worn off yet and the side effects hit her like a train.

"For all his diplomas, Dr. Waxen doesn't seem to know what the hell he's talking about," Terrence said through chattering teeth. He was only wearing a wrinkled white t-shirt and boxers. The only warmth they found was from each other's hand.

They raced across the cattle field, avoiding cow patties like landmines, until they reached the road. Evelyn recalled the path that the twin had drove down and started that way. They grimaced as they stepped on the rough road with their dirty bare feet.

"Where are we going?" Terrence asked, struggling to keep up with Evelyn's speed walk.

"Home," she replied. "It's a few miles down this way."

Terrence cursed. "It makes no sense that we walked that far without waking up."

"I don't know what to tell you, Terrence. You know as much as me."

"Whatever we have, it's not a normal medical condition."

"Really?" Evelyn said sarcastically.

"This is way past screwed up," Terrence mumbled.

"Hey, at least we don't have guns this time," Evelyn said to make up for her husband's lack of optimism.

"We might have. Who knows anymore? I sure don't." Terrence grumbled. "Hell, it might be good to have weapons in the middle of nowhere."

"You're acting uncharacteristically grumpy," Evelyn pointed out.

"I feel grumpy," Terrence retorted angrily.

Evelyn kept her mouth shut. About a half mile into their journey, their jog died into a painful walk. No cars drove by. No lights illuminated the street. They navigated inky blackness, feeling their hairs stand whenever they heard a critter or movement just out of sight. An hour passed, or at least what felt like an hour, it could've been more, before they reached Quenby Avenue. With lazy footsteps, they stayed on course until they reached the red brick path. Evelyn sneezed and Terrence coughed. Despite the walk, the cold never seemed to leave their bodies.

Through the long columns of trees, the mansion slowly revealed its tall, white colonnades. Panting, Evelyn and Terrence shambled towards the house. A crescent moon hung above it. There was a light on the second-story window. Evelyn and Terrence turned to one another.

"Did you turn that on today?" Terrence asked.

Mouth still dry from the long walk, Evelyn said, "No."

Cautiously, they pushed open the unlocked front door and stepped into the dark foyer. She marched to the kitchen and armed herself and Terrence with knives before proceeding up one of the curved stairways. Evelyn walked on the sides of her feet or heels due to the tenderness of her soles. They reached the second floor and silently walked through the long hall. The floor groaned and creaked, causing them to pause and trade looks with one another. Evelyn wished she had the shotgun as she approached the closed door with light streaming out from its seams.

Getting on either side of the door, Terrence turned the knob slowly and opened it into the nursery. The light was on. The toys were in the same place Evelyn saw when she last visited the room. Not seeing anyone inside, Terrence entered. Evelyn followed. The ceiling fan whirled above their heads.

"There's no one here," Terrence said with relief.

They turned back to the door, only to see the little blonde girl and the tall man in a white mask staring at them from the doorway.

Evelyn opened her mouth to scream. The light suddenly cut out.

With a gasp, Evelyn shot out of bed in her Sunnyside Motel room. She looked at Terrence, who was sleeping soundly beside her. She took inventory of herself. *It was a dream,* she said, feeling her heart pounding.

Drenched in sweat, she swiveled her legs over the edge of the bed. Her tender feet touched the cheap-carpeted floor. Evelyn didn't like that feeling. She lifted one foot and studied the bottom of it. It was bruised, raw, and dirty. Panicking, she pulled the covers off of Terrence. His feet were dirty too.

"Terrence," Evelyn rolled her husband over. His body was limp. His head was covered by a featureless white mask.

8

THE CALL

The tight cotton mask encased Terrence's face, almost as if sucking at his skin. The point of a crude knife had cut out the two crude eye holes the size of buttons, and the two ear holes the size of peas. A burnt musk lingered on the mask. Terrence's stomach rose and fell with every breath. Band-Aids decorated his fingertips. Evelyn looked at her husband with fear and uncertainty. Her muscles were tense and her breathing ragged. She brushed her fingers across the smooth cotton texture before clenching the mask in her hand and tearing it off her husband's face. Still sleeping, Terrence's head rolled limply.

Evelyn faced the mask as if it were a decapitated head. When she looked into the dark eye holes, the crackling of fire and the screams of a little girl filled her ears. Without hesitation, Evelyn threw the mask at the wall. It hit with a soft pat and plopped to the ground, wrinkled like a tissue. She turned back to Terrence.

Like worms, red veins reached to brown irises as Terrence stared at her with wide eyes.

Evelyn scooted away from him as a horrifying thought

snaked into her mind. Whoever she was looking at wasn't really her husband. He may look like him, he may smell like him, but he wasn't her Terrence.

"What happened?" Terrence asked. "Baby, you look worried."

Evelyn didn't speak. She stared at him, ready to bolt out of the room in an instant.

Sensing Evelyn's worry, Terrence sat up.

Evelyn got out of bed.

"Babe--"

Evelyn interrupted him. "What happened in the child's playroom last night?"

Terrence cocked his head in confusion. "Playroom?"

"Don't play coy. The nursery."

"I don't--" Terrence swiveled his feet out of bed.

"Stay there!" Evelyn shouted.

Terrence put his hand up in a non-threatening manner and stayed in the bed. "Okay, okay, I'm not going anywhere. Evelyn, I'm not going to hurt you."

"Were you thinking about hurting me?" Evelyn asked with frustrated suspicion.

"What? No, Eve, of course not. I'd never." Terrence replied. "Why would I?"

Evelyn didn't have a solid answer. "Something happened last night when we were at Quenby House. Whatever it was caused you to wake up with *that* on your face." She pointed to the white mask scrunched up on the floor.

Terrence gulped when he looked at it. "I was wearing *that*?"

Chewing her thumbnail, Evelyn nodded.

Terrence's eyes turned to glass. "The last thing I remember is taking the medication and going to bed with you."

Evelyn felt the breath leave her for a moment. "The

pasture, our walk, the little girl and masked man, you don't remember any of that?"

"I'm telling you the truth. I can't remember anything. You gotta believe me, babe." He looked at his dirty and raw feet with horror.

Evelyn paced, trying to get control of her frustration and fear. It only made it worse. Usually, she was good at hiding her emotions. Not now. She swept away a tear before it could fall.

"I'm scared," Terrence wiped his eyes. *Where those real tears or was it an act?* Evelyn wondered. She couldn't shake the pit in her gut that said this was not her husband.

"What the hell is happening to us?" Terrence asked.

Evelyn hated the words she spoke, but she could find only one explanation. "It's that house."

Terrence turned to Evelyn, giving her his undivided attention.

"Before we arrived, we lived normal, crappy lives, but not a single thing has made sense since we walked through that mansion's front door." Evelyn forced herself to be honest. "I don't know if demons, or karma, or spirits, or any of that unexplainable hocus pocus is real, but there is something going on here that defies explanation."

"Evelyn, maybe we're just sick," Terrence said softly. "Or the side effects of the medication--"

"Let's be honest with ourselves, Terrence. This happened way before we met the creepy doctor. Sick people don't paint the Sistine Chapel on their hallway when they can hardly doodle. They don't claw on the basement wall without reason."

Terrence stretched out his bandaged fingers. "That's what I was doing?"

Evelyn glared at him.

Terrence pursed his lips and averted his eyes.

Evelyn continued, "This all ties back to the girl, the mask, and somehow my father."

"Girl? Mask? I don't understand," Terrence said honestly.

Evelyn felt herself squirm. "Just trust me, all right?"

"I do," Terrence said feebly. "But... what should we do? Run? Burn the house down? Call an exorcist? How does any of this information help us if we don't have a solution?"

Evelyn ran her hand through her disheveled blonde hair and up her scalp. "We've been out of the house for a few days. Waking up with that mask proves that there is still a connection to the mansion even when we're away." Evelyn didn't know if her words were phony or gospel, but it sounded right and made a miniscule amount of sense in some weird way.

Startlingly quick, Terrence got out of bed and bee lined for the deflated-looking suitcase on the ground.

Evelyn took a step back, hitting her spine against the wall behind her. "What are you going?"

"Getting the hell out of here," Terrence said with vigor as he jammed dirty clothes into the suitcase.

"I just told you it won't make a difference," Evelyn argued.

"I get you want answers," Terrence said as he began putting on new clothes. "You're an investigator, I don't fault you for that, but, at the moment, I don't care about truth or the explanation. I care about my safety," Wearing his shirt on backwards, he shoved the wrinkled pajamas into the suitcase. "And I care about yours. To hell with the rest. Get packed. We're leaving."

Not since Terrence pulled Evelyn's broken body from the crashed car all those years ago had he ever been so demanding. Not wasting time to take a shower, Evelyn threw off her pajamas and put on jeans and an orange and black striped long-sleeved shirt. Holding a bobby pin between her teeth, she put her hair into a loose bun. Terrence zipped up the bag and reached for the wad of cash next to the Gideon bible. Evelyn grabbed the money before Terrence could touch it. Off his confused look, Evelyn replied. "I'll hold on to it. You get the suitcases."

Not wanting to argue, Terrence heaved up both suitcases. The cords of muscles in his arms went taut as he hustled out the door. Evelyn slung on her double-breasted raincoat and shoved the money in the inner pocket. If there was something wrong with Terrence, she needed to make sure she was prepared to survive on her own.

The grass was still dewy and the sun was low and golden. In the nearly desolate parking lot, Terrence shoved the suitcases in the back cargo hold of the minivan. He slammed the truck so hard that the van's windows rattled, and he clambered into the front seat. Evelyn took shotgun with hesitation, hoping that her suspicions of her husband were wrong as he turned the key in the ignition.

The minivan puttered to life and reversed so fast that the tires screamed and another hubcap fell off. Terrence put the vehicle into Drive and raced down the road flanked by pastures and a few pine oaks. The car wasn't a speed demon, but that didn't stop Terrence from stomping the gas. They had left so quick that Evelyn forgot to return the room key… and pay the landscapers. Running away from it all felt weak and impulsive, but her life was on the line. Evelyn rested her head against the window and watched spotted cows and red tractors reaping hay blur by. Less than an hour later, the green sign for Adders, Georgia was in their wake.

They drove in silence and slowed to the speed limit. In a few hours, they would be out of the state. Many hours after that, they'd be home. Evelyn wondered what she'd tell her kids, if she could ever have children, when they asked about their grandfather. She thought she'd lie to them, tell them she knew nothing about the mysterious Maxwell or where he lived. All of what happened in Adders would be mere memory. One locked away till the end of her days.

Evelyn watched the road and felt a wave of tiredness flood over her. *Must stay awake. Must keep an eye on Terrence.* She tried to blink the sleep away. It didn't help. The rumble of the road calmed her much more than the mansion's bed ever had. She wanted to shut her eyes.

Only for a second.

She awoke to the smell of gasoline and fumes. *Another nightmare.* Her neck cried out in pain. Her nose throbbed. She opened her eyes to the cracked windshield and the tree beyond it. It was dark outside. A gasp of pain escaped her lips as Evelyn sat up and rubbed her neck. She tasted blood on her lips and noticed a crimson smudge on the dashboard in the shape of her nose. A million questions raced through her mind. She twisted to Terrence before answering them. Her husband's face was buried in the deflated airbag. His arms were limp by his side.

"Terrence." Evelyn's voice cracked. "Wake up."

She shook his shoulder, causing his whole body to rock. He didn't react. Dread fell over Evelyn. She pushed her fingers on his neck. Nothing.

"Oh God," Evelyn whimpered and readjusted her fingers.

Nothing.

"Oh God," Evelyn felt herself cry as she readjusted her fingers again.

The faintest pulse thumped against her fingertips. Evelyn inhaled deeply. Adrenaline coursed through her veins. She unbuckled her seatbelt and fished her hand into her pocket. The simple action caused pain to shoot through her body. Dialing 911, Evelyn staggered out of the car, leaving her unconscious husband to rest.

"*State your emergency,*" said the mechanical-sounding dispatch lady.

"Car crash. My husband and I." Evelyn felt the ground move as she put her feet down. The world tilted. She blinked a few times, finding her balance.

"What is your current location?"

Evelyn waddled around the side panel of the vehicle. Over the white fumes wafting out the crumpled and corroded hood stood the mighty Quenby House backed by a pregnant moon and thin, drifting clouds.

"My house," she said with defeat before she gave the dispatch lady the address and let the phone fall from her hand with a *clack* on the red brick road.

Fate stabbed her with a knife and twisted the blade in her chest. Her car, her only means of escape, was jammed into an oak tree running alongside the path to the house. Her husband was unresponsive and possibly a replacement of his true self, and the theory about her connection to this place was unfortunately true.

She sank to her knees.

"What do you want from me?" she mumbled to whatever force was toying with her.

The midnight wind shrieked in reply.

IN A FURY of flashing lights and screaming sirens, the ambulance and police cruiser arrived. The young and strong EMTs that looked like poster boys for 1950s America dragged Terrence from the car and loaded him onto the gurney. Grabbing either side of the stretcher, they carried Terrence into the back of the ambulance.

"Have you ever been in a car accident before?" The brown-eyed and brawny EMT standing by her asked.

"Once. Years ago," Evelyn said, her eyes a thousand yards away and looking at the house. "When I tried to kill myself. Terrence saved me."

She had no clue why she told the boy her darkest secret. Not even Terrence knew the cause of the accident.

"Well," the EMT said, unsure how to reply. "Your neck appears to be okay. It's just a minor sprain. Likewise with your nose. All things considered, you're very lucky. We'll take you to the hospital while a tow truck takes care of your vehicle."

"And Terrence?" Evelyn asked.

The EMT gave her a pitying smile. "He's alive, but we can't say much else right now."

A police officer approached Evelyn after the EMT left, asking how much she had to drink that night.

"My husband and I are sober, Officer," Evelyn replied with a little more attitude than she intended. "We got distracted on the way home and he hit the tree. I think it must've been deer." Evelyn lied with a straight face.

The officer eyed her for a moment and then jotted down the answer.

In the sterile-smelling white walls of the hospital waiting room, the nurses gave Evelyn aspirin and a small neutral-colored cup of water. She quickly downed the items and slouched back in the uncomfortable but cushioned chair. With every heartbeat, her nose throbbed. *Did Terrence black out or did he mean to drive us home?* Both answers scared her.

"Mrs. Carr?"

Evelyn didn't hear the man approach. The handsome doctor had a square jaw and big eyes with streaks of natural silver in his dark hair. Putting her palms on the arm rests, Evelyn tried to stand, but he said otherwise. "You need your energy."

"Dr. Gregory," Evelyn read his nametag. "Any word on Terrence?"

"He's still unconscious. The airbag cushioned most of the impact. We believe the force of the accident rattled his brain, but honestly, we don't have a definitive answer. His vitals are fine. There's no reason why he shouldn't be waking up."

Evelyn had nothing to say. If Terrence were here, he'd make a positive quip. *"Hey, at least I'm alive."* But Evelyn didn't have much optimism before, and there was even less now. *Maybe it was good he wasn't waking up.* Evelyn shunned that thought the moment it passed through her mind. After spending five years with the man, she couldn't imagine a world without her good-natured husband.

"I noticed that your health insurance is out-of-date," the good doctor said. "Would you like to discuss payment plans now or tomorrow?"

Evelyn almost laughed at the amount of crap being dumped on her.

"Now," she replied, and felt the wad of cash in pocket that would be much smaller come this time tomorrow.

"You may stay here for the night if you wish. We have a few extra rooms," Dr. Gregory said as he handed her the proper paperwork. Evelyn glanced about the empty waiting room.

"Is it free?" Evelyn asked cynically.

"I'm afraid not."

Evelyn nodded to herself, paid her dues, and vanished out the hospital's double doors.

She saw a nurse approach Dr. Gregory before the machine doors shut. With the breeze brushing her hair against her cheek and lip, Evelyn pulled out the picture of the little blonde girl, torn at the top where the nail had been planted.

The doctor raced out of the door. "Mrs. Carr!"

Under the streetlight and with apathetic eyes, Evelyn turned back to the winded doctor.

"I've decided to cover your expenses." Dr. Gregory handed the money back to her.

"Why?" Evelyn asked skeptically.

Gregory stared at her. "I didn't realize that you're a Quenby. Come back inside. I'll get you something to eat."

Her cramping stomach replied for her. Gregory opened up the cafeteria door and flipped on the lights.

"No one's supposed to be in here this late," Gregory said as he slipped behind the counter and into the kitchen. "That never stops the nurses though."

Evelyn stood in the large room with rows of tables. "I didn't realize my family name carried so much clout," Evelyn yelled to Gregory.

Gregory returned with a few yogurts, apples, and juice cartons. "For many years, the Quenbys donated to this hospital. We're indebted to you."

Evelyn was taken back by that, wondering how much sway her family had over this town. "Do you know about Maxwell's disappearance?" Evelyn said while she accepted the food.

Dr. Gregory paused at the question. "My guess is that he ran away. He probably went stir-crazy in that mansion and wanted to say goodbye to it all. See, Maxwell wasn't the most well-liked of the Quenbys. When he vanished, things were... better."

"Tell me about him," Evelyn insisted.

"Prideful," Dr. Gregory said with venom. "He thought he was untouchable in his big house. Never worked, took whatever he liked and, unlike his father, he was stingy with his money. That's normally not an issue, but the Quenbys had a reputation for generosity, and many facilities relied on their annual donations. When Maxwell decided to withhold his support, he lost a lot of friends."

"You don't seem to like the man very much," Evelyn said.

Dr. Gregory's smile betrayed him. "I did, actually. At one time." His fingers drummed on his juice carton before he gulped it down. "It's nearly 11. I must get going, Evelyn. Do you mind if I call you that?"

"I don't see why not," Evelyn replied.

The handsome doctor smiled in a way that would melt many girl's hearts. "Enjoy your meal, Evelyn. I'll see you tomorrow."

Taking her food with her, Evelyn ventured down the hall into the room the nurses had prepped for her. She requested that the nurse lock the hospital door while she slept. Suspicious, the woman granted the request.

In the clean and crisp hospital room, Evelyn flopped onto the stiff mattress. She couldn't sleep even if she wanted to, which she didn't. She locked her fingers together on her slender stomach and thought how best to find the blonde girl or her body.

Sunlight crawled over the carpeted floor, up the bed, and across Evelyn's determined face. The nurse unlocked the door and entered with a metal tray. An orange juice carton and eggs rested on the tray top. Evelyn ate quickly, for energy over taste. "Tell Dr. Gregory I said thanks," Evelyn said mid-bite.

"You sure you don't want to tell him yourself?" the nurse replied.

"No time," Evelyn said and slung on her jacket. "Call me if Terrence wakes up."

She took a cab back to Quenby House. The landscapers were working feverishly as always. The tractor rumbled in the hay fields. Everything seemed… normal. Evelyn glanced at the plastic bumper left behind at the base of an ancient oak and went inside of the mansion. She marched to the foyer and through the hall of portraits. Moving aside the corner of one painting and turning the key, she slipped into her father's private study. She scoured every inch of it, finding a wide-brim fedora from the 1940s, stacks of old National

Geographic, and various religious texts and textbook examinations of the supernatural. *Was Father looking for answers too?* Evelyn pulled open the drawers of the desk, put aside the documents, and opened various travel brochures. One was from Hawaii, and the original stamped plane tickets were tucked away inside.

Evelyn kept sifting through old knick-knacks and Antebellum-era artifacts stored away for safekeeping. She found two ruby earrings covered in a sheen of dust and an empty ring box. Evelyn wondered if they were owned by her mother. She discovered a large stash of crosses hidden under the bed and a slit in the mattress used to store small objects. Evelyn reached her hand inside, feeling feathers and cotton but not finding anything. As she walked around the room, Evelyn felt a loose floorboard under her foot. Stopping, she looked at the wooden plank before putting her fingertips underneath and pulling it up. Inside was a green hair ribbon and a lock box. Evelyn removed both objects and blew on them. The dust rolled off like a miniature sandstorm. She clenched the hair ribbon and re-examined the photo of the little girl. Atop the girl's sunny hair was the vibrant green ribbon tied into a bow. Evelyn used her lock-picking tools to open the box and found a stack of children's drawings. It showed a tall man and a blonde girl standing out of a crude rendition of the Quenby House, another with them in the cotton field and in a series of other locations. The hairs of Evelyn's neck stood when she realized they shared the same orientation as the blonde girl and masked man in the mural Evelyn had painted.

Evelyn flipped the drawings to their back. Written in crayon, the text read, "Max and me."

Evelyn lowered the children's drawings.

"What did my father do to you?" Evelyn asked aloud.

The house was silent. She needed more evidence. She

needed to know this girl's name. She researched *"Adders, Georgia murder"* on her phone. There was a story about a husband who shot his cheating wife in 90s, but that had nothing to do with a little girl or Maxwell. She tried more in-depth searches but found nothing under murder. She leaned back in the leather desk chair and scratched her swollen nose. She winced at the action and searched, *"Adders, Georgia kidnapping."*

No results.

"Adders, Georgia missing girl."

A hit. Actually, multiple hits. But one with a familiar face stood out. Evelyn clicked on it.

Evelyn opened the photocopied version of a news article on her small phone screen. June 29, 2003 was the date on the news article, over a decade ago. It displayed a picture of a cute blonde girl with big blue eyes, a wide carefree smile, and faint freckles on the bridge of her nose and under her eyes. Mary Sullivan, seven years old, left in the morning to visit friends, the report said, before vanishing. She was known to bike everywhere and frequently left the house. Her guardians didn't report her absence until 8:42 pm that night. No trace of her was ever found.

Evelyn glanced through the rest of the web pages. There were reports of other girls missing over the last three decades, but nothing more on Mary.

Using a photocopied version of the Mary's missing person poster, Evelyn found the names and contact information of Jack and Angie Sullivan, her aunt and uncle/legal guardians.

Evelyn dialed the number.

After a few rings, she heard a *"Hello?"* It was a male's voice, gruff and brutish like a frontiersman.

"Mr. Sullivan?" Evelyn's voice echoed slightly in the hidden study.

"Whatever you're selling, I'm not buying."

"It's about Mary."

She could practically hear the air leaving Jack's room. *"What about her?"*

"I want to help you find her. My name is Evelyn Carr. I'm a private investigator."

"Mary's long gone. Don't waste your time."

"All I need is a few moments with you. It won't cost you anything, I swear."

"It will cost me, Investigator Carr. Only I'll be paying with my peace, not my wallet."

"Can we meet this afternoon?" Evelyn asked, not willing to take no for an answer.

Sealing up the secret study, Evelyn headed to the Sullivan residence. It was a single-story house with drab paint and junk-littered front yard. Multiple big dogs barked at Evelyn from a wide, fenced-in pen beside the house. Jack opened the screen door upon Evelyn's approach. He was a tall man with a keg-like torso, more muscle than fat, and a bushy, soot-colored beard that covered half of his face and fell a few inches past the V-neck of his white t-shirt. Deep lines were etched around his unreadable blue eyes, and wrinkles snaked over his untamed brows and across his forehead. His breath smelled like PBR and, from what little Evelyn could see beneath the mustache that ran over his upper lip, his teeth were slightly crooked and yellow.

"What happened to your nose?" Jack asked.

"My husband's a bad driver," Evelyn replied, stepping past him and into the dirty home.

"I've heard that one before," Jack said behind her.

Dog fur and dirt gathered in the corners of the house, a handful of dirty dishes jutted from the sink, and a black splinter crack disrupted the image on the large living room TV screen. The home's sour scent combatted the cheap air fresheners plugged into nearly every outlet. Evelyn noticed there were no pictures of Mary on the walls or anywhere for that matter. When asked about it, Jack replied, "You wouldn't want to be reminded of your failure all day, either."

Evelyn took a seat on the couch with cat claw marks on the lower portion of the armrest. In between the cushions, she could see powdery Doritos fragments and loose change. *Was the messiness a reality of Mary's childhood, or a result of her vanishing*? Evelyn wondered.

A willowy woman stepped out of the bathroom and seemingly floated to the nearby recliner. Angie's arms and leg looked like sticks of skin and bone jutting out of her yellow floral dress and sandals. Her upper ribs pressed hard against her pale skin and could be seen at her neckline. Sunken and touched by age, her green eyes spoke of sorrow. Her hair was cut evenly just below her jawline and was splashed with the color of wet ash.

The Sullivans waited for Evelyn to say the first words. "I want to know about Mary's disappearance."

"You aren't local, and never has an outsider cared what's happened in Adders. Why does my niece concern you?" Jack lingered nearby with his arms crossed over his broad chest.

"I make my living looking for the forgotten," Evelyn said.

"You said this was free," Jack reminded her.

"It is," Evelyn retorted. "Mary has some significance in my life, let's just leave it at that. Now are we going to talk or waste even more time?"

Jack and Angie traded looks and then gestured for Evelyn to proceed.

"Tell me about Mary. What was she like?"

A tiny, sad smile formed on Angie's hollow face. "Mary loved to play. She loved the outdoors. Every summer day, she'd ride that bike of hers. Up and down. Up and down. It had little tassels on the handlebars. Do you remember the tassels, dear? The little ones on the handlebars?"

Jack stared at her a moment. "Yeah," but the word sounded more like a grunt than anything.

"Did she act any different leading up to and on the day she vanished?" Evelyn inquired.

"No," Angie replied, her reminiscing smile fleeting. "The only change is that she never came home for supper."

"Describe her home life," Evelyn asked.

Angie gave Jack a sharp look. "Peaceful. Happy. Normal." Something about her tone suggested a more sinister reality.

"Discipline and order, that's what keeps a house in line," Jack said with gruff resolve.

Evelyn began to realize why Mary was away so often. "Was there anyone who wanted to hurt Mary?"

"Apparently someone did," Jack said.

"Did she have any stalkers or people you suspected after she vanished?"

"There was one," Angie said, looking Evelyn in the soul with her jaded eyes. "Maxwell Quenby."

9

THE TRIO

Jack boiled at the mention of Maxwell's name. He grumbled what seemed like the foulest assortment of curse words he could muster.

Evelyn ignored him and spoke to Angie. "Tell me about Maxwell."

"He lived in that old plantation house outside of time," Angie said. "Some days, Mary would bike down his street. Maxwell would give her candy and other gifts. We thought he was harmless, truly, but then Mary vanished."

"That police, incompetent as they are, wouldn't arrest Maxwell," Jack said. "Not enough conclusive evidence, they said. To hell with them. Everyone knows that the Quenbys donate to the department every year."

Evelyn jotted down the information, realizing that her family had their hand in a lot of honeypots. "Did Mary visit Maxwell often?"

Angie and Jack traded looks.

"I don't know," Jack admitted. "Mary would bike all over the place. God knows the people she met during her travels."

Evelyn tried pressing them for information regarding

Mary's other friends and the times she'd stay out late. Jack and Angie answered the best they could, but time had clearly muddled their memories. None of the information was useful. Before she left, Evelyn asked a final question. "What happened to Mary's parents?"

"One's in jail, and the other is dead." Jack glared at Evelyn. "Don't have an affair."

He let Evelyn piece the rest of the story together. After the meeting, Evelyn called a cab and thought of her next move. Her mind drifted back to her father, a man she'd never seen, and his odd reputation. She wondered what it must be like to live under a parent's shadow and to shoulder that burden alone. Maybe he did run away? Or did he become the man in the white mask and Mary was his victim? If that was true, what did that mean for Evelyn? Would the revelation be enough to end her and Terrence's plight?

She returned to Quenby House. The white flowers on its vines shimmied in the breeze. *Such a beautiful place for such evil.* Evelyn entered the house. The afternoon sun vanished as she shut the door behind her. She rested her back against it and took a deep breath. Her busted nose throbbed and had her head pounding. *If my father is a monster, what am I?* Evelyn struck down the thought. She'd never defined herself by her parents or lack thereof. Why start now?

She glanced up at the mural of trumpeting angels painted across the domed ceiling.

"Help me," Evelyn mumbled to the cracked mural of heaven. She noticed something shift on the ceiling, almost as if the paint was moving. Suddenly, the baby-faced angels began to swirl around the inside of the dome. Their little mouths opened to scream, but no sound escaped. Within seconds, their snowy skin blackened as if they were being grilled. The paint blue sky turned black. The puffy white clouds turned blood red. All the angels screamed and burned, yet no sound escaped their lips.

Evelyn clenched her eyes shut. The air inside the house became thick. *Stop. Please stop.*

After counting to ten, Evelyn reopened her eyes. The ceiling painting had returned to normal. The atmosphere was normal. Evelyn hunched over, feeling like she'd vomit. She was uncertain if this was a vision or a hallucination.

She noticed that the foyer had grown dark around her. It was 1 p.m. when Evelyn arrived. She twisted back to the door and windows, seeing the sunset. *No way.* She looked at herself. Specks of dried paint were splattered on her fingers and shirt. She noticed the door to the hall was open. She stared at it cautiously. Half of her wanted to see what lay within; the other half wanted her to run like hell. Remembering that the car would put her back in the house no matter what, she carefully approached the door. Heart racing with fear and anticipation, she peeked her head into the pitch-black hall.

Evelyn found herself holding her breath as she flipped the light switch. The bulbs flickered in ceiling-mounted glass cases. Across the very same wall where she had painted the last mural, there was another, fresher painting that was triple the size and stretched over the entire wall, door to door. Ceiling to floor.

With the ceiling lights still flickering, Evelyn stepped into the hall. With each flash, a portion of the mural revealed itself. The nearest showed a road that looked a lot like Quenby Avenue. A blonde girl on her pink bicycle was in the process of stopping in front of three people wearing white masks. Black splotches had been used for their eye holes. From them, inky tears dripped down the wall and unto the hall's floor.

Another light flicker later, and Evelyn saw the next part

of the mural. The girl was riding her bike into the woods as three masked figures chased after her.

The light kept strobing.

The third part of the mural showed the masked figures carrying away the blonde girl while her bike was abandoned by a fat tree with an owl hole.

Evelyn walked through the hall that seemed to blink out of this existence every other second.

The fourth showed three figures dragging the girl by the plantation house and towards a cotton field.

The fifth and final aspect of the mural displayed an orange, yellow, and red fire blazing up from the center of the cotton field. The masked figures stood around it. Two looked into the flame. One looked directly at Evelyn.

Evelyn covered her mouth, involuntarily tasting the paint on her palm. She felt herself shake. Her steel resolve shattered. The lights suddenly stopped flickering and returned to normal. The wet mural began melting away the images.

"What do you want me to do?" Evelyn asked the house, which felt like the most insane and most sane things she'd done since she first heard that scratching sound in the basement. A cold breeze drifted through the house. She felt her chest tighten as she looked at the painted fireball dripping away.

Evelyn exited the house and allowed the clean Georgia air to circulate through her. "If I find those men, will you set me free?"

Silence. Like always.

Evelyn tucked her blonde hair behind her ears. She knew she was on her own.

She walked down the red brick road and onto the street. Evelyn tried to imagine herself as Mary. The little girl's hands on the bicycle handlebars. Her tiny feet churning the pedals. Evelyn turned to her right. The single-lane street ran in a line, well past Quenby House and into a more heavily trafficked street that was too far away to be seen.

Evelyn kept on, keeping an eye out for any evidence left behind after a near twenty-year murder. The odds were slim, but she had to try. She walked into the trees opposite of her property.

Twigs cracking beneath her shoes, Evelyn marched deeper into the woods. Soon the road vanished in her wake and only sentry oaks surrounded her. Their points reached to the cloudy heavens. Their shadow cast over Evelyn in oddly-shaped blobs while unseen birds screamed out of sight. Beetle and other ground bugs scurried under felled leaves upon Evelyn's approach. Evelyn stopped in front of a massive oak with an owl hole. Evelyn twisted about the wooded area. No bike. Figures. With a case this cold, she was grasping at straws. If the killers were smart, they would've hidden the evidence.

That's when she saw it. The pink plastic casing from a handlebar pressed into the earth by time and nature. Tattered but glittery plastic tassels streamed out of the end of the casing. *Just like Angie said.*

Evelyn was alone, yet she felt someone's eyes on her, seemingly watching her from all directions at once, if that was possible. Evelyn shut her eyes, collecting herself. *You're tired. That's all,* Evelyn lied to herself. Deep down, she felt like a pawn in someone else's game, meddling with forces of which she had no comprehension.

Digging her fingernails into the packed dirt, Evelyn removed the handlebar's plastic casing from the ground. The rest of the bike was nowhere to be found. On her hands and knees, Evelyn crawled and dug around the area, looking for more of Mary's items. She saw a corner of a half-inch binder sticking out from the earth. Evelyn pulled at it, removing the white, three-ring binder from the soil. The papers inside were completely washed out and decomposed into small misshapen squares. One laminated page survived, with faded Sharpie writing. "6-29-2003."

Evelyn shook off the loose dirt on the drawing and used her hand to get rid of the rest. Created with crayon, it showed a little blonde girl clutching a doll in one hand and using her other hand to hold the hand of a beardless man in front of a huge house with pillars. *Maxwell and the Quenby House.* Evelyn recognized the doll, too. If she wasn't mistaken, it was the same one she found in the scorched cotton field. A shiver danced down Evelyn's spine.

The picture included three more stick figures in the background. They had frowns and angled brows, watching in the distance. All three looked nearly identical, except one had long brown hair and the other two had short hair.

Evelyn brushed her thumb across the three jealous stick figures and removed some excess dirt from their faces. *Mary knew she was being stalked. Why didn't she tell her guardians?*

Evelyn studied the back of the drawing. She re-read the Sharpie note. The date stuck out. June 29, 2003. The day Mary vanished. Evelyn removed her phone and reviewed her picture catalogue. She opened the photos she took of her father's secret study and swiped through the images until she found one of Maxwell's plane tickets to Hawaii. That was dated 2003. He left June 27th and got back on July 2. Her father couldn't have taken Mary during that time. Unless, Evelyn thought of another possibility, Maxwell returned home during that vacation time. It was unlikely, but he had a few days to do so. Also, Hawaii seemed like such a random destination.

Evelyn focused on the three stick figures. These were the people she needed to find.

Brushing the dirt off herself, Evelyn left the woods and contacted the cab driver.

"Have you lived in Adders for a while?" Evelyn asked the driver as he rolled to a stop twenty minutes later.

"My whole life," the man replied. "This town has a way have sucking people in and keeping them forever."

Evelyn tried not to be creeped out by the man's cryptic answer and asked, "Do you know about the disappearance of Mary Sullivan?"

The man thought for a moment, pulling at one side of his thick mustache in a provocative manner. "Many believed she was murdered, not kidnapped."

"Why say that?"

"Because Mary wasn't the only person who vanished. None of the others were ever found either."

Evelyn remembered the Missing Persons reports from all those decades ago. "You think the same guy took them all?"

The cab driver shrugged. "I have no idea. Besides, that's old news. The little girl was the last one to go."

Evelyn processed the information. "Did anything else happen that year?"

"I don't think so. If you're so curious, I can take you to the police station. Sheriff Yates knows more about it than anyone."

"Take me to him," Evelyn commanded.

Looking at Evelyn's paint-stained hands and swollen nose in the rearview mirror, the drive said. "You're not very normal, you know that?"

"Good, I'll fit right in."

The driver took Evelyn to the sheriff's office. The building was rectangular and brick with an American flag post jutting out of the front lawn. Unsure how long the meeting would take, Evelyn told the cab driver to go on.

Evelyn bounced up the steps and pushed through one of two glass doors with the sheriff department decal on it. She approached the young woman at the receptionist's desk, who didn't look a day over twenty-one. She had short blonde hair, a cute, naive face, and a yellow blouse. A deputy wearing a green uniform and black felt hat leaned on the counter with a lusty grin on his face. "Come on, Sunshine. Come out with me tonight. I'll show you my secret spot."

"I'd love to, Deputy, but Avery's already invited me to go line dancing tonight."

The deputy frowned. "Your loss."

He straightened his posture and brushed by Evelyn, turning back to check out her bottom before he left.

Evelyn approached the desk.

The girl smiled sweetly. "My name's Claire. My friends call me Sunshine. How may I help you?

"I'd like to discuss something important with the sheriff. Is he available?"

"Can I have your name?"

Evelyn told her and waited by patiently while the receptionist picked up the old cord phone and dialed one. She smiled at Evelyn as she waited. "Yes, Sheriff. It's Sunshine. There's a woman here who'd like to discuss something with you. She says she has evidence for a case regarding Mary Sullivan… Uh huh… Thank you… Yes. I'll get you coffee too… Thank you." Sunshine hung up. "He's ready to see you."

Sheriff Garrett Yates opened the door for Evelyn and allowed her passage into his office. Yates had red hair and a red beard touched with gray on its sides and seemingly painted on his face. By the air of maturity about him, Evelyn could tell he was much older than he looked.

"What can I do for you?" he asked and sat at the rim of his clean desk.

Evelyn showed him the laminated drawing. "Mary Sullivan drew and had this laminated the day she vanished."

Yates grabbed the drawing in both hands and studied it.

"I believe the three men in the background are responsible for her disappearance," Evelyn continued.

Yates set the drawing on his desk. He put his hands in his pocket. "Could be. But this was drawn by a seven-year-old. It's not exactly foolproof."

"I guess you're not going to reopen the investigation?" Evelyn said.

"I never closed the investigation," Yates replied. "But we've hit enough road blocks that it's not a priority at the moment. May I ask why it concerns you?"

"My father was Maxwell Quenby. He may be responsible."

"You are a Quenby, huh?" the sheriff said. "I didn't know there were any of you left."

"Here I am," Evelyn replied. "Will you help me prove my father's innocence? My family gave a lot of money to this department over the years. I think it's time to cash in on the investment."

Yates chuckled. "Just like a Quenby. I'll tell you what: you bring me something solid, I'll prioritize this case. Deal?"

Evelyn let out a sigh. "Deal. Can you answer a few questions first?"

"Sure."

"Who were the suspects?" Evelyn asked.

"Maxwell for one, but the plane tickets proved otherwise."

"How about the scorch mark in his cotton field? Was that evidence?"

"Never noticed it." Yates replied casually.

Evelyn nodded, suspicious of the man. "Any other suspects?"

"Andrew Doyle," the sheriff replied.

"Where can I find him?"

"In the Adders cemetery. Six feet underground," Yates said, charmed by his own wit.

Evelyn wasn't amused. "How did that happen?"

"That's another case, Mrs. Carr."

"Cut me some slack," Evelyn pressed. "Why did you suspect him?"

"Because his body was recovered the morning after Mary vanished with a self-inflicted gunshot wound. There was evidence that he was moved and dumped there," the sheriff said. "My wife says I'm forgetful, but I never forget a case."

"There was no information of the murder online," Evelyn said.

Sheriff nodded. "You must be new to Adders. Let me give you a tip. We live in a bubble. It's a nice bubble, but a fragile one. One poke and POP, the whole town goes poof."

Sunshine walked in and gave Yates his coffee. He sniffed the steam in ecstasy. "Look into Doyle or don't," the sheriff said. "It's not going to change the fact that Mary Sullivan is long gone. If you'll excuse me, Mrs. Carr. I have work to do."

Suspicious, Evelyn left the sheriff's office. She looked up Andrew Doyle on her phone's Internet web search and, after about twenty minutes, found his obituary. He was thirty-two when he died. Andrew was a stone-faced man with a big nose, soft eyes, and silky hair. Something about him looked familiar. Evelyn noticed the date of his death. June 8, 2003. The day after Mary vanished. At least she knew the sheriff wasn't lying. No cause of death was listed. The obituary read, "lived on by his brother and sister: Catherine and Stephen Doyle." Evelyn searched for them as well, finding a picture of Stephen on a farming website. She recognized him as the twin who entered her house uninvited. Evelyn felt the hairs rise on the back of her neck, starting to connect the dots.

Evelyn couldn't find Stephen's address. She recalled the place where she woke up in the cow pasture and headed that way in a cab. After driving down a single-lane country road, she spotted an old two-story house tucked away at the end of a long driveway. She had the cab driver pull up to the front, and Evelyn knocked on the door. Hands in her pockets, she waited for someone to answer.

After a moment, Stephen opened the door. His bug-like eyes scrutinized her. His mouth was tightly closed above his sharp jaw. His short hair was silky smooth and nicely cut. He wore a white polo, khaki shorts, and gray slip-on shoes.

"Hi Stephen," Evelyn said.

"What do you want?" he asked, looking past her and at the cab. "Did you leave something in my pasture when you were sneaking around, or are you here to threaten to call the cops again?"

"Nothing like that," Evelyn reassured. "Have you ever heard of Mary Sullivan?"

"No."

"She went missing years ago. Your brother died the day after."

Stephen clenched his fist so tightly that the blue veins bulged. "Get off my porch."

"Stephen--" Evelyn said.

The man stepped out of the door frame and glared down at Evelyn. He shoved his finger at her. "Go!"

"Can't we--"

Stephen did not wait for her to finish before he turned back around and slammed the door in Evelyn's face.

Evelyn looked like an idiot standing on his front porch. Any other case, she would've pressed him for more information, but this was a delicate game. She needed to rethink her strategy.

Ring!

Evelyn's heart nearly stopped at the sound of her own phone. The light ceased its flicker. Evelyn didn't recognize the number.

"Hello?" she answered, unable to take her eyes off the mural.

"Mrs. Carr, this is Dr. Gregory. I have some good news. Your husband is awake."

"Tell him I'm on my way," Evelyn said and hung up. She gave the Doyle house a final look before rushing to the hospital.

Terrence rested against the backboard of the hospital bed, dressed in patient's garb. His dark face seemed gaunter since Evelyn last saw him. A nurse stood by, checking his vitals on the monitor.

"Could you excuse us?" Evelyn asked when she entered. It came out much ruder than she would've liked. Giving Evelyn a disgusted look, the nurse exited, keeping the door open. Evelyn shut it and turned back to her husband.

"They said I was in a car accident on the way back," Terrence said, almost disbelieving. "Is your nose hurt because of that?"

"Yeah, but it doesn't matter." Evelyn replied.

"Of course it matters," Terrence retorted. "I could've killed you. Eve, this is--"

"Shut up and listen to me, Terrence," Evelyn said quietly as she moved towards him.

Terrence opened his mouth to speak but then shut it and reluctantly gave Evelyn his attention.

Evelyn still felt that heavy, inexplicable feeling inside that she couldn't trust him. Nonetheless, she needed an ally. She twisted back to the hospital hallway to make sure no one was listening and then turned back to Terrence.

"I think I understand what's happening now."

10

DEATH AT THE DOORSTEP

Evelyn paced as she explained the case to Terrence. "Three people killed Mary. Two had short hair. One had long hair. That translates to two guys and one girl. Andrew, Stephen, and Catherine Doyle. When Maxwell was away, they came to his house and committed the murder. Maxwell wasn't arrested, but his reputation was destroyed. He ran off or maybe killed himself. I don't know, but I feel this is more about the girl than my father. If we catch these killers, the girl finds peace and all our problems end."

"Evelyn," Terrence said with hesitation. "Should we be getting involved in this?"

Evelyn glared. "Yes, Terrence. It's the only way."

"But how do we know?" Terrence asked.

"The murals, as I explained. It's all linked together. Don't give me that look. You were the one who drove us home."

"You can't blame me for that. You know I had no control over it," Terrence argued.

Or did you? Evelyn wanted to ask but knew it would get her nowhere. For the sake of her sanity, Evelyn needed to trust that the man was her husband.

Terrence averted his eyes. "I only want us to be safe. Confronting someone who burned a seven-year-old for no reason doesn't sound very safe."

Evelyn approached, got on her knees, and took his hand in her own. She looked into his eyes. "Please, Terrence. I have never begged for anything in my life."

Terrence looked at her with empathy. "I'm with you, Evelyn. I'll always be with you. I only--"

Evelyn pulled close to him and planted her lips on his. She felt her courage returning. Their kiss ended when the door opened. Dr. Gregory stood in the threshold. "Am I interrupting?"

"Yes, but we're finished now," Evelyn said, turning back to him.

"I'm going to have to steal your husband away," Dr. Gregory said.

Evelyn and Terrence traded concerned looks.

"Why?" Evelyn asked.

Dr. Gregory replied, "There are still tests to be done. His condition, it's an abnormality and must be evaluated before he can leave."

"How long will that take?" Terrence asked.

"Three or four days at the most," Dr. Gregory said. "It's for your safety."

Terrence leaned into Evelyn and whispered, "Can you wait that long?"

Evelyn whispered back with fiery determination. "We need to end this, Terrence. Once and for all."

For a moment it looked like Terrence was going to protest. Instead, he turned to the doctor. "We're checking out now."

"I would not recommended it," Dr. Gregory said, friendly but stern. "The hospital has already taken care of the fee. Take advantage of the opportunity."

"We appreciate everything, Dr. Gregory, but we have something we must do." Evelyn rose from the floor.

"This is not a jail. I'm not going to lock you up," Gregory said, trying to keep a lid on his frustration. "But if anything happens, like another car accident perhaps, it's on your heads."

"We understand the risks," Terrence replied. "Can I get my clothes back?"

Once Terrence had changed back into his jeans and tan button up shirt with little instruments on it, they exited the hospital.

"How *are* you feeling?" Evelyn finally asked as they waited for the cab. Stars speckled the night sky.

"Could be worse," Terrence said. "I'm still in one piece. What's the plan?"

Evelyn explained it to him.

EVEN AT NIGHT, the flat Georgian landscape was alive with green grass and wildflowers outside of the small town. Clusters of ancient trees spotted the fields. The cab driver let them off on the side of the road, flanked by two cattle pastures. Evelyn fished out some cash and thanked the driver for his services. He drove off. Terrence approached the fence. It had wooden pins connected by wire mesh. A number of black and white cows grazed on the tall grass spotted with dung. Terrence turned back to Evelyn. "I should've brought my cowboy hat."

"Just climb the fence," Evelyn said, a small smile betraying her seriousness.

After checking the streets for any oncoming cars, Terrence planted his hands on top of the post, put his feet into the mesh, and heaved himself over. His feet landed on the other side, narrowly missing a cow paddy. Evelyn followed Terrence over. Under the cover of darkness, they scurried across the open pasture. Terrence had suggested they bring a flashlight, but Evelyn knew that would draw unwanted attention.

They swatted off bugs and steered clear of the livestock. Evelyn wondered if the blackout led her here because the supernatural force knew the Doyles were guilty. It seemed plausible. Were the shotguns for the Doyles too? They said they were looking for something. Evelyn didn't know. She felt dread sink in, still unsure what Terrence and her shot that night.

Jogging until their calves were sore and their shoes were stained with dried poo, they noticed the silhouette of a two-story house in the distance. Light streamed from its windows. There was a sedan parked in the driveway. Terrence and Evelyn hunched low to the ground as they neared the property. By the time they reached the fence, they were completely prone and crawling up the itchy grass on their bellies.

"House or shed?" Evelyn asked herself.

"This is my first breaking and entering, but I'd say shed. If we find what we need, there's no reason to go inside," Terrence whispered, keeping his eye on the house. It was an old building made in the thirties with a covered porch, wooden window shutters, and a symmetrical box design.

"Stephen's truck is not here," Evelyn noticed.

"Do we come back later?" Terrence asked.

"No. The night Stephen picked me up out here, he was driving around at 4 a.m."

"Doing what?" Terrence asked.

"I have no clue," Evelyn replied honestly.

They waited a half an hour, but it felt much longer than that. Finally, the lights in the house shut off. After a moment, Terrence and Evelyn hurried over the fence. They ran up the driveway and to the shed. It was a rectangular structure made of unpainted wood. There was a window on each side made up of four glass panes. The door had a wooden X on its front and a master lock on its rusty metal latch. Terrence flipped over the surrounding rocks.

"Looking for a key," he replied off of Evelyn's look. The moon reflected on the sweat of his bald head.

Evelyn checked her pockets and pulled out her lock-picking tool. "Never leave home without it."

She fiddled with the lock until it popped. Keeping the open lock on the latch, she opened the shed door. The interior was musty and cramped with tools, lawn mowers, and old car parts.

"Keep guard," Evelyn told Terrence.

He nervously looked around while Evelyn pulled out her smartphone and turned on the flashlight. Every sharp rake or paint can that the light brushed across cast long shadows through the room. Evelyn tiptoed across the dirt floor. She spotted a few gasoline tanks over varying capacities and liquid levels. One of them had rust spots on its tin frame and dated back to 1988. Still, there was no possible way she could link that to Mary's death. Evelyn headed to the back of the shed. She glanced at the wall of hammers, screwdrivers, and other tools. There was a heavy-duty metal tool trunk beneath it. Evelyn popped the latch and opened it. She removed the tray of tools from inside. Her eyes widened and her heart quickened as she looked down at the white cotton mask lying at the box's bottom.

It's him. Evelyn knew at once.

"Evelyn!" Terrence called with a loud whisper.

Evelyn twisted to the door in time to see the large truck pulling into the driveway. Its headlights grew closer by the second. "Close the door!" Evelyn commanded.

"What?" Terrence replied, panicking.

"Do it!"

Reluctantly, Terrence shut Evelyn inside and fiddled with the lock to make it look like it was set. He rushed by the right-side window and vanished behind the shed. Evelyn turned off the light on her phone and ducked down. The truck's high beams sliced through the slits between the shed's plank walls and created jail bars over Evelyn's chest and face. She held her breath as the vehicle shut off.

The door opened, spilling country music into the night.

Evelyn stayed still.

The music died with the headlights.

The door slammed. Someone yawned.

Footsteps neared the shed.

Turn around. Evelyn silently commanded as the figure approached the shed's door. *Why are you coming here?*

A key ring rattled together.

Evelyn looked for a place to hide. She ducked behind the ride-on lawn mower.

The figure outside hesitated as he saw the door. He lifted the unlocked lock and pushed open the door. Evelyn hunched low and covered her mouth. The figure was silhouetted in the door frame. He glanced around the room and lifted his t-shirt. A holster with a small pistol was tucked between his belt and pelvis. He withdrew it, clicked off the safety, and took his first step inside.

Evelyn frantically looked for a weapon as beads of sweat trickled down her brow. Her hands found a hand shovel made for gardening. It had a pointed edge. It would have to work.

The man took another step inside, fully entering.

Evelyn could hear his nasal breathing. His hand reached for the beaded string dangling from the ceiling light bulb. His fingers wrapped around it, preparing to tug.

Evelyn clenched the small spade in her paint-stained

fingers, ready to lunge the second the light turned on.

Crash!

The man and Evelyn both twisted back.

The noise sounded behind the shed.

The man rushed out of the room and ran around back.

Evelyn leapt to her feet and started running. She slipped on something, nearly smashing her face on the paint cans. She looked at what caused her to stumble.

It was her minivan's hubcap.

Evelyn didn't investigate further. She ran like hell out of the shed and over the pasture fence. She dropped prone in the tall grass and watched the man walk around the shed in search of the cause of the noise. Evelyn spotted Terrence crouching behind the air-conditioning unit behind the house.

Gun raised, Stephen approached Terrence's hiding spot.

Don't move, Terrence. Don't move. Evelyn wished she could yell. She could see Terrence tense up and get looking for a place to run.

Stephen got closer and closer. Evelyn picked up a rock, ready to throw it at the truck in hopes the car alarm would deter him.

Stephen stopped about six feet from Terrence, scanned the area, and holstered his gun. He walked back to the shed and entered. The light flicked on and he closed the door. Keeping low, Evelyn moved up parallel to the shed and, at a distance, peered through the window as Stephen lifted the cotton mask and looked it in the eyes. By the time Evelyn pulled her phone from her pocket and got the camera ready, Stephen had put the mask away.

Terrence clambered over the fence and gestured for Evelyn to run his way. Reluctant, Evelyn followed after him. When the house was just a black blob in the distance, they slowed their sprint and caught their breath.

"That was too freaking close," Terrence panted, drenched in sweat.

Hunched, Evelyn rested her palms on her knees. Perspiration glued her blonde hair to her forehead. "It's him, Terrence. I saw the mask."

"So him and his twin are the other two killers?"

Evelyn nodded. "That's my theory. They had our hubcap, too."

"What? How?"

"He followed us to the motel," Evelyn said, her mouth still dry from the run.

"But no one knew we were there," Terrence replied.

"He did," Evelyn said. "Let's get back home before he starts looking for us. Tomorrow, we'll call the cops, tell them about the hubcap robbery, and get them to search Stephen's shed. If they find the mask, pray to God they arrest him."

The walk was long and sticky. By the time they reached Quenby House, Evelyn's feet were screaming to get out of her shoes. With slumped shoulders and defeated eyes, the couple shambled toward to the plantation house.

"I'm not going to be a happy camper if we sleepwalk tonight," Terrence said as they stumbled through the front door.

"I don't know how you can still joke after all this," Evelyn hiked the foyer stairs, using the railing to heave herself up. They reached the master bathroom and climbed into the tube and turned on the upper shower head, washing away the sweat, dirt, and cattle dung.

Still wet, Evelyn and Terrence flopped on their bed and stared at the canopy. Evelyn's heart still pounded, though she couldn't tell if it was from the excruciating walk or the encounter with Mary's killer. A small fear pinged in the back of her mind. *Stephen saw you. He is coming.*

Under the watchful eye of their Sony video camera,

Terrence and Evelyn struggled to keep their eyes shut. Evelyn gripped Terrence's calloused hands and waited anxiously for dawn to break.

At 3 a.m., something broke.

Evelyn and Terrence shot out of bed at the sound of glass shattering.

They turned to one another, only able to see each other's silhouette and the whites of their eyes. Evelyn opened the dresser drawer, feeling around for her extendable baton and smartphone. Terrence leaned over the bed. He returned with his fingers coiled around the grip of a wooden slugger.

"Wait here," Terrence whispered.

"No," Evelyn replied.

That was the extent of their argument.

Together, they headed for the door. Terrence flipped the light switch with a Band-Aid-wrapped fingertip. No light came to their aid. Before they left the room, Evelyn headed for the oil lamp. Terrence grabbed her wrists and shook his head. He picked up the camera off of its tripod, fiddled with the buttons, and turned on night vision.

Pressed shoulder to shoulder, they looked at the monitor of the camera. Its verdant glow illuminated their sharp chins and eyes. On the screen, the room before them was shades of dark green and black, but clearer than that, the abyss in which they currently stood. To ensure they could both see their path, they needed to walk closely together, constantly bouncing their eyes between the monitor and the real world. If Evelyn had it her way, she'd hold the camera and be on the offensive. But in reality, it would be too jarring. Terrence must've realized this, as he handed the camera to Evelyn before tightening his grip on the baseball bat.

One hand on the baton and the other on the camera, Evelyn was ready to see what they'd find. The bedroom door creaked as Terrence pushed it open. They stepped into a hall, hearing the old floorboards groan beneath their weight. Apart from that, the house was as silent as death.

Side by side, Evelyn and Terrence walked the hall, scanning the walls and doors with the camera's large black lens. They approached the grandiose inner balcony that overlooked the foyer and stopped at the railing. The window nearest the front door was shattered. The howling wind stirred the large curtains, causing them to flap like crimson capes.

Before Evelyn could say call the cops, she saw a figure clad in black with a white cotton mask staring at her from the base of the curved foyer stairs. She didn't see the gun until the muzzle flash flickered, and the gunshot thundered through the house.

"Run!" Terrence yelled before Evelyn knew what the bullet hit.

They twisted back around, noticing all the hallway doors were slung wide open. *What the--* Evelyn couldn't finish her thought as she heard footsteps racing up the foyer stairs. Evelyn and Terrence ran past the first door: a bedroom with an old bed frame and 19th century marble-topped dresser, but nothing else. In the monitor screen, Evelyn saw the back of a gorgeous woman, late 30s, in a glossy jade dress that accentuated her hourglass body. The woman peered over her shoulder, looking at Evelyn with sultry green eyes. A rivulet of thick blood seeped from her jade neck ribbon into her bosom.

Evelyn's jaw dropped. She wanted to scream, but nothing escaped her lips. Not even the faintest breath. She kept running and glanced in the next room. It was a spare bathroom that once had a tub full of leaves. In the monitor screen, there was a naked fat man with an oblong head, stretch marks, and sagging tits watching Evelyn run by. A long horizontal slash across his meaty belly revealed his innards.

Evelyn felt her eyes water. Instinctively, she followed Terrence into the third door.

The nursery.

As soon as they stepped through the door, it slammed shut, along with every door in the hallway. Terrence cursed. Evelyn shushed him. The blood had left her face and she couldn't remember the last time she blinked.

The wall paint was pink and chipped. The bed was tiny and broken in on itself. A massive dollhouse—an exact replica of the plantation--rested on a big table. On the floor, toys and dolls from a bygone era sat in a semi-circle facing Evelyn and Terrence.

Through the thin walls, they could hear footsteps moving through the hall. A nearby door opened and slammed shut.

Stepping over the spectating toys, Evelyn rushed to the window. She put down the camera and the baton and tried to slide open the window. Seeing her struggle, Terrence rushed over to assist her. He grimaced as he put his damaged fingertips under the window.

"It's jammed," Terrence barked.

Evelyn tried to lift it again. Her face turned cherry red. A vein bulged in her neck. The window didn't budge. Winded, she turned to Terrence. "Hide."

Another door opened. It was closer. Much closer.

Terrence rushed behind the dollhouse and ducked under the table. Grabbing her equipment, Evelyn rolled under the broken bed. Feathers from the split-open mattress brushed across her swollen nose.

The doorknob jiggled.

Evelyn laid on her belly. She watched the door swing inward and the masked figure step inside. In the darkness and clad in black, the stranger looked like a floating head. He kept his gun in both hands. He slowly scanned the room, eyeing the corners. His muddy boot stomped a doll. Cocking his head, he studied the odd arrangement of toys. He stepped toward the bed.

Click.

Down the hall, the bedroom lamp flickered on and spilled golden light across the hall. The masked figure turned back and walked out of the nursery to investigate.

Evelyn crawled out from under the bed, and Terrence removed himself from behind the dollhouse. He removed his cell phone and dialed 911. A mechanical high-pitch screech rang into his ear. Terrence quickly pulled it away and looked at the phone that had just spontaneously fried its circuitry. His already horrified expression became ten times worse.

Grabbing the camera and the baton, Evelyn tiptoed to the doorway and peeked her head out, seeing the lights on in the master bedroom but no sign of the figure. With her baton, Evelyn gestured for Terrence to follow her into the hallway. Sprinting silently, they ran out into the hallway and to the balcony railing.

Bam! Bam! Bam!

Bullets zipped past their heads. Staying low and zigzagging, Terrence and Evelyn separated and dashed down the left and right side of the stairs. Evelyn tripped on the third step and watched the world spin as she careened headfirst down to the bottom of the steps. She landed with a *thunk!* She mouthed a scream and clenched the top of her head. Hundreds of black specks danced in her peripherals. Eyes watering, she looked up from the floor and the muddy boot in front of her.

Trembling, Evelyn glanced up at the figure with a white mask arcing a woodcutting axe over its head. The glistening edge cut through the air and down on Evelyn's pretty face. She rolled to the side as the axe head slammed into the wood.

Still on the ground, Evelyn reached out for her baton that had rolled against the wall.

The female figure yanked the axe from the floor, leaving behind a two-inch deep notch in the hardwood.

Evelyn swatted the baton against the figure's knee. The stranger grunted as their leg bent inward.

"Get away from her!" Terrence shouted as he charged the axe woman and swung the bat. The slugger bashed in the figure's forehead and it staggered back, a crimson rose blooming on the white cotton mask. Terrence brought the bat down on the figure again, knocking the stranger prone.

"Terrence," Evelyn screamed.

Her husband turned back to the inner balcony railing and the mask aiming a gun at him. He opened fire.

Suddenly, all the lights in the mansion flickered. The jiggles of arcade machines screamed through the house, louder than the gunfire that rained down on Evelyn and Terrence. The front door was too far. They ran for the nearest exit, leaving the cracked video camera at the bottom of the stairs. The masked gun looked around at the chaos, cursed aloud, and then headed for his limp partner's axe.

Evelyn and Terrence dashed through the hall of portraits. The lifeless, painted eyes seemed to follow their trek.

"This way," Evelyn commanded and stopped before the portrait of her overweight ancestor. She pushed aside the corner, revealing a keyhole. She pulled out her key fob and shoved the proper key within. Terrence guarded her back. The key clicked and a three-foot wide rectangular portion of the wall opened from floor to ceiling, revealing a tight, dusty corridor with walls made of unpainted wooden slats.

"He's coming!" Terrence yelled. Evelyn didn't look back. She pressed onward toward her father's hidden study. Terrence slammed the secret door behind them and followed.

THUMP!

An axe battered the portrait wall.

Evelyn and Terrence pushed through the study door that was already battered from an assault a decade ago. The hinges were warped. The wood around the doorknob was splintered. The lock was broken.

THUMP!

The flickering light and screaming arcade sounds seeped through the new hole in the wall behind them.

Evelyn and Terrence slammed the door behind them and shoved a chair under the knob. Terrence rubbed his hand up his bald head. "He's going to smash through that wall within the next five minutes."

Evelyn felt her heart cramp. She put her hands on her father's desk, shifting her thoughts away from the horrific and the unexplainable to how she would survive.

"We're going to need to make a stand," Evelyn declared.

Terrence's jaw tightened. He nodded. "Two of us. One of him."

"We get rid of his gun, we win," Evelyn said, wiping sweat from her brow.

THUMP!

She turned back to Terrence. "I'm sorry I brought you down here. We should've stayed in Detroit."

"Hey," Terrence brushed aside a hair from Evelyn's cheek with his bandaged thumb. "No time for regrets. Besides, we've faced worse odds."

Evelyn cracked a smile. "You only lie that bad when you're trying to get into my pants."

"Can you fault me?"

Wood cracked and the mumbled curses of the masked figure could be heard through the three-foot wide corridor.

Evelyn and Terrence turned to the concealed study door.

"He's here," Evelyn said, their moment ending.

Boots thumped through the corridor and an axe head slammed into the study door. Evelyn and Terrence stood on either side of the doorway, ready to hit the masked man the moment he breached.

Evelyn's skin crawled as the room temperature plummeted twenty degrees. She noticed Terrence's teeth chattering and felt someone's eyes on her. Both Terrence and her twisted back to the seven-year-old little blonde girl and the tall, white masked figure standing beside her.

Both Evelyn and Terrence froze in fear.

The axe splintered the door's face inward.

While looking at Evelyn with emotionless blue eyes, freckle-faced Mary Sullivan raised her right arm and pointed at the mahogany desk.

Evelyn and Terrence turned to one another. The axe head punched a hole between them. It started to wiggle free.

Mary kept pointing at the desk.

The man with the white mask watched Evelyn through the black button-sized eye holes on his tight white cotton mask.

Evelyn dashed to the desk and looked across the piles of old documents on top. "What is it?" she screamed at Mary.

The little girl remained emotionless and silent.

The axe punched another hole into the door, spitting splinters on the floor.

Terrence readied his bat. He bounced his eyes between the door and his wife.

Evelyn saw a finger-sized hole on the floorboards beneath the desk cubby. Using her index finger, she opened the trapdoor, revealing a circular pit, tight enough for a person, black as tar and similarly endless. Evelyn gulped and turned back to Terrence.

The axe smashed through the door. One more hit and the gunman would have enough space to aim his gun.

Evelyn didn't wait for that. She nodded at Terrence and slid into the abyss.

She slid down the slick metal chute, feeling jets of wind against her face. Maybe she was a fool to trust the little girl. Evelyn would know when she hit the bottom. The tunnel twisted and a moment later, she was free falling into a black pit.

Bottom first, she hit the ground. She gasped in pain as something jabbed into her thigh. Her hands felt something hard, dry, and chalky. Her eyes tried adjusting to the darkness. They didn't. The world was black and cold. She lifted her thigh and grabbed hold of the curved pointy thing that nearly pierced her flesh. She pulled it free. The wound was tender but didn't feel deep.

The ceiling grumbled and spit Terrence out. Evelyn moved to the side to allow him to crash down nearby. He groaned. "The trapdoor shut behind me... Where the hell are we?"

"I don't know," Evelyn whispered. "I can't see anything."

Evelyn felt someone grab her shoulder.

"It's me," Terrence said.

Evelyn stayed tense.

Around the room, lantern hinges on pointed metal hooks lit up. Their tiny flames cast an amber glow throughout the massive room, across its brick walls, and down its cratered floor. Evelyn and Terrence sat at the center, bathing in dry bones. Evelyn dropped the curved pointy thing--a human rib--into the rest of the pile of human vertebrae, pelvises, femurs, and skulls.

Before she could process the horror, footsteps approached from all sides. Evelyn looked up from the pile of bones and saw the emotionless people surrounding her: the sexy slashed-throat woman in a green dress, the naked fat man with a horizontal cut across his torso, a teenage goth girl bleeding from the back of her head, an old man in a sweater vest with blood flowing from his lips, a seventeen-year-old boy in a football jersey missing his right wrist, and sweet Mary Sullivan.

Terrence pulled close to Evelyn and stuttered. Evelyn held him tightly, feeling his warmth for the last time. Tears streamed down her face. "What do you want from us?" she screamed.

Mary locked eyes with them. With her small, childish voice, she said, "Help us."

The others echoed her plea. "Help us. Help us. Help us."

Their cries grew louder and louder, echoing off the brick walls where Evelyn first heard the sound of scratching.

Thank you so much for taking the time to read my story!
Writing has always been a passion of mine and it's incredibly gratifying and rewarding whenever you give me an opportunity to let you escape from your everyday surroundings and entertain the world that is your imagination.
As an indie author, Amazon reviews can have a huge impact on my livelihood. So if you enjoyed the story please leave a review letting me and the rest of the digital world know. And if there was anything you found troubling, please email me. Your feedback helps improve my work, and allows me to continue writing stories that will promise to thrill and excite in the future. But be sure to exclude any spoilers.
I would love if you could take a second to leave a review:
Click here to leave a review on Amazon!
Again, thank you so much for letting me into your world. I hope you enjoyed reading this story as much as I did writing it!

11

BLACK BIRD

Clad in black and pasty-skinned, fifteen-year-old Zoey Pinkerton shielded her eyes from the oncoming high beams. The light bounced with the vehicle as it sped down a cattle pasture-flanked road. Like most nights in Adders, Georgia, the world was an inky black void. Just the way Zoey liked it. Or at least that's how she branded herself with her use of black eyeliner, black hair dye, and black lipstick. In truth, she loved nature, animals, and art of all varieties. She was even a sucker for those cheesy rom-coms her other girlfriends enjoyed, though she'd never admit it.

The car slowed to a stop beside her. It was an expensive, fuel-efficient BMW. Zoey crossed her arms over her chest and raised a brow.

The window rolled down. The black interior of the car shrouded all but the man's soft hands. Hands that had never worked a day in their life. It was probably another middle-aged creep looking for a cheap thrill with "damaged goods." Even in a small town like Adders, pigs like this weren't that rare.

"I'm not interested in whatever you're doing," Zoey said snarkily. As an only child, making her demands known was never difficult.

Completely silent, the man's hands tightened and loosened their grip on the steering wheel as if he were using a stress ball. Goose bumps rose on Zoey's skin. She took a step back from the car and flipped open the phone within her hoodie pocket. She wasn't going to threaten to call the police. She was going to call them now.

"I'm sorry," the man said. His soft but stoic voice lent to a handsome face, though Zoey still could not see it. As she subtly dialed 9 on her number pad, Zoey opened her mouth to ask "why?" but the glint of the abnormally long and skinny barrel shut her up with its quiet *pint* sound.

A sharp pinch hit her throat. Her hands touched the long-feathered dart protruding from her flesh.

The ground came up and punched her jaw.

Her limbs disobeyed her.

The world twisted, becoming ever so dark.

Zoey dreamed of falling into a pit. Her parents were watching her from high above. Their expressions were judgmental and their frowns heavy. Zoey's tongue was thick in her mouth, preventing her from speaking. She felt weak.

The teenager awoke in a sprawling hay field with an electric lantern on the ground a few feet away. In the light, black beetles and ants scurried under stomped hay. Zoey pulled her wrists. They were tied to the arms of an old wooden chair whose right front leg was a little shorter than the rest.

She jerked in her binding and looked out at the endless field. Eyes watering, Zoey screamed. "Somebody! Help me!"

The night sucked up her cry.

The wind screamed back.

Grass crunched behind Zoey.

Zoey trembled. *He's behind me.* Her breathing became disjointed. Her heart pounded.

"I've killed a lot of people," the man admitted, almost with pity. "Poison. Knives. I haven't found a method that I like. That's weird, is it?"

"Untie me," Zoey said through her teeth. She had to clench her jaw. It was the only way to keep it from chattering. "Do it."

"I can't, Zoey. God knows I've tried for many years."

How does he know my name? Zoey felt dizzy. "Who are you?"

He bent down and whispered his name into her studded ear. Zoey trembled. It didn't make any sense. Why him? Why was any of this happening? The man grabbed the crown of her head and held it in place. Zoey attempted to shake out of his grip, but he was stronger than he sounded. As she struggled, Zoey noticed a large building in the distance. In her peripherals, she saw the man lift something sharp and pointed.

"Hold still. You really don't want me to miss," he said.

Zoey clenched her eyes shut, telling herself to wake up from this nightmare, but with each passing moment, fear built and the man lined up the sharpened stake for the kill.

12

BED OF BONES

In the black of night, rain fell on the quaint town of Adders, Georgia. Homestyle restaurants, Baptist churches, and ancient barns were silhouetted in the inky blackness. Far beyond the rolling pastures and barbed wire fences resided a single-lane red brick road fit for a horse-drawn wagon. Towering, moss-covered oaks flanked its side. Tattered lichen dripped from the trees' high and sprawling branches that arched over the road and touched each other's skeletal fingers. At the end of the wet brick road stood Quenby House: a symmetrical 19th century masterpiece.

Bowling green grass blanketed the front yard while large trees bordered the massive seventeen room, three-story estate, emphasizing the home's importance. From the distance, the mansion was monumental. Up close, it was breathtaking. Drooping white flowers spotted the vines that climbed the mansion's chipped white walls and its grand colonnades--one set across the house's face, and a second like it but rising out of the second-story balcony. Above that, arched windows jutted out of the wide truncated roof.

Muddled noise and flashing lights escaped the mansion's many windows.

The window nearest the front door spilled shattered glass across the red carpeted foyer--a massive hall with a parallel curving staircase that ended at the opposite ends of the interior balcony. Bordered by gold leaf frames, authentic early 19th-century oil paintings of the mansion and its surrounding lands decorated the high walls.

Every light, even those on the massive multiple-tier chandelier, flashed rapidly. Annoying arcade jingles screamed from the billiard room packed with hoarded 1980s gaming paraphernalia. The distorted sound rattled the window and shook the walls, crescendoing louder and louder as the stutter of every light quickened.

In the cluttered basement, past the mountain of sheet-covered furniture and dust-dressed Antebellum relics stood an unassuming brick wall. Droplets of dried blood crusted in its coarse ridges where fiddle-maker Terrence Carr had mindlessly clawed at it weeks ago.

If one pressed their ear against the cold brick, they would hear faint scratching on the other side, but not the voices. Those were reserved for someone else.

WEARING cyan boy shirts and a low-cut black t-shirt, thirty-three-year-old blonde and slender Evelyn Carr sat on a bed of bones. Chalky femurs, ribs, and human skulls pooled over her toned legs and dug at her flesh. Just like the tears running down Evelyn's pale cheeks, beads of wax leaked down lit and dying candlesticks that systematically lined the four doorless and windowless brick walls.

Evelyn's only warmth in the frigid room came from her husband's hand. Lost in fear, Terrence squeezed so tight that pain crippled Evelyn's palm and fingers. She was too terrified to resist.

Band-Aids wrapped the tips of Terrence Carr's fingers. His skin was dark, his head was bald, and his face was well-structured and kind with a little black beard on his chin. He wore pajamas decorated with little string instruments. Foggy breaths escaped his ajar mouth. Like hungry snakes, red veins squiggled toward his dark irises.

Under the hole of the secret ceiling chute, the married couple sat in the cratered floor where the dry human remains seemingly sucked them in deeper into the nearly two-hundred-year-old plantation house.

Six individuals stood around them.

An old man in a sweater vest and white slacks. His thin hair was combed to the side and his eyes were flat black. Thick blood leaked from his lower lip and down his shaven, sagging chin.

Next to him was a gorgeous woman wearing a glossy jade dress to accentuate her hourglass figure. Like her dress, her eyes were green and sultry. Her hair was thick, luscious and velvet red. Crimson seeped into her full bosom from the slash across her skinny throat.

Naked and with a horizontal opening across his belly, a fat man with an oblong head stood next to the woman in green. His face was neutral.

By him and wearing a 90s football jacket, a seventeen-year-old male with devilishly handsome features and dimpled chin seemed in perfect form apart from the wet nub where his throwing hand once resided.

Then there was the goth girl. Fifteen, raven black eyeliner to match her black hair and black lipstick. There was a hole in the back of her head.

Lastly, seven-year-old Mary Sullivan with sandy blonde hair and freckles spotted under her blue eyes and across the bridge of her nose. Her killer--a man in a featureless white cotton mask--was upstairs, looking for a chance to put a bullet in Evelyn and Terrence's skulls.

In her tiny voice, Mary repeated her plea. "Help us."

The other five mimicked her words. "Help us. Help us. Help us."

Their cries echoed off the cold walls of the fully enclosed chamber and into Evelyn's mind, drowning out all sounds and thought, seemingly taking root in her skull.

Evelyn searched for the right words, but she could barely control her breathing. Her heart pounded until it cramped in her chest. Goose bumps grew across her body. Dust from the ceiling rained down upon Evelyn's messy golden hair as Mary's killer stomped around upstairs. The masked man was one step away from finding the trapdoor that ended in this candlelit pit.

Suddenly, as quick as the mangled strangers had appeared, they vanished. All that remained was their plea resounding off the walls and the corners of the doorless and windowless square room.

Evelyn and Terrence sat in the cold quiet, lost in the sound of their ragged breaths and racing hearts. The world had returned to normal, but under the surface, Evelyn's foundation was shattered. The divide between life and death blurred along with reality and fiction. In a stir of confusion and fear, a million questions raced through her mind. No one could answer them.

Terrence let go of Evelyn's hand. He stood, taking a moment to steady himself. Pain thumped in Evelyn's hand, but that seemed to be the least of her problems.

"Are they..." Terrence's voice faded.

"I don't know," Evelyn answered his unspoken question. For all she knew, the ghastly strangers were hiding just out of sight. They could return any second and shred Evelyn apart, and she'd have no way of stopping it. As a generally self-sufficient woman, being stripped of control left Evelyn feeling as exposed and naked as the bloody fat man that branded her thoughts.

Terrence's body trembled. He craned his head up to the circular holes cut into the ceiling. The chute in the middle led to Maxwell Quenby's hidden office: the place where he wrote his last will and testament to Evelyn before vanishing a decade ago. Evelyn never knew her father. Their only connection was the key to this accursed estate. She recalled his crinkled note.

To Evelyn, my daughter. My heir. I failed you in life. I will not make excuses or justify my actions. I will leave you with the only thing I have to give: my estate. Enclosed within this note is the key to our family home. May it give you more peace than it did me. Your father, Max.

Terrence stretched out his shaking hand to Evelyn. It took her a moment to process before she accepted his gesture and allowed him to pull her to her feet. Evelyn turned back to the bones and saw the world twist. She steadied herself on her husband.

"We need to get out of here," Evelyn declared.

"Funny," Terrence said weakly. "I was thinking the same exact thing."

13

FAMILY

Leaning on each other, Terrence and Evelyn shambled out of the bone pit and onto the wood floor. The icy kiss from the dusty surface made their toes curl. Terrence looked at the wax candles in sconces on the wall and shivered. Their spontaneous ignition wasn't even on the top ten list of abnormal events that transpired tonight or any night in Quenby House.

They approached the nearest brick wall. Terrence put his ear on the surface and knocked. He tried his knuckles at different locations while Evelyn kept watch. There was a chance that the killer still lurked upstairs. Evelyn clenched the rib bone that had been digging into her thigh. Its point wasn't sharp but with enough force and jammed in the right place, it could be deadly. Evelyn attempted to forget the fact that it originated from one of the six people that had loomed over her. The rib's dry texture and odd density did a horrible job of hiding that fact. The idea made Evelyn queasy.

Terrence pulled away from the wall. "It's hollow. We just need a way to bust through."

They needed a sledgehammer. Evelyn wasn't crossing her

fingers. The room was a pile of bones away from being empty. A morbid thought came to mind as she looked at the bones and the wall, but the skeletal remains were too old and brittle to MacGyver anything.

Evelyn sniffled. The cold was getting to her. They needed to get out of this room or risk getting sick. Or worse, starve. Terrence traced the walls with his hand. He pressed on random bricks, disappointed by the lack of result. In any other place Evelyn would've laughed at him, but her father's mansion was full of secrets. Like the hidden wall in the hall of ancestral portraits that had been axed apart by the masked killer.

If there was a way to the ceiling, Evelyn would try it. But even on Terrence's shoulders, Evelyn feared that she wouldn't be able to hoist herself into the corpse chute. She wondered if any of the bodies down here were tossed before they died. Alone, cold, bleeding and surrounded by death, it was hard to imagine a worse fate. As a pessimist, Evelyn could probably think of one, but she'd rather not.

Terrence, an optimist at heart, "pressed" every brick he came across, but to no avail. Evelyn turned her sights on the bones, gulped, and knelt beside them. She brushed aside skulls, vertebrae, and knuckle bones. In the near darkness of the room, it reminded her of a Halloween party game where the participants are blindfolded, feeling different objects and trying to guess their not-so-sinister reality. In this case, the reality was pretty glum. Terrence twisted back to her at one point, opened his mouth to speak, but thought better of it. He mumbled something and went back to "pressing" bricks.

Pushing aside the bones quickly became a frustrating process as they kept falling back on her hands every time. Instead, Evelyn set them aside, unintentionally categorizing the skeletal remains. Skulls in one spot, arms in the other, etc. She blamed it on her methodical investigative skills.

Soon Evelyn got the pile organized. She looked at the dip. It was nothing but a structural weakness in the hardwood. She plopped to her bottom and hugged her knees close to her chest. She looked up the ceiling chute, feeling the paranoia cripple her. *Get your head on straight,* she commanded herself. It didn't work. She watched Terrence press away, seeing his movements becoming rushed and frustrated.

Taking in the surroundings, Evelyn put her P.I. skills to the test. She found putting herself in the missing person's shoes helped her retrace their path. In this case, she thought about the killer who designed the place. Firstly, she'd assume that the room was a body dump, not a torture chamber. Still, the killer would want to account for any potential escapees. The victim would be beyond desperate and try every nook and cranny for an escape. Assuming that the candles were not lit, the victim would be fumbling blindly. The smart placement for a switch would be in a high place. Somewhere out of reach but not inconvenient. If the killer was six feet, the switch wouldn't be higher than eight feet to toggle. Evelyn scanned the room. The candle sconces matched the height. *Tell me you're more creative than that.* She got up and started feeling the various candlesticks, wondering if Terrence would make some innuendo-esque comment.

"You sure this is your first time?" Terrence joked as he felt up the wall.

"Ha. Ha." Evelyn replied dryly. Wearing a small smile, she turned back to the task at hand. If they weren't laughing, they'd be crying.

After five stiff candlesticks, what little hope Evelyn had fleeted. She pinched the bridge of her slightly swollen nose. It was 3 a.m. when the killer broke into her home. It was probably 4ish now, but after her trek to Stephen Doyle's house hours before, exhaustion hit Evelyn like a steam train.

The only thing keeping her on two feet was the threat against her life.

Evelyn tried another candlestick, wishing the killer wasn't that creative. On her way to the candlestick, she noticed a brick jutting a little farther out than the rest on that wall. Holding her breath, she pressed it. Nothing. Irked, Evelyn hammered her fist against it. "Stupid--"

Cha-Chunk

Something rattled in the wall. Evelyn stumbled back, bracing herself. No rolling boulders. That was a relief.

After a moment of stillness, Evelyn outstretched her skinny arm and pushed against the wall. The five-foot section of the wall opened, meeting resistance on the dirt floor. Evelyn pulled a candle off its stand and held it out like a torch. The amber glow lapped against the packed dirt and periodic vertical wooden posts holding up the damp, mine-like tunnel. A tear of hot wax slithered down Evelyn's fingers as she stared into the abyss. Terrence joined her in her scouting.

"It was the first brick you pressed, wasn't it?" Terrence asked.

With pursed lips, Evelyn nodded.

Deadpanned, Terrence replied, "Neat."

Grabbing a candle of his own, Terrence walked with Evelyn through the corridor. The ground dipped and widened at random intervals, but the path stayed straight. Insects, worms, and other deep-earth creatures wiggled away from the candlelight. By the time Evelyn and Terrence reached the old wooden crop cart and sketchy ladder beyond it, their hands were stiff with hardened wax dripping stalactites from the bottom of their fists.

At the center of the decrepit crop cart was a faded maroon stain. *Body cart.* Evelyn wondered if the killer stripped the victims before or after trotting them down here.

After all, there were only dry bones in the basement. No articles of clothing.

Seeing Terrence's tension, Evelyn allowed him to climb the ladder first. The aged rungs groaned under his weight. He pushed hard against the trapdoor. It didn't budge. Locked from the other side. Terrence got off the twelve-rung ladder.

He planted his dirty bare foot on one of the long cart's handle and pulled the wooden pole to him. Forehead vein bulging, he yanked back as hard as he could. There was a snapping noise underfoot and then the handle broke away. Terrence sucked air, handed the broken handle to Evelyn, and lifted his foot. Grimacing, he extracted a long splinter burrowing into the front layers of his sole. Hopping on one foot, he returned to the ladder and used the rounded tip of the broken handle to ram against the wooden slats of the trapdoor. Setting her dwindled candle aside, Evelyn grabbed ahold of the bottom end handle and helped punch the trapdoor. The rusted hinges loosed. Evelyn and Terrence proceeded to hit it a few more times until the rusty hinges gave way and the trapdoor fell towards them. Evelyn and Terrence ducked out of the way, avoiding an unnecessary headache.

Taking a breath, Terrence climbed up. After a moment, he gestured for Evelyn to follow. As she climbed, cool wind chilled her skin. She glanced about the shed before fully exiting the portal. Old gardening equipment and rusty tools were scattered about. A scrunched-up rug had been used to cover the trapdoor. Though windows were covered with old towels, small slivers of light escaped through moth holes. Terrence opened the shed door, allowing both of them into the back yard.

A flock of birds scattered across the dark indigo sky. The sun peeked up the long grassy field. Hay bales spotted acres of field. Cotton plants swayed not far from a cotton gin and six servant cabins. Down a dirt road, the back of the Quenby House faced Evelyn. Unlike the mansion's front, there were no colonnades, but the upstairs porch was more accessible. There was a number of raised flower gardens and chipped Roman-esque statues in the back lawn.

Arms around one another's shoulder, Evelyn and Terrence dragged their bare feet across dewy grass and toward the mansion. Their only key was inside. Evelyn walked around front. No vehicles. Terrence didn't say anything, but Evelyn knew they had the same question. *Are the killers gone?* They peered into the shattered front window. A portion of the red carpet floor was soaked with rain water. The masked killer's partner that Terrence had beat with a bat no longer rested at the foot of the foyer stairs. *Alive or dragged away?* Evelyn didn't like either option. A corpse would've been concrete evidence that they defended themselves.

The front door was slightly ajar. Evelyn grabbed the fist-sized metal knob. Before she could twist it, Terrence put his large, calloused hand on her shoulder. He shook his head. Evelyn took a step back as Terrence pull out his cell phone. There was a large black smudge on the back where the circuitry had spontaneously fried last night.

Evelyn withdrew her own cell phone from the small pockets on her cyan boy shorts. After seeing the results of Terrence's cell phone use and not having service underground, Evelyn hadn't tried hers. Arm outstretched and body spinning, a little bar appeared on Evelyn's screen. Good enough for 911. She dialed, half expecting the mobile device to explode. Maybe the night was finally over. Maybe it was all a bad dream. She peered through the shattered window and at the video camera on the floor. Terrence bought it after they had started sleep-walking. Last night, it was used to see the first guest, the woman in the jade green dress. That would be their proof that they were not crazy.

. . .

SQUAD CARS and an ambulance rumbled down the red brick road. Their flashing lights illuminated the moss-covered oaks and then the vine-covered house. A duo of officers--Davis, 30s, a short and stout man with an angry mug, and Bailey, a granite-faced woman with fiery red hair and Georgia twang--pressed through the front door, hands on their holstered pistols. Through the open front door, Evelyn watched the officers sweep through the vast foyer. Davis and Bailey stopped at the bloodstain at the base of the curving stairs. They drew their handguns and vanished into the hall of portraits.

It seemed like forever before the duo returned. Evelyn attempted to read their expressions, but like Evelyn, they did well at hiding their demeanor. Truly, the only person Evelyn was transparent with was Terrence.

“It’s secure,” Officer Davis replied. “You said something about bones?”

Evelyn walked them to the shed, recounting the home invasion. She kept the story simple: invaders broke in at 3 a.m., Evelyn and Terrence knocked one out and ran to the private study. That’s where they found the trapdoor and landed in the bone pit. That was the gist of what happened, anyway. The reality was much more complicated.

Davis and Bailey traded looks. Terrence gave Evelyn a worried look of his own.

Evelyn pushed open the shed door. “We’ve only been in town for a few weeks. I inherited this house from my deceased father.”

They descended down the ladder and into the dirt corridor. The officers moved with caution and kept a close eye on Evelyn. She didn’t blame them. This could almost be construed as a trap. They entered the bone room. The candles had died down, so Officer Davis held his huge flashlight. He illuminated the multiple piles of bones organized into different categories next to the dip in the floor. Evelyn felt her heart spike. She forgot to put them back in the pit after looking for a key.

"Did you do that?" Davis inquired about the organized bones.

"Yes," Evelyn painstakingly admitted. "I was looking for a way out."

The officers glanced at one another.

This is bad.

"We'll get Forensics down here," Davis said. "Y'all wait up top."

Officer Davis led them back to the front of the house. He didn't ask any questions and didn't take his eyes off Evelyn. In her boy shorts and low-cut t-shirt, the officer was getting an eyeful, but something about his gaze hinted that he was looking for a deeper truth. Evelyn felt the hairs on her neck stand. *He doesn't trust us.*

Terrence leaned in to ask Evelyn a question. She shook her head. "It can wait." The reply was curt, but the last thing she wanted was to have their words twisted against them.

Davis's radio buzzed. He answered.

"Stephen and Catherine Doyle are not at their home," said the officer on the other end. *"We're putting out an APB."*

Over the next two hours, the forensic photographers, analysts, and more people from the state arrived. Only having a population of twenty thousand, Evelyn assumed Adders didn't have its own forensics unit. Soon, bones were being carried out in bags and tarps. The officers bombarded Evelyn with questions about her father and the house. She had little information to give.

By the time it was dealt with, it was almost dark. The specialists gave Terrence and Evelyn odd looks. A few chatted quietly about the freshly painted mural across one of the downstairs halls. Days ago, Evelyn had blacked out and painted seven-year-old blonde and freckled Mary Sullivan being stalked by three white masked figures and then being burned alive behind Quenby House. Before the blackouts, she couldn't draw a stick figure to save her life. The work inside was a disturbing masterpiece. Evelyn found plane tickets that proved her father, Maxwell Quenby, was out of town during the days Mary went missing/was murdered. Nonetheless, she did not know Stephen, Catherine, and Andrew Doyles' motivation behind the killing or why they chose Maxwell's property to do it.

Finding missing people, Evelyn could do. Solving murders was a different ball game.

"We advise you to stay in a hotel for the coming days," Officer Bailey said. "We'll reach out if there's any developments."

"Thank you," Terrence said with relief.

"Uh huh," Bailey replied. "Y'all be safe now."

Evelyn and Terrence hunkered down in a cheap hotel for a few days. They religiously watched the news for Stephen and Catherine Doyle. Both had vanished without a trace. The news only reported the discovery of the bone pit. There were five complete skeletons. Mary Sullivan and the decade-dead phantom in the cotton mask--Andrew Doyle--were not among those, but Evelyn knew they both died on the property, and that was enough to lock them in the house for eternity. As for the twins Stephen and Catherine Doyle, they were gone.

"Do you think *they* got them?" Terrence sat on the edge of the bed and watched the TV, his shoulders slouched.

Evelyn stared at the screen intently. They hadn't talked about the encounter in the pit since they got out. "I don't know, but we need to go back."

"What?" Terrence protested. "I don't know if I can stomach that, Evelyn. We don't know if they're a threat, and even if they aren't, I see no reason to go back."

"They need our help," Evelyn said.

"But... they're dead."

"They may know about my father."

"The truth will come out."

Evelyn glared at him. "We came down here to sell the mansion, but now it's so much bigger than that. This is my family home. It's my responsibility."

Terrence looked in shock. "I didn't know you felt that way."

"I didn't," Evelyn admitted. "But seeing them... I don't know, Terrence. I can't shake the feeling that I have to do something."

Terrence took a breath and turned off the TV. He smiled softly at Evelyn. "Whatever you want to do, I'm with you."

After picking up their minivan from the mechanic and burning through a layer of their dwindling cash bundle, they parked in front of Quenby House. Its shadow grew like the angel of death. Evelyn and Terrence slammed their doors in unison and hiked toward the front door. The excitement and awe Evelyn had felt when she first found out this property was her inheritance twisted into uncertainty and fear that crawled beneath her skin.

Terrence and Evelyn took a breath and pushed against the front door covered with zigzagging caution tape. Creaking like a death rattle, the entrance opened into the foyer. Gusts of wind bombarded the plastic sheeting on the nearest window. They stopped at the center of the room. On the painted domed ceiling, trumpeting angels with cracked faces watched Evelyn with lifeless eyes and innocent smiles. For a moment, it almost seemed like they were swirling across with artificial clouds.

"Mary?" Evelyn called out. Her voice bounced off the hall walls.

Outside, wind whistled and Evelyn swore she heard whispering.

"Evelyn," Terrence said in a shaky voice. His eyes locked onto the interior balcony.

In a yellow dress with a belt, the little girl sat cross-legged behind the wooden bars, staring at Evelyn with dry, unblinking blue eyes. She murmured an indistinguishable chant.

Words lodged in Evelyn's throat. She took a step forward. The massive crystalline multi-tier chandelier flicked briefly as the little girl cocked her head. At the motion, thin blonde hair flooded down the girl's freckled cheek.

"What do you want from us?" Evelyn asked, mindful of the chandelier dangling from rust-spotted copper chains above her head.

Mary stood and slowly walked down the curved steps. Her little hand glided down the smooth railing. Terrence went tense. Evelyn fought to keep her composure. The little girl approached, eyes unblinking, and turned into the hall.

Seriously questioning their life choices, Evelyn and Terrence followed the ghostly girl. Every ceiling light Mary passed under flickered, casting a glow across the massive mural Evelyn painted from one side of the hall to the other. The paint failed to dry properly. Inky droplets melted away the featureless white masked strangers. There were three in all. Two male and one female, the Doyle family. From their blotchy eye holes, black tears hardened. Terrence shuddered when he looked at the artwork. Evelyn walked closer to him. Their shoulders scraped. They traded glances and looked back at the little girl a few feet ahead.

As a private investigator, Evelyn could travel to the seediest locations with only her wit and extendable baton to keep her safe. From swapping orphanages for her first eighteen years to couch surfing and hitchhiking across the country, Evelyn had learned to survive. There was no other choice. All that said, it got her nowhere when she got into her car "accident" that etched her body with deep scars. The grooves across her back were reminders of her old life. One of substance abuse, deceit, and more meaningless vices. But the moment Terrence pulled her from the wreckage of her car, everything changed.

Tall, handsome, an all-around blues lover, Terrence came from a line of lower-class musicians and union workers and took up the luthier trade--someone who makes string instruments. Unlike Evelyn, he was always good for a laugh, drank his glass half full, and liked playing the peacemaker even if it compromised his agendas. Also, his parents were the sweetest couple you'd ever meet. His father, a tall man with white curly hair, laugh lines, and a love of suspenders, was poor, but more generous than anyone Evelyn ever knew. His mother, a short plump woman with a welcoming smile, could cook like Betty Crocker and always knew the right thing to say. However, Terrence was not without faults. It wasn't until after their wedding that he admitted to having an eleven-year-old daughter somewhere in Ann Arbor, Michigan. Nonetheless, she couldn't imagine spending her life with anyone else.

Keeping her eyes ahead, Evelyn interlocked her fingers with Terrence, her last and only anchor in this crazy world.

Getting progressively colder with every step, they tailed Mary into the lounge. The room was devoid of light and consisted of bookshelves packed with dusty books, an unlit fireplace, and an assortment of lounge furniture. Evelyn passed through the threshold.

Suddenly, the fireplace burst to life. Its warm glow lapped against the wall. Lamps flickered on. A wisp of smoke climbed from the Sherlock pipe held in the old man's chapped lips. He wore a neutral-colored sweater vest and intense gaze. His white hair was trimmed and combed to the side. When he pulled the pipe from his mouth, blood leaked from his lower lip like sap from a tree.

The sexy woman in the glossy jade dress slouched in the loveseat, free of all the cares in the world. Her plump lips curled into a smile on her perfect heart-shaped face. Her lipstick was as red as the blood pumping from her slashed throat.

Sitting cross-legged on a nearby recliner, the goth girl read an old book with stained yellow pages. She wore black jeans with torn-out knees and a zipped-up hoodie decorated with pins that read "Save the Earth" and "Go Green, Idiot!" She glanced up at Evelyn and Terrence with an apathetic expression. Though Evelyn couldn't see it at the moment, she knew there was a bloody gash on the back of the girl's head.

In the corner, the naked fat man with an oblong head "watered" withered flowers with an empty watering can. Humming to himself, he paid Evelyn and Terrence no mind.

Lastly, the one-handed jock stood at the center of the room. He wore a varsity jacket with the number thirteen sewn on it. He rubbed his right wrist just below the place where someone cut off his hand. Seeing him, Mary smiled and took off into a sprint. With a dimpled grin, the jock lowered to a knee and allowed the little girl to jump into his arms.

The goth let her gaze linger on the handsome football player before quickly returning to her book. The jock hoisted Mary up with his good hand and faced Evelyn. The whole cast of bloodied strangers turned to Evelyn and Terrence with expectant looks.

Terrence mumbled something.

Trembling, Evelyn bounced her wide eyes between them. With the crackling of fire and wisp of smoke, the room seemed like something out of a lucid dream. How did her life come to this? She traced back the confusion to the moment she had inherited this house.

Silence filled the lounge.

The old man cleared his throat.

Evelyn and Terrence give him their attention.

"I'm Barker." the old man declared, using the top of his hand to wipe the blood from his lower lip. He gestured to the naked fat man with an oblong head and who was probably in his early forties but looked much younger. "That's Winslow. He's a few cards short of a full deck."

Winslow bared his teeth in what could be interpreted as a smile. His underbite was horrendous.

"That fox is Alannah," the old man continued.

"A pleasure," the woman in glossy green said, her voice silky and smooth. The slash in her neck moved as she spoke. Wearing a devious smile, Alannah studied Terrence. Eyes wide, Terrence slowly turned to Evelyn with a look of pure horror.

Barker gestured to the goth girl. "And there's--"

"I can speak for myself," the goth replied and, with dismal enthusiasm, said, "My name is Zoey."

Barker smiled widely at the comment he was about to make. "All you need to know is that she's angsty, and she has her eyes on Pe--"

"Shut it!" Zoey threw her book at him. Barker sidestepped out of the way, careful to keep his pipe from harm.

"I'm Peter," the jock introduced himself with a million-dollar grin. "This is Mary, the mastermind of this whole operation."

The little girl kept a neutral face when looking at Evelyn. Evelyn wondered why she wasn't gory like the rest of the specters. She had been burned in the cotton fields behind the house. Surely there must be some residual effect. The answer hit Evelyn as she looked at the pattern. *Her heart must've given out before the fire got her.* Perhaps there were rules to the ghostly dimension: the killed kept the wounds that ended them.

Standing in the shadow of the farthest corner, the man in the white cotton mask stepped forward. The black eye holes were the size of buttons. The ear holes were the size of peas.

Terrence cursed and took a step back. Evelyn familiarized herself with the nearby table lamp.

"That's Andrew," Barker declared with disgust. "He keeps to himself."

Andrew Doyle, Evelyn knew. His body was discovered the day after Mary vanished. *Stephen, Catherine, and Andrew must've killed Mary, but did they murder the rest?*

The masked specter stood firm and followed Evelyn's movements with his head.

Evelyn struggled with the words. She closed her eyes, trying to think of them as normal people. It didn't help. "I'm Evelyn," she finally said. "This is my husband, Terrence."

"Hi, Terrence," Alannah said with seduction in her voice.

"Uh... hey."

Mustering a little courage, Evelyn addressed the room. "You want our help. Tell us what we need to do."

14

ROMANCE

Mary's eyes were dry, uncanny and deep blue. In her sweet and tiny voice, she said. "You need to stop the boogieman."

Evelyn's spine tingled at the words. Her vision bounced between the massacred victims and their brutal wounds. Bile crawl up the nethers of her throat. She fought it down.

"We've been trapped here for so long," Mary continued.

"So, you possess us?" Evelyn retorted. "Make us sleep-walk? Make us claw on the brick walls or wake up in a cow field?"

"Don't yell at her," Barker said. "She's only a little girl, and she's much stronger than you think."

"I needed to talk to you," Mary said. "I needed to make you understand."

"Understand what?" Terrence asked feebly, finally finding his voice.

"That we can't free ourselves," Mary said seriously. "Only you can. You must stop the boogieman."

Zoey combed her black hair with long black fingernails. "And then we can leave this crappy world."

Evelyn tried her best to process it all. "How do you know that will work?" she asked daringly.

Alannah sat up. "Because we feel it, darling." She got off the loveseat and, hips swaying, walked up to Terrence. He took a step back as she grabbed his hand and put on her bloody chest. "We feel it right here. Don't you?"

Completely in shock, Terrence watched blood pool around his fingers. "You're so warm."

Boiling, Evelyn grabbed at Alannah's wrist, but her hand swiped through the woman's arm.

"My apologies," Alannah said to Evelyn. "Married men are my weakness."

She released Terrence, and locking her sultry eyes on him, backed to a comfortable distance. That is, if there ever was a comfortable distance for a woman like that.

"Keep away from my husband," Evelyn told her and then glared at Terrence.

"... Yeah, stay back," he replied, not as firmly as Evelyn would've liked.

"Who is the boogieman?" Evelyn asked Mary.

The little girl shrugged. "I don't know. I don't remember."

Evelyn turned to the crowd. "Do any of you remember?"

They were silent.

Barker spoke up. "It's not easy, you know, recalling one's death. There are some things better left forgotten."

"Yeah, except that doesn't help us or you," Evelyn replied. "Did Stephen Doyle do this?"

"Maybe," Mary said softly. "I think so."

The man in the white mask said nothing.

"Did Stephen, you know, to all of you?" Evelyn asked.

Peter shrugged. "We don't know. That's why we need your help. The moment you find the killer, we're out of here. Otherwise, we're benched in this house."

Breathing loudly, Winslow nodded many times in agreement.

The jock continued. "If we had a better play, we'd tell you. So far Mary's been the only one able to reach out through Terrence and you."

"Did you deal with the gunman from the night of the attack?" Evelyn asked.

The ghosts traded looks and shook their heads. "We scared him away."

"Well then, Stephen is our best bet at a lead," Evelyn said. *And our only lead.*

"So you'll help us?" Mary asked.

The ghosts looked at Evelyn, awaiting a response. Evelyn looked to her husband, who looked at his hand that was completely clean of blood. "Your call," he said quietly.

Thinking back to why she became a private investigator, to help the downtrodden and neglected, Evelyn replied. "Yeah. We'll help, but no more blackouts."

Mary smiled. "Deal."

Barker chuckled to himself and put his pipe back in his mouth. "Boy, am I glad to hear that."

Within a blink, the room fireplace snuffed out, the dust on the furniture and books returned, and the specters were gone. Evelyn and Terrence stood in the musty room.

"Did that just happen?" Terrence said, rubbing the hand that touched Alannah.

Evelyn studied her quiet surroundings and empty chairs. It felt like the longest dream. When she awoke, she would be back in Detroit, in the small apartment that smelled like wood finish. However, a deeper truth screamed inside. One that said it was all real. "We need to find Stephen Doyle."

"He tried to kills us," Terrence argued. "He killed them."

"Terrence, this is probably the most significant moment

in our lives." Evelyn did not want to sound dramatic, but it was true. "And the only thing that makes sense is that those people need rest."

"What if they're wrong and we're hunting a serial killer for no reason?" Terrence replied.

Evelyn grabbed his hand, the one that touched the woman, and took it in both of her palms. "If it were me, wouldn't you do the same?"

"I'd go to hell and back," Terrence said with the passion that made Evelyn's heart skip beats.

"They're no different," Evelyn replied. "We're all human. We all deserve a chance."

Terrence inhaled deeply and then cracked a smile. "I knew there was a reason why I married you."

"That's not the best thing to say after groping another woman," Evelyn replied with a deadpan expression.

Terrence fidgeted. "You can't blame me for that. The woman had me spellbound."

"You're really not making a good case for yourself," Evelyn said and headed for the door.

"Babe. Come on," Terrence pleaded in the way men do.

"I'm going to the Doyle house," Evelyn said as she left the room. "You coming with?"

Terrence looked back to the place where the sexy woman once stood and then followed after his wife.

They climbed into their minivan. It was a sad vehicle with a chipped hood spotted with brown and burgundy rust. Evelyn tossed Terrence the keys and let him drive. Down Quenby Avenue were pastures of short green grass with clusters of tall trees every now and again. The sun was high and the sky blue. With the windows down, Evelyn let the country breeze soothe her soft skin. Her blonde hair danced in the wind and blew against her cheek. Cows and tractors blurred by. She thought that calling the police would be the best way to find the killer, but Mary's plea was more personal. *"You need to help us."* The words replayed in her mind, getting progressively more direct and personal each time. If she could get the police to help, then great. If not, Evelyn braced herself for the days to come. She was under no illusion that this would not get messy. By the bullet holes in her house and the bones in the basement, it had already gotten messy.

The old two-story farmhouse came into view beside two cattle pastures picketed with wooden posts and wide metal mesh. The house had a symmetrical design with wooden shutters like washboards and a covered porch that had three stairs leading into the jaws of the house. Evelyn and Terrence checked for cop cars. None. Since days had passed since the Doyles had vanished, the sheriff possibly assumed that they had skipped town. They may have gotten a warrant to search the premises. Evelyn didn't know. The only thing she was sure of was that answers awaited her inside.

She stepped out of the minivan. Gravel crunched beneath her heel-less black boots. She wore a long-sleeved violet shirt and form-fitting jeans. Terrence was dressed in a short-sleeved collared button up with a violin patch above the right pec. At Evelyn's command, they both wore plastic gloves.

A shed stood beside the house. That was where Evelyn saw Doyle's white cotton mask. She would've taken a picture of it to send the police, but Stephen returned a moment later. Keeping her extendable baton attached to her waist, Evelyn peered into the windows. Curtains kept her from seeing what lay within.

"What should we be looking for?" Terrence asked while Evelyn lifted the welcoming mat, revealing disturbed pincer bugs and dirt.

"First the key." Evelyn stood on her toes and ran her fingers across the top of the door frame. "Then anything that might tie Stephen or his twin sister Catherine to any of the victims."

Terrence checked inside a nearby flower pot. No luck.

"Screw it," Evelyn said and pulled out her lock-picking tools. It would leave scratches on the lock, and if the police came back to the premises, they'd know someone broke in. But Evelyn was not one to waste time.

"Aha," Terrence said, removing the key from under a rock. He hiked up the stairs and twisted the key while Evelyn put her lock-picking tools away. The door opened smoothly into the welcoming residence. Pictures of Stephen and Catherine, both in their 40s with hooked noses and slender frames. Their eyes were buggy. Catherine had a lazy one. More family photos spotted the various stands. A few even showed Andrew Doyle, the other brother who was a few years away from his siblings, who had a similar nose and intense eyes.

Closing the door behind them, Evelyn and Terrence scouted the house. When they knew they were alone, they started their investigation. There were dishes on both sides of the sink and leftovers in the refrigerator. All the cupboards were closed and there was a rag on the stove.

"I don't think they ever came back here," Terrence said.

"Or they did, but only grabbed the things they needed."

The living room had an outdated box TV and blue sofa. There was a DVD player and a tall stack of country rock CDs. Upstairs, both of the twins' bedrooms were roughly the same size. They had a bed, dresser, and other furnishings common in most houses. Terrence tried one room and Evelyn tried the other. When they were both done looking, they would trade to make sure neither of them missed anything. Evelyn pulled open the bedside drawer, finding sleeping medication, a box of pistol ammo, and a

Cosmopolitan magazine. She didn't know what to think about that.

Under the bed were a number of plastic containers filled to the brim with old clothes fit for a Goodwill drop-off. She put them back, finding more women's fashion magazines. She thought she was in Catherine's room for a moment until she saw the big wooden letters above the inner door that said Stephen. She returned the items and tried the closet. As she walked to it, she heard Terrence rummaging in the other bedroom.

"Anything?" Evelyn asked.

"Um, I don't really know… what we're looking for," Terrence replied honestly from the other room.

Evelyn curbed her frustration, remembering that he'd never done any investigative work. "Journals, photographs, mementos from the victims. Think Barker's pipe for example. Or Alannah's brassiere."

"It was an accident!" Terrence shouted back.

Evelyn smiled to herself.

She opened the closet doors and sifted through a number of all-season jackets and hunter garb within. On top of the horizontal coat rack were a series of shoeboxes. Evelyn took them down, one by one, examined the contents, and put them back where she found them. In the second to last box, Evelyn found a number of keepsake items. Most of them were souvenirs from various national parks along with accompanying brochures. Evelyn sorted through them, taking a trip down Stephen's memory. He had quite the road trip from Georgia to Yellowstone. Oddly, he was alone for most of it. Before Evelyn put back the box, she noticed a cardboard flap cut to the size of the box and intent on hiding an item below. Evelyn had seen plenty of these in her P.I. work. Most people used them to hide ecstasy tablets or naughty pictures. Things that helped launch Evelyn's investigation. Sticking her finger in the circular hole of the cardboard, she removed it from the shoebox.

Her eyes went wide as she looked at the picture of a younger Stephen and Alannah sharing a smoothie with two straws. It was dated 1998.

"Terrence," Evelyn called out. "I think I got something."

15

BREATH

There was no doubt about it. Stephen Doyle had a connection with Alannah. But, why didn't the ghost reveal this information, and how did her body end up in the bone pit? Evelyn recalled her first encounter with Stephen. He and his sister showed up at her front door, invited themselves inside, and started taking pictures of the foyer. *"It's not your house,"* Stephen replied when Evelyn demanded that he leave. Evelyn hadn't thought much of the statement, but it seemed to carry weight now. Was it because of the bones that he said such a thing, or was there any other reason Evelyn hadn't accounted for? Perhaps it was just empty words from a homicidal maniac.

Evelyn racked her brain, trying to link the investigation back to her estranged father. She had two connections that drew Maxwell Quenby in these murders. Number one and a huge red flag, the bones were hidden in his family estate. Number two: Maxwell's connection to Mary. By the hair ribbon found in his secret study and the number of Mary's drawings that showed them together, the two of them shared a bond. Evelyn hoped it was innocent, but her pessimism seemed to get the better of her.

The rest of the time spent searching the Doyle house turned up fruitless. If anything, Evelyn garnered a new outlook on her sadistic neighbors. Stephen owned a lot of polos, shorts, and slip-on shoes. He ate a lot, a whole lot, of chicken broth, and the most expensive thing in his house was a new washer and dryer. The Doyles lived simple lives: hand-washing dishes, folding clothes, watching old reruns of *I Love Lucy* on the tube. They had a few stuffed game trophies mounted on the walls, a leaning stack of board games inside the storage closet, and an uncompleted game of Scrabble on the kitchen table. Judging by old pictures of the house and their droopy-faced grandparents, the Doyles were long-time Adders locals. Evelyn made note of that. She needed to suspect that Stephen and Catherine knew the town and its secrets.

Evelyn and Terrence double-checked the rooms to make sure everything was put back in its proper place and then reconvened in the minivan.

"Back to the mansion?" Terrence asked.

Evelyn nodded. Soft blues filled their silence.

They bumped down the red brick road, passing under the sprawling branches that dripped clumps of moss. They hopped out of the car and cautiously returned to the lounge. The room was dark and dusty, just how they left it.

"Alannah? Mary?" Evelyn called out into the empty room. She felt completely stupid as she waited for a reply.

"Hello?" Terrence asked the lounge. "We have some questions about your relationship with Stephen."

A few moments passed.

"You've got to be kidding me," Evelyn said.

"Maybe they didn't hear us," Terrence said, trying to cheer her up.

Evelyn sucked up her pride and asked again to speak with the dead. No reply.

"If you want our help, show yourselves," Evelyn demanded.

As seconds ticked by on the wall clock, seeds of doubt grew in Evelyn's mind. Was the first encounter a vision? The sights, the smells, and everything else felt so real. By Terrence's perplexed face, he had similar doubts. That was a good thing. It meant that he definitely saw it, too. Nonetheless, after having blackouts and a number of uncanny visions, reality blurred and Evelyn didn't trust her mind. Unfortunately for her, the mind was her most reliable tool.

Tick-tock, the clock kept on. Waiting around wasn't getting them anywhere. Evelyn felt a crushing weight to solve this mystery and return to her life with some semblance of normalcy. *Good luck,* a little condescending voice told her.

"What's the play?" Terrence asked.

Evelyn glanced about the room. "We proceed without them."

Part of her longed to learn more about the other victims, but she needed to prioritize. If she couldn't find Alannah, she would need to find someone else. Leaving the lounge behind, Evelyn booted up her computer in the upstairs study because the secret study in the downstairs hall of portraits was in need of serious repair. The cotton-masked person, Stephen or his sister, took an axe to the thin wall and inner door. It wouldn't help the resale value, nor would the discovery of human remains beneath it. Some people were superstitious. They might think the place was haunted.

Terrence had the video camera set out on the desk. Its tumble down the foyer stairs cracked the lens and distorted the footage. He attempted to replay the footage from the night of the invasion, catching glimpses of Alannah in her jade green dress and naked Winslow. Terrence shuddered. "I don't think I'll ever get used to that."

"We might not be supposed to," Evelyn replied, getting quick flashes of leaking wounds in her mind. Her pity for the victim was the only thing keeping her from vomiting.

Sitting upright in the leather rolling chair, Evelyn researched local missing persons on her laptop. It wasn't hard to find the news column in such a small town press. The first picture showed Alannah's perfect face and alluring smile. The second image showed police officers surrounding a red convertible parked off the road.

"Missing: Alannah Gimmerson, age 38," Terrence read. "Authorities discovered the local performer/songwriter's vehicle parked on the side of Meadows Road. The front tire was flat, undamaged but lacking air, and bags of groceries spoiled in the trunk. Authorities are seeking any information regarding Alannah's whereabouts."

Evelyn tapped the screen. "March of 2001. Mary Sullivan vanished in 2003."

"And Mary was the last victim, right?" Terrence asked.

"To our knowledge, yes," Evelyn replied. "Alannah could've been the pre-ultimate one."

Terrence pulled at his little chin beard. "Hmm. What if... never mind."

"What?" Evelyn asked.

Terrence continued. "What if the flat tire wasn't random? If the killer let the air out, knowing that Alannah would pull over. The car looks clean to me and the doors are closed. It doesn't look like Alannah resisted her attacker."

"I was thinking the same thing," Evelyn replied. She looked up at Terrence and smiled. "You're not bad at this."

"Maybe I can be the big-time investigator and you can be the humble guitar guy," Terrence joked.

"I'd rather not."

"You can wear my cowboy hat," Terrence bargained.

"Tempting," Evelyn replied dryly.

She swiveled back to the laptop. The screen's glow reflected in her bloodshot blue eyes. She researched further, finding archived newspaper slides. There was a small section from a paper a few years back, inviting anyone to Alannah's funeral where they buried an empty casket. Alannah's mother, Ida, organized it. Doing the math, Evelyn figured that Ida was retirement age and sought out retirement homes and local assisted living facilities. She got a bite for an ALF facility a town over and headed that way. Terrence joined her.

The building was single story, with diamond-shaped tiles across the floor. Brochures seemed to be set out on every surface of the entrance area. The receptionist, a short and kind woman, asked, "What is the nature of your visit?"

Evelyn flashed her P.I. license. The receptionist used the intercom to contact Ida and then led Evelyn and Terrence to the dining area. The room was largely barren this time of day apart from several round tables in the back where residents mingled. An elderly couple nodded at Evelyn and Terrence as they walked into the social area. The receptionists pointed at an elderly woman dressed lavishly with a fashionable cloth scarf around her neck. Drinking hot tea, she worked on a puzzle that displayed an 18th century ballroom. Pieces were missing from the picture, but Ida was moving along nicely.

"You have visitors, Mrs. Gimmerson," the receptionist said before she headed back to her desk.

Terrence and Evelyn sat down opposite of Ida. Like Alannah, the woman had dazzling blue eyes that seemed untouched by the age of the rest of her body. Her gray hair was cut into an expensive bob. Gemstone rings decorated her fingers and a silver necklace sparkled under the ceiling light. Evelyn introduced herself and Terrence.

"I don't get many visitors," Ida said. "Especially ones as handsome as you." She winked at Terrence.

"You're very polite, ma'am," Terrence replied.

"Oh, and you're a gentleman," Ida said with a small smile curling up her seventy-seven-year-old but still pretty face. "And please don't call me ma'am, it makes me feel dreadfully old."

"I'm under the impression that women age like fine wine," Terrence replied.

Oh, brother.

"You're a beautiful liar," Ida said, chuckling. "I know you didn't come all this way to woo an old woman."

"I've taken an interest in your daughter Alannah's case, Mrs. Gimmerson," Evelyn stated.

Ida's eyes glossed over. She blinked a few times and her normal demeanor returned. "My, it's been a long time since I heard that name."

"I want to bring closure for your daughter and you," Evelyn said.

"Dear, I found closure when I put that empty casket in the ground," Ida replied. "What you bring is a scalpel to my stitches."

Evelyn pursed her lips. Guilt plagued her heart. "That's not my intention."

"Intentions are funny things," Ida said, looking into the mug of tea. "Roads paved on good ones lead to disastrous ends."

"Evelyn is the most brilliant investigator you'll ever meet," Terrence reassured her. "If anyone can find out the truth about your daughter, it's her."

Evelyn held onto her husband's compliment.

Ida sipped her tea, adding another lipstick stain to the mug's rim. She bounced her piercing eyes between Evelyn and Terrence. "It beats looking at this puzzle for another hour. What do you wish to know?"

"Let's start with her disappearance," Evelyn said. "What do you recall about the days leading up to that?"

"Alannah took after me. A little too much," Ida reminisced. "She preferred more challenging men, and that often got her in trouble. For years, she had been living on her own. Writing songs, singings at private galas across the nation, and enjoying the wealth her boyfriends showered her with. She lived like that until the end. I noticed no change in her mood."

"Was she seeing anyone during that time?" Evelyn asked, taking out her notepad.

"Alannah always had a warm bed. Whether or not those were long-term arrangements, I cannot say. I don't know any names. She abhorred kiss and tell."

"Was there anyone that showed up at the funeral that you may have suspected?"

Ida sighed. "Despite her copious amount of lovers, Alannah's burial was quite barren. Angry wives don't allow their husbands to send off their mistresses. Surprising, I know. Still, for such a loving girl to leave this world alone, you would think she'd at least receive some flowers."

Evelyn let the words sink in for a moment and then asked about Stephen Doyle.

Ida smiled to herself. "Oh, Stephen. Such a sweet boy."

Evelyn and Terrence traded wide-eyed looks.

"Sure we're talking about the same person?" Terrence asked.

"The twin," Ida clarified. "He had a heart for Alannah since they were children."

"Did they..." Evelyn let Ida fill in the blank.

"Oh heavens, no. My daughter had her eye on bigger fish, and poor Stephen was like a lost pup. In his schooling days, he'd bike all the way across town to see Alannah with hands full of wildflowers or cheap candy. He even bought the same tabloids as her so they would have something to talk about. As Alannah filled out, so to say, Stephen's visits became more frequent, though I doubt he got far in his romantic endeavors."

"Do you know the state of their relationship during the time of the disappearance?"

"Unchanged, but at a lesser degree. Alannah's lovers didn't like having him around. After my Alannah--" Ida choked on the words. "After it happened, Stephen would visit me daily."

"To comfort you?" Evelyn asked.

Ida looked out the nearest window, blinking away the wetness in her eyes. Failing, she turned back to Evelyn. "That's how it started, but then he changed."

Evelyn lowered her pen, engrossed in the story. "How?"

"He turned bitter." Ida's words were loaded with venom. "He became obsessed with finding her and admitted to driving all hours of the night in search of some clue. Foolish boy, but I respected his efforts. The police had given up at this point. Stephen was all I had. A few months later, he burst through my front door, shouting something about a lead. *I found Alannah's killer.* He said it with a crazed fire I'd never seen in anyone since." Ida locked eyes with Evelyn. "*Maxwell Quenby.*"

Evelyn sucked air. She held it in her lungs as fears about her father became realities.

Ida continued. "He tried to explain how he came to that revelation. It had something to do with Maxwell being seen following my daughter, but he was speaking so fast I couldn't make sense of it. The next time I saw him, he arrived with his twin sister and quiet brother. The brother, I didn't mind so much. He was an odd duck but never a threatening person. The sister I knew, however. Back in her schooling days, she became notorious for killing and dissecting squirrels and other small critters. And when she got her camera as a teenager, Alannah told me rumors that Catherine took pictures of roadkill and other dead things. Catherine was the only one who came into this meeting with a smile, I remember, while Stephen was fuming and Andrew was trying terribly to hide his discomfort."

Ida peered into the dark liquid in her mug. "*He took away what I love. I'll take away what he loves.* Stephen vowed it. I didn't see him until the funeral four years later, and he left before it was through."

"Maxwell went missing during that time gap. Mary Sullivan too," Evelyn thought aloud, forming the timeline in her mind.

"I can't say if Stephen hurt anyone because of my daughter," said Ida. "I've learned in my age that there are things I don't wish to know about the world and its evils."

"Is there anything else you can give me?"

"Yes. Don't bother with Alannah," Ida said and smiled sadly at Terrence. "Enjoy your time with the living."

Under the table, Evelyn took Terrence's hand.

"Now if you'll excuse me. This puzzle requires my full attention," Ida said.

Unable to get any more information, Evelyn said farewell to Ida Gimmerson. *I have a puzzle of my own.*

As they left the assisted living facility, Evelyn said to Terrence, "You were quiet in there."

"I'm used to carving wood and tightening guitar strings. This is a different ball game. Don't get me wrong, solving crimes and stopping bad guys was a childhood fantasy, but I didn't expect the viscosity of it all. We've been seeing visions, learned about murders, broken into someone's house. It's an adrenaline rush, but I don't know how you do this on a daily basis."

"It takes some getting used to," Evelyn admitted. "This case especially. There are reasons why I don't like to talk about work. I understand if--"

"I never said I'm backing down," Terrence interrupted. "I told you that I am with you, and I won't make myself a liar."

They arrived back at Quenby House at sunset. Scarlet rays blasted over the massive white and vine-covered plantation house. Thin clouds stretched across the sky like pulled cotton.

She yawned, thinking about the bedroom. Sleeping in their massive canopied bed would never be the same, but despite the long and grueling day, Evelyn knew there was still much more work to be done. She resolved to herself that she wouldn't be getting rest anytime soon.

They stepped into the large foyer. Terrence shut and locked the door behind them. They hiked up one side of the curved stairway, and at the top of the inner balcony, Evelyn noticed splintered wood on the railing. She crouched down next to it.

A bullet. From the night of the house invasion, no doubt. "The police missed it," Evelyn told Terrence.

He didn't reply.

With a crinkled brow, Evelyn turned back to a figure in a featureless white cotton mask. Shoulders broad. Clothes black. Little button-sized eye holes stared into Evelyn's soul. Speechless, Terrence backed a step away from the figure.

"Andrew?" Evelyn asked with doubt as she stood.

The man in the mask didn't reply.

"Say something," Evelyn demanded, able to keep a still face but not a steady heart.

If this was Stephen or Catherine, Evelyn had nothing to defend herself with. All it would take was one simple bullet or a shove over the balcony and it was lights out. No more P.I. work. No more planning a family with Terrence. *Will I come back like one of them*? She didn't know if she wanted that. They were trapped here, forced to "live" with the blow that killed them. Perhaps it was better than the alternative... or miles worse.

The figure raised its hands and grabbed the sides of the mask. Carefully, it pulled it from his head, revealing a man with a hard mug, soft eyes, and silky hair. There was a hole in the back of his mouth that was a clear shot through the back of his head. It was Andrew Doyle.

Before Evelyn could speak, Andrew grabbed Evelyn's shoulders and pushed her against the balcony railing. He locked his silvery blue eyes with her. Her body became like pudding. The walls and floor began to melt into blackness. She saw a glimpse of Terrence grabbing at Andrew, but he fell through the phantom.

Blackness swarmed in... but only for a moment.

In brief flashes, only a breath length long, she saw through the small eye hole of a cotton mask. The taste of booze lingered on her tongue. Sweat stuck the fabric to her face. Two more figures in masks dragged the screaming blonde girl into the clearing amidst the cotton field. *So young.* A thought raced through Evelyn's mind. It was not her own.

The breath ended and another began. She was looking at a tower of fire rising up in front of her and into the blue Georgia sky. Her gloved fingers held an empty can of lighter fluid. The two other figures reveled at the flames. One took joy in the vengeance. The other, in sadism. Evelyn felt nothing but dread. *You're here for the family. Doyles stick together.*

A breath.

One of the figures blasted the little charred bones with a fire extinguisher. The other watched apathetically. *We all deserve to die.* In her hand, Evelyn felt the cold weight of the pistol.

A breath.

Evelyn looked down the weapon's iron sight. At the other end of the barrel, the masked figures stared at her in confusion. "Andy," one said condescendingly.

A breath.

The mask was pulled up past Evelyn's nose. She smelled the pillar of black smoke. She tasted the metal barrel in her mouth. The masked figures were moving in, arms out in a non-threatening manner. One said. "Andy, now you wait a--" She squeezed the trigger.

Suddenly, Evelyn was back at Quenby House and in her own skin. She looked into Andrew's eyes, tasting gunpowder residue in the back of her throat.

"Let go of her!" Terrence shouted at the man holding Evelyn by the shoulders. Andrew listened and backed away. Terrence instantly jumped in front of Evelyn.

"Evelyn, babe, are you okay?"

"...yeah," Evelyn replied whimsically.

Andrew slid on his mask and walked away, vanishing into the darkness of the upstairs hall.

Terrence twisted back to Evelyn. His eyes were intense and damp with terror. "What did he do?"

"He showed me how Mary died. How he died." Evelyn said, still trying to make sense of it all.

"Okay. We're leaving this place," Terrence declared

"No," Evelyn said defiantly. "We're in this, Terrence, like or not."

"But--"

"--If you saw what they did to Mary Sullivan--"

"--I saw her body," Terrence cupped his hands on Evelyn's cheeks and looked her in the eyes. "I feel the responsibility too, but they're abusing us, Eve. As much as I pity them, they are stripping us of our will."

"They're communicating with us," Evelyn counter-argued

Terrence stepped away and paced in frustration. "We know it's Stephen Doyle. Police are already going after him. Case closed. What can we do?"

"Stephen and Catherine killed Mary," Evelyn said. "But they didn't kill Alannah or the rest. Ida's testimony, Stephen's motivation, it all proves that Stephen is not the serial killer."

"Then who murdered the other five other people in our basement?" Terrence asked, meaning the question to be rhetorical. Evelyn didn't take it that way.

"I intend to find out."

16

BROKEN LIVES

Though their eyes were closed, Evelyn and Terrence lay awake in the king-sized bed. An uncanny silence hung in Quenby House, as it did every night. In any other time or place, the quiet would've offered a certain comfort of being alone and private.

Not here.

The spirits of the dead could be watching Evelyn at this very moment, but there would be no tell of their presence. Evelyn bundled up under the thick covers and allowed the divine mattress to swallow her up. She listened to her husband's soft breaths and remembered a time where the biggest stress was paying the bills and getting clientele. It wasn't as easy then, and that conflict was only put on hiatus, but it seemed so trivial now. There was something about helping the dead that brought a fulfillment Evelyn hadn't felt in a long time. She wondered if Terrence felt the same way.

Evelyn got up at the crack of dawn. She took a hot shower while standing in the bathtub and got dressed in her typical dark blue jeans and a white t-shirt. She kept her black, belted, double-breasted raincoat nearby. The forecast predicted another incoming storm. She sipped black coffee from her mug and stood at the threshold of the lounge. Her ringed eyes scanned the places where the victims had stood and sat. *Are you watching me?* Evelyn wondered.

Dust danced in the air. There was a slight depression in the loveseat's second cushion. Evelyn couldn't recall if it was always there. She took another sip from her mug and returned to the kitchen.

Terrence was up and about, making scrambled eggs on the kitchen stove. He wore a collared shirt, pants, and two mismatched socks with different sets of instruments on them. "Morning."

"Morning," Evelyn replied.

Terrence pulled out the block of cheese from the fridge and grabbed Maxwell's grater from a drawer. "I counted our money."

"That good, huh?" Evelyn replied and glanced about the room, wondering if anyone was eavesdropping.

"It might be a smart choice to start selling some stuff," Terrence said, grating the cheese over the fluffy scrambled eggs.

"Will we make it till the end of the month?" Evelyn asked.

Terrence handed her a plate. With hesitation, he said, "I think so. If we're not dealing with any more car issues, motel stays, and hospital visits."

Evelyn took her plate and ate a bite, staring at nothing in particular.

"Maybe our roomies will lead us to a hidden stash of money," Terrence said, trying to lighten the mood.

Taking her plate, Evelyn headed to the study. Terrence tagged along. They booted up the laptop and started their research. Alannah and Mary were the only two victims that Evelyn knew the last names of. She had a fair understanding of their disappearances and personalities, but the others were still strangers. She jotted down a list of the names. Barker, Winslow, Zoey, and Peter. Today, she'd focus on them and hopefully establish a strong profile for each one. A guarantee that Evelyn gave all her clients was her ability to work quickly.

Several locals vanished between the 1980s to the early 2000s, but Evelyn's search in Quenby started in 1998 with Dr. James Barker. In the black and white photo online, he wore his signature sweater vest and slacks with an elegant tobacco pipe in his hand. He vanished at the age of 74. No trace of him was ever discovered.

In 1999, Winslow Darvey, age 42, vanished from the butchery where he worked. In his picture, his smile was crooked and ruined by his underbite. No trace of him was ever discovered.

2000, varsity player Peter Calhoon, 17, vanished without a trace. The local news described his loss in great detail and made mention that a recruiter from University of Georgia had visited on multiple occasions though he was only a junior in high school.

2001, Alannah Gimmerson, 38, vanished.

2002, Zoey Pinkerton, 15, never returned home. Her missing person picture was blurry and not chosen with much care.

2003, Mary Sullivan, 7, vanished, though Evelyn believed that her disappearance was connected to Stephen Doyle, not the killer of the other five individuals.

"There's a pattern here," Terrence stated the obvious.

"A victim a year for five years," Evelyn said. She studied the missing persons reports, tracing the killer's descent into evil. He/she started with an old man and ended with a girl. Younger and younger the victims became and then suddenly all the vanishing stopped. That meant one of three things: the killer was over a decade dead, the killer had run away, or the killer was lying dormant.

As much as Evelyn wanted to focus on the killer, there was not enough information to build a location profile. She needed to look at the victims, starting from the beginning: James Barker. After some digging, Evelyn discovered he worked as a professor in East Georgia State College, which was about a two-hour drive from Adders. He retired at the age of 65.

Evelyn would've liked to ask him where he lived but, alas, the phantom did not reveal himself. *Are you testing me?* Evelyn wondered. *Or am I doing something wrong?*

She contacted the number on the Missing Persons page. It was out of commission. She contacted the college.

"We cannot disclose any of his personal information," one of Barker's old colleagues said over the phone.

"I'm a P.I," Evelyn explained in what she expected would be the first of many times today. The man gave her the runaround for a bit before Evelyn pressed him. "No one else is looking for your friend. At his age, they probably suspect he is dead. Give me a chance to find out the truth."

The colleague grumbled on a bit about college policy, but at the end of it all, he revealed Barker's retirement address, which was in Adders. Light rain pattered the windows of the mansion and turned the world steel and gray.

Evelyn pulled her black double-breasted coat on while Terrence grabbed the car keys. A sudden chill gripped them.

"What? You aren't going to say goodbye?" A voice said behind them.

Barker stood at the railing of the inner balcony, looking down on them with a smoking pipe in his hand. He used the top of his other hand to wipe the blood leaking from his tight mouth.

Terrence and Evelyn exchanged glances and felt the tension in the room.

"The two of you need to relax," Barker said with small smile. "You look like you've seen a ghost."

"Good one," Terrence said, unsure how to react.

Evelyn couldn't get used to this, no matter how many times she'd encountered the supernatural. Taking a step forward, she said, "We're going to visit your home."

"I think you'll like the place. Sally's a great interior decorator." Realizing that Evelyn was unfamiliar with the person he mentioned, Barker clarified. "Sally. My wife. She's the most beautiful, lively, and intelligent woman you'll ever meet. A little snarky, I might add."

"We could just ask you about your demise," Evelyn said, crossing her arms.

"It's a pathetic story. Old man goes on a walk as per the doctor's request and then… the rest after that is blurry. Apart from the chlorine." Barker's face went bitter. "I can still taste that."

He hit his pipe. Smoke and blood fell from his lips.

"He made you drink…" Terrence said, becoming wheezy.

"He, she, I don't know." Barker admitted, wiping his chin. "Scotch has always been more my poison."

"Did you know my father?" Evelyn asked.

"I knew the name. I mostly called him the guy in the big house."

"Do you think he did this to you?"

Barker looked around the vast foyer. "I'm in his house, aren't I?"

Evelyn felt her stomach drop. She couldn't draw a conclusion. Not yet. But the evidence was building. "Is there anything you want to say to Sally?"

Barker seemed stunned by the question. He recomposed

himself. "Tell her… tell her that she made life a joy and to keep on living until I come home."

"We'll tell her," Terrence promised.

Barker stared through them, seemingly unable to hear Terrence's words. Blood seeped from his lips. This time, he didn't wipe it away.

EVELYN KNOCKED on the front door of the ranch home. Weak rain pelted its cobblestone exterior while wind swayed the small and pointy evergreen trees sprouted across the house's face. Terrence held the black umbrella over Evelyn's head while a little rain pattered the back of his charcoal gray fleece that Evelyn bought him one Christmas. With Evelyn wearing black, too, they must've looked like they were returning from a wake.

A Hispanic woman in blue scrubs answered the door. "Yes?" she asked suspiciously.

"Does Sally Barker live here?" Evelyn asked.

The Hispanic woman nodded slowly. "She won't be taking any visitors."

"What happened?" Terrence asked with concern.

"I'm afraid her health is failing."

"We'd like to talk to her about her husband. Could you tell her that?" Evelyn asked.

The woman eyed her. "Wait here." She vanished inside without another word. She returned a moment later. "You may enter, but her nap time is nearing, so be quick."

Terrence frowned at the woman's rudeness, but Evelyn kept her expression flat. This was nothing new to her. There were very few lights on in the house, and the walls were shades of blues and grays. Pictures of James and Sally in their 50s and 60s backed by the Louvre, the Leaning Tower of Pisa, the unique colorful buildings of Amsterdam, and more breathtaking European travel destinations. Terrence cracked a smile. He nudged Evelyn. She didn't share the same enthusiasm. Not because she didn't long to see the world, but because she knew she'd never have time.

They entered the bedroom. Whatever bed had been there before was replaced with an adjustable one from the hospital. The woman lying on it had long white hair, paper skin, and a sunken face. An IV needle was trapped into her inner elbow. Her gaze was cast at the rain cascading down the window. Evelyn could feel the dread hovering in the room and knew that time was not on Sally's side.

"You can go, Lucile," Sally said in her froggy voice.

The Hispanic woman whispered, "Don't upset her. Her heart can't take such things."

She slipped into the hall, leaving the door open behind her.

Sally turned to them. "Did you find my husband?"

"In a manner of speaking," Evelyn replied as she approached the bedside. Terrence followed behind.

"Did he run away or is he gone?"

"Gone," Evelyn replied honestly. She couldn't lie to a woman nearly a century old.

Sally shut her eyes for a long while. Her breath was so faint that Evelyn thought that she may have left them. "How?"

"We're figuring that out," Terrence said.

"Tell us about him?" Evelyn asked.

"A talker. A doer. More of the former," Sally said with a slight smile. "He stole my heart when we were fifteen."

"Before he disappeared, did you notice a change in his attitude?"

"James was James. He was never one to stay mad for long, though he did complain a lot. Also, he would always smile before he made a witty remark. I rolled my eyes to show him how impressed I was."

Evelyn looked at her blank notepad. "Did he have any enemies or anyone angry with him?"

"Restaurant waiters," Sally nodded seriously. "He was a lousy tipper."

James chuckled.

"The last thing James ever said to me was, *I'm going on a mundane stroll. I'll be stinky and sweaty when I get back, so have the bath ready.* That was it. Never saw him again. I waited beside the cold bath water for an hour before I went after him. Old Sycamore Trail is the place where he hiked. Five-minute drive from here. Police found nothing." Sally said and turned to Evelyn. "There are days when I... feel him, but now that I know he's gone. Really this time. There's not much left to hold onto."

Terrence took the woman's hand. "He's not as far away as you think."

Sally's brown eyes widened.

"We've talked to him," Evelyn said, overcoming her struggle to admit to the ghostly encounter. "A part of him still remains."

Terrence nodded in agreement.

"How--What did he say?" Sally asked with a small voice.

"He said, you made life a joy."

Sally shivered and cried softly.

"And to keep on living until he comes home."

"Oh, James," Sally said through her tears. She talked to the ceiling. "You promised we would leave this world together. I'll wait on you for another nineteen years."

The nurse lingered in the doorway with her hands on her hips.

"Get your rest, Sally," Evelyn said. "We'll get James home much sooner than that."

Evelyn and Terrence left and traveled to Old Sycamore Trail. In the rain and without talking, they walked the smooth path through the woods, but found nothing that hinted at James Barker's disappearance.

"You think we should've told her?" Terrence asked as they drove back.

"We gave Barker our word," Evelyn replied.

"I know but... what if we fail and he's stuck in the mansion for good?"

"Hey, there's only room for one pessimist in this relationship."

"You're right," Terrence replied. "I was just hoping we would've learned more from her."

"We have three victims left," Evelyn reminded him. "One of them will know something."

Following the killer's chronology, they started with Winslow, the second victim. A little ways outside of town, Evelyn and Terrence arrived at a large, drab, industrial-style building that had multiple semi-trucks shipping grass-fed meats across the state. Tipton's Slaughterhouse.

Avery Tipton greeted Evelyn and Terrence at the front door as he said he would over the phone call. He was a man of average build and height, with the beginnings of a second chin and a thin crown of hair around his head. He wore a blue collared shirt and welcomed Evelyn and Terrence aside.

"I'm glad you're taking an interest in Winslow. God, I loved that boy. My wife and I helped raise him. Well, ex-wife." Avery said as he led them to the office. Evelyn noticed his finger swelling around his undersized and weathered wedding ring.

"Did you adopt him?" Evelyn asked.

"Not officially," Avery sat on the edge of his metal desk and moved his hands when he spoke. "The boy's father was never in the equation, and his mother would beat him and call him names. Nasty stuff. I was locking up the church one afternoon and saw the boy sitting on the steps. The mother left him there and skipped town. For the better I think. I took him in, originally for just a few days, but he had such a gentle heart, my wife and I kept him. We raised him with our other two boys." Avery fidgeted. "My ex-wife and I."

"You gave him a job here?" Evelyn asked.

"Winslow wasn't..." Avery searched for the right word, but didn't find it. "He had strengths and weaknesses like the rest of us. One of the traits was strength. The boy could lift a cow, I kid you not. Eat a whole one too." Avery sighed. "Yeah, I miss him. He worked a lot harder than the clowns I have now."

"He was forty-two years old when he went missing," Terrence recalled. "How old was he when you adopted him?"

Avery rubbed the back of his neck. "To be honest, I was never quite sure. Communication wasn't Winslow's strong suit. I was in my early thirties when I got him. He was probably seventeen or so. Innocent as a child though. I'll always see him as a boy, despite the age factor. What made you so curious about him anyway? Someone hire you?"

"It's a personal project," Evelyn said. "My father went missing too. I'm seeing if there is any connection. Maxwell Quenby. Heard of him?"

"Quenby. Yeah. I heard of him." Avery's face twisted to disgust. "I never knew he had a daughter."

"Yeah, sole inheritor," Evelyn replied. "What's your issue with Maxwell?"

"Nothing personal, but I'm sure you've heard of the Sullivan girl."

"Mary."

"I'd bet my bottom dollar that Maxwell had something to do with her disappearance."

"Any reason you think that?" Terrence asked.

Avery frowned heavily and shook his head. "Just made sense. Maxwell lived in that big house all by himself. He looked down on us normal folk. He had so much money and clout, cops wouldn't even give him a speeding ticket. If anyone could get away with murder, it was Maxwell Quenby. That's why I'm glad he's dead and gone. No offense, but this town has been quieter since no one's been in that house."

Evelyn changed the topic. "Tell me what happened to Winslow."

Avery stopped leaning on the desk. "Let me show you."

They walked into the meat locker.

Massive slabs hung from hooks across the ceiling. Cold fog thumbed through the icy room.

"I hope blood doesn't make you squeamish," Avery said.

"Not anymore," Terrence replied.

In the far corner of the room, Avery pointed at the gash in the wall and then went back to hugging himself.

Evelyn approached and brushed her fingers across the groove. "Meat hook?"

"Yep," Avery said. "Winslow was manning the graveyard the night he vanished. In the morning, I learned he was missing, the back door was open, and there was this scrape on the wall. The police said that there was a fight. That Winslow used a hook to defend himself. But they found no blood. A few days later, I realized one of my curved butcher knives was gone. If that doesn't scare you, nothing will."

Evelyn recalled the long slash across Winslow's belly. "Anything happen leading up to the attack?"

"Something," Avery said. "Winslow was flipping out. I didn't understand what he was saying, but I knew he was scared. I told him that it was nothing and to get to work." Avery shook his head. "Boy, I was wrong."

17

THE LOST

Peter Calhoon was a poster child for any high school, anywhere. He had a clean-shaven boxed jaw with a dimpled chin and shy smile that kept girls swooning. His blond hair was cut neatly, and his grade card boasted a 4.0 GPA in all advanced placement classes.

"No one could've asked for a better son," Mrs. Sheerly Calhoon said. She was in her early fifties, with highlighted blonde hair and small rectangular glasses that made her look like a sexy secretary.

Evelyn placed the school photo back on the fireplace shelf and looked at the picture of Peter. Kneeling in a football field, he wore an indigo football jacket with yellow sleeves and text. *He died in that jacket,* Evelyn thought.

"He was varsity captain and named junior prom king," Mrs. Calhoon explained.

Mr. Calhoon, a middle-aged version of his son with the same chin, dashing looks, and silky hair, rocked in the fluffy recliner. "Nearly broke the school record with the longest pass. A fifty-seven yard missile right into the end zone."

"Your son sounds like he was really something," Terrence

said, admiring the glass trophy case that seemed to fit perfectly in the McMansion. "I played a few years myself."

"Yeah?" Mr. Calhoon said. He stopped rocking. "What position?"

"Wide receiver," Terrence replied.

"Really?" Mr. Calhoon exclaimed. "Shotback?"

"Split-end," Terrence said proudly. "Only for a few years, though."

"Coach moved me between shotback and flanker. It pissed me off when I was young. Everyone wants to be quarterback."

"I enjoyed my position. Still, I'm glad your son got to live that fantasy for you."

Mr. Calhoon licked his molar and mumbled, "Yeah. He was going to be the next Fred Crawford. I could see Pete throwing an eighty-five yarder to a legend like Eddie Kawal."

Mrs. Calhoon used her index finger to rub away a tear welling in her left eye. She blinked a few times.

Evelyn turned away from the fireplace and looked up the large living room. Though it was a selfish thought, Evelyn found it hard not to compare homes. Quenby was bigger for sure, but the modern classiness of this place seemed much more functional than her pre-civil war relic. Evelyn refocused. "What do you think happened to your son?"

Mr. and Mrs. Calhoon traded looks. "Murdered."

"What makes you think that?" Evelyn asked.

"He would never run away," Mrs. Calhoon said. "His future mattered to him too much."

"Our son was happy," Mr. Calhoon added.

"Is there anyone you suspected of harming him?"

With red-rimmed eyes, Mrs. Calhoon said, "Everyone."

"People were jealous of Peter," Mr. Calhoon added.

Mrs. Calhoon looked ill. "Behind their smiles and compliments, they couldn't stand that my son was better than theirs."

"What are your thoughts on Maxwell Quenby or Stephen Doyle?"

"I don't know any Doyles," Mr. Calhoon said. "Maxwell, though. He attended a few school board meeting events. At first I thought it was his chance to chase some tail. He had this mysterious way about him that drew in women. But after my son's disappearance and women started going missing..." Mr. Calhoon balled up his fist. "I'm glad Max is gone."

Evelyn gnashed her teeth. The more people suspected her father, the less she wanted it to be true. Blame it on her rebellious nature or her empathy for the underdog, but if she could prove her father was innocent, it would be a beautiful thing.

Without getting more help from the Calhoons, Evelyn sought out her final lead: Zoey Pinkerton.

The house was at the other end of town. It was quiet, quaint places with a few mares grazing in the fenced-in pastures. Wind chimes hung on the porch. Unmowed grass carpeted the earth. Gnats and chiggers leaped between leaf blades and weeds. Evelyn and Terrence exited their crude minivan as the day neared its exodus.

Zoey was the final victim before Mary. Evelyn reflected on what she'd learned while she waited for the next of kin to answer. Firstly, the killer was testing the waters in the beginning. He killed an old man, then a middle-aged one and followed by a teenage male. Then he switched to an adult female and then teenaged girl. Mary's killing would've been the logical step, but that was the Doyles' doing. So what stopped the killer, and where did he go?

As for her father, she knew Maxwell had a friendship with Mary, was disliked by seemingly everyone, and seemed to draw in women. Also, Maxwell knew of the plantation mansion's secret study. If he was the killer and died, the phantoms would have peace, right? Unless they wanted Evelyn to chase a ghost. A fool's errand that would be. Either Maxwell lived, which there was no proof of, or the killer was someone else who knew the house's secrets.

The door opened. Dressed in a wrinkled shirt and faded Levis, a short man with a shaggy goatee and tired blue eyes stepped out. Evelyn introduced herself. The man inhaled deeply through his nose. "Come in. I'm making tea."

The house was minimalist, but not in a stylish way. The kitchen table was devoid of cloth. Sparse paintings decorated the neutral-colored wall. There were a few pictures of Zoey as a kid. She had lush brown hair and a big smile. Between ages 9 and 15, something changed. It could be puberty that led her to her goth persona.

"Is it just you?"

"Wife passed a few years ago," the man said.

"I'm sorry," Evelyn replied.

"She made her choice."

Evelyn averted her eyes. She remembered her own "choice" years ago. It ended with Terrence, a complete stranger at the time, pulling Evelyn's broken and bleeding body out of the ruins of her car. If only everyone had such luck.

David gave them mugs of hot tea and took a seat at the head of the square dining room. They crowded around three of the four seats. "Did Zoey run away or was she killed?" David asked.

"Killed," Evelyn said. "The news will disclose the victim's information soon enough."

"My wife was right after all," the man said.

"I promise you, Mr. Pinkerton, we are doing everything in our power to make sure your daughter finds peace."

"Why?" the man asked.

"Eve and I believe that we can help the restless find closure," Terrence said. "In doing so, we hope you'll find peace."

"And you're doing this for money?"

"Any other case, yes," Evelyn admitted. "Not this one."

"Then what do you hope to gain?" David Pinkerton eyed her.

Terrence and Evelyn looked into each other's eyes. "The truth." *And some overdue peace and quiet.*

Mr. Pinkerton chuckled sadly. "If my wife knew there were people like you when our daughter first vanished, things might have been different."

"Tell us about Zoey."

"She was a hermit with a brilliant mind," David said. "She hid behind shades of black, but her heart was good. She was good, even if I didn't agree with her in most things. I only wished I had told her that instead of doing *what was best.* She vanished after we had a big fight about her music and attitude. I was a different man back then."

"Did she say where she was going?" Terrence asked.

"She didn't say, but I knew. It was to her godfather's house." Tired lines etched around his eyes. "Maxwell Quenby."

Evelyn's heart skipped a beat. "Godfather?"

"Yeah, I gave Quenby the honors. I worked his land. Taught him how to ride horses. If there was ever a man who was misunderstood, it was Max."

Finally. Someone who doesn't hate him. "Tell me about him."

"I thought you were here for Zoey?"

"I'm here for both," Evelyn replied swiftly and with fire.

David raised his brows. After a moment, he returned to a normal tone. "He didn't want the family name. The Quenbys were always movers and shakers here in Adders. They liked keeping an eye on the town and its money, and made sure the old blood stayed in power. They had blackmail material on everybody and when they made an investment--cattle for example--they'd cripple the competitors. Some people believe that's why Adders never grew in size. In a small town like this, most people were okay with that. It was the outsiders who got the shaft."

"But Maxwell was different?"

David nodded. "Night and day compared to his father. Maxwell had no desire to flaunt his wealth or extort anyone. After his father died, Maxwell wanted to live a quiet and peaceful life with a family and kids. The town's institutions--police, judiciary, big business, small business, you name it--wanted his family's knowledge and continual donations. They pressed him day in and day out. There was a time where he had different guests every day, some would stay from breakfast to dinner. Maxwell hated it. After a while, he voiced his opinion but no one listened. To open their ears, Maxwell destroyed his family's blackmail material, stopped all funding, and shut himself in."

"Why name him Zoey's godfather?" Evelyn asked.

"I swore I'd take that to the grave."

Evelyn leaned over the table. "Please."

David grumbled. "All I can say is this: he had to give up his own daughter for reasons unknown and the mother was never in the equation. Because I counted him as my closest friend, I let him help raise Zoey. It brought some joy back to his life. Though our parenting styles differed back then. When Zoey was around fourteen, I kept her away from Max. A few years later, he found someone else to fill that emptiness inside. Little Mary Sullivan."

Evelyn let the revelations sink in.

"Evelyn is Maxwell's daughter," Terrence told David.

He studied Evelyn. "You don't look like him. Why did you come back?"

"She inherited the plantation," Terrence explained. "We came down here to sell it, but… our plans changed."

"What else can you tell me about my adoption?" Evelyn said, ignoring all that Terrence had said.

"I'll tell you when you find my daughter's killer," David bargained.

"You're kidding, right?"

"Not at all. You find who killed my daughter and I'll tell you everything I know."

Reluctantly, Evelyn agreed. "Did you ever suspect Maxwell hurt Zoey?"

David locked eyes with her. "Never. Not in a million life times."

"What if I told you her remains were found hidden in his basement?" Evelyn asked.

The vein in David's neck bulged. "Then I'd call you a liar."

Evelyn decided not to say any more about it. She asked more questions about Zoey's disappearance. Just like the other victims, not a trace was ever found.

Five victims in five years, and not a shred of evidence. Whoever Evelyn was up against was good. Very good.

Terrence and Evelyn ate dinner at a local mom-and-pop restaurant in the heart of town. It couldn't get more Southern than country fried steak, green beans with bacon bits, and a glass of sweet tea. Unlike the rest of the family patrons enjoying their Thursday evening, Evelyn and Terrence had trouble keeping their eyes open. The emotional roller coaster of the day ended with more questions and heavier stress.

"I'm going to need a vacation for my vacation," Terrence said, midway through thc meal.

Evelyn cracked a smile.

They returned home. Evelyn gazed up the painted angels on the domed ceiling. Terrence took a shower and crashed on the bed. Evelyn wasn't as fortunate. At about 2 a.m., she was staring at the ceiling growing frustrated, but she couldn't turn off her mind. She walked downstairs to the hall of portraits. The oil painting of her fat ancestor was cast to the side and the wooden wall with a secret door had a massive gash on it. The broken planks formed crooked teeth around the hole like a circular jaw. Evelyn didn't bother unlocking it with the old key. She stepped through the portal.

The hallway to the secret study was three feet wide and seven foot tall. Unpainted wooden planks made up the interior. Dust flowed through the creaks. The floor groaned under Evelyn's slippers. At the end of the short hallway, the door to the secret study was wide open, with an arm-sized axe hole at its core. During the night of the invasion, Evelyn and Terrence fled here while the masked killer took an axe to the door's face. Mary pointed Evelyn to safety using the secret trapdoor beneath the ancient mahogany desk. It spit them into the bed of bones.

Evelyn scanned the decimated room. It looked like the killer knocked over every light, tore every book from the shelf, and turned over the various Antebellum antiquities. Evelyn picked up some of the clutter. Many of the books were classics in their earliest edition. If they were in a little better condition, they could fetch a good price. She approached the desk and swiped her hand across its top. Within lay the original land deed and slave purchase receipt. Evelyn guessed this was where the blackmail material used to be as well. Quenby House was built on blood and deception, and her father wanted to make it right. Evelyn liked that thought. She pulled open the drawers and shuffled through the contents. A small picture of freckle-faced Mary Sullivan was lodged in the back corner. Evelyn stared at the child, wondering what it would've been like to be raised by Maxwell. Evelyn had seen Mary's drawings. They were always pleasant. She put the photo aside, allowing the small thought to warm her in this dark, cruel world.

Something else caught her eye. A knob the size of tack at the back of the upper drawer. Evelyn pulled it, revealing a small cache. It was made for a notebook that could fit in her palm. Evelyn opened the thin leather bindings. Within were a number of random names. Some were circled while others were crossed out. She didn't recognize any of the names. A lot of them were terribly misspelled. *Drunken text or a code.* She turned page after page of misspelled names until she reached the end of the first third of the booklet. There was one blank page, but the page following it had a list of dates and locations. Six in all, and each coinciding with one of the victims found in the basement. Even Mary Sullivan, whose remains were ash somewhere on Quenby land.

Evelyn stared at it for a long while. *Why would you have this?*

Evelyn must've fallen asleep because she awoke in the master bedroom and Terrence wasn't beside her.

She got up and took a shower. Getting dressed in a blue and black striped long-sleeved shirt and dark capris, she headed downstairs. "Terrence?"

Voices seeped through the foyer. Cautious, Evelyn followed the noise to the mural hall. She silently pushed into the lounge. Terrence sat in the loveseat with his eyes glued on his laptop.

"What are you doing in here?" Evelyn asked.

Terrence looked up from the screen. She realized he was watching the news.

"I needed to see if *they* knew anything about this," Terrence said in a harrowing tone.

"About what?" Evelyn scooted in next to him.

He tilted the screen her way.

The local news anchor spoke objectively. "At eleven

o'clock last night, local nine-year-old girl, Bella Day, vanished. Authorities are looking for any information about her current whereabouts."

Evelyn felt a chill. She glanced behind her, seeing Barker, Alannah, Zoey, Mary, Winslow, Peter, and Andrew standing sentry.

Immediately, she knew that the killer's cycle had just restarted.

18

THE VANISHING OF BELLA DAY

With rich brunette hair cut at the shoulders and big brown eyes, Bella Day would be a looker when she grew up. If Evelyn could rescue her.

She twisted back to the phantoms. "Do any of you know about the Day family?"

Terrence looked them up and down, unable to take his eyes off their fatal wounds.

"To take a girl that young…" A look of disgust scrunched Peter's handsome face. He put his one hand on Mary's shoulder.

Barker took a puff from his pipe and wiped the blood from his chin. "It stinks of the same bastard who killed us. I can feel it."

Evelyn stood to face them better, but also to keep the couch as a barrier between her and the phantoms, not that it would help. "You've got to give me something. All our leads are busts. So think. Andrew showed me how he died. Can't the rest of you do that?"

The phantoms turned to Andrew. His featureless white

mask displayed no hint to his expression. He glared at Evelyn through the black, button-sized eye holes.

The blood left Terrence's face. "Evelyn. I don't think--"

"That little girl is going to die," Evelyn barked at her husband. She redirected her attention on the victims. "Please."

Zoey, the goth, said, "You're going to regret this." It wasn't a threat. It was a warning.

"Try me," Evelyn replied.

With a sad smile, well-endowed Alannah reached over the back of the loveseat's backboard and put her hands on Evelyn's cheek. "I'm sorry, darling."

"Hey," Terrence yelled at the woman in the jade dress. "What do you--"

Evelyn didn't hear the rest of it. She was too busying having her throat slashed. Her red fingernails dug into the old wooden chair's arms. Her long, perfect legs kicked in all directions. Her heels crunched away at the dirt. In the night, tall yellow hay swayed around her as crimson seeped from her opened throat and into her bosom. Her blurry eyes met the glowing lantern set on the stomped grass a few feet in front of her.

Evelyn returned to the lounge, grasping her neck. She staggered back and sucked in air. The phantoms had formed a circle around her. Alannah stepped back. Peter put his only hand just above Evelyn's chest.

Terrence stared in horror.

Evelyn was back in the field, seated on the wood chair, looking at both her hands bound at the forearms. They were Peter's hands. She glanced up at the silhouetted figure standing between her and the lantern. He raised the meat cleaver. Moonlight reflected on the polished metal. Then the blade cut the air and dropped on Peter's right wrist. A quick splash and then cold shiver.

The vision ended. The shakes didn't.

Winslow grabbed Evelyn's shoulders with his large hand. His meaty nude body and slash across his belly made Evelyn queasy. Winslow mouthed something, but the underbite made it impossible to interpret.

"Get off her." Terrence tried to pull at him, but phased through the body.

Evelyn stood in a meat locker. Something moved in the other side of room, swiftly passing between the slabs of dangling meat. No one was supposed to be here, she knew. Papa won't like that. She grabbed a loose hook from the rack and readied herself. Though the room was freezing, Evelyn--in Winslow's body--was sweating profusely. She saw something running to her from the corner of her eye and swung the hook at them. It scraped against the wall. She blinked and awoke, suspended with her bound wrists dangling from a hook in some sort of basement that wasn't Quenby. Winslow closed his eyes--Evelyn couldn't see either-- as the figure worked the blade across her belly. No one heard the screams.

Evelyn was back in the lounge. She opened her mouth to speak but couldn't find words. Her whole body was burning up, but she was shivering.

Barker stepped up and took her hand in his that was cold and clammy.

The next kill began in the same basement, seated at a table and drinking a tall glass of chlorine while feeling a gun barrel on the back of her head.

Evelyn could taste the chemical as she returned. The enfeeblement of every vision clung to her like her only slice of hell. "No..." she mumbled.

Terrence pulled at her, trying to get her out of the circle, but some unseen force locked her in place.

With a look of guilt, Zoey stepped up and put her hands

behind Evelyn's head. Tears fell down Evelyn's red face. They met eyes and Evelyn saw the approaching car on Quenby Avenue, the shadow-shrouded driver, odd tranquilizer gun, and hay field where a sharp metal pole was jammed into the back of a skull.

Back in the lounge, Evelyn crumbled to the floor. Her body trembled. Her eyes were blinking but lifeless. Her body was an empty shell, imprisoned by the sights and feelings of five deaths.

Terrence rubbed his hands up his bald head and stared at the phantoms with utter horror. After a moment, he dropped to his knees and held Evelyn's wrist to stop her from shaking. "Eve, baby. Oh, come, baby, stay with me."

Evelyn tasted the chemicals on her tongue. She felt the cold blade across her flesh in every place the victims suffered injury. The fear made her heart beat rapidly and then slowly and then rapidly again. Her chest cramped. Images burned into her mind, horror and nightmares she couldn't escape.

Yellow hay sprouted from the floor and swayed in the darkness. The walls of the room fell away and she was back in the chair. She saw a house in the distance. Quenby? She couldn't tell. She heard a mechanical scream as some unseen power tool turned on right behind her head. A circular saw neared her head. This wasn't from one of the visions. What the hell was happening?

Terrence twisted back to the victims, "What the hell did you do?"

Mary stepped forward. "They showed her."

"Whatever you did, reverse it!" Terrence demanded.

"We can't, darling," Alannah replied with pity. "What's seen can't be unseen."

Terrence turned his shaking hands into fists. "Get out," he fumed. "Get out of my house!"

The phantoms stared at him, almost confused or hurt by his words.

"Go! Go!" He grabbed the lamp off the couch table and slung it through them. It shattered on the wall.

The phantoms stepped back. In a blink, they were gone and Quenby House was deathly silent.

"Terrence," Evelyn said weakly from the floor.

Terrence turned back to her and brushed her blonde hair away from her cheek. "What did they do to you?"

Still in the hay field, Evelyn saw her husband's wide eyes. Suddenly, the world returned to normal and she was back on the floor of the lounge.

"Don't blame them," Evelyn said, cycling through the five deaths in her mind. "They don't remember. They never saw his face."

Terrence helped Evelyn sit up. Evelyn rubbed her hand down her sunken face that seemingly aged twenty years in two minutes. The feelings of the victims' deaths faded, but didn't disappear. How long the phantom pains would remain, Evelyn didn't know. She looked ahead at her next goals. "We need to visit the sheriff. See if he's learned anything about the bones and Bella Day."

"Evelyn, this is insane," Terrence argued. "I know you want to do the right thing, but *they've* gone too far."

Evelyn forced herself to stand. She closed her eyes until the sense of vertigo left her. "I wanted them to show me."

"You didn't know what you were asking."

Evelyn pursed her lips. She hated that her husband was right. "If the cycle restarts, more good people are going to die."

"And why is that our responsibility?" Terrence retorted. "I make fiddles for a living. You--you find missing people. Living people. For money. I went along with you for so long, Evelyn. First, it was sneaking into Stephen Doyle's shed. That ended with two gunmen under our roof. Then, I followed you to this lounge where I find myself questioning my sanity with every second that passes, and now we're going after some little girl we don't know because there's a chance a serial killer has her. I could go on about the sleepwalking, death visions, the way you looked at me like I was some monster some days ago, but that was only the start of the fiasco. It's the finale that worries me. How do you think it's going to end? Tell me. Because I don't know."

Evelyn soaked in his words, finding logic in them and growing angry because of it. She shut her eyes and attempted to clear her mind. "The evil that happened here has caused a ripple in so many lives. Don't tell me that doesn't affect you?"

Terrence looked like he was chewing gravel. "It does, but we have our own lives to worry about." Terrence approached her and put his hand on her belly. Evelyn tensed up. Terrence didn't let go. "And whatever life we bring into this world."

Evelyn tried to imagine Terrence and the son and daughter they talked about during those late nights. She could only think of the wounds of phantoms and the broken families they left behind.

Evelyn put her hands on Terrence's. Gently, she removed it from her torso. She thought he would be mad and mentally braced herself for resistance.

Terrence was as silent and hollow as the mansion.

Evelyn brushed some dust off her pants. "I'm going to visit the sheriff. See if he can't put me on as a consultant."

Terrence averted his eyes.

Unable to find anything more to say, Evelyn left the lounge and walked down the hall displaying a mural of Mary Sullivan's death. There was another that needed saving now.

In the driver's seat of her rusty minivan, Evelyn pinched

the bridge of her nose, trying to kill the headache but failing. She shoved the key into the ignition and twisted it harshly. With a sad sputter, the vehicle awoke.

She put the car into reverse when the passenger side door opened and Terrence climbed inside.

"I'm not changing my mind," Evelyn said.

"And I'm not letting you go alone." Terrence slammed the door behind him.

Is this a mind game? Evelyn looked at him for a moment.

Terrence stared back at her expectantly. "Well? Are we going?"

Evelyn held her breath and reversed the car. She didn't let it go until they were halfway down the red brick path.

THE SKINNY, blonde, peppy receptionist named Sunshine greeted Terrence and Evelyn as they entered the sheriff's office.

"Have a seat," Sunshine said with the friendliest smile. "The sheriff will call you in when he's ready."

If not for the sheriff's seal on every wall and window, Evelyn would've thought she was waiting for a dentist appointment. After a few moments, Terrence grabbed a Forbes magazine off the stack.

As soon as Terrence opened the front page, Sunshine said. "He's ready."

Perturbed, Terrence slapped it back on the stack and followed Evelyn into the office.

Sheriff Garrett Yates had red hair and a red beard touched with gray on its sides and cut so short it was seemingly painted on his face. By the air of maturity about him, Evelyn could tell he was much older than he looked. Standing behind his desk, he clenched his tall mug of coffee in both hands and sniffed the divine aroma. With closed eyes, he took a gulp, a small smile curled on his face as he savored the moment.

Evelyn cleared her throat.

Yates opened one eye, looked at her while he finished his gulp, and then pulled the coffee from his thin lips. "Mr. and Mrs. Carr, I've been meaning to have someone check up on you. How have you been feeling since the, for lack of a better term, home invasion?"

"We're surviving," Evelyn said curtly.

Yates took another sip of coffee. Another sip of his own personal heaven. "On behalf of the town, I apologize. In Adders, stuff like that just doesn't happen."

Right. Evelyn kept her expression neutral. "I want to consult with you on the Bella Day case."

Yates raised his reddish-gray brows. "Wow. You come right out of the gate with it."

"I believe the same person who took the girl is linked with the bones found in my basement," Evelyn said.

Yates set his coffee on the desk. "That's quite the accusation."

"Nothing like this has happened in over a decade," Evelyn explained. "And now this whole town is in a fritz."

"You know what's funny?" the sheriff asked rhetorically. "Adders was quiet before you two arrived."

Evelyn crossed her arms. Terrence glared at Yates.

Yates grinned. "That was a joke. Eh, there are a few grains of truth in it. You have been visiting an awful lot of people lately. Disturbing the peace, some might say."

"You've been following us?" Terrence asked.

"I'll tell you what I told your wife on her first visit. Adder's a bubble. Inside it, everyone knows everybody and everything."

Evelyn replied, "Except for the whereabouts of Bella Day,

and who killed Zoey Pinkerton, Peter Calhoon, Alannah Gimmerson, Winslow Darvey, and James Barker."

The sheriff eyed her for a moment with a small disbelieving smile on his tan face. "You know, those names haven't been released to the public."

Evelyn felt her heart skip a beat. "I researched disappearances online and compared them to the decay on the bone. It made the most logical sense those were the victims." It was only a partial lie.

Yates looked at Terrence. "Your wife is a private investigator *and* forensics analyst? Anything else you want to tell me about her?"

"She sees dead people," Terrence replied.

Yates studied him for a moment. Then, he chuckled. "You two are something else. Tell me what you want to do on the Day case and I'll see if I can help you out. For your father's sake. Speaking of which, have you thought about donating? The department could use your support."

Evelyn ignored his request. "I want to see the crime scene."

"There's not much of one," Yates replied. "The parents called it in last night after the girl didn't return home from their neighbors. The neighbors told us that Bella never came over at all."

"I still want to look around."

"Be my guest," He jotted down the address. "Deputy Painter is already over there on his second sweep. Now I have a question for you: why do you think her disappearance is linked to the murders over a decade ago?"

"Something about the timing feels *off*. I guess you can call it a gut feeling." Evelyn replied.

"Or you've been asking too many questions."

Evelyn and Terrence exchanged looks.

"Do I need to fill out any paperwork?" Evelyn asked.

"For simplicity's sake, we'll say you're an--" Yates made hand quotes, "--*unofficial* consultant. You get something big, we'll talk about a contract form."

Evelyn and Terrence headed to the door.

"Oh," the sheriff said, stopping them. "We haven't forgotten about Stephen and Catherine Doyle. We believe they've left the state. I'll contact you if that changes."

"Thanks, Sheriff," Terrence said.

Evelyn drove to Berry Street, where little Bella Day went missing. Like most neighborhoods in Adders, the houses were very spread apart. The Day residence and their neighbor's house were separated by a twisted road flanked by towering trees.

Evelyn slowly drove down the road. The shadows of tall oaks fell over her vehicle. Terrence sat in relative silence, as he had since they left Quenby House. Up ahead, Evelyn saw Deputy Painter. Mid-thirties, wearing a green uniform and black felt hat, Painter had a steel-colored five o'clock shadow and shark eyes. He leaned against his squad car and took a drag from a dwindled cigarette. Evelyn pulled up behind him and exited the car with Terrence.

"Yates call you over?" the deputy asked, giving Terrence a nasty look.

Evelyn nodded. "I'm a P.I. Terrence is my assistant and my husband."

"Husband?" Painter asked, his Southern twang showing.

Terrence smiled awkwardly. "That surprises you?"

Painter shrugged. "We don't intermingle as much as you city folk do."

"No?" Terrence asked, playing the peacemaker.

"Hey, I don't think it's a bad thing," Painter flicked his cigarette. The amber bounced on the road, spilling ash on the concrete. "Different, that's all."

"This is where Bella Day went missing, right?" Evelyn asked, feeling it best not to continue this conversation.

"Uh-huh," Painter replied.

Evelyn glanced at the cigarette butt, wondering if she should mention the fact that it was disrupting the crime scene. She had a feeling that the deputy wouldn't care either way. "Mind if we looked around?"

"Sure," Painter replied. "Call me if you find anything. I ain't had no luck."

Evelyn and Terrence split up while Painter stuck his hands in his pockets and craned his head up to the sky. Evelyn couldn't tell if Sheriff Yates was a bad judge of character or if he put Painter here because of his laziness.

Evelyn walked by the ditch that rutted beside the asphalt road. She found dirt, rocks, and Styrofoam cups. There were no tire marks, meaning either the abductor slowed to a stop or he was on foot. Evelyn searched on her side of the tree line. A few yards back from the road was a wire fence staked in the ground and linked together by green metal shafts. She found a tuft of brown and white hair tangled around the wire. By its density, it belonged to an animal. Cow, maybe. Not finding anything on the road side of the fence, Evelyn climbed over. The woods quickly turned into a pasture, spotted with crusty cow patties. She walked out into the field until she could see both the Days' residence and the neighbor's home. The stretch of woods was only a few hundred feet long. Beyond that, someone would've seen the little girl getting into a stranger's car. The abductor must've known this. It was why he took her at this location.

Evelyn returned to the road. The deputy was away from his car. Terrence was waiting for her return. "I found something."

Evelyn followed him to the far ditch on the opposite side of the road. Painter was crouched down in the rut, examining a sunflower-shaped earring. It was cleaner than the rest of the ground's surface, which mean it wasn't there for long. *This was where she was taken.*

"Good job," Evelyn told her husband.

Terrence didn't reply. He was still not happy pursuing this lead.

Evelyn headed to her next stop. The Days' residence. The parents were visibly and rightfully distraught. The husband wore horn-rimmed glasses and casual wear, and the woman wore a long-sleeved shirt and a skirt.

"We've answered all the police's questions already," Mr. Day said.

"Has Bella's attitude changed in the last few weeks?" Evelyn asked.

Mrs. Day replied this time. She patted her red nose with a tissue. "Apart from her allergies, nothing has changed. She followed her weekly schedule like always."

Evelyn glanced at the calendar. Piano practice Monday, doctor's appointment Tuesday, choir practice Wednesday, babysitting Thursday, second choir practice Friday, clean-up day Saturday, and church Sunday. Most of the steps were repeated weekly.

Evelyn pressed the Days for more information about their daughter. They said typical parent stuff. "She was an angel." "Why would someone do this to my baby?" More things that didn't help the case.

The Days squeezed each other's hands. The wife looked into her husband's tired and downtrodden eyes and said, "We worked so hard to give this child a good life, and now that she's gone…"

"Not gone," Mr. Day said. "Missing. She can still be found."

Mrs. Day glanced at Evelyn. "Do you think you can do a better job than the police?"

"I can offer my services, but nothing more than that."

"Why help Bella?" Mr. Day inquired.

Because there was no disappearance before the bones found in my house were broadcasted on TV. "Because I'd want someone to do the same for my daughter if I had one." Evelyn gestured to the calendar. "You mind if I take a picture of that list?"

Mr. Day gave his approval. Evelyn snapped a picture. "I'm going to need her tutor's contact information too."

Once she got it, Evelyn started with the piano instructor.

With screeching brakes, Evelyn pulled up to the woman's house and raced out her car. The first forty-eight hours of any missing persons case were crucial. Evelyn had no time to waste.

The instructor's house had tall glass window frames and, if seen from the sky, was in the shape of a golf club. Approaching the front door, Evelyn could hear the piano playing. It was a familiar tune, but Evelyn couldn't put her finger on it.

"Clair De Lune by Claude Debussy," Terrence said.

Evelyn punched the doorbell with her finger. Soon after, the music stopped and the door opened. The piano instructor was middle-aged, wearing a long red shirt and black pants. Her hair was gray and tied off in a ponytail. Her face was angular and centered by a sharp nose. She smiled awkwardly at them. Her name was Lola.

Evelyn made the introductions brief and got straight to business. "We're looking for Bella Day."

Eyes watering, the instructor let them in. "It's a horrible thing, isn't it? Such a talent."

Terrence and Evelyn walked into the open hall that branched into the living room and dining room. Lola took them to the living room and took a seat on the piano bench. Evelyn and Terrence sat on the couch. Musical decor decorated the walls, whether it was old framed sheets of music, a metal treble clef, or simply artistic black-and-white photos of pianos. Upon the piano bench, dozens of photos of little girls and boys hung.

"You're doing quite well for yourself," Terrence said.

Lola wiped a tear. "It's nothing really, I'm just following in my mother's footsteps. She taught most of the town's children too. Piano, that is. If not for Bella's disappearance, I would've been meeting her today. Right now."

"We're sorry," Evelyn said.

"I'm just glad an outsider is taking such an interest."

"I'm not that far of an outsider. I'm Maxwell Quenby's daughter and sole inheritor," Evelyn explained.

Lola's jaw dropped. Suddenly, her sorrow twisted into disgust. "Oh," she said.

Terrence leaned forward in his seat and asked, "Is something the matter?"

"No… It's just… I…" Lola searched for the words. She finally spit out, "My head hurts and I'm not feeling well."

"Not a fan of Maxwell?" Evelyn asked.

Lola stood up. "I'd like you to leave now."

Evelyn crinkled her brow. "Tell me what the issue is."

"Please leave," Lola said, her face going blood red and her eyes watering. "I will call the cops if you don't leave."

Evelyn fished out her business card from her wallet and put it on the table. "Call me if you're interested in saving Bella Day."

As soon as Terrence and Evelyn were out the door, it slammed and locked behind them.

"What the hell was that all about?" Terrence asked.

Lola closed the curtains.

Evelyn heard the start of her phone call.

"You would not believe who just showed up at my house… Yes, asking about Bella," Lola started. Her voice faded as she left the living room.

"I guess her head didn't hurt after all," Evelyn said.

Evelyn pulled out the address for the choir practice. It was much closer than the doctor's office.

The GPS took Evelyn to the Baptist church: a white steeple on a hill with a sign that said "Only Jesus saves." Nearby, a cross had been set out and painted white, with spray-painted pools of blood where the hands and ankles would be. Evelyn gave the door a knock. An elderly man answered. He was tall with short hair and loose skin. A burgundy birthmark bloomed above his right eye.

"You Thomas?" Evelyn asked.

"I am."

"I want to talk to you about Bella Day but need your assurance you aren't going to slam the door in my face."

"That would be absurd," Thomas replied.

He welcomed them inside. Parents and children alike chattered at the far end of the church, no doubt getting ready for practice. "The children's choir will practice tonight. We will feel Bella's loss but are praying for her swift return."

He opened the door to a small conference room that consisted of a table, a few chairs, and tapestry that displayed the most renowned bible stories. Thomas poured them all glasses of water from the glass pitcher. Holding three glasses, he gingerly walked to the table and put them on top. "Mary likes music. She likes singing. But I believe her involvement with such activities were more her parents' executive decision. I know Mary and how much she loves adventure and the outdoors, something that was safe in Adders at a time."

"Is there anyone you might suspect that would harm Mary?"

Thomas shook his head. "No. There are sinners, yes, but none this great in many years."

"What happened many years ago?" Evelyn asked, playing ignorant.

"A series of events that I would not like to see repeated."

"Such as..."

Thomas bounced his eyes between Evelyn and Terrence.

"We need to know," Terrence said.

"Not to breathe life into any rumors, I'll tell you the facts. A series of individuals went missing. Whether it was coincidence or something else, I don't know enough to say, but the discovery of bones in the old Quenby House makes me question a darker reality."

"I get the feeling people suspected Maxwell Quenby," Evelyn said.

"I can't say. To falsely accuse a man is wrong. However, in light of recent evidence, I think it's fair to say he had some involvement, whether voluntary or involuntary."

"Is there a chance Bella could've run away?" Evelyn asked.

"There's always a chance," Thomas said. "But that just is not something Bella would do. If anything, home would be the first place she'd run to."

Thomas studied Evelyn. "You aren't from around here, are you?"

"Would you hate me if I said I'm Maxwell Quenby's daughter?" Evelyn asked.

"No, but I know some would."

"Why's that?"

"Those rumors from all those years ago, a lot them were directed at Maxwell. A lot of people hated him." Thomas replied.

"How did they know it was him?"

"How could they know he wasn't, and now the bones in his basement are confirmation." Thomas checked his watch. "If you'll excuse me? Practice starts soon."

In the parking lot, Evelyn asked Terrence if he could get in contact with his friends--the band he agreed to build a guitar for during their first week in Adders.

Terrence shrugged. "They won't be happy that I never finished their custom guitar."

"Tell them that your wife has been driving you crazy," Evelyn replied.

Terrence cracked a small smile.

That's what I wanted to see.

Evelyn put her hands in her pockets. "I can drop you off at their place and swing around the hospital to talk to Mary's doctor."

"I don't have access to a phone," Terrence replied. "Mine is still fried."

Evelyn handed her cell to Terrence. "Use mine to call them, then text with theirs when you're done."

After a moment of thought, Terrence agreed. "Alright. You sure you're okay being on your own?"

Evelyn patted her concealed extendable baton. "I think I can manage."

Terrence dialed the number. "Hey, it's me. Sorry I haven't got back to you… Yeah, my wife has me running around church and piano practice."

When the call was finished, Evelyn took him to the small ranch home where the band practiced. The members, wearing skinny jeans, cowboy boots, and cowboy hats were sitting on the porch, drinking cheap beer. Terrence said goodbye and got out of the car, his smile returning. Things would be better this way. Spending some time with the guys would calm Terrence down, and Evelyn wouldn't feel the guilt of her unrelenting stubbornness.

She drove to the hospital, missing the noises of Detroit. In the city, no one would care how her father was or wasn't. She'd be judged by her merits and work ethic as she climbed the ladder. Not that all small towns were bad, but Evelyn's experience in Adders hadn't been pleasant. Now, the best of both worlds would be to live off the land with only her and nature for miles. No people. No BS.

Evelyn walked through the hospital's mechanical doors and asked to speak briefly with Dr. Waxen. He was in another appointment, so Evelyn took a seat. She waited for a solid hour before Waxen approached her. He was a tall man with hollow cheeks, blue eyes so light they were almost silver, and thin white hair. His smile was small, secretive in a way, and his glasses were circular with a gold rim.

"Mrs. Carr, I expect the blackouts subsided?"

"Yeah." *No thanks to your medication.* "I never knew you were a children's doctor."

Waxen looked at her. "In Adders, we tend to fill many roles. What's the nature of your visit?"

"You had an appointment with Bella Day a few days ago. Now that she's missing..."

"Doctor-patient confidentiality keeps me for disclosing any information about Day."

"I know," Evelyn said, slightly peeved. "I'm concerned with her attitude. Was she scared? Nervous?"

"All children are," the skeletal doctor said coldly. Evelyn wasn't surprised when the doctor looked like death incarnate.

"More so than usual?" Evelyn clarified.

Waxen studied her for a moment, his hands folded behind his back. "If anything, Bella was in high spirits."

"Why?"

"Maybe she got a new doll," Waxen replied.

Evelyn couldn't tell if he was being sarcastic or serious.

"Anything else you can tell me?"

Waxen shook his head. "Sorry for wasting your time."

Evelyn got up to leave.

"Wait," Waxen said. He walked close to her. So close she could smell his breath that reeked of onions. He whispered.

"They say bones were found in the basement of Quenby House."

"Yeah," Evelyn replied and glanced over to the desk worker up front. The worker was texting, not remotely aware of what was happening.

Waxen looked at Evelyn with acute facilitation. "They say when you found the bones, you organized them into categories. Heads in one. Femurs in another. I find that curious."

"I wasn't thinking clearly," Evelyn tried to take a step back. Waxen subtly blocked her off.

"Do you know where Bella Day is?" Waxen asked, his intense eyes looking into her with unwanted intimacy. His skinny lips twitched into a grin. "Doctor-patient confidentiality. I won't tell."

Evelyn pushed him away. "Get away from me." She headed for the door, trying to cause as little a scene as possible.

She got into the minivan, feeling her racing heart. With lips slightly parted, she turned back to the hospital, waiting to see if Dr. Waxen would follow. He didn't. Evelyn drove on, trying to make sense of the interaction and feeling a growing pit of dread in her stomach.

On her way to pick up Terrence, she dialed Bella's babysitter. *"Hi, this is Kimmy."*

"Hey, Kimmy. This is Investigator Evelyn Carr," Evelyn said, halting at a stop sign. "I want to talk to you about Bella Day."

"Have you learned anything?" the babysitter asked with concern.

"Not much, frankly. I want to ask you about her. Do you have the time?"

"Umm. I'm heading over to my dad's office. We could meet there."

"Okay. Where does he work?"

"Town Hall. He's the mayor."

Terrence and the band strummed guitars on the porch steps and didn't stop when they saw Evelyn pull into the driveway. With Band-Aid-free fingertips, Terrence played on, nearly losing himself in the twangy blues.

Evelyn watched him. An unintentional grin curled on her face as he looked her in the eyes and picked away. When the song came to a close, he strummed one final time and then handed it back to one of the band members, a shaggy-haired man with a hide-colored cowboy hat.

"Ready?" Evelyn asked guiltily.

"Yeah."

Terrence said goodbye to the boys and got into the driver's seat of the minivan.

"Did you have fun?" Evelyn asked.

"I did," Terrence replied. "It made me realize…"

"What?"

"How far we've come," Terrence replied. "I've learned some things."

"What's that?"

Terrence looked at her intensely. "The last time someone pieced together the slew of missing persons, there was a witch hunt. He said that there was vandalism, death threats, and more."

"Then we need to find this girl," Evelyn replied.

"I don't think you understand," Terrence explained. "The boys told me that you need to stay out of it."

"Because of my father?"

Terrence struggled to find the next words. "Because they might suspect you."

Evelyn scoffed.

Terrence put his hand on her thigh. "I'm serious. When the cops get desperate, who are they going to point at? Us. The curious strangers who happened upon five skeletons in their basement, and who've taken an acute interest in a missing girl. Heck, more has happened to us in two and a half weeks than they've seen in decades."

Evelyn played with the possibility. Terrence might be right, but she couldn't dwell on it now. She needed to meet with Kimmy.

Evelyn and Terrence headed to the downtown area. It was made of historical brick buildings, mom-and-pop shops, a general store, and more trademarks of a Southern town. The town hall was an old colonial building with a tall flight of stairs, four pillars, and a long rectangular frame. Below its peaked roof, a massive clock ticked away the day. A few pedestrians strolled by. One was walking a dog, another pushing a stroller. They stared at Evelyn and Terrence. Somehow the air became much colder.

Evelyn hiked up the steps and entered into the foyer. It was clean and simple, like most interiors in Adders. Old 1920s and 1930s photos were in frameless glass on the walls, showing off the town of Adders after electricity was established. A receptionist, a crone with a heavy frown, flashy beetle broach, and a tucked-in neck scarf glared at Evelyn with judgmental eyes.

"Evelyn?" A voice said behind her.

Evelyn twisted back to Kimmy Timberland, twenty-four, a tall and slender cutie with a purple headband, a rich chocolate ponytail, and dark mascara. She wore a white blouse and lady's business skirt. "I look more like a lawyer than a babysitter, I know," Kimmy said. "Babysitting has been a habit since high school, honestly."

"Was Bella a good kid?" Evelyn asked.

Kimmy smiled shyly. "Yeah. You want to talk in a different room?"

Evelyn and Terrence traded looks and shrugged. Evelyn

surrendered her cell phone and baton. They moved into an empty conference room.

"I help fill in as my father's secretary while the others are away." Kimmy shut the blinds and turned back to Evelyn with worry. "This Bella thing scares the crap out of me."

Evelyn went over the basic questions and got the usual results.

Kimmy thought for a long moment, "Bella is typically untrusting of strangers. I took her to a store once and she wouldn't even look at the cashier."

"So you think someone close took her?" Evelyn asked.

"You would know better than me," Kimmy replied. "But if there's no sign of a struggle, it's the only thing that would make sense. Bella was even untrusting of some of her distant family, too."

Evelyn thought back to all the people she had talked to today: piano tutor, choir orchestrator, the sheriff, the deputy, Bella's parents, her doctor, and Kimmy. All of them had different responses to Bella's vanishing and to Evelyn's family name. They were all old enough to have partaken of the murders starting a decade and half ago. Evelyn needed evidence.

"Evelyn Quenby is your real name, right?" Kimmy asked out of the left field.

"Maiden name, if you can call it that. My father put down a different name on the adoption papers," Evelyn explained.

"You know, I met your father," Kimmy said.

Evelyn sat up, giving the girl her complete attention.

"When I was young, he invited my father over to the plantation. What a beautiful house."

"Tell me about Maxwell."

"He was intelligent, handsome... sad," Kimmy explained. "He didn't talk too much. Just listened and sipped his wine. My father and Maxwell were good friends, but I felt the relationship was one-sided. Maxwell… he was a hard man to read, but always good with kids."

"Kids and ladies, from what we've heard," Terrence chimed in.

"Those were the rumors," Kimmy said. "But Maxwell seemed like a one-woman type of guy, and that is why I think he was so lonely."

"How did he die?" Evelyn asked.

Kimmy opened her mouth to speak when the doorknob jiggled. Kimmy opened it to a man in a business suit. On his rectangular head, his eyes were brown and his mouth was wide with a smile that creased his clear face. "I was looking for you, Kim."

When he saw Evelyn, the man's smile faded.

"Dad, this is Evelyn Carr and her husband Terrence," Kimmy gestured to them.

"Hey," Terrence replied

"This is my father, Mayor Joshua Timberland."

Timberland bounced his eyes between Evelyn and Terrence. "The two of you should go."

"Dad--"

Evelyn stood. "It's alright. Come on, Terrence."

Reluctant, Terrence stood.

Timberland stood aside. "I know your game. Stay away from my daughter."

"I don't have a game," Evelyn replied.

"Your father said the same thing. Go."

Without resistance, Evelyn collected her things and returned to Quenby House. Off Terrence's pressing look, Evelyn said, "My father had blackmail material, remember? He didn't make himself many friends."

"You'd think he'd try to help us if Maxwell burned the blackmail material against him."

"Not if it was ammo against his enemies, too."

The giant vine-covered mansion under the moonlight welcomed them. Evelyn and Terrence double-checked the door locks and window bolts,

"Goodnight," Evelyn whispered down into the lounge before closing the door.

In the master bedroom, Evelyn and Terrence lay in bed. Evelyn closed her eyes and could see the hay field. She felt the edge of a knife on her throat.

CRASH!

Evelyn and Terrence shot up out of bed.

Someone else was in the house.

It wasn't a phantom.

19

CRAWL SPACE

Evelyn and Terrence followed the noise through the creaking hallway. The old house groaned. They tried the light switch. Click. Nothing. They would be walking through the abyss. Evelyn relied on the ancient oil lamp and matches to guide her through the long halls of Quenby House. They whispered the names of the phantoms. No reply.

Terrence coiled his fingers around a bat. Evelyn kept one hand on her heavy baton and the other hand on an oil lamp. The puny flame cast its orange and yellow glow across the old wallpaper and thin red carpet. A chilling breeze coasted through the house and painted Evelyn with goose bumps. They reached the inner balcony of the foyer. The firelight reflected off the massive multi-tiered chandelier at the center of the domed ceiling.

Standing beneath it were all seven ghosts: Zoey, Barker, Winslow, Andrew, Alannah, Mary, and Peter. They stared at Evelyn.

Evelyn loomed above the railing. "What?"

In unison, the phantoms raised their left hands and

pointed to the hall of portraits. Evelyn gulped and hiked down the steps. The phantoms kept pointing. Evelyn pressed her back against the wall by the threshold. She peeked around the corner. At the far end, past the great patriarchs of the Quenby family and one female portrait of the plantation's founder, the kitchen door was flung open. Evelyn and Terrence walked that way.

They reached the kitchen. The room could fit multiple cooks and had spacious cabinets and multiple walk-in pantries. A wooden island marked the room's center, where the servants and slaves would prep meals for dozens of esteemed guests. The metal-faced refrigerator upgraded the old icebox and an electric stove stood in the spot where the old gas stove sat. The mansion's first brick stove remained. Soot blackened its mouth like a child after having ice cream. Like when Terrence and Evelyn moved in, most of the kitchen remained untouched. They investigated cabinets and pantries but had never used them, which was why the open pantry door terrified them.

Terrence stepped ahead of Evelyn. He held the bat at the ready and used the side of his foot to scoot the door open the rest of the way. Empty shelves lined three of the four sides. Dust bunnies gathered on the upper one. A squashed cockroach twitched its last remaining leg at the foot of the doorway. Terrence leaned his head inside of the confined space. He tapped the bat on the floor, tilting his head slightly as he listened for hollowness.

"The wall," Evelyn pointed at the left wall.

Terrence tapped his bat on the upper tier shelf, middle tier, and then just below the bottom shelf. The wood sounded different there. In his boxers and white t-shirt, Terrence squatted and brushed a hand over the lower portion of the wall. A small section pushed in. With a click, it pushed back out to Terrence an inch. He glanced up at

Evelyn and then pulled it open. Evelyn crouched next to him. She outstretched the flickering oil wick, looking into the dusty crawl space: about three and half square feet. Its walls were wooden planks, the same as the secret passage to the hidden study.

"This is right about the time we should call the cops," Terrence whispered.

Evelyn shook her head. "We can do this."

Terrence sighed. "I go first."

"You sure? I thought you'd want to look at my butt." Evelyn said.

Terrence pondered it. "You had to make this hard, didn't you?"

Evelyn shrugged.

Grumbling, Terrence climbed in first.

"Your loss." Evelyn followed behind.

"Don't remind me," Terrence replied.

They traveled into the corridor, Terrence at the helm. He held the oil lamp and bat. They walked straight to the back of the house, Evelyn believed. It turned right and reached a fork. Straight ahead, up a ladder, roughly where Evelyn thought the backyard was. Sweat drenched them after a few minutes. Their knees were red and raw. Musty dust hung in the air and launched Evelyn into a sneezing fit. Terrence bumped his head on the ceiling at one point, and he groaned as dirt fell on his bald head like snow.

The idea of turning back tempted Evelyn, but she realized too late that these tunnels weren't made for turning around. Evelyn wondered why they were created. Her only guess was that they were escape routes in case of a slave revolt. *Did my father know about this*? Evelyn didn't know. More time passed and her joints were killing her.

She wondered where it would spit her out.

Finally, the claustrophobic corridor came to an end at a

seven-rung ladder. "How deep are we?" Terrence asked. He put the lamp aside and climbed. Meeting little resistance, he pushed open the hatch. The black night and stars carpeted the sky above his head. In a moment, he had exited. Evelyn shoved the retracted baton in the left side of her boy shorts, grabbed the oil lamp, and climbed the ladder.

They stood in a wooded area, far outside the property. In the far distance, Quenby House looked like a little box car.

They looked around the woods, listening to night creatures, owls, and bugs, knowing that the mansion had a million more secrets.

Back in the bedroom, Terrence sat at the corner of the mattress and clicked open the metal box. He pulled out a small stack of fifties. "We can stay at a motel for a few nights, and then we're out of our savings."

"No," Evelyn said. "We need that money in case something happens."

"Someone knows how to get in and out of the house. I don't know how I feel staying here."

Evelyn pinched the bridge of her nose. She glanced at the clock. It was nearly 4 a.m. "We'll keep the doors locked and barred and hope that our roommates will warn us of any trouble."

"If you think we can trust them."

"They need us," Evelyn replied. "If we fail, they're stuck here." Evelyn climbed into bed. "Get some rest. There's still a lot that needs to get done."

He glanced around the room for a moment and then scurried up to his pillow and under the covers. Thanks to her sore palms and knees, Evelyn was so beat from going through the tunnel that sleep came swiftly. So did the morning sun.

After getting dressed, Evelyn ventured down to the lounge and found the girl she was looking for: Zoey. The goth sat sideways in the recliner with her legs slung over an armrest and an open book on her lap. Evelyn didn't recognize the title, but she could tell it contained a plethora of dark poems within.

Evelyn sat down the loveseat nearby. Zoey glanced over to her. Black eyeliner encased her apathetic eyes. She said nothing and went back to reading.

"I spoke to your father," Evelyn said.

Zoey's flat expression wavered for a moment and then returned to its normal, callous look.

"He wished that he hadn't been so overbearing and regrets the way the two of you parted," Evelyn said.

Zoey closed the book and turned to Evelyn. "You told him I was... like this?"

Evelyn shook her head. "I didn't want to risk sounding insane."

"You are a little psychotic," Zoey said dryly. "Most people would've run far away."

Evelyn cracked a smile. "We tried that once. Mary drove us back here."

They sat in silence for a moment.

Evelyn spoke up. "You know I help a lot of girls like you. Potential runaways, that is."

"Is that how you see me? Some damaged little girl?" Zoey shot back.

"We're all damaged," Evelyn replied. She turned her shoulder to Zoey and pulled down the back of her shirt's neck. Deep scars engraved her flesh. Once Zoey got a look, Evelyn repositioned herself.

Zoey averted her eyes, pondering.

Evelyn scooted to the end of the seat. "Your father told me Maxwell was your godfather. Why didn't you tell me?"

Zoey shrugged. "Did it matter? I'm dead. Maxwell is dead."

"You saw him die?" Evelyn asked.

"I saw him get taken from this house."

"By whom?" Evelyn asked anxiously.

Zoey shrugged again. "I don't know. People. It happened pretty fast. The screams were pretty convincing though."

"You couldn't follow him?" Evelyn asked.

Zoey shook her head. "There's only two of us that can do that. Andrew and Mary. The rest are bonded to these halls."

"What was Maxwell like?" Evelyn asked.

Taking her legs off the armrest, Zoey sat up normally. "Relaxed, around me at least. I would come over, and he'd give me free rein over the house. Unlike my parents, Maxwell didn't mind listening to my music at full blast and allowed me to stay out late. He was a great listener, too. Me, being a kid at the time, could talk to him for hours and felt like I wasn't speaking to a brick wall. Unlike my father and mother. At the end of my venting, he'd share some sage advice about letting go or looking past the drama and at your future. I think that's how he lived. Thinking about tomorrow, but enjoying the fruits of today."

"Sounds like quite the father figure," Evelyn replied.

"Yeah, he wasn't perfect. There were still areas where he'd draw the line. Like how much wine I could have or making sure that I always had money put back into savings. My father didn't see that. He thought that Max was corrupting me and banned me from coming over here when I was fourteen. Max respected my father's wishes. He would reach out in other ways though, like buying me a new book or CD on different holidays." Zoey sighed. "When I saw Max in passing, he looked so lonely. I think he wanted his own family, but despite his fortune, he never found it."

Evelyn soaked in the large lounge and antique furniture.

"I think sometimes about what my life would've been like if I was raised here. I know you didn't love your parents, Zoey, but be grateful you had them. Everything I have, I've had to earn myself. Every skill, I had to teach myself. It wasn't until I met Terrence that I realized I didn't need to shoulder the weight alone. But I'm sure he can attest that there are days where I certainly don't act like that."

Zoey pondered that.

"Let me ask you something," Evelyn said.

Zoey gave Evelyn her full attention.

"Is there a chance my father is still alive?"

Zoey thought about it for a moment. "I guess."

"Is there a chance he's behind these murders?"

"Never," Zoey replied swiftly and with fire. "Not Max."

"Then who?" Evelyn asked.

"Someone who hates him so much they used the basement as a body dump."

"Barker!" Evelyn called out.

"Hmm?" the old man appeared, pipe in mouth, sweater vest on his person. "What is it?"

"Now you answer my call," Evelyn said in disbelief.

"Sometimes we hear you, sometimes we don't," Barker said. "We have lives outside of talking to you, you know."

Evelyn gave him a look.

"Okay, maybe you can't channel us because you're not open to it. I don't know. Do I look like a clairvoyant? I taught Humanities, for Pete's sake."

Evelyn crossed her legs. "You've been here the longest. Did you see who carried in the bodies?"

"Good question," Barker replied. "The answer is no."

"Why not?"

"He'd look blurry. Out of focus."

"Was he a phantom?" Evelyn asked with concern.

"Heavens no! That would be ridiculous. I could see

everyone else here fine, but not him. The others have the same issue. My theory is that we can't see who killed us."

"That's a stupid rule," Evelyn said.

The phantoms nodded in agreement.

"Welcome to the supernatural," Barker said. "Some things just don't make sense. When I tried to look at the killer, I found myself spitting blood everywhere. It wasn't an experience I wanted to repeat."

Evelyn stood up. "Was Maxwell home during the times the killer dumped the bodies?"

The phantoms exchanged glances. "Never on those nights, but the killer always came in through the tunnel in the shed, and when the killer was away, Maxwell was in complete focus."

Evelyn throw up her arms. "Why didn't you tell me this?"

Barker pulled the pipe from his mouth. "We never expected you'd blame your own father. That's just sick."

Evelyn opened her mouth and then closed it before she said things she would regret.

"So you're telling me my father might be alive and there's a good chance he's not the killer the town thinks he is?"

Zoey and Barker replied in unison. "Yes."

Evelyn cursed. Loudly. "Where did he go?"

"We have no idea."

Evelyn waited around until the other phantoms arrived. They had the same response.

Alannah said, "I'm sorry, darling. I wish you the best of luck in finding him."

Evelyn rushed upstairs. *Does my father know who the killer is?* Evelyn wondered. She got Terrence out of bed. "There are some people I need to talk to. You tagging along?"

Terrence bounced his eyes around the master bedroom and its dusty furnishings. "If you think I'm staying in this house alone, you got another thing coming."

They drove out of Adders and into the nearest town that was larger and had a proper hospital. Evelyn and Terrence marched through the mechanical doors and requested to speak with Dr. Gregory.

"I like this guy," Terrence said as they waited. "He was very nice to pay for my stay."

"He seemed to have a friendship with Maxwell at some point, and maybe our best shot at locating him."

"What about Bella?" Terrence asked.

"I'm not giving up on her but until we can get a lead, there's not much to do. I don't want to be sitting around either."

Wearing a white doctor's coat, Dr. Gregory, in his fifties, waltzed to them. With every step, his silver-streaked brown hair seemed to bounce. His piercing brown eyes were full of concern. "Evelyn. Mr. Carr. What seems to be the issue? Is it your health?"

Evelyn looked around the semi-packed waiting room and the strangers staring at them. "Can we talk somewhere private?"

"Certainly," Gregory replied. He led them back to a small office with a patient bed, countertop, and stool. He gestured for them to sit. Evelyn claimed the stool. Terrence took the bed.

With his arms crossed, the handsome doctor waited anxiously for a response.

"It has to do with Maxwell. I think he may be alive," Evelyn said.

Gregory's eyes widened. "You've been keeping your ear to the ground."

"You knew?" Terrence exclaimed.

"I wouldn't go that far, but a body was never found," Gregory said.

Evelyn fumed. "Am I the only one who's out of the loop?"

"I'm a man of certainties, Evelyn," Gregory explained, choosing his words carefully. "I don't go spouting off gossip, nor do I pay mind to rumors. But, if you come to the conclusion that he may be alive, then I cannot deny it because I am uncertain myself. Forgive me for not being more forthcoming with the two of you."

Terrence flashed a smile. "Apology accepted. Tell us what you know about Max, Doc."

Gregory glanced back to the door, making sure it was closed. "Those last few months, Max was very nervous, and with good reason. Most of the townspeople blamed him for the disappearances of all those people, especially Mary Sullivan. However, with the police on his side, the people felt betrayed. They threatened Max, vandalized his property, and wouldn't serve him at any store. One night, he vanished, but all of his belongings remained. Some say he ran away to kill himself, others say he was murdered by a vengeful parent. The theory that has resurfaced of late is that he went into hiding. Until now."

Terrence and Evelyn traded worried glances.

Gregory continued. "The bones found in his basement convinced people that he was the killer. That little girl going missing a day and a half ago confirmed his existence."

Evelyn ran her hand through her hair. "Is that why the townspeople won't talk to me? They think my father is a killer?"

Gregory took a breath and nodded. "Petty, I know."

"How about you?" Terrence asked. "Do think that Max killed those people?"

"You tell me," Gregory replied.

Evelyn studied him for a moment. "You can't deny the facts."

"They are pretty damning," Gregory said, lost in thought. After a few seconds, he returned his attention to them. "If you need anything, here's my contact information. I have to return to my patients."

"Thanks," Terrence replied. Evelyn accepted the card with his address and phone number on it.

With pursed lips, Gregory smiled. "Stay safe. I would rather not see you on my operating table."

The doctor hurried out of the room and onward to his next patient.

"What now?" Terrence asked. "There's still no proof he took that girl."

"I know," Evelyn replied. "Let's head back home."

As Terrence drove, Evelyn watched the cattle pastures and old farms blur by. The AC jostled her blonde hair. She wanted to ask her father so many things. *If you're alive, why haven't you reached out? Why leave me the house in your will? Why did you put me up for adoption? Who is my mother?* She pulled out the small ledger and looked at the dates that coincided with all the abductions, even Mary Sullivan's. *Why did you have this? Were you chasing the killer or were you working with him? Did you bring me back here to find you or keep far away?* Evelyn needed to find him, now more than ever.

She dialed Sheriff Yates and put it on speaker.

"*This is the Adders sheriff's department, Sunshine speaking. How might I assist you?*" the pretty receptionist replied.

"It's Evelyn Carr. I need to talk to Yates."

Sunshine patched her in.

"*Hello? Yates speaking,*" the sheriff answered.

"Any update on the Day case?"

"*Nada. We've organized a few search parties though. Hopefully that will bring some results,*" Yates said. "*It's really starting to smell like a body.*"

"Well, that's horrible," Terrence mumbled.

"Why say that?" Evelyn replied.

"No ransom. All next of kin have alibis. These are the signs of a tragic ending, or no ending at all, if you catch my drift."

"Do you think Maxwell Quenby is behind it?" Evelyn asked.

Yates spit coffee. *"What gave you that idea?"*

"People seem to think he's back."

"Be praying he isn't."

"Why's that?"

"The locals know that the Quenby House has all sorts of secrets. If they believe Maxwell has returned, I don't have the manpower to stop them from searching your land, whether you give them permission or not."

"If that happens, Sheriff, I expect I can count on you, whether you're ready or not," Evelyn said curtly.

"Yeah."

Their conversation ended soon after.

Terrence shook his head. "This is unbelievable. What's the chance that some attack will happen?"

Evelyn smirked. "We should've never buried those shotguns."

"We wrapped them up," Terrence replied. "It's not too late to get them out."

Back at the plantation, they grabbed shovels from the shed and hiked beyond the cotton field and past the hay. They found the rock that they placed over the burial and started digging. Three feet down, they found the two shotguns swaddled in an old rug. Evelyn unwrapped it while Terrence went to dig up the ammo box.

She felt the weight of the weapon in her palms. The gun was a decade or more old and not the most trustworthy of firearms. It beat having no weapon though. After getting the guns and ammo, they returned inside and opened up gun cleaning tutorials on the Internet. Keeping the news playing, they periodically glanced up to see if there was any more information on Bella Day.

Nothing.

They looked up from the dining room table, noticing Mary Sullivan standing in the doorframe.

"You need to stop them," Mary said. Her eyes were wide and dry, her voice small and emotionless.

"The police are looking for Catherine and Stephen Doyle," Evelyn told the girl.

"They won't find them," Mary replied. "*You* need to find them."

The girl turned around to exit. Evelyn got up and followed. Mary was gone.

"We have a full plate," Terrence said.

"It seems to only get fuller."

After they finished cleaning the shotguns, they went outside and fired a few rounds. The weapons worked. For now. They stashed them under the bed, still wondering where the two rounds they fired went after they sleepwalked with the armaments so long ago.

They spent the rest of the afternoon looking up information on Maxwell and Bella. After recalling the conversation with Bella's parents and double-checking the abduction site, they realized it was time to rethink their strategy. They returned to the lounge and found Alannah relaxing in the loveseat, Winslow watering his flowers, and Andrew standing off the corner, observing them with black holes in his white cotton mask.

Alannah smiled wickedly at Terrence's arrival. "You're looking handsome."

"Uh, thank you," Terrence replied, trying to take his eyes off the woman's slashed throat and failing.

Evelyn approached Andrew. "What can you tell me about your brother and sister?"

Andrew said nothing.

Evelyn asked again and got the same reply: an empty glare.

Terrence asked Alannah if she remembered seeing the killer drop off any bodies or lurking about. Alannah thought on it. "I saw nothing at all. The last time I tried to look, it felt like a cold blade was opening my neck again."

The clock ticked on. It was nearing the forty-eight-hour mark since Bella Day vanished. Evelyn double-checked the bone pit beneath the house. Empty. She tried out the servant cabins outside of the house. No Bella. The killer may not have dumped the body on her property, or Bella Day might still be alive.

That night, they made sure the kitchen pantry was especially sealed off. Putting a chair under the master bedroom doorknob, Evelyn and Terrence were ready to go to sleep.

That night, they heard another noise in the house.

"Someone's here," Evelyn whispered. Terrence pulled the bedside lamp switch. Mary stood at the foot of the bed. Her head was slightly tilted, her blonde hair flowing down the side of her freckled face and her eyes seemingly lifeless. "Downstairs," she said.

Evelyn swiveled out of bed and slid on the jeans that were scrunched on the floor. Terrence put on his shorts and socks while Evelyn grabbed the shotguns. She checked the chamber. Fully loaded. Terrence accepted the weapon with hesitation. As quiet as they could, they removed the chair from under the doorknob and ventured into the hall. Every step they took seemed to groan too loud. Mary watched them leave.

Evelyn reached the foyer, keeping the gun up but her finger off the trigger. They turned on the light, brightening the massive foyer. Terrence went down one of the curving steps and Evelyn went down the other. They reconvened at the center, watching each other's backs. They headed down the hall of portraits and unlocked the kitchen. They flipped on the light. All of the doors and cabinets were closed, but lying on the kitchen island was a folded note.

While Terrence scanned the room, Evelyn picked up the letter in one hand and opened it.

It read: "I want to meet with you -- M," and listed a set of coordinates.

Evelyn re-read the note, and then re-read it a third time. She put it down so Terrence could study it.

"Could it be..." Terrence's voice trailed off.

"Yes," Evelyn replied, her heart racing. For the first time in her life, her father had reached out to her personally.

"It doesn't say when," Terrence pointed out.

"Tomorrow, I suspect. I'm not risking it tonight," Evelyn said.

"Should we risk it at all?" Terrence asked. "There's still a chance that your father killed all those people."

"When did you become cynical?" Evelyn asked with a raised brow.

"I'm not, but... we should call the police, nonetheless." Terrence suggested.

"So they can arrest my father for murders he didn't commit?" Evelyn shook her head.

"Will you bet your life on that?" Terrence asked.

Evelyn glanced at his shotgun and then his eyes. "We won't need to."

Terrence paced. "I don't know, Evelyn. I don't know if I can pull the trigger if push comes to shove."

"You can," Evelyn replied, though she doubted herself as well. She put the gun on the island and pressed close to Terrence. "We will if we need to."

After propping the gun against the nearest counter, Terrence wrapped his strong arms around Evelyn, pulling her close. Evelyn reciprocated. She rested her cheek on his shoulder.

"You owe me big time," Terrence said. "For this and many things."

"Keeping tabs?" Evelyn asked.

"Something like that," Terence replied.

Evelyn kissed him and then pulled away. They searched the room for another hidden entrance. It seemed that the note was delivered a different way.

The rest of the night, Evelyn tossed and turned, barely able to keep her eyes closed. Her heart beat in a combination of fear and anticipation. She didn't know if she should be weeping for joy or utterly terrified. Looking out the window at the pregnant moon, Evelyn knew she'd find out soon.

Tomorrow, Evelyn would meet her father.

20

ENCOUNTER

Evelyn studied the glowing computer screen and map it showed. The coordinates listed in the note pointed to a wooded area a few miles outside her property. No roads stretched that far out. She would have to walk.

At daybreak, Terrence drove to town on a water run. Evelyn stayed in Quenby House, admiring its size and Antebellum-era interior design straight out of a civil war movie. She opened up the master bedroom closet. It smelled of mothballs and had multiple racks of blazers and men's sports coats dangling on twisted wire hooks. With her palm, she brushed them aside, momentarily distracted by the idea of Terrence dressed in one of these. They might fit him well, however, none boasted the tiny instruments that decorated ninety percent of his shirts and socks. At the bottom of the closet floor, Evelyn found the backpacks. They were nearly twenty years old but sturdy. Evelyn grabbed it by the straps and lifted one up. It had multiple pockets on both the inside and outside, a waterproof exterior, and was surprisingly heavy. By the expert construction and suturing, she knew she wouldn't find this at Walmart. *Father must've been a hiker.* Being a city girl most of her life, Evelyn would enjoy exploring nature with her family. She struck down the thought, reminding herself that her father was a stranger and possibly a killer.

By the time Terrence returned, Evelyn had set the dining room table with loaded shotguns and travel packs. She put her blonde hair into a ponytail with a few loose strands tumbling down the side of her face. She wore jeans, a belt with her extendable baton clipped to the right hip, and a short-sleeved olive green V-neck.

As he walked into the dining room, Terrence paused to stare at her and then bounced his eyes to the weapons. "It's not our typical breakfast platter."

"It is a little abnormal," Evelyn pointed out.

"We can still call the police," Terrence not-so-subtly reminded her of his stance on the issue.

Evelyn felt resistance in her gut. It was a common side effect of her bull-headedness. She couldn't fault her husband for thinking rationally. Calling in backup would be safer, and probably smarter, but if her father saw them coming, he might slip into the woods and out of Evelyn's life again. Whether or not they shared a family bonding moment, Maxwell could be the key to sending home the phantoms and freeing Evelyn from her burden.

"We do this alone," Evelyn declared.

Terrence put the twenty-four-count water pack on the table. "I thought you might say that."

Without much else to say, they prepared for their deadly venture. They packed light and put the minivan's first-aid kit in Terrence's backpack. Evelyn strapped one of the shotguns on her shoulder and hung it in an upright position, with the barrel pointed to the blue sky. She grimaced under the weapon's weight. It would be a long walk.

They started out the back door, not wasting a moment to

turn back to the vine-covered mansion. Brushing past the mossy stone furnishings, they followed the dirt path by the six slave cabins. The single-room buildings had wooden walls, dirt floors, and flat roofs. Through the musty windows, decaying and collapsed feather beds could be seen. Soon, the path branched out into the hay and cotton field, the latter being tainted by a black scorch mark at its white and weedy hair. Terrence shuddered when he glanced at it. Hooked-nose Stephen Doyle and his siblings murdered Mary in that very spot, and it seemed the blackened earth would never be the same.

They ignored the cotton field and went around the cut hay. Yellow bales spotted the smooth terrain. Beyond it, the trail pattered into nothingness and disappeared into the trail line. The instant Evelyn and Terrence stepped into the woods, society, safety, and the clear path vanished, leaving behind the sounds of odd birds and insects in search of something dead to consume. The terrain seemed to roll and dip. Evelyn's only guidance was the map book with a red line toward the coordinates.

The land here had no owner. Evelyn and Terrence kept an eye out for anyone or anything. Explaining why she had weapons but no hunting permit was something Evelyn needed to avoid. Every forty-five minutes, they drank water and sat on rocks or felled trees in order to readjust their weapon's weight and get the kinks out of their shoulders. Terrence would yawn a few times or squeeze a half-drunken bottle of water on his well-structured face, and then they would set out again.

The woods seemed alive. Ferns and other greenery spotted the dirt while trees of different shapes and leaves bent out in all directions. Every few moments, Evelyn forced herself to looked up from the ground and out at her surroundings. Behind any tree or boulder could be a predator, whether beastly or human.

Only getting turned around once, Evelyn neared the destination as the afternoon sun breached the canopy. Loose strands of hair were sweat-glued on her pale cheeks. Her clothes were stained, and though she was physically exhausted, her mind stayed alert and her hands prepared to equip the gun at a moment's notice.

In the distance and amidst the trees, a rusty tin roof jutted out of tall shrubbery. Tall briars concealed the dark wood walls of the lopsided home. The age of the building and the reason for its strange locale left Evelyn wondering. By its outwardly appearance, the structure had to be someone's home because it was far too big to be a cabin. What few window panes remained suffered elemental damage that left spider web cracks across their faces. Evelyn guessed it contained a bedroom, living room, kitchen, and closet. Restroom facilities were in the nearby outhouse with a moon cut on the door's face.

"Do you think Maxwell's been living here all this time?" Terrence whispered as they huddled behind a tree.

No light shone from the house. Evelyn would be shocked if the building had access to electricity. "The place looks dead."

She unslung her shotgun.

"Shouldn't we wait to do that?" Terrence asked. "I don't want him getting the wrong impression."

"And I don't want to be defenseless if someone starts shooting."

After a moment of hesitation, Terrence unslung his shotgun.

Staying hunched, they moved from tree to tree, getting closer to the house with every movement. Evelyn's blue eyes scanned the decrepit house's windows, keeping an eye out for any protruding gun barrels. Though no threat was present, Evelyn's heart raced. Her sweaty palms clenched the heavy weapon tighter, imprinting her hands with the pattern of the forestock and grip. If push came to shove, Evelyn hoped these weapons would fire. Being at least over a decade old, she couldn't know their reliability, even after they had test fired the weapons several times.

With no more cover, Evelyn and Terrence stepped out into the "yard." Shin-high grass brushed against their pant legs. They reached the front door. Evelyn pressed up beside it and peered in through the cracked window. Dust swirled in the living room. There were a few wooden chairs, but no couch or any sort of entertainment setup. Evelyn leaned back and knocked on the door.

Nothing. She peered back into the window.

"Maybe he wants us to wait for him?" Terrence theorized.

Evelyn chewed her lip nervously. *He should be waiting for us.* "Try the door."

Terrence twisted the knob. He glanced at Evelyn and shook his head.

A crow cawed at the clear Georgia sky. More unseen crows answered its cry. Leaves rattled and branches swayed in the breeze. Apart from the sounds of nature, the place was unnervingly quiet.

Evelyn mustered her courage and gave the door another knock. "Max? Maxwell Quenby?"

It somehow felt wrong to talk in her normal voice, almost like it was too loud for such a harrowing place.

"I don't like this," Terrence said, his eyes widening and his fingers further coiling around the gun.

"Let's check around back," Evelyn suggested.

Silent, Terrence followed her around the corner of the building. They turned sideways to slide between two far-reaching thorn bushes. Through the window, the basic kitchen could be seen. It had a few cupboards, counters, a water bucket for a sink, and a small table. They made it around back to the kitchen door. In the back yard--which wasn't so much a yard as it was a sprawl of green weeds and tall grass--a stone well rose out of the earth. It had a wooden A-framed roof and lowered bucket. Evelyn took a detour from the house to check it out. The inside was a circular black abyss. She pulled at the retrieval rope and watched the wooden bucket climb into her sight. A dead and bloated rat bobbed at the surface of the murky black water.

"No one could survive like this," Terrence said with a sickened expression.

Evelyn let the bucket splash back into the deep but nearly diminished well.

They returned to the building and tried the back door. Locked as well. Evelyn slung her weapon back over her shoulder and pulled out her lock-picking tools.

"Evelyn, should we--"

"Yes," Evelyn replied as she listened for that sweet clicking sound. After a few moments, she heard it and the house was open to her. Re-equipping her gun, Evelyn stepped into the kitchen. The clacking noise from her foot on the wood floor bounced off the wall. Terrence followed her inside.

"Maxwell?" Evelyn called out to the old house.

There was no sign of a refrigerator or any sort of cold storage. She briefly opened the cupboards, finding dead insects either on their backs or swaddled in spider webs. The dining area was similar in its emptiness. Evelyn moved into the living room. The three wooden chairs at the center seemed to have been pulled from the dining room table. Two of the chairs sat side by side. The third faced the corner. Evelyn noticed the lack of dust on the two chairs and dirt caked on their legs. Someone brought these outside, and not too long ago from the looks of it.

There wasn't a hallway to the bedroom, only a closed door branching off from the living room. Evelyn gestured for Terrence to keep his gun ready while she pushed the door open. A rusted spring bed frame supported a skinned mattress. The stained yellow sheeting that once sutured it was nailed above the window to make some sort of makeshift curtain. Containing a little bit of dirty spring water, crinkled plastic bottles and mason jars rested on the dresser's top nearby a stack of mystery novels with bent bindings. The ajar top dresser drawer revealed a matchbox, pocket knife, and compass. A portable hot plate with charred meat melted to its surface sat at the base of the dresser.

"Someone's been living here," Evelyn stated.

They turned to the closet.

Evelyn kept her gun aimed while Terrence took the initiative. He pulled open the door, revealing the deceptively large windowless room. Two ruffled sleeping bags with the head opening at the opposite ends were laid out on the floor. Next to it was a bloodstained shirt.

Terrence turned back to Evelyn with a worried expression.

Evelyn felt her mouth dry out. "We need to leave."

Terrence gave her a look full of concern and fear. "What?"

"Maxwell didn't write that letter."

"Then who did?"

Evelyn rushed into the living room and grabbed the front door knob when she saw the figure outside the window. The man with a featureless white cotton mask and a raised pistol. She dropped to her belly. Terrence mimicked her. Evelyn's heart pounded. *Did he see me?*

Terrence army-crawled to her. "That's Stephen Doyle. What is he doing here?"

Rolling on her back, Evelyn aimed the shotgun at the front door. The weapon trembled in her hands. Her vision bounced between the entrance and the windows. She waited. *Come on. Come on. Come on.* Her heart twisted. A bead of sweat snaked down the bridge of her nose.

Terrence tapped her shoulder and pointed to the dining room. He was right. They needed to get out of here. Not taking her eyes off the entrance, Evelyn returned to her hands and knees and scurried as quickly and quietly to the dining room as she could. As she rounded the corner, the front door knob jiggled. By the time they were halfway past the table, the front door opened with a loud creak.

A boot stepped inside. Terrence and Evelyn pressed themselves up against the nearest wall, trusting their hearing to locate the masked gunman. Slowly, he stepped into the room, leaving the door open behind him. Terrence, being closest to the living room, straightened his back against the wall and positioned the gun to point upward at the door. Perspiration dotted his dark skin and upper lip. His finger slid on the trigger.

Evelyn slowly began scooting away. Somehow, even that simple movement made some noise. She froze and listened.

Stephen wasn't moving.

Was he listening too?

Evelyn didn't want to wait to find out. She turned her head to the open kitchen. The back door wasn't far. If she ran...

The gunman's footsteps neared. Terrence tensed up. In three seconds, Doyle would be around the corner.

They needed to run.

Two seconds.

Dread pitted in Evelyn's stomach. Two sleeping bags, she remembered. Two enemies.

One second.

Evelyn aimed the gun.

The back door opened.

Evelyn saw the burgundy-stained white mask. The woman wearing it wielded a woodcutter's axe. With a hollow shriek and her weapon raised, Catherine Doyle charged at Evelyn.

Evelyn shut her eyes and held her breath.

The masked woman tore through the kitchen, her little feet pattering on the hardwood, and swung down the glossy edge of her deadly axe.

Evelyn heard it cut the wind.

Unable to wait any longer, Evelyn forced herself to squeeze the trigger.

The gunshot blast rattled the whole house. The weapon's stock punched Evelyn's shoulder. The masked woman lurched back, red mist bursting from her flat chest.

"Nooooo!" Stephen yelled and curved the gun around the doorway. Terrified, Terrence pulled his shotgun's trigger. Jammed.

With no time to think about the person she had just doomed, Evelyn grabbed Terrence and they ran as Stephen blindly fired the pistol at them. Bullets zipped by their heads, only inches away from instant death. Evelyn jumped over Catherine's twitching body. The woman's mask had fallen off. She had a hooked nose, lazy eye, and a bruised and pus-filled forehead. A massive red soup puddled on her chest. By the time Terrence jumped over, Catherine Doyle was dead.

Evelyn ran for the woods. Her vision tunneled. Adrenaline screamed through her veins. Thorns raked against her arms. She ducked below skinny branches. Keep running, her instincts told her. Keep running and never stop.

Evelyn didn't know how far she went. There were no familiar landmarks or trails. She slowed down amidst trees and bushes. Her stomach cramped and the weight of the weapon had returned. She couldn't escape the fact that she had killed the woman.

Guilt-ridden and panting, Evelyn turned back to talk to Terrence. He wasn't behind her.

"Terrence," she called out, her voice hoarse from the sprint. "Baby?"

Quiet.

She observed the woods. No sign of him. No sign of any movement.

Holding the gun in one hand, Evelyn used the neck of her shirt to wipe down her soaked and dirty face. She couldn't remember when she lost track of him. The events replayed in her mind. She grabbed him by the shoulder, let go to hurdle over the dying woman, and ran. Evelyn's heart skipped a beat. She tried to recall if Doyle had gotten another shot off after she escaped the house, but her own killing made the rest of the world and its noises a blur. There was a chance Terrence never made it out of the house.

Evelyn looked to the blue sky and forced herself to think about her next move. She cocked her gun, watched the empty shell shoot into the air, and then turned back the way she came. Moving swiftly but with caution, she realized just how far she'd run. Nothing looking familiar, and the more she traveled, the more fears pinged in her head: you've already gone past the house, you're going the wrong way, your husband is dead. The world seemed to tilt. Evelyn rested her hand on the rough bark of the tree. Her husband needed her. She couldn't let this guilt and physical pain crush her. She pressed on.

Her throat became parched. She thought about getting water from her backpack but couldn't bring herself to stop again. The house still hadn't appeared in her view. Doubt swarmed inside her. She thought she ran in a straight line, but maybe she didn't. She picked broken leaves from her hair and felt stinging from the thorns in her forearms. Little spiked seeds dangled off her shirt and jeans. Her ankles seemed to swell in her boots. She hated admitting that Terrence was right. They should've called the cops. The Doyles had tricked them into coming out here. They'd probably been hiding here since the house invasion and wanted to lure her out. If Terrence died because of her decision, Evelyn didn't know if she'd be able to live with herself.

In the distance, she saw the rusted tin roof. *Thank God.*

She crouched behind a tree and took aim with her shotgun. She could barely make out the back door where Catherine's lifeless body seeped crimson. *Where are you?* Evelyn asked Terrence, though he could not hear her.

A twig snapped.

The hairs on the back of Evelyn's neck stood.

She twisted back in time to see the axe head swinging to her face and pulled the trigger.

The tree bark behind him exploded into wooden shrapnel as the masked axe man staggered to the side. He went in for another swing before Evelyn could cock the shotgun. Momentarily shutting her eyes, she blocked the axe head by holding the shotgun horizontally in both hands. The force of the impact sent a shock up both her arms. For the one second they stood like that, Evelyn looked into the button-sized eye holes on the featureless white mask.

Evelyn put the toe of her boot into the man's groin. Grunting, he staggered back. As soon as Evelyn cocked the weapon, the axe head hit the side of the barrel, causing the weapon to fly from Evelyn's grasp.

She reached for her baton. The masked man grabbed her neck and slammed her back into the tree. Her wind left her. She swung the baton down on the side of the man's head. With a thump, he staggered back. Evelyn went for the shotgun. Stephen took off his mask, revealing his disheveled gray/black hair, hooked nose, small boils, and crazed eyes.

He went back for a swing of the axe when he found himself looking into the barrel of Evelyn's shotgun. Gnashing his teeth, he took a step back but kept hold of the axe.

"Where's Terrence?" Evelyn demanded an answer.

Stephen's face turned blood red. "You murdered my sister, whore."

"Tell me where my husband is!" Evelyn yelled.

"He's bleeding out somewhere. From my gunshot," Stephen bragged.

Evelyn struggled to hold the gun steady. Her eyes watered.

"You going to kill me?" Stephen asked. "Get your fill of justice? It's not as satisfying as you might think. I learned that when I burned Mary Sullivan alive for what your father had done. None of this would've happened if he hadn't killed my Alannah. People thought I was crazy, but I saw Alannah in that house long before you showed up. I tried to tell you it wasn't your home. It's a graveyard for your father's victims. My sister even had proof on her camera before you deleted it."

"My father is innocent," Evelyn said through her teeth. "You killed that little girl for nothing. You lured me out here for nothing."

Stephen locked bloodshot eyes with her. "You're wrong. Maxwell is every bit the monster they say he is."

"Alannah told me otherwise," Evelyn replied.

The words struck Stephen.

Evelyn raised the weapon. "I'm not going ask again. Where is Terrence?"

Stephen frowned heavily, "He's bleeding out with every

second you waste talking to me. So, go ahead, pull the trigger. You've already killed once. It'll be easier now."

Evelyn held her finger on the trigger and no matter how hard she wanted to pull it, brokenness in the man's eyes prevented --

BOOM!

In a blink, most of Stephen's head was no more. His body spiraled in the air and then flopped on the ground.

Warm tears of blood dripped down Evelyn's horrified face and into the neck of her shirt. Her trembling hands lowered the shotgun that she hadn't fired.

Slowly, she turned her head to the man standing beside her.

A bushy gray beard fell down past his skinny frame. Long and wavy soot-colored hair flowed down his bony shoulders. What little could be seen of his face was tired and wrinkled. Deep crow's feet etched out from dark eyes. With tattered gloves, he held Terrence's shotgun. A wisp of smoke snaked out of the barrel.

Evelyn opened her mouth to speak, but no words could escape her. The stranger stepped toward her and grabbed her shotgun. Evelyn wanted to resist, but her will was weak. With a weapon in each hand, the old man gave her final, unreadable look and then headed into the woods.

"Dad?" Evelyn finally got the word out.

The stranger paused for a moment. Then he continued on, soon vanishing into the thick foliage.

21

DAYS BEFORE DEATH

On her way to her friend Janet's house, cute nine-year-old Bella Ann May biked down the tree-flanked street, blinked, and awoke, facedown, on the floor of the damp concrete basement.

Her head throbbed. Her vision blurred. Around her, the compact basement seemed to swirl. She put her palms against the ice-cold floor and pushed herself up. Her elbows wobbled. Nausea flushed over her.

She managed to plop onto her bottom before forgoing all further movement for now and possibly forever. She felt a bump on her pink neck. The flesh felt tender and caused her to wince. Did a bee sting her? If she did, she didn't remember.

"Mommy?" Bella called into the dimly lit room. "Daddy?"

Gray walls seemed to absorb her cry. A moth fluttered around the exposed, glowing light bulb screwed into the ceiling.

With her tiny fingers, she brushed her rich brunette hair away from her pretty hazel eyes. The basement consisted of a dusty metal shelf, a brick-sized air vent high up on the wall, a few plastic buckets containing one oddly shaped sponge used to wash the car, and eight wooden steps leading to an unassuming door.

Bella's eyes watered. She forced herself to her feet. Her pencil legs felt like jelly. She brushed off her little khaki shorts and midnight blue t-shirt as she stumbled to the door. The steps groaned beneath her. She tried the doorknob.

Locked. Fidgeting nervously, she gave the scary basement another glance before yelling for her parents.

No reply.

She hammered both fists on the door. "Let me out!" She screamed until her voice cracked and her bottoms of her hands were purple. Turning back to the basement, Bella sank down to the top step and pulled her knees close. She wiped tears from her angular face and sniffled. Fear, confusion, and anxiety swirled inside her.

Where were her parents? Why would they do this? Bella didn't remember doing anything bad. That wasn't completely true. She did steal chocolate from her mother's secret stash and faked a bellyache to get out of chores, but was that deserving of such a harsh punishment? Unless it wasn't her parents… Bella shuddered. It couldn't be her teachers. School was out for the summer, and her friends would never do something this cruel. Bella's head hurt thinking about it. Her crying worsened. The worst part about crying was how she looked doing it. Everyone said that she had such a cute face, but when she wept, her nose turned red and her cheeks looked puffy. It only made things worse. Maybe whoever took her made a mistake, and they'll come back to get her soon.

Minutes, hours, in the basement, time met nothing.

Bella had run out of tears ages ago, and she was antsy waiting for help. She screamed until she couldn't talk. She beat the door until her hands were numb. She asked countless questions but found no answers. One thing was certain. She was alone in this basement, and no one was coming to save her.

When her body mellowed out, Bella got up and paced about the room. She looked up at the shelf and at the small vent nearby. She knew she couldn't fit, but had nothing to do but try. She grabbed the shelf and tried to move it below the vent. It didn't budge. Moping, she started to climb. The metal rattled under her shaking. She got to the top and reached for the ventilation grate. It was too far. She reached farther.

Snap.

The top metal shelf broke beneath her weight and her back hit the floor. She gasped and rolled to her side. Whimpering, she curled up into a ball. Even after the pain faded, Bella didn't move. She watched the tiny cockroach scuttle up a wall. She remembered the sweet song her mom used to sing her but couldn't remember the words. She hummed it instead, feeling the emptiness of the room bearing down on her.

She closed her eyes, clenching her rumbling stomach, and dreamed about horses. They were big, beautiful, majestic animals trapped behind a white fence. Bella dreamed she broke them out and was running free with them, through the rolling green pastures and by the red brick school. Above, fat clouds surfed on blue skies. Mommy and Daddy and all her other friends were there, welcoming her and her animal companions with open arms.

"Hey." A muffled voice woke Bella from her slumber.

Bella quickly got up from the concrete floor, feeling a crick in her neck. She brushed her long hair from her face and listened.

"Are you awake?" the muffled voice asked.

Bella blinked away the sleep and charged up the stairs. She grabbed hold of the doorknob. It didn't twist.

"Help me! I'm trapped!" she said in her tiny voice.

The man on the other side of the door replied. "I know."

"Then get me out!" Bella begged. "Please. I'm sorry I stole Mommy's chocolate. I'm sorry I pretended to be sick--"

"Bella," the muffled voice said calmly.

Bella sniffled. "I don't want to die, Mister."

"You're not," the man said. "Not today at least."

"Are you trapped too?" Bella asked innocently.

The man chuckled kindly. "No, Bella."

"Then why can't you help me?" the little girl asked.

"Because," the man said as if that was an explanation.

"I don't understand," Bella moaned.

The man sighed. "I've hurt a lot of people. I don't rightly know why I do sometimes. I've liked it since I was younger than you. Maybe it's an ego thing, or genetics. I don't know."

"You don't need to hurt me. I can be your friend," Bella replied, confident that would work. "Friends make everything better."

"I wish that were true," the man said. "I'm old, Bella, and I have this... emptiness inside of me. If I don't fill it, then I lose my mind and make stupid decisions."

"I can help you," Bella said.

"You are," the man replied sincerely. "See, the thing about this emptiness is that I don't know the best way to sate it. I've opened a beautiful woman's throat. I made an old man drink poison. I took off a young athlete's throwing hand. None of that did it."

Wide-eyed and heart racing, Bella took a step back from the door.

"Every great killer has their method." The man continued. "Some use knives, others guns, some cannibalism. Even after all these years, I haven't found mine. That's why I brought you here."

The steps creaked beneath Bella's feet as she distanced

herself from the door. The man behind it didn't seem to care. "I'm going to starve you, Bella. When you're near death, I'll come back and look into your gorgeous brown eyes, watch the light flicker out, and see if that does the trick."

"Please," Bella begged. "I don't want…"

"I'll see you soon," the man said and walked away from the locked door.

Trembling, nine-year-old Bella Day clenched her cramping stomach and listened to its gargled rumble.

22

CRIMSON TEARS

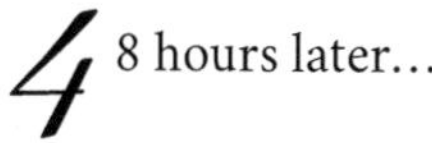

48 hours later…

Birds screamed and scattered at the thunderous boom of the twelve-gauge shotgun.

Their black wings fluttered desperately across the indigo sky.

Like raindrops, warm blood slithered past wide blue eyes, down pale cheeks, and leaked into the neck of a short-sleeve olive green V-neck. Blood-covered, blonde and slender, Evelyn Carr lowered her shotgun. Her body trembled as she looked down at the nearly headless corpse of Stephen Doyle, the man who had killed a child a decade ago and lured Evelyn into this trap.

Slowly, Evelyn turned her horrified gaze to the stranger nearby. Pale smoke wisped out of his shotgun's barrel. Dressed in faded camo, the gaunt man had long ashen hair with a lengthy beard to match. Like the scars on Evelyn's back, deep wrinkles etched the man's dirty forehead and around his black eyes. He lowered his shotgun, which was actually Evelyn's husband's, and approached. Too shocked to resist, she let the man take her weapon. Silent, he turned back to the woods from whence he came. Twigs crunched beneath his boots. Holding the choke of the twelve gauges in each hand, he stepped over a felled tree dressed in green and white fungi.

Evelyn opened her mouth, as if trying to speak for the first time.

"Dad?" she managed to call out

The stranger paused, his shoulders slumped under the weight of the weapons. After a breathless moment, he walked on, soon vanishing into the Georgia wilds.

Evelyn's knees hit packed dirt and dry leaves. Her thoughts transported her back to the lawyer's office where she received her estranged father's will. It was a simple letter, rather cold in nature, and heavily wrinkled. *"Ten years,"* the lawyer explained. *"That's how long the deceased instructed me to wait before delivering it."*

"In his will, he said that if he was presumed dead. What does that mean?" Evelyn replied.

The lawyer locked his fingers on the desk and leaned in. *"Maxwell vanished from his home. All of his possessions were accounted for. However, a body was never recovered."*

The tall oaks began to warp into an amalgamation of brown bark and pointed green leaves. Stephen's blood crusted on Evelyn's soft skin. She remembered the man's words, back when he still had a mouth to speak them. *"He's bleeding out somewhere. From my gunshot."*

Terrence, Evelyn thought. Her husband, her anchor, the man who pulled her from her crunched car years ago, was dying somewhere in these woods.

She forced herself to blink and shielded her eyes from the warm cadaver. There was another body back at the cabin.

This one was Catherine Doyle, Stephen's sadistic twin sister that had charged Evelyn with a raised axe and forced Evelyn to squeeze the trigger. Though she was painted with Stephen's blood, it was Catherine's blood that would forever stain Evelyn's hands.

"Evelyn!" A voice in the woods cried out.

Footsteps neared. "Evelyn! Where are you?"

The person paused.

Evelyn glanced up her husband, expecting to see a fatal wound. Terrence's dark skin was free of any cut or blood. Sweat dotted his bald head and well-structured face. The top four buttons of his beige button-up were undone, revealing the few small hairs on his upper chest. With bloodshot brown eyes, he bounced his vision between his bloodied wife and the limp body ten feet away.

After his gawking ended, Terrence rushed to Evelyn, dropped to his knees in front of her, and looked her in the eyes. His dark irises seemed to tremble as he studied her. "Oh, God, Evelyn."

He pulled a crinkled, half-filled water bottle from the back pocket of his khaki cargo shorts, poured some of the crystalline water into the palm of his hand, and washed away the blood from Evelyn's cheek. The dried crimson thinned out to light red droplets and snaked down the curvature of Evelyn's jaw. She had a beautiful but intimidating face that became more broken with sorrow the more it was cleaned.

"Where's your gun?" Terrence asked softly.

"My father took it," Evelyn mumbled back.

Terrence stopped brushing his thumb across her cheek. "Maxwell was here?"

Evelyn nodded slightly. "He took your shotgun too. Used it on..."

Terrence didn't need to glance back at the corpse to know

it was right behind him. "I tossed my weapon after it jammed, how did he--why did he take it?"

Evelyn turned her eyes away. "Whoever owns the weapons is guilty of these murders."

It took Terrence a second to realize what she was saying, and then he squeezed her. With trembling arms, Evelyn reciprocated and grabbed fistfuls of the back of his shirt. Minutes ago, she thought Terrence was dead. Now, she didn't want to let go.

Terrence eased Evelyn off him and helped lift her by the hand. Leaning on one another, they traveled through the woods, leaving the cabin and the bodies of Stephen and Catherine Doyle in their wake.

The hike back to their plantation home took hours. Once, Evelyn saw a few hunters on ATVs. She and Terrence ducked behind a hedge of dirt. Dirty, worm-like roots jutted from its face. Soon, the camo-wearing hunters were far away. Evelyn wondered if they'd heard the shotgun's boom. It was too late to go back. If law enforcement found the bodies and pinned it on Evelyn, she wouldn't resist. She was far too tired for that.

The falling sun painted the world scarlet. The clouds above were thin and stretched like pulled cotton across the darkening sky. A sliver of the moon appeared in a rare moment where it shared the sky with the sun. Out of the tree line, stubby, cylindrical, yellow bales of hay could be seen spotting acres of trimmed field. In another field nearby, thorny weeds climbed rows of deep-rooted cotton plants with a massive charred smear at the field's center. The burnt scar reminded the world of seven-year-old Mary Sullivan's demise at the wrath-filled hands of Stephen, Catherine, and Andrew Doyle. They hated Evelyn's father Maxwell because they believed he took the life of sultry Alannah Gimmerson, and many more. Whether the accusation was gospel or fiction, it didn't stop them from taking Mary's life, the child who Maxwell treated like a daughter.

Beyond the crops, six decrepit slave cabins--three on either side--flanked a wide dirt road that wound down to the massive seventeen-room, two point five story mansion dressed with green vines and little white flowers. Bordered by trees, exquisite stone statues, and a flower garden decorating the backyard, the Quenby House was the epitome of post-civil war Southern ideas: symmetry, hierarchy, and order. It was a marvelous building built on blackmail, deceit, and bones. Though its exterior showed life and was a mastery of human architecture, the dead walked behind the house's beautiful jaws. *A blessing and a curse,* Maxwell had described it in his will. That short, handwritten document was the only communication Evelyn Carr had ever shared with her father. She had nothing from her mother.

Pain and fatigue jabbed at Evelyn's heel and calf with each step. Sweaty clothes stuck to her flesh like a second layer of unwanted skin. Terrence, usually one with a good laugh, kept quiet apart from his tired panting.

Away from the crops and drab cabins, the couple shambled through the bowling green backyard, past raised gardens spilling over with long grass and multicolored flowers, and by old statues with blotches of green moss on their smooth stone skin. Unlike the mansion's face, the back lacked colonnades and had a second-story porch a third of the size. Evelyn imagined her greatest ancestor, a gorgeous Scandinavian woman with pale white skin, tall blonde hair wrapped in braids, and a stunning heart-shaped face, looking over her lands in the early 1800s.

Terrence stepped ahead of Evelyn and turned the knob of one of the two double doors. Holding it open with his back, he allowed Evelyn passage into the dark house. It was quiet, apart from their footsteps clacking across the hall's rickety floor. Past a few sideboard tables decorated with old vases and authentic 19th century oil paintings, they reached another set of double doors that spit them into the massive foyer, stopping just below the two curving stairways that covered the interior balcony above Evelyn's head. The floor was blanketed with thin red carpet and, beyond the balcony, the foyer opened all the way to the second story. Hanging from the high-domed ceiling was a massive, crystalline multi-tier chandelier that had been updated in the last century to use dimmed, flame-shaped bulbs that gave off the illusion of real fire.

Beneath the chandelier stood two figures. The first was a short little girl in a belted yellow dress. She had blonde locks that tumbled down her shoulders and adorable freckles across the bridge of her button nose and under her dry and lifeless blue eyes.

The tall figure next to her wore a black long-sleeved shirt with matching pants and a featureless white mask that hugged his entire head. Button-sized holes were cut out over his unreadable eyes. Holes the size of peas were cut out on his ears.

They both stared blankly at Evelyn and Terrence.

Deathly silence hung over the Quenby House.

"I thought you'd be gone," Evelyn said to Mary Sullivan. "Catherine and Stephen are."

Suddenly, the little girl charged Evelyn. Before she could react, the little girl had her arms wrapped around Evelyn's torso and the side of her face pressed against Evelyn's flat stomach. Evelyn held her arms up, unsure how to react. She traded looks with Terrence, whose eyes were wide and his lips parted.

"Thank you," the little girl said in her tiny voice, tightening her embrace. Hesitant, Evelyn wrapped her arms around Mary Sullivan, feeling the icy-cold body. But somehow, deep within her, something felt warm. Alive.

The man in the featureless white mask, Andrew Doyle, who took his life on the day he helped take Mary's, watched the scene. Was he touched? Jealous? Amused? His emotions were unreadable.

Mary let go off Evelyn and gave Terrence a hug.

"Strong girl," he chuckled.

When the sweet moment ended, Mary pulled away and headed for the front door. Trading a look, Evelyn and Terrence followed her. They glanced up at the interior balcony behind them, noticing the five spectators: a sweater vest-wearing old man, a sultry woman in a shapely and glossy green dress, a teenage football player with a handsome face and dimpled chin, a girl with straight black hair to match her black eyeliner and lipstick, and a naked fat man with an oblong head and extreme underbite. All of them suffered from the wound that killed them, but at this moment, Evelyn looked past the gore and into their watering eyes.

Mary pulled open the front door and skipped between the tall colonnades and down the steps before running for the brick road that was flanked by ancient, moss-covered oaks. From the doorframe and with fingers twined together, Evelyn and Terrence watched the girl running to her newfound freedom. She twisted back and smiled widely at the couple before continuing her sprint and eventually dissipating into ash that was taken by the wind long before it hit the ground.

Feeling a burden lifted from the house, Evelyn and Terrence turned back to Andrew Doyle and allowed him room to exit. He turned his head to Evelyn and then to Terrence. Without a word, he twisted around and headed for the back door and scorched cotton field beyond. Though the door slammed behind him, all knew that he was here to stay… possibly for eternity.

On top of the interior balcony, the other phantoms departed throughout the house. The last one to go was the sweater vest-wearing Barker, who gave them a nod before turning back into the hallway. If their true killers were the Doyle twins, they would've left with Mary. Evelyn felt pressure growing in her heart, knowing she had more work to do.

But first…

Hot water from the copper showerhead spilled down Evelyn's face and bare body, splashing softly to the bottom of the old tub. Pink water swirled down the drain as the final bit of hooked-nosed and creepy Stephen Doyle washed from her pale skin. Other mysteries required her attention: finding her father, finding the killer of her five lingering houseguests, and finding Bella Ann Day. Like a thread tacked to a cork board, all three mysteries were linked together. It was merely a matter of finding the true connection, and as a private investigator by trade, Evelyn was confident the rest would fall into place.

Evelyn turned the shower dial and stepped out of the tub. She grabbed a towel off the rack and swaddled herself with it. Putting her palms on the icy marble sink counter, she waited for the fog to clear on the chipped, gold-rimmed mirror. Like golden seaweed, wet hair dangled over her face and clung to her high cheekbones. Wrinkles branched out from her blue eyes. A brush of indigo swooped under her tear ducts. Beneath her still gaze, she saw mask-wearing Catherine Doyle charge at her and felt the shotgun's recoil punch her shoulder. Evelyn's fingers squeezed the rim of the sink and then she pulled herself away from the mirror. She may be thirty-three years old, but she felt ancient.

Holding the towel up, she walked out into the bedroom.

With the canopied bed, untouched jewelry station, and various antique furnishings, it looked like a screenshot from *Gone with the Wind.* Still dripping from his bath in a different restroom, Terrence--wearing his boxer briefs--sat at the corner of the tall, king-sized mattress with his face buried in his hands.

Evelyn stood before him and lifted his chin with her finger. She met his downcast face to her own. He looked tired. Beaten down. Just like Evelyn.

She kissed him.

He grabbed her waist.

Leaving the damp towel on the bedroom floor, they let the night slip away.

ARMS UNDER HER FLUFFY PILLOW, Evelyn opened her eyes to her husband. Resting his spine against the bed's backboard, Terrence studied the open laptop on his covered lap. Sunlight and the chirp of morning birds spilled into the room.

"Hey," Evelyn said quietly.

"Hey," Terrence replied in kind. "Sleep well?"

With pursed lips, Evelyn nodded. She didn't remember dreaming. She didn't remember falling asleep. Stretching, she forced herself up and rested her back against the backboard. She glanced over at the computer screen. The local news broadcasted an update on nine-year-old Bella Day. The flashing caption read, *"Missing for Seventy-Two Hours."*

Evelyn felt the day's weight crush her like a boulder.

"Remember when our biggest problem was selling violins?" Terrence asked.

"Barely," Evelyn replied. She pecked Terrence on the temple and swiveled her legs out of bed. Her toes curled on the cold hardwood floor.

With raised brows, Terrence followed her trek to the dresser. The scars painting her bare back were reminders of her car "accident."

As Evelyn threw on the day's clothes, Terrence asked, "Where are you going?"

Evelyn slipped on a long-sleeved black t-shirt. She twisted back to her husband. "To cash in a promise." She held a bobby pin in her teeth and fixed her hair. "You coming?"

Terrence closed the laptop and set it aside. Stretching tall and wide, he got ready for the day.

As they hustled down the curved foyer steps, they heard someone clear their throat. Evelyn and Terrence turned back to the interior balcony. Fifteen-year-old Zoey Pinkerton, the goth girl with black everything but her pasty white face and mortal wound on the back of her head, rested her elbows on the balcony railing. The buttons pinned on her black hoodie boasted mottos from The Green Party.

"I'm going to see your father," Evelyn answered the girl's unspoken question.

"Why?" the girl asked with snark.

"He said he'd tell about me about Maxwell when I solved your case," Evelyn replied.

"You're doing a really good job," Zoey replied sarcastically.

"Watch the house while we're gone," Evelyn commanded, ignoring the comment.

Zoey scoffed and turned her chin away from them.

Terrence smiled at her. "I can't wait to have teenagers."

Zoey turned around glared at him.

Evelyn and Terrence headed out the front door, locking it behind them.

Their rusty minivan sputtered down the red brick road to Quenby. Fat, moss-covered oaks flanked both sides. Their long branches reached over the road and touched fingers, turning the path into a tunnel. It ended at a horizontal single-line street: Quenby Avenue. Directly opposite off was a small wooded area, but on the side was rolling farmland with the occasional cluster of trees or cattle-watering pond. Pastures and tractors blurred by as Terrence sped into the town of Adders, Georgia.

Like most deeply rooted rural towns, the main street was lined with mom-and-pop shops, home-cooked restaurants, and churches. There was a big farmer's market stocked with plump black berries, freshly harvested vegetables, eggs, and homemade donuts. A barn-shaped building advertised line-dancing twice a week and live music. A luthier by trade, Terrence would know more about that than Evelyn. String instruments were the heart of bluegrass, country blues, and Southern rock.

Evelyn's skill set contained tracking, surveillance, and imitation; perks that helped her make a small living as a private investigator in Detroit. Though Adders was quiet and had crisp country air, Evelyn was conflicted on which home she liked better. Detroit was hard living in their small, one-bedroom apartment. Sirens wailed through the night, and the endless climb to earn the month's rent beat her down like a sledgehammer. Nonetheless, the two and a half weeks Evelyn spent in "quiet" Adders thrust her into more life-threatening situations and exposed her to much more horror than she ever personally saw in the Motor City.

Main Street vanished, and they were back to farmland. Down a winding road, their rusty minivan crunched gravel and sputtered to a stop at the quaint house's long driveway. A fenced-in pasture enclosed a large area around the sides and back of the property. Within, a handful of horses grazed and galloped playfully.

Wind chimes hung on the house's front porch. Unmowed grass carpeted the earth. Small green bugs leapt between weeds. Evelyn and Terrence exited their cruddy minivan. They hiked up two steps and knocked on the door. Under the awning's shade, they waited for David Pinkerton.

"You're going to be waiting there for a long time," a voice with a rich Southern twang yelled out. From the inside of the horse pen, David leaned on the white fence in the same way his daughter had on Quenby House's interior's balcony. Standing five-foot-six, David had a shaggy gray goatee, mop of black/gray hair, and drooping blue eyes. Just like their first meeting, he wore a wrinkled shirt, Levis, and mud-caked boots.

"How you doing, Mr. Pinkerton?" Terrence asked politely.

"I've had better days," David replied. "Come to follow in Maxwell's footsteps? I got a new mare that needs breaking in and will be happy to teach y'all. Won't be free, of course."

Evelyn bounced down the steps and approached the fence. The stench of horse dung grew stronger. "I wanted to talk about my father."

David swatted away a fly. "Yeah, me too. After you find my daughter's killer. That was the deal, investigator."

"Maxwell is alive, Mr. Pinkerton," Evelyn said, avoiding the runaround. "I saw him." In a flash of memory, she heard the deafening shotgun blast and felt the warm blood spatter.

The old farmer eyed her suspiciously. "He visited you?"

"In a way," Evelyn replied. "The point is, I need to find him again. You named him Zoey's godfather. If anyone knows where he's been hiding, it's you."

David tugged at his goatee. "You know our relationship went south after he fueled Zoey's bad habits. I haven't seen him in fifteen years. Last time you were here, you asked what I would do if I learned Zoey's remains were found in Max's basement. What the hell did that mean?"

"It means I need to find my father to find Zoey's killer," Evelyn said sternly.

David stopped resting his arms on the wooden fence and put his hands in his pockets. Chewing the inside of his cheek, he studied the clouds drifting over the blue sky. Evelyn could tell he was trying to keep a lid on his frustration, but couldn't stop his reddening cheeks and glossy eyes.

Terrence spoke up. "We don't want to believe Maxwell did this to your daughter, but we need to get to the bottom of this situation."

"When you first came here," David said, "you said that you wanted to help the restless find truth. Not for profit, but the closure for those who lost their loved ones. I respect that more than I can express. Hell, I didn't believe there were people like that anymore. Not since I met Maxwell. A man who took other's burdens for the simple reason that it was the right thing to do. And now, you say he killed my daughter. Maxwell and I had our differences, but I would never pin something like that on him."

"Help us then," Evelyn pleaded. "We find him, we learn the truth about Zoey, his disappearance, and who killed those people all those years ago."

With glassy eyes and a heavy frown, David Pinkerton studied her for a long while. "I don't know where to find Max, but I know someone who might."

Evelyn crinkled her brow, listening intently.

"Your mother."

23

THE FAMILY NAME

"Who is she?" Evelyn asked as she did when she was just some ugly kid in an orphanage. Back then, she only got vague replies and pitying smiles.

A stirring of emotions twisted inside Evelyn at David's words. She was overjoyed to hear about the woman who had brought her into this world but enraged that she had been abandoned. Many nights in her youth, Evelyn had wondered about her mother. Her first thought was that the woman was dead. Perhaps via some horrible accident, fatal disease, or some other tragedy that forced her to surrender Evelyn. A more guilty thought followed, suggesting that Evelyn had killed her during childbirth. On the few rare nights when Evelyn was able to get past those scenarios, her mind went to crueler places. Her mother had surrendered Evelyn because she hated her or the responsibilities of an unwanted child. Evelyn held spite in her heart for that one until she was much older and understood the complexities of the world and humanity. Maybe her mother was living it up in Vegas, or taking care of ten more children and couldn't mentally or physically handle another. Evelyn could go on theorizing forever. She refocused on David Pinkerton.

"Her maiden name is Lily Copperdoe," David explained, with grazing horses and blue skies to his back.

At the age of thirty-three, Evelyn finally learned her mother's name. She felt her chest tighten. She didn't expect the revelation to hit this hard. Terrence noticed and put his arm around her shoulder.

"Very pretty woman," David reminisced. "Smart but complicated, much like my daughter."

"What can you tell me about Lily?" Evelyn asked.

"Gossip and other things you don't want to hear," David replied.

"Try me," Evelyn said.

"She was married when her and Max… you know."

An adulteress. Wonderful. "Who was the man?"

David shook his head. "Nah uh. I promised Max I wouldn't talk of her or the situation to anyone."

"I'm her daughter." Evelyn wanted to wring the guy's neck and scream at him.

"And I'm a man of my word," David replied.

"You're very frustrating," Evelyn told him. "Can you tell me where she's at or is that off limits, too?"

David frowned at her. "I know she's around. I don't have an address."

"Who can help us?" Terrence asked.

"Maxwell," David replied.

Evelyn shook her head. "How does that work? I need Lily to find Maxwell. Not the other way around."

"There's definitely some flawed logic there," Terrence interjected.

"I don't know what to tell you," David replied, feeling Evelyn's building frustration. "Lily, for lack of a better word, exiled herself after having… you."

That was a lovely thought.

David went on. "Lily's parents are dead now. She had no siblings. The only person that might be in contact with her is Max. That's why she's your best lead."

"She's not if we can't find her," Evelyn thought aloud.

David's frown sank lower. "If I knew more, I'd tell you."

"We appreciate everything," Terrence said sincerely. "We're going to head back to the house and see if we can't make heads or tails of this."

"Call me if you learn anything about my daughter or the man who did her in," David said. "I'll give you a shout if I think of anything else about Lily or Max."

"That's all we ask," Terrence said, always the peacemaker.

Too lost in thought, Evelyn left David to his horses without saying another word.

The ride back was somber. For everything Evelyn learned, it still felt as if she was stuck in swamp muck. Someone would have to know where Lily went, but Evelyn was drawing blanks as to who. If she knew Lily's husband, that could help pinpoint Lily's location, but the man could be any of the twenty thousand locals that lived in Adders.

Evelyn pinched the bridge of her nose and closed her eyes.

She felt Terrence's big hand squeeze her knee. "We'll find her."

I wish I shared your confidence. Evelyn propped her head against the glass. On top of all this mom stuff, she was still trying to process last night's shootout, the phantoms lurking in her halls, and countless other issues she'd faced. "I should've gone after him."

"Your dad?"

Evelyn nodded. "He was right there. I should've stood up and just confronted him."

"I'm glad you didn't," Terrence replied.

Evelyn turned to him.

Terrence kept his eyes on the road. "A man's head exploded in front of you. If you were able to play twenty questions with your pops after that, I would be seriously worried about your mental health. Personally, I would've been screaming and running the moment I saw Maxwell with my gun."

"I'm glad you don't think I'm crazy all the time," Evelyn replied. They drove a little farther up the road. "My father was--is--meticulous in his documentation. Remember the plane tickets to Hawaii and the Quenby's first slave receipt?"

"What are you getting at?" Terrence asked.

"Maxwell might've saved Lily's address somewhere."

"It's worth looking into, but it's a pretty big property for a little piece of paper."

The Quenby Plantation consisted of twenty to twenty-five acres with multiple cabins, sheds, cotton storehouses, and other buildings. Obviously, the address would be in the house, but Evelyn didn't want to box herself in case she didn't find it in one of the seventeen rooms of the two point five story mansion. Not included among those was the basement and the secret room behind it where Evelyn and Terrence had found the bone pit. For such an uneventful little town, a lot had happened to Evelyn in a few weeks.

It was late in the morning when they got home. A line of birds lingered on the mansion's truncated roof. The most curious aspect of the articular design was that the domed ceiling in the foyer was not visible on the exterior. It must've jutted out in the attic, behind a wall somewhere.

While Terrence flipped grilled cheese on the stovetop, Evelyn drew a rough sketch of the house and labeled the rooms accordingly. Her doodle was painfully amateur, but readable. Somewhat.

She started in the most obvious place: her father's secret

study. The hall leading outside of the kitchen had windows on one wall and a series of large oil paintings on the other. Apart from the first, which showed the beautiful blonde Scandinavian woman, the other dozen and half portraits displayed the various patriarchs of the Quenby family. There were men with dark hair, dark eyes, some with strong jaws and others with big noses. A few were gaunt and skeletal while others were pudgy and inclined to plumpness.

One in particular had the cotton gin painted behind the subject's head. It was through that clue that Evelyn found the key to unlock her father's secret study behind the painting itself a while back.

Evelyn stopped before the gaping hole in the middle of the wall and cringed at the estimated repair cost. When Stephen Doyle had invaded the house on the night that changed Evelyn's life, he took an axe to the portrait and wall before charging through the three-foot-wide wooden corridor to do the same to the door beyond whose lock was broken long before Evelyn showed up. To survive, Evelyn followed Mary's instructions to dive into the trapdoor beneath the desk. That landed Evelyn and Terrence in a hidden bone pit where she met the other five phantoms.

Evelyn slithered inside of the small, dusty room. There were piles of old books spilling out of a dusty bookcase, a big mahogany desk, an old globe with an orangish tint, a rusty bedframe and lived-in mattress, and dirty plates, cups, and silverware. There were antiques and Antebellum-era toys as well.

Evelyn had searched inside the desk before where she found documents that had survived since the house's inception in 1827. That was back when Adders was still a trading post. More significantly, Evelyn had discovered the drafts to Maxwell's will. She had unballed them and put them in a neat stack inside the upper drawer. The top one started with,

"To my beloved, in a less cruel world, we could've been together. It was never my desire to send you away, but sometimes sacrifices must be made for your safety and for mine. I write to you with my final breath. Come home..."

Evelyn held the paper close to her chest. After a moment, she put it back on top of the stack and sifted through the rest of the old documents. No address for Lily. She searched under the bed, in the slit in the mattress, inside the small drawer in the lamp stand, and in every other nook and cranny in the room. Fruitless, she reminded herself of the palm-sized notebook she had discovered in a hidden compartment within the desk drawer. She flipped through pages of misspelled names, unsure if there were some sort of code or Maxwell was drunk when he wrote them. There was one blank page a third of the way through, but the page following it had a list of dates and locations. Six in all, and each coinciding with one of the victims found in the basement. Even Mary Sullivan, whose remains were ash somewhere on Quenby land. Evelyn didn't know why her father had this. It would've been no surprise that he heard of the murders during his time, but to catalogue them was a little suspicious.

Evelyn ventured upstairs to the main study: a room that was much larger and lined with tall bookshelves, chairs with cracked leather cushions, and a number of wilted flowers that decorated the windowsills and tabletops. She searched that desk too, but found more useless documents. Disappointed in the lack of results, Evelyn returned to the kitchen and ate her grilled cheese, which was cold now. She found Terrence hunched over in the pantry. The wooden slat covering the long crawlspace was open.

"Hey," Evelyn said.

Terrence pulled his head out of the crawlspace and turned back to her.

"What are you doing?" Evelyn asked.

"I was thinking of a way to seal it up," Terrence declared. "If Stephen Doyle could sneak in here, who else can?"

Terrence had a good point. The serial killer who dumped the bodies in the basement either dropped them through one of the multiple hidden chutes or carried them through the secret dirt tunnel that connected the shed and the basement.

"Whenever you're finished, you're invited to help me look for Lily's address."

Terrence cracked a smile. "That sounds like it's more than a suggestion."

Evelyn shrugged and continued her search in the master bedroom. She opened up every drawer on the jewelry dresser and, at the sight of their emptiness, ran her hand up her hair. It seemed like her father had nothing of Lily's, and Evelyn wondered if their relationship was as shallow as a one-night stand. *Romantic,* Evelyn thought sarcastically.

The grueling search grew tiresome. She followed the upstairs hall to a closed door and opened it. It was a small corridor with a stairway that folded in on itself. The top step entered directly into the attic. As she ascended, the hotter and darker the room became. Grabbing aimlessly, she snatched up the beaded light string and gave it a good tug.

Flickering two or three times, the dim light illuminated the attic. The ceiling was much lower and crooked nails spiked out of the wood. Cardboard boxes had fallen in on themselves and naked, milk-skinned mannequins were standing around. There were at least seven or eight of them, all female.

There were two upright posts connected at the top by a horizontal pole. Women's dresses from different eras hung on the horizontal pole via metal coat hangers. Old rectangular suitcases from a bygone era sat at the base. Evelyn approached them, curious about any shared connection with her mother. The floor creaked beneath her feet. Dusty marbles hugged the wall, hinting at an uneven surface.

Coat hangers screeched against metal pole as Evelyn slid them over one by one. The dresses they held were marvelously beautiful. From a flowing, golden-yellow empire-waist dress to a tight, dark-violet maxi, each of the twelve dresses boasted a different design and color. A small tag was clipped on the dress's chest area, labeling each with a different month. September, October, November, etc. Tacked onto the rack itself was a small note that opened like a little folder. In fine cursive, it read "To Lily, a dress for every season."

Evelyn cracked a small smile. Perhaps Maxwell was a romantic. Then she remembered Stephen's death and felt sick to her core. Evelyn glanced about the room and rubbed her damp forehead. The attic grew muggier by the minute. She wondered if all the items inside were gifts to her mother.

With her fingers, she popped open the latches of an old travel trunk and found it stuffed full of wrinkled women's shirts and pants from the seventies. Evelyn closed it and took a step back. She examined more suitcases and luggage bags, finding clothing from all different sizes and eras, the oldest being a flapper dress. *These must be from all the Quenby ladies.* Most of the articles were expensive and a few were custom-fitted. If this were a Goodwill, Evelyn would be having a field day. Then she remembered the estate and all its contents were hers now. Or were they? Now that Maxwell was proven alive, what did that mean for the inheritance?

Evelyn felt conscientious about disturbing the various items. *If Maxwell wanted the estate, why would he leave it to me?* Nonetheless, Evelyn put the dresses back and hiked to the back of the attic. The farther she went, the darker and hotter the long room became. The light from the dim bulb struggled to reach this far and caused a long shadow to grow out of Evelyn and the surrounding coat stands.

Evelyn blinked, feeling salty sweat stinging her eye. To clear up her vision, she wiped her eyes with her moist hands. It barely helped. A nearby hat stand wobbled.

Evelyn froze. Her pulse quickened.

"Hello?" she called out.

No response.

A shadow grew under her feet and stretched out beside her own.

Raspy breathing filled her ear. Its rank stench violated Evelyn's nose.

Dreadfully, Evelyn clenched her fist and turned back.

Only dresses, suitcases, and mannequins.

Beneath the lightbulb, the beaded string swayed.

Evelyn held her breath and scanned her surroundings.

No one.

Cautiously, she turned back around to the far end of the basement.

With cold dead eyes, a naked fat man stared at her. He had a saggy chest, stretch marks, and what stood out more than his misshapen head and horrible underbite was the massive horizontal slash across his belly. Red organs and other disgusting gore slowly leaked out of the open flesh

Evelyn took a step back.

The man breathed heavily. The corner of his upper lip twitched.

Staring down the fat man, Evelyn collected herself.

"Winslow?" Evelyn asked.

The man bared his big teeth into what could barely be considered a smile.

"What are you doing up here?" Evelyn asked. Out of all the phantoms, Evelyn had communicated with him the least of all, but Evelyn remembered what he showed her when she asked to see how the phantoms had died. Winslow, in his 40s though looking much younger, was strung up by his wrists, stripped, and had his belly opened with a knife used to cut cattle meat. Evelyn felt wheezy thinking about it.

Winslow turned around and waddled to the back corner of the room. Evelyn stayed where she was, unable to calm her heart. *You're here to help these people. There's nothing to be scared of.* Evelyn put on a hard face but couldn't shake her uneasiness.

Winslow returned with a turquoise necklace on a silver chain and presented it in his massive hand.

"For me?" Evelyn asked.

The naked man nodded.

Gingerly, Evelyn accepted the gift.

Winslow "smiled" again and waddled to another part of the attic.

Evelyn studied the necklace and the three little gems dangling from it, unsure what to make of it. She pocketed it and wondered what other hidden treasures lay within. Evelyn traveled deeper into the attic.

Surrounded by odd and end furnishings, a circular wooden pedestal sat against the far wall. An old leather-bound tome rested at its center. The lamp with a stained-glass shade sat at the pedestal's base. Cautious, Evelyn approached. With her palm, she brushed away the sheen of dust on the book's cover. Written in black ink, the title read, "Quenby."

Evelyn turned the fat book in her hand. A leather strap with a tiny rusty keyhole sealed the book's pages. Evelyn gave a good pull. That didn't get her anywhere. She glanced around the pedestal and surrounding floor for a key. Nothing.

"Eve," Terrence called out as he hiked up the stairs. "Sorry it took me so long. You up here?"

"Yeah," Evelyn shouted back.

Terrence got to the top of the stairs.

"Hey," Evelyn said, still studying the book. "Can you get my lock-picking tools and the house key from the bedroom?"

Terrence opened his mouth to say something. Instead, he slumped his shoulders and obeyed. He returned moments later and gave her the necessary items. Evelyn tried the key. It was just a little too big. She relied her on lock-picking tools instead. After a moment of fiddling with the lock, it gave way. Terrence leaned over Evelyn's shoulder as she opened the front cover.

That musty, old book smell wafted from the ancient pages. To Evelyn's surprise, a yellow Post-It note was stuck to the front page. It began with the word "Evelyn."

Terrence and his wife exchanged looks. They started reading again. *"I'm sure you've realized that there was no key to this book. In all honesty, I purposely hid it from you."*

"Why would he do that?" Terrence interrupted.

Evelyn shushed him. "Let's keep reading."

"If you're like me, a curious sort, you've found a way to access these pages anyway. Thusly, you've earned your reward. Since Cecilia, our greatest ancestor, arrived on the shores of America..."

Evelyn turned the sticky note over.

"She made clear documentation of our family's history. As per tradition, the following heads of Quenby were required to add their account as well. Your origin lies within these pages, Evelyn. Kill your ignorance. Read it and see what it means to be a Quenby. In doing so, you'll see who I am and learn the truth about your mother."

"Whoa," Terrence said. "Lucky find."

Evelyn glanced at the pedestal. "It wasn't luck. Maxwell wanted me to find this."

They moved downstairs to read the book more. The pages had a yellow tint and were thin. Prone to tearing. The first page started with Cecilia Hagan and the murder of her family.

Born into a wealthy Norwegian manor during the Napoleonic invasion of 1802, Cecilia spent her early years locked away and eating rationed food as the war had brought a great famine to Norway. With a sickly father and mentally unbalanced mother, Cecilia's one hope was to marry another noble and share the wealth and food stores. At fourteen, after the war had ended but her family still suffered, she married Erik Eriksen, a handsome but abusive man. One night, before a great family feast, Cecilia went on a horse ride through the meadows beside her manor. However, a snake scared her steed and it bucked her off. Cecilia awoke where she fell during a great storm that night. Lost and cold, she staggered back home and found her mother, father, husband, and his relatives dead at the dinner table, their heads in pools of their own blood.

Poisoned, the investigators believed.

For two years, she lived alone as a widow and the only survivor of her family in those cursed halls until a stranger came to visit. He was a lowly Englishman from a small house that was destroyed during the war. He claimed that he was passing through the area and needed lodging for the night. Pitying him, Cecilia allowed him to stay. While they were together, Cecilia realized how lonely she had been. She could sense the man's loneliness, too, and in what could only be described as love at first sight, Cecilia consummated their relationship on the night of their first meeting. The man stayed with her, teaching her English and speaking of prospects overseas. Cecilia, tired of living in halls stained with blood, grabbed her money and lover then headed to America. Under the man's guidance, they bought a large plot of land away from the rest of the world. The man personally oversaw the building of the plantation.

His name was Abel Quenby, and Cecilia never met his family.

In her writing, Cecilia described Abel as a quiet and patient man who always seemed to show up at just the right moment. Feeling cursed by her family's demise, Cecilia didn't allow them to marry until she was gray and full of years, thus the Quenby name lived on and Hagan died away. Cecilia's final account read as follows. *"With his usual kind smile, Abel brought me a gift to celebrate our two year anniversary. A fine Norwegian wine coated in dust. I remembered its vintage as the same one my family drank during their final feast."*

The next account began with their eldest son Alistair Quenby and his discovery of hidden passages in the walls. *"My father built something here,"* Alistair described. *"Much grander than I could've imagined. The purposes of such tunnels, I know not, and when I confronted him about it, he took a switch to me as he did the slaves each morning. I will not confront him again."* Alistair proceeded by listing the locations of such tunnels.

The pantry, all five bedrooms, two of the three bathrooms, the lounge, the billiard room, the study, dining room, living room, the foyer, the art room, and the nursery. In summary, fifteen out of seventeen rooms. The only ones that didn't have passages was the downstairs bathroom, second extra living room, and the upstairs hallway.

Evelyn lowered the old, leather-bound book. "What the hell?"

"I don't know if this is the coolest thing we've discovered or the most terrifying," Terrence replied.

Evelyn glanced around the foyer, and it suddenly seemed much larger and intimidating. On the domed ceiling from which the chandelier hung, painted angels with cracked faces, little smiles, and golden trumpets watched them with lifeless eyes.

"Does it say how to access them?" Terrence asked.

Evelyn skimmed over the following pages, careful not to tear them. "It does not." She glanced at the book's three-inch girth. "At least not right here."

"I say we explore," Terrence suggested. "But first..."

He rushed upstairs and returned a moment later wearing his seventy-dollar white cowboy hat.

Evelyn raised a brow.

"Every great detective has their hat. Besides, if we weren't having little fun, we'd probably be in a mental hospital."

Evelyn pondered the statement. He did make a good point.

They started with the master bedroom. They pulled the paintings off the walls and pushed aside the wardrobe. Terrence searched under the bed. Evelyn searched behind the dresser. They brushed their hands over the wall, feeling for hidden switches. Minutes rolled by. Evelyn's index finger found a depression behind the wallpaper.

"Terrence," she beckoned him over.

He felt it too. "That could be it."

Evelyn pursed her lips, wondering if she wanted to tear open the wallpaper on a guess. Terrence poked it, trying to test if it was a clear hole or just a depression in the wood.

Pop. His finger punched through it and his body went tense. Slowly, he turned to Evelyn with a guilty expression. "Oops."

Evelyn crossed her arms.

Terrence slowly removed his finger from the wallpaper. Evelyn gestured for him to step aside while she peeked in. She saw blankness and sniffed dust. Terrence grabbed a flashlight and shined it within. There was a two or three-foot gap between it and the other wall. The rusty nails within were bent down to keep whoever traveled within from harm.

"How do we get in?" Terrence asked.

Evelyn tried to get a better look at the tight corridor but could not.

"I don't know," she admitted and turned back to see the peephole aligned with the canopied bed. *Classy,* Evelyn thought.

They moved to the bathroom in search of another breach there. No peephole, which was good news. Upon trying to move the mirror, Terrence discovered it was built into the wall. "You thinking what I'm thinking?"

"Two-way mirror," Evelyn replied.

Terrence shuddered. "Why would he build this stuff? To watch his own family?"

Evelyn perused the old tome as they walked the hall and into the next bedroom. Terrence ran his hand across the wall, feeling for more depressions.

"Listen to this," Evelyn said, resting the heavy book in her hand. "*When I came of age, my father told me that any man can make money, but information is where true power lies. The realization dawned on me as to why he hosted so many gatherings with local and foreign businessmen. To learn of their secrets and trap them with it.* That was written by Harvard Quenby, son of Alistair, in 1867."

"So they were using these before the civil war," Terrence thought aloud. "I bet it kept them afloat after the Confederacy fell."

"Precisely." Evelyn said. "Judging by what is written in the following pages, the Quenbys were advocates of the Southern cause and had ties to many Confederate states."

Terrence absorbed the information with a serious face. "How did they treat their… you know?"

Taking a breath, Evelyn skimmed through the following pages. "Not well."

"How bad?"

Evelyn read the description. "Very. After the war ended,

they didn't want to let them go, but the law prevented the Quenbys from keeping them. It says they grabbed guns and lined them out in the field. Told them that if they wanted freedom, they'd have to run for it."

Averting his eyes, Terrence nodded to himself and went back to his search.

Evelyn closed the book and set it aside before joining her husband in his searching. They found hints of a hollow wall but avoided making another hole in the wallpaper. They tried the guest bathroom. The mirror there was also built into the wall. Despite all those, Evelyn had not discovered a doorway. Perhaps the crawlspace in their kitchen went through the whole house? She made a deal with herself to check out the billiard room before destroying the work Terrence put into securing the crawlspace.

The billiard room didn't fit with the rest of the house. It was cramped with old arcade cabinets, pachinko machines, and noisy carnival games with lots of lightbulbs. 1980s electronic devices that had been gutted for their parts sat on top of the pool table. Terrence flipped the light switch. A wave of arcade music, distorted electronic buzzing, and flashing lights screamed to life. Overwhelmed by the noise, Terrence toggled the switch again. The mansion fell silent. Evelyn found the old power brick and unplugged the various machines. She nodded at Terrence. He flipped the switch. This time only the lights came on.

Terrence wandered through. "This is some pretty cool stuff, though."

"I guess," Evelyn replied.

Terrence rapped his knuckles on one of the dusty arcade cabinets. "We should take one of these back to Detroit with us."

"If it can fit in the van," Evelyn replied.

Terrence willfully ignored the comment. "Your dad must

either be a collector or had the best childhood any boy could ask for."

Evelyn was glad they were back to talking about less serious things. Evelyn's family weren't saints. When she was an orphan, that didn't matter to her. But the more she learned, the more the Quenby history became a part of her. As a woman who paved her own way, Evelyn didn't know what to think about it. Was it her blood that defined her or her actions? She always thought it was the latter, but, thinking back to her life decisions and morally-flexible early adult years, she wondered how much of her choices were influenced by her ancestors' genetic breadcrumbs

"Come over here," Terrence said.

Evelyn followed his voice to the back of the room and found him standing before an arcade cabinet. Carved onto its side were the words *"to the book reader."*

"You think Maxwell wrote that for you?" Terrence asked.

Evelyn squatted down and brushed her thumb over the words. He had used a knife to carve it. "Help me push it."

Terrence and Evelyn pressed on one side of the cabinet and pushed. Their faces went red and Terrence's forehead vein bulged. After a moment, they gave up.

"It must be nailed to the ground or something." Terrence rubbed his shoulder.

Evelyn crouched in front of the cabinet and found a small knob on its front. She twisted and pulled it. With a click, it opened to the inside of the arcade machine. Behind the jungle of loose wires was a square hole that led into the wall and the dark corridor beyond. On her hands and knees, Evelyn squeezed inside. She found herself inside of the two-and-a-half-foot wide tunnel that was unpainted and filled with countless bent nails on both sides. Broad shouldered, Terrence could barely fit. With a grimace and a determined spirit, he made it into the walls.

Dust particles circled and danced through the air. Like thin white hair, stringy cobwebs stirred in the soft breeze. The corridor went both left and right. "Do you want to split up?" Evelyn asked.

"I don't think I'm ready to die."

Sliding sideways, Evelyn navigated the uncomfortable tunnel using the flashlight. She found a little cubby where she could peek into the guest bathroom. There was a double-sided mirror. They traveled the tunnel and reached another two-way mirror in the master bedroom.

"I feel creepy," Terrence said.

"Me too," Evelyn admitted.

They heard scurrying behind them. Terrence and Evelyn turned back in time to see the massive rat zigzagging beneath their legs and vanish in the darkness of the tunnel.

Terrence cursed and shuddered. "Yeah, I don't like this place."

Like the attic, the hidden corridor seemed to trap heat. As she moved through the upstairs, she felt like she was in a microwave. Terrence wasn't faring much better. They reached a vertical shaft that descended into the ground floor staircase and climbed to the attic. Evelyn leading, she put her hands on the foot-long rungs and lowered herself into the darkness. She held the flashlight between her teeth. Her shoulders knocked against the shaft's wall. Halfway down, a rung spun under her foot and she slid to the bottom. The impact sent a burst of pain up her feet and ankles.

"You good?" Terrence asked with concern.

"Uh huh." Evelyn winced and took the flashlight from her mouth. Her teeth hurt from biting down on it.

Terrence began his careful descent.

Evelyn stepped away from the shaft and flashed light down the corridor.

A shadowy figure watched at the very end.

"Winslow?"

The figure didn't reply. He seemed to be at the far end of the corridor.

"Zoey? Peter? Barker?" Evelyn called out.

"What is it," Terrence's muffled yell came down the shaft.

"I can't tell," Evelyn replied, looking at the stationary figure. "Let me back up there," Evelyn whispered to Terrence.

"I'm stuck," Terrence replied.

Evelyn watched the figure, seeing if he would step into her light.

He didn't move.

"Whoever you are, I demand you show yourself!" Evelyn's shout traveled down the dark tunnel.

The figure said nothing. It stood as still as a statue.

"Terrence," Evelyn barked.

"I'm trying!"

The figure took a step forward.

Evelyn took one back.

"I'm... almost... up. I'm up," Terrence yelled down the shaft.

Evelyn took another step back.

The figure took a step forward.

Evelyn lifted her foot to back up again when the figure charged her.

Before Evelyn could twist back to the rungs, the man was standing right in front of her. He wore all black and had on a featureless white mask.

Evelyn cursed aloud. "Andrew. You scared the crap out of me."

The masked figure looked down at her through the button-sized eyeholes.

"Your family is gone. You need to leave this place," Evelyn said, much crueler than she had anticipated.

Andrew reached out his gloved hand. Evelyn's back hit

the ladder's bottom rung. The man's fingers moved toward her cheek. Evelyn swiped at his hand, but it phased through.

"Stop. Now." Evelyn demanded.

"Hey, what's happening?" Terrence yelled from above her.

"It's Andrew, he's…"

With a slightly cocked head, Andrew kept on reaching until he was an inch from her cheek. Evelyn pulled her head back as far she could, knowing he could grab her and she couldn't resist.

Evelyn felt her hair stand and the presence of his finger a centimeter from her skin. Without warning, Andrew Doyle was sucked backwards. He reached both hands out to Evelyn as some invisible force pulled him away. He vanished.

Evelyn collected herself as she bounced the flashlight beam through the claustrophobic corridor.

"What the hell was he doing?" Terrence asked.

"I don't know," Evelyn replied. She felt a dreadful feeling gathering in her stomach. *Andrew Doyle is trapped here forever and he knows that...* Evelyn didn't know why, but that thought sent shivers her spine. She looked up at Terrence. "Come on. Let's keep exploring."

"You sure?"

"No, but we'll do it anyway," Evelyn replied dryly, and gave Terrence room to climb down.

As they moved through the ground floor, Evelyn found multiple places to spy into the foyer. Two holes were cut in the carpeted curved steps, allowing the peeper to look out at who was coming and going. There were a few more behind certain paintings. Evelyn realized that the compilation of vantage points created a full canvas of the foyer. There were little strings that ran up through little holes drilled into the corridor above. By pulling them, a little bell in the upstairs corridor jingled. Evelyn theorized they were for communication with the people upstairs, possibly to warn them when a guest was coming up. If they were stealing blackmail material from the guest rooms, it made sense that they'd want to have certain safety measures in place.

"Sorry it took me so long," a voice said.

Evelyn and Terrence directed their attention to Peter Calhoon, seventeen-year-old varsity football player. He was a handsome kid with a dimpled chin, nice smile, and a varsity jacket. Bound for the big leagues, Peter's father had told Evelyn. That was before his throwing hand was removed with a meat cleaver and he bled out on the spot.

"You startled us, man," Terrence said.

"I had to make sure Andrew was gone," Peter admitted. "He hasn't been the same since Mary left."

"It's only been a day," Evelyn replied.

"Yep. We're all glad she got out, but it hurts too. I liked that girl. Treated her like a sister."

"You'll join her soon," Evelyn declared. "I'll make sure of it."

"Thanks. All of us are pretty anxious to go home, wherever that may be."

Peter seemed like a normal kid if not for the bloody stump at his right wrist. Evelyn remembered seeing his death through a vision he gave her. He was bound to a wooden chair in the middle of a hay field. It only took one brutal swipe at his wrist to kill him. Evelyn still had no clue why the killer used different methods on his victims. Old man Barker was forced to drink chlorine, naked Winslow had his gut cut open, Peter lost his hand, sultry and curvy Alannah's throat was slit, and goth Zoey was impaled by a spike in the back of her skull.

"Thanks for the assist with Andrew," Evelyn said.

"I'll keep y'all safe." Peter said. "I got to make sure our MVPs finish the game."

Peter said his goodbye and vanished down the corridor.

Evelyn and Terrence kept sliding through the tight space until they reached the lounge area. The tunnel moved in a U-shape around the back of the brick fireplace. Terrence discovered a wooden sliding hatch nearby. It opened the back of a bookshelf and offered a view between two books that leaned together like a right triangle. Wearing the jade green dress that accentuated her hourglass figure, Alannah danced alone in the center of the room. Her sultry green eyes were shut, and her lips were plumps and red. Blood seeped from the opening in her throat down into her bosom.

Barker, gray-haired and wearing a sweater vest, took a puff on his pipe. Crimson leaked from his lower lip and down his chin. He wiped it away with the top of his hand.

Alannah opened an eye and looked at him. "Sure you don't want to join me?"

Barker flashed his wedding ring. "Taken."

Alannah smiled wickedly. "What happened to *till death do us part,* darling?"

Barker placed his Sherlock pipe on the corner of his thin lips. "How many years have you been trying that line on me?"

"Too many," Alannah said and kept dancing.

"You make a good point, though."

"I know, darling, but you'll still say no."

"Aye. I will." Barker replied. "I got two left feet anyhow."

Terrence backed away and found Evelyn glaring at him. "You can't still be mad that she made me touch her whatever," he said.

"I might be," Evelyn said.

Terrence's shoulders sank.

Evelyn cracked a smile.

"You're teasing me?" Terrence asked with uncertainty.

"Maybe," Evelyn replied.

Terrence opened his mouth like he was going to speak but then thought better of it.

Sometimes it was funny watching him squirm.

Evelyn continued around the back of the brick fireplace when she noticed an envelope nailed into the brick. Carefully, she removed the loose nail and opened the envelope. Inside was a small piece of paper.

"You've come this far," the note read. *"Go to pages sixty-four and twenty-eight."*

"Come on, let's find a way out of here," Evelyn told Terrence. It took them a while, but they found their way back to the billiard room. Evelyn didn't doubt that there were other exits, but she didn't have time to look for them now. Evelyn sighed when she got out of the wall. Dust covered her head-to-toe and her clothes were soaked with sweat. Terrence got two glasses of water while Evelyn searched for the appropriate page number.

Following Maxwell's instructions, she went to page sixty-four. Marian Quenby authored this portion in 1901. *"I wanted additions to the basement, so I added them. I wanted to use the chute in the basement's ceiling for something more than a place for dropping pickpocketed items, so I changed their function. After completing the tunnel, I was able to begin my work. It would be easy to bring the animals inside now and far easier to dispose of them."*

"What was he doing there?" Terrence asked.

Evelyn got a hunch and pulled up the web browsers on her phone. She researched early Adders newspapers and found a photocopy of what she was looking for: an article titled "severed hands and feet found outside of town. Bodies never recovered."

"You don't think..." Terrence voice.

"Maybe. I'm more concerned as to why Maxwell wanted us to see this page."

"The phantoms said Maxwell was innocent."

"They think he's innocent," Evelyn corrected. "They said that they could not look directly at their killer."

Terrence said soberly. "There's a lot of death surrounding this house and your family."

"Tell me about it." Evelyn massaged her forehead. "We need to find my mother."

Page twenty-eight mentioned the addition of statues in the backyard. That was where Evelyn and Terrence went next.

The sun was falling. Their search had eaten up most of their day. Crickets chirped and frogs croaked. Side by side, Evelyn and Terrence walked behind Quenby House. There were a number of raised gardens, overflowing with an unhealthy mixture of weeds and flowers. Nearby, different stone benches and statues stood about. Most of the statues were of men with their chins up high, with stone leaves to hide their private parts. There were a few women, too. Between two trees, a stone slab sported both a man and a woman, looking into each other's stone eyes and grasping each other's hands. Thin moss spotted their gray skin. Vines snaked up their legs. The woman's face had a crack down the middle while the man was short a nose. The whole scene was romantic in a creepy way.

Evelyn opened up the book and kept reading page twenty-eight. *"I added The Lovers last,"* Jonah Quenby penned. *"A visage of my wife that I eternally immortalized in stone. Though she may be gone from this world, I remain, and so will these stones."*

Evelyn glanced around the backyard, trying to figure out what her father wanted her to find. She walked around the statues, studying their rock faces that the years had faded. In the back was a copper plaque that had turned green over the years. "The Lovers," it read. Evelyn noticed that the screws were loose. She didn't need to tell Terrence to get the screwdriver. He was already on his way.

He returned and made quick work of removing the plaque. An airtight lockbox sat in the stone indentation. Evelyn popped it open, revealing another note.

"You've seen the fruit of our family. Death, lies, and ruin. I aimed to change that. To give you a better life. As you know, fate had different plans. This statue is where I professed my love to your mother. Our relationship was not orthodox, but I vowed to make it work. To start a family and to right the wrongs my ancestors had committed.

"I failed.

"Listed below is your mother's address. If you wish to know more heartache, visit her. If you want to be done with this mess, be done. Evelyn, you are your own woman. Make your choice and live with the consequences. -- Maxwell."

24

TATTERED HEARTS

Terrence stayed home as Evelyn requested.

"See if you can't learn more about Bella Day and the others," Evelyn told him as she climbed into the minivan.

"Eve, you don't need to do this alone," Terrence reminded her.

"She is my mother. I should be the one to confront her," Evelyn said with determination.

Terrence held her upper arms softly and gazed into her eyes. The shadow of The Lovers' statue cast over them. "I don't want you to shoulder this burden alone. After all we've been through, it doesn't seem right."

Evelyn studied her husband's tired and well-structured face. Hints of stubble painted his dark, gaunt cheeks. "The people in this town don't like me, but they might like you. Reach out to any of your contacts in that band you met and research old newspapers for anything that points to someone other than Maxwell as our killer."

Lips pursed, Terrence nodded. He gave her a strong hug. "I wish you luck with your mother."

"Thank you," Evelyn said quietly. Not accepting Terrence's support nagged at her, but her mind was set.

"I'll pick up a new cell phone and text you the number. Make sure we're on the same page if anything happens," Terrence declared.

After a moment, Evelyn separated herself from him, took a quick shower to wash the dust off her, and then got dressed in her black double-breasted raincoat, dark jeans, and heel-less boots. From the second-story balcony, Terrence waved her goodbye as the rusted minivan putted down the red brick path.

Lily Copperdoe, Evelyn thought with a smirk as the small farm town of Adders vanished behind her. *What a name.*

It was a grueling and anxious two-hour drive to Montezuma, Georgia. Blooming from a few families in the 1950s, Montezuma had a population of thirteen hundred plus residences. It made Adders look big in comparison. Passing through the historic downtown flanked by interconnected brick buildings and out beyond the town's borders, Evelyn found the doublewide trailer. The decorated building was tucked in the deep woods, up a winding dirt road running by rushing creek spotted with mossy rocks. Large gardens were planted on either side of the trailer. One garden produced peppers, carrots, cabbage, and other vegetables while the other had mint, oregano, and various leafy herbs. By the way the trees seemed to encircle the trailer, it seemed like this place was built deliberately away from the clutches of society.

Evelyn parked beside the tarp-covered Harley Davison motorcycle. She stepped out, listening to the sounds and cries of unseen birds. Dead bugs swirled in the shallow water of the metal birdbath. From end to end, hand-painted sunflowers decorated the trailer's front wall. The yellow petals were misshapen and the green stems bent and leaned in different directions. Still, there was something enduring about the artistic imperfections.

The isolation, the gardens, and artistry told a tale of the owner's disconnection to the world.

Evelyn knocked on the door, waiting to see if her mother truly lived here or if the ten-year-old address was a bust.

Locks clicked. A loose knob jiggled.

Hands in her coat pockets, Evelyn watched the door open.

The woman who stepped out was short and skinny with a strong posture and faded jean jacket over a tucked-in gray shirt. She had long and wiry gray hair that tumbled down her shoulders and ended at a point on her back. She had a hard leather face with timeless blue eyes amplified by black eyeliner. She looked Evelyn up and down, seeing if her guest had something to prove. After a brief moment, the home-owner's look changed from an uninvited glare to a respectable acknowledgement of a fellow woman who had also visibly walked a hard life.

"Are you Lily Copperdoe?" Evelyn asked.

The homeowner squinted at her. "Who are you, girl?"

Evelyn flashed her P.I. license. "Evelyn Carr. I'm looking for Mrs. Copperdoe. Does she live here?"

"What do you want with her?" the woman asked suspiciously.

"That's a private matter," Evelyn replied, a little harsher than she had intended.

"In my experience, people with secrets aren't to be trusted," The women stated.

Evelyn didn't know why she hesitated to say, but she did. "I'm her daughter. My maiden name is Quenby."

The woman's face went stark white. She tripped over her words and decided not to speak. Without warning, she wrapped toned arms around Evelyn and squeezed her tightly. Evelyn tensed up. She kept her arms off the strange woman. A confusing barrage of fear, anger, and joy hit Evelyn at once.

"I never thought I'd see you come home," the woman said.

Remembering all the years spent lost and alone, Evelyn pried the stranger from her body.

Shocked by Evelyn's resistance, the woman took a step back. "I'm Lily. Your..."

"Yeah," Evelyn replied. "We need to talk. Inside, preferably."

The tough woman blinked the glossiness from her eyes and recomposed herself. She stepped aside and allowed Evelyn to enter.

The house smelled of wet paint masked by cinnamon and other natural spices. A clear tarp covered the living room floor. An easel stood at the center. Paint of all colors and density splattered the white canvas: it was the beginning of some interpretive piece of art. Not only did artwork hang on the walls, but even the interior of the house was uniquely painted. One wall displayed a massive field of swaying wheat stalks. Another showed an indigo sky speckled with stars and a crescent moon. The third had tall evergreen trees blanketed by rolling vistas in the sunset. All were beautiful, unique, and imperfect. Evelyn found herself gawking. Even the ceiling had been painted with spiraling birds of different breeds and colors.

Flowers and cacti lined the windowsill. Dripping paint cans stained the wooden tabletop. More paint drops hardened on the carpet floor.

Lily leaned in the doorway, with her arms across her chest and a sincere but crooked smile on her tanned face. "It's something, isn't it?"

"I've never seen anything like it," Evelyn admitted. Standing in this drab trailer, she felt lost in another world.

"I reckon you won't ever again," Lily bragged. "Count yourself lucky. Only a handful has ever seen my work."

Apart from the disturbing mural Evelyn painted during a blackout, she struggled to draw a stick figure. If this work was truly her mother's, Evelyn counted herself impressed.

Lily walked inside and closed the door. She headed for the dented refrigerator and pulled out a foggy plastic pitcher. "Tea? It ain't that sweet stuff, but it'll stain your teeth all the same. Grew the leaves myself."

"I'm alright," Evelyn replied, studying the walls.

"Well, too bad." The woman filled two cups anyway.

She handed one to Evelyn, who cautiously accepted. Lily gestured to the wall painting of the swaying wheat. "That's my first. Truth be told, I got my inspiration from Quenby's hay field. Most of the art came from places I won't return to but are still worth remembering. I should show you around back. Have you hike the trail I cleared last spring. You'll like it."

Evelyn turned to the woman. "We're suppose to bond now like nothing's ever happened? You put me up for adoption and provided no means of contacting you. Not even your name."

A look of conviction flooded over Lily. It only lasted a second, then her normal hard demeanor returned. "You're naive if you believe the world is black and white, and every decision a mother makes is clear cut."

"You see yourself as my mother?"

"I got the scars to prove it," Lily argued.

"You weren't there," Evelyn barked, feeling years of pent-up rage boil over. "You never made an effort. You know what that's like? Feeling unwanted? Neglected for all those years?"

"Don't be a drama queen," Lily said. "You're a stronger woman for it."

"Stronger?" Evelyn chuckled in frustration. "I didn't want to be stronger. I wanted a family."

Lily shut her mouth, averted her eyes, and took a sip of her bitter tea. Evelyn paced a few steps away and faced one of the walls. She closed her eyes and listened to her rage-filled heart. It was not like how she had imagined the overdue family reunion, and she didn't know why her emotions were all out of whack. *Family. That's why.*

"I'm sorry," Lily struggled to admit. "I know those words don't mean much from an old woman you just met, but it's all I have to give you. Unlike your father, I'm not George Vanderbilt."

"Where is Maxwell?" Evelyn asked, back still turned to the stranger.

"That's a long story," Lily said. "One I'll tell, if you answer my questions."

With red-rimmed eyes, Evelyn twisted back to the woman. "You had thirty-four years to ask me anything."

"Thirty-three," Lily corrected. "Your birthday is not until the fourteenth of next month."

Evelyn was taken aback by that.

"What? You don't think I'd remember the day I brought you into this world? You were an ugly, pink screamer."

Evelyn gnashed her teeth.

"I didn't want to let you go," Lily finished.

"But you did," Evelyn replied.

"I did," the woman said.

The two women stood in silence. The soft hum of the window air-conditioner echoed through the doublewide trailer.

"Answer one of my questions, I answer one of yours. Deal?" Evelyn reluctantly negotiated.

"Deal," Lily agreed. "But I'm asking first."

Evelyn unclenched her fists in her coat pocket and waited for the woman to ask.

Lily sipped her tea. "How did you find me?"

"Out of everything you could've asked me, that's what you want to know?" Evelyn asked with hostility.

"I'm not going to scrutinize your questions. I expect you to show the same restraint."

Evelyn breathed heavily out of her nose. "Maxwell's old family journal put me on a scavenger hunt of sorts that ended at a statue in the backyard. It contained a note with your address on it."

Lily cracked a sad smile. "That's my Max. Always had a flair for the dramatic. Alright, ask away."

"Why did you put me up for adoption?" Evelyn asked.

"You're not going to like that story." Lily said, "I'll give you more than you bargained for, starting with young Maxwell Quenby and going into his disappearance. You may want to sit down."

Evelyn pulled up a wooden chair from the corner of the room and sat down, waiting for the woman to start.

ADDERS, Georgia

Spring of 1965

DRESSED in a short-sleeved blue and white tent dress, six-year-old Lily Copperdoe sat in the azure blue backseat of the classy and black 1960 Lincoln Continental. Through the window, she watched the massive gnarled branches arc overhead. The red brick path rattled their bulky vehicle. She caught an appetizing whiff of her parents' tinfoil-covered casserole next to her in the backseat.

"How are my lashes?" Alexandra Copperdoe, a scarlet-haired woman in her finest blue dress, asked her suit-wearing, stout, and balding husband, Ralph.

"Beautiful as always, dear," Ralph replied, keeping a hand on the steering wheel and his olive-green eyes on the road ahead.

Alexandra slapped his arms. "You didn't even look."

Ralph turned his head, locked eyes with his self-conscious wife, and forced a smile. "Wow, so beautiful."

Alexandra scoffed and went back to curling her eyelashes in the side mirror.

"There's the bastard's house," Ralph said as the massive, two point five story mansion came into view. Its walls were white, with small vines sprouting up a few feet around the base of the first-floor colonnades. Bowling green yard and expertly-pruned trees only bolstered the house's perfect grandiose appearance.

"You best be nice to Mr. Quenby," Alexandra reminded him sternly. "We're trying to mend bridges, not burn them, as you do so well."

Ralph squeezed the steering wheel tighter. "I'll tuck my tail between legs and cower. What a day to be a man."

They parked on the brick circle outside the mansion and the dapper-dressed house servant allowed them entry.

Lily looked up at high-domed ceiling and mural of angels. The walls, the stairs, the help, everything in the mansion dwarfed the little girl. She tugged on her father's slacks. "Why don't we have a house this big, Father?"

Ralph forced a smile. "Because Mr. Jonathan Quenby is extorting all of Daddy's money."

Alexandra elbowed her husband and spoke hastily. "Ralph, build. Don't destroy."

Ralph's false grin faded, but then instantly returned when Jonathan and Alice Quenby waltzed down one of the foyer's curved stairways. Jonathan wore a tailored suit with a scruffy blazer and Alice wore a flowing red dress. They were both beautiful people but had the same dark circles under their dark eyes

"Jonathan, Alice, you look spectacular," Alexandra exclaimed.

"You're so sweet," Alice Quenby said, taking Alexandra's hands. "Come, dinner shall be served soon."

The men shook hands. "You've been avoiding me, Ralph." Jonathan said. "I hope it's nothing I said."

"Of course not, John. Been busy."

"With the new slaughterhouse?" John asked.

"Ah, you know," Ralph replied dreadfully. "It's another venture to throw my money at."

"I can't wait to hear all about it," John replied.

"I'm sure you already have," Ralph grumbled.

Chatting, the adults walked off, leaving Lily alone in the foyer. Dressed in slacks and a sweater vest, a little boy, six years old, with a combed mop of rich dark hair and nearly black irises, entered through the foyer's back door. He stared intensely at his hands that were loosely closed together.

"Hi," the little boy said upon noticing Lily.

"Hi," Lily replied nervously. She was never good at talking to boys her age. To be honest, they scared her.

"Do you want to see something?" the boy asked.

"Um, yes," Lily replied, remembering what her parents told her about being polite to the Quenbys.

The strange boy slowly opened his hands, revealing two little eyes. Lily's jaw dropped at the fattest toad she'd ever seen sitting in the boy's hands.

"I found him in the backyard," the boy bragged with a grin. "He's a real fatty--do you want to pet him?"

Lily reached out her little fingers and brushed them across the toad's slimy and warted back. "Ew, he feels funny." Lily scrunched her nose and chuckled shyly.

The toad croaked. Lily squealed and jumped back. She felt her heart race. The boy smiled proudly.

"You want to hold him?" he tempted. "Come on. He won't bite."

Hesitant, Lily let the boy put the toad in her cupped hands. Her palms got wet and she dropped the toad. "He peed on me!"

"Gross," the boy laughed.

The toad bounced away.

"I'll show you the restroom so you can wash your hands," the boy said.

After dinner, Lily's father and Mr. Quenby became really good friends and talked about going into business together. The boy, named Maxwell, showed Lily the statues in the backyard and the secret hiding places in the mansion.

"If I had these in my house, my mom would never find me," Lily explained as they climbed into the billiard room crawlspace. She held on to Maxwell's shirt as he bravely navigated her through walls and looked into the secret eye holes where she could view his parents' room.

"Doesn't it scare you to come back here?" Lily asked him.

"A little," Maxwell replied. "But that's why it's so much fun."

When it was time to go, Lily didn't want to leave. There was so much to do at the mansion, and Maxwell was really nice.

As they drove away, Ralph said, "I guess I should start calling him boss now."

"It could've gone a lot worse and you know it," Alexandra replied.

"He could've bankrupted us, sure, but what would the great John Quenby benefit from that? No, he wants us to split our earnings in exchange for keeping the IRS from knowing about our little project. Same blackmail stunt he's been pulling for years."

"Are we coming back here again, Father?" Lily asked from the backseat.

Ralph sighed. "I'm afraid so, dear."

Lily smiled to herself.

For the next couple of years, Lily's visits to Quenby grew more frequent. Maxwell would always have some new thing to show her, like the creepy cabins in the backyard or the old cotton gin. Lily would "ooh" and "awww" at those things, but as the years went on, her real interest was in Maxwell. At fifteen, he had grown tall and handsome. But, like his parents, circles formed beneath his dark eyes. Lily was glad to call him friend. She had very few guy friends at school and none as close as Maxwell. Even if he was a little odd, like the time when he proudly showed her the dead possum.

"That's sad," Lily said when she looked at the dead animal on the forest bed. "How did it die?"

"I don't know," Maxwell said with acute fascination. "It looks like someone smashed its head."

One summer afternoon, while their parents discussed business over a game of pool, Maxwell took Lily's hand and led her outside. His palms were clammy, and he could barely look her in the eyes.

"Is everything alright, Max?"

"I, um, want you to see something," Maxwell explained. He stopped in front of The Lovers' statue.

"I've seen this before," Lily replied, unsure why Maxwell was acting so nervous. He let go of her hand.

"Yes, I know," Maxwell said. His mouth dried. "Lily, I… we've known one another for so long--as friends, and I… well, I was hoping we could--"

"Max!" Alice called from the second-story balcony.

Maxwell's eyes widened and the blood left his face. He turned to his mother.

"Your friend is here," Alice Quenby proclaimed.

The back door opened and out walked sixteen-year-old Vincent Gregory. He moved with a sort of swagger and was dressed to match the year's style. His shoulder-length brown hair was thick and heavy. His jaw was strong. Lily knew immediately that this was the type of boy that could have his pick the girls. He approached Maxwell and gave him a firm hug. "Good to see you, man."

"You too," Maxwell said with a downcast face.

He let go of Maxwell and smiled widely at Lily. "I didn't know you hung out with such pretty girls, Max."

Lily blushed and introduced herself.

Gregory turned back to Max. "I'm going swimming down at the Hole. Thought I'd give you a ride."

"We should go," Lily exclaimed. She playfully pulled at Maxwell's sleeve. "It'll be fun."

Maxwell's face had gone from pale to green. "I'm not feeling well."

"Oh," Lily said with disappointment.

Maxwell noticed. "Go ahead, Lily. Have fun."

"Really? Are you sure?" Lily asked.

"Yeah--yes. Please. Don't wait for me." Max replied with a shaky grin.

Vincent looked at Lily in a way that made her blush. "I'll show you to my car. It's a Plymouth."

Lily tucked her blonde hair behind her ear. "Cool."

"See you around, Max," Gregory said.

Maxwell wished them a good day and with sunken shoulders, returned inside.

When Lily started dating Gregory, Maxwell didn't act the same. Though he never refused to see her, Max was distant. He wouldn't talk as often or show her anything new. That didn't stop Lily from talking his ear off though. He sat on the edge of his bed and listened. Unlike Gregory, he didn't shower Lily with advice. Maxwell waited patiently and asked questions.

"Oh, you are such a good friend, Max," Lily said, hugging him.

Maxwell smiled sadly.

A year later, Ralph Copperdoe's business bombed thanks to Mr. Quenby, and Lily stopped seeing Maxwell. At the age of twenty, Gregory proposed to Lily. He was halfway through college and planning on attending med school after. Lily's parents forbade her from letting any Quenby at the wedding. Three months later, she learned that Jonathan and Alice Quenby were killed in a fatal car crash during a similar time. The brake lines were nearly cut through and snapped the rest of the way when they were speeding down a back road. The police had no suspects. Maxwell inherited the Quenby estate.

It was a stormy winter night. Adders was too far south to get snow, but that didn't stop icy slush from smacking the windows and disrupting the roads. Gregory walked inside. His hair was soaked and his nose was red. Lily grabbed a towel and rushed to him. He took it forcefully and dried off his hair.

"You okay, Vincent?" Lily asked with concern.

"I heard you saw Max today," Gregory said.

"I did," Lily admitted, taken back by Gregory's tone. "After what happened with his folks, I didn't want him to be alone."

"Ah," Gregory said.

"What's wrong?"

"Last week you saw Jackson and now you're seeing Maxwell. There's just a lot of men in your life, that's all." Gregory said, taking off his tie and avoiding eye contact.

Lily felt a flush of anger rising inside. "First of all, I met with Jackson to discuss seeing my artwork. Secondly, I'm not nagging you about all the girls you talk to."

"That's different," Gregory said, setting his rolled-up tie on the small sideboard Lily's mother had given them. The house they lived in was much bigger than they needed it to be, thanks to Gregory's parents, but most of their items were given to them by both their parents.

"Well why are you so mad all of sudden?" Lily asked. "Nothing happened with Max and I. Nothing will ever happen."

Gregory stomped to her. "That's not the point. I don't want you seeing anymore men."

Lily noticed that his eyes were bloodshot. "Have you been drinking?"

"No, and I'm sick of your backtalk."

"Sick of my--what are you talking about?"

Gregory grabbed her by the scruff of her shirt. She felt her stomach drop and fear grip her. "I work all day and come home to hear you've been out and about with a half-dozen men. I'm really not asking for too much. Just that you're faithful."

"You're hurting me," Lily said, her fear turning to anger.

"Are you going to obey me?"

"No, Vincent," Lily defied him. "I'm your wife, not your house slave."

The next thing Lily knew was that she was on the floor. Her left cheek was on fire and her eyes were watering. Vincent's hand was still raised from the slap he gave her. In his eyes was a hate she'd only seen hints of before. "You are my wife now. You're going to be held to a higher standard."

Saying no more, he marched into the bedroom.

Lily stayed on the floor, rubbing her cheek. *He's a good man,* she reminded herself. *He's only stressed out. It's only one slap.*

In the coming months, Lily learned quickly it wasn't just one slap. She would forget to wash the dishes, Gregory would slap her. She didn't fold his shirts properly, Gregory would slap her. She talked to someone he didn't approve of… the list went on.

Gregory's mood swings occurred constantly. When they were out with friends, he'd shower her with compliments, play footsie with her, and kiss her in a way that made her forget about the strife. The moment he closed the door for the night, the kind smile quickly fell away. He berated her for the condition of the house and complained that she wasn't working. Every time Gregory hit her, he struck harder. Slaps became punches. Lily felt like a prisoner in her home. When she walked outside, she felt like she was suffocating, knowing what would happen if she left the house without Gregory's permission.

One night, when they were having dinner at her parents' house, Lily called aside her father and asked him what he thought of the soon-to-be-doctor Vincent Gregory.

"He's a keeper, Lily," Ralph said. "I hurt you and your mother with my business practices, but Gregory is beholden to no man. He will go far in life."

Lily opened her mouth to tell him about how he called her names and hit her, but found she couldn't find any words. Perhaps it was out of fear of what Gregory would do when he found out. Or it was because, somehow, deep down, she still loved him.

Lily went home that night holding on to her secret.

As Gregory undressed by the bed, he said. "I like your parents. They're good company."

"Thank you," Lily replied with uncertainty. She couldn't say when it started, but she had become cautious of every word she said. Not just to Gregory, but to everyone.

"I should thank you," Gregory said.

Lily got an eyeful of his abs and muscles.

"Why?" Lily asked sheepishly.

"You did everything right tonight," Gregory said with the smile that used to make her blush. Now, it made her shiver.

He grabbed her hips. "I think we're finally ready to have children."

Fear twisted Lily's heart. "No. I don't think..."

"It's a great idea," Gregory said, completely ignoring her. "You'll finally have something to occupy your time. After my long classes, I'll be able to tuck the kid in. It's the perfect picture."

"Vincent, please. I can't." *If I have this kid, then there's no escape.*

Gregory brushed his thumb over her lips. "Of course you can. You're strong and beautiful. You'll make a great mother."

Don't believe his lies, one voice told Lily, but her heart fluttered when he complimented her for the first time in years.

"I love you," Vincent said into her ear.

"I love you, too." Did she? Lily didn't know if the response was out of fear or genuine affection.

"You so are perfect now." Vincent whispered. "We're going to be happy." He put his hand on her belly. "This child will be the joy this relationship needs. No more discipline, Lily. You don't need it anymore."

Lily could feel her rationalization fall away as her husband's words felt like life to her soul. *Run, you stupid girl!* a voice told Lily. She shut it up and made love with her husband while holding on to the smallest ember keeping the relationship alive.

Lily awoke in the dead of night and slowly crept out of bed. She got dressed and bundled up her clothes. Without saying goodbye, she left her house behind and drove to the only safe place she could think of.

Chewing her lip nervously, Lily hammered her fist on the

mansion's front door. “Please open up,” She mumbled. Minutes passed. She knocked again. Tears welled in her eyes. She couldn’t stay out here all night. She’d need to get to home.

The door opened. Black hair disheveled and eyes tired, Maxwell stood in the threshold. He was in his pajamas and had a shaggy black beard.

“Can I come in?” Lily asked.

“You’re always welcome here.” Maxwell allowed her to enter.

In the dining room with a single light on, he poured Lily and himself cups of coffee. Though it was not particularly cold inside, Lily’s teeth chattered.

With a look of concern, Maxwell waited for her to speak.

“I feel so lost, Max,” Lily admitted since the first time she’d gotten married. “It’s like I don’t know who I am anymore.”

“You’re you,” Maxwell put his hand on her own. Lily quickly pulled it away.

Lily clenched the hand he touched and stood up. “I’m sorry. Coming here was a mistake.”

“Don’t go,” Maxwell said. His eyes looked so tired. “Please.”

She glanced at the clock. It was four a.m. Vincent would be up in two and a half hours. Lily sat back down and took a sip from her steaming mug.

“Lily, what you ever tell me won’t leave these walls, I promise you.”

“It’s Vincent, he…” *Tell him, you idiot.* No words came. She forced herself to stand and started lifting up her shirt.

Maxwell cast his eyes away. “Lily, I…”

“Look,” Lily’s voice wavered.

“No. This--it’s not right.”

“Max,” Lily pleaded.

Hesitant, Maxwell cautiously glanced up at Lily. She held her shirt up just below her breasts. Misshapen purple bruises painted her flat belly. Maxwell's eyes watered and he covered his mouth with his hand.

Lily put back down her shirt. "Do you understand?"

Mouth still covered, he nodded.

"What should I do?" Lily felt her legs go weak. "I can't keep living like this."

Maxwell thought for a long moment. Lily thought he would say to call the cops. That would be the most rational thing to do. Instead, Maxwell said, "Stay with me."

"He'll be furious," Lily said fearfully.

"He'll never know."

But somehow he did, and two days later his car screeched to a stop in front of the mansion. Face blood red, handsome Vincent Gregory slammed the car door and started his march to the house entrance.

"That's far enough," Maxwell said from the second-story balcony. She could hear him from the guest bedroom and walked to the window to get a better look. Seeing Gregory sent chills down her spine. Vacation was over. Time to go home.

Gregory glared up at Maxwell. "Where the hell is my wife?"

The night Lily arrived, Maxwell parked her car behind the cotton store house far away from the mansion.

"She's not here," Maxwell said.

"You're lying, Max. If she wasn't, you'd welcome me with open arms."

That was when Maxwell pulled out the shotgun. "Go home, Vincent."

Gregory clenched both of his fists. "You going to shoot me for the woman that chose me over you? Give me a break, Max. Let me have her."

Maxwell cocked the shotgun and aimed it at him.

"Get off my property or I will kill you," Maxwell said with a scarily calm voice.

Gregory shook with rage. He opened his hands and turned back to his car. Without another word, he turned the ignition and screamed down the road.

Maxwell lowered the gun. He watched the red brick to make sure Gregory wasn't coming back and then returned inside. Lily met him on the interior balcony of the foyer.

He flipped the safety and rested the weapon on his shoulder.

"You didn't mean that, right?" Lily asked.

"I did," Maxwell replied. He brushed past her and put away the weapon.

Lily felt anxious over the next couple of days. She watched the red brick road, expecting Gregory to show up and take her back. He didn't.

A month passed. No sign of him.

Maxwell knocked on her door. She fixed her hair and opened it. Maxwell's face was stern. "There's something I want to show you."

Nervous, Lily followed him down the steps and through the hall of portraits. *Did Gregory show up when I wasn't looking? Did Maxwell kill him?* They turned into the kitchen. A tiny vanilla cake with a single lit candle sat on the kitchen island. The cake wasn't as big or as beautiful as the ones Gregory had bought her, but somehow that made it more appetizing.

"Tada," Maxwell said with a little grin.

"I don't know what to say," Lily replied.

"Make a wish before wax gets on the icing I spent all morning making."

I wish I had a different life. Lily blew out the candle.

Maxwell cut her a piece and watched her eat.

"Aren't you going to have some?" Lily said as she lifted the fork to her lips.

"This is your treat," Maxwell replied.

"I want to share with you."

"Alright, but know that I have a voracious appetite. There may not be much left when I'm done," Maxwell warned.

They traded smiles.

Maxwell served himself.

When they had finished, Maxwell said, "There's something else."

He led her out back to the statue of the two lovers. The chiseled man without a nose looked into the eyes of the stone maiden with a cracked face. "Remember this?"

"I do," Lily replied, reminded of her childhood when she was happy and actually looked forward to waking up in the morning. It seemed so long ago Lily forgot that time even existed. Until now.

"Here," Maxwell produced a gift box a little bigger than his palm.

"You're so sweet," Lily replied. "But you've done so much already."

"Open it," Maxwell said.

Feeling guilty, Lily pulled the ribbon and opened the box. Inside was a fat toad made of plastic.

"I tried catching a real one," Maxwell said. "It didn't work out."

Lily chuckled. She took out the toad and put it on the stone slab between the lovers' feet.

Maxwell looked at his toes. "Lily. I brought you here when we were fifteen, remember?"

"Yeah," *It was the day I met Vincent.*

"Do you know why?" Maxwell asked.

Lily took his hand and looked him in the eyes. "Because you wanted to kiss me."

Maxwell seemed shocked at first, and then his expression softened. "May I?"

Lily nodded.

Maxwell leaned in and planted a small kiss on her lips. He pulled away when Lily leaned in for another. Rain fell on them.

"I love you," Maxwell said, the downpour lapping against his face. "For so long, I've wanted to tell you."

Lily forgot all about her marriage to Gregory and the abuse she endured. All that mattered now was the moment.

Locked at the lips, they rushed inside and up the stairs.

Sheets of rain battered the old mansion.

It wasn't long before Lily learned she was pregnant.

"We'll make this work," Maxwell said to her, his leg slung over the side of the bed. Lying on her side, Lily pulled her pillow close to her, wishing the canopied king-sized bed would just eat her up.

"You don't get it," Lily said. "Vincent, he'll..."

"Let me worry about Vincent," Maxwell said.

"Do you even want this?" Lily asked, rolling to her side so she could face him. "I mean, we're both so young."

Maxwell smiled softly at her. He looked handsome when his hair was ruffled and his beard shaven. "More than anything."

Lily sat up and tried to rub away her migraine. "Max, I'm married."

"I know a lawyer. He handled my inheritance. I'm sure he can take care of the necessary arrangements."

"Vincent won't want that," Lily said dreadfully. "Everything is happening too fast. Maybe we can try again. Some other time."

Maxwell crinkled his brow. "What do you mean?"

Lily gave him a look.

Maxwell's eyes went wide. He stood up and paced around the room.

"It's my decision," Lily said firmly.

Maxwell stared at her like she had blasphemed. "I don't think that's fair."

Lily glanced at her belly. She was wearing one of Maxwell's t-shirts that looked like a dress on her.

"I want this family," Maxwell stated. For a brief moment, he reminded her of Vincent Gregory.

Lily's fear bubbled up. Had she fallen into the trap of another horrible man? Would this be her fate?

Maxwell took a deep breath. "For so long, I've had this emptiness inside of me."

"Since your parents died?" Lily asked.

"Way before then," Maxwell admitted. "Lily, you're the first and only person to give me peace. I understand that this child, our child, is not something you want--"

"I do want it," Lily interrupted. "But just not now. It seems like I only moved in yesterday."

"But we've known each other our whole lives. This is the logical progression of our relationship." Maxwell tried to keep a lid on his frustration, but it was building.

Lily sniffled. "Vincent will find out. He'll come to the hospital, just you watch."

Maxwell walked around in front of her and lowered to his knees. He took both her hands in his. "Then let's have the child here. No one needs to know. We can get an in-home doctor. I have all these antique toys and a dollhouse we can put in the nursery. If people ask, I can say it's my niece or something."

"How do you know it's going to be girl?"

"I don't , but I want it to be someone like you."

Lily smiled sadly at him. *I'm not as good as you think I am.*

"Will you do this with me?" Maxwell asked.

Eyes watering, Lily nodded. “Yes. I will.”

Maxwell pampered her in the months leading up to the birth. Every day, he smiled, sung, sometimes danced with her in the foyer--a skill she never knew he had. Lily tried to share his joy. The morning sickness made it hard. As promised, the doctor showed up every few weeks to check on Lily.

A few weeks before the birth, Lily heard Maxwell talking privately with the doctor in the upstairs hallway. Lily pressed her back against a corner and listened.

“You're twisting my wrist here, Quenby,” the gaunt doctor said. He was a tall, skeletal man with circular glasses, thin lips, and thinner chestnut hair. “I can't keep canceling on my patients.”

“You do this, I burn those files--the ones about the mysterious deaths.” Maxwell said. “But if you fail me or her, I'll destroy you. Do I make myself clear?”

“Crystal,” the man said with a twitching lip.

Maxwell shook his hand. “Be happy I haven't called the cops already.”

“That wouldn't be the Quenby way,” the doctor said with an angry grin.

“I suppose not.”

Lily rubbed her belly, thinking about the child and the house it was being brought into. She'd be bound to the same family that bankrupted her parents after one bad sale. Lily felt like something squeezed her heart.

Lily gave birth in one of the guest bedrooms. Her screams echoed through the hall. Maxwell watched with pure horror as Dr. Waxen performed the emergency C-second. Lily remembered the pain and the blood puddling on the bed sheets and dripping on the white hardwood floor. It seemed like the room spun. Lily clenched her eyes tight.

"Women have been doing this since the beginning. You'll make it," Maxwell said. His voice seemed faint and far away.

Suddenly, the screaming stopped. There was a soft cry. She opened her eyes and saw the pink child swaddled in a cloth and cradled in her arms. The baby looked so fragile and small, like a small breeze would break her.

"What should we call her?" Maxwell asked.

"Evelyn," Lily replied, relieved the worst of it was over. "It means life."

"Evelyn it is," Maxwell said with a tired smile.

After Lily had recovered and Maxwell burned the doctor's old case files, they stared at the child sleeping in the nursery's crib.

"She looks a lot more like you," Maxwell said.

"Maxwell," Lily said seriously. "I think we should put her up for adoption." Lily cut him off before he could protest. "I'm twenty-two years old. I know I sound like a broken record, but it's just too much."

With a heavy frown, Maxwell said. "Let me raise her. You can leave and visit if that's what you want."

"Vincent will find out, and he'll hurt you," Lily said.

"I don't care," Maxwell replied.

"He'll hurt me and her."

"He won't," Maxwell said with determination.

Lily showed him the letter she fetched from the mailbox that morning. "It's from Vincent. He wants his child back."

"His child?" Maxwell asked suspiciously. "Lily, what does he mean?"

"It means she's not safe," Lily said. "You're not safe."

"I can fight back," Maxwell argued.

"It's not just Vincent," Lily replied. "It's the lies, the blackmail, everything that your family does."

"And you think I'm like them?" Maxwell said with offense.

"Aren't you? I saw what you did to that doctor."

"That was different."

"It was the deceit and constant threats that got your parents killed. How do I know the same won't happen to you? Your loneliness kept you safe because you had no weakness. Now, you have me and you have Evelyn. She could be out one day and some vengeful person from your past could take her. Use her against you."

"I can change," Maxwell's said. "It may take time, but I can get rid of my family's evil, if that's what you want."

"Put her up for adoption, Maxwell," Lily begged. "Not for my sake, but for hers."

For the first since she had chosen Vincent over him, Maxwell looked sick with grief. "I know she needs to be with good people..."

"That's not us," Lily affirmed his words. She felt guilt crushing her.

Without a word, Maxwell left the nursery. Lily looked down at the child and wept. "It's better this way," she whispered.

EVELYN GNASHED her teeth and looked at her hands. The AC buzzed. The trailer's painted walls seemed to close in. Evelyn wanted to smash something.

"Maxwell listened to me." The gray-haired woman refilled her iced tea. "He wasn't mad, but... broken. I couldn't live with myself because of it. I couldn't live with him because of it. So, the night after the adoption, I packed my bags and left him. Left Adders. Never remarried. Never made myself beholden to another man. I became my sole provider."

Evelyn's heart raced. She couldn't bring herself to face the woman.

"Maxwell changed, as he promised he would. It took a

few years, but he cleaned up his family name. But it came a little too late. After people started going missing, old and new enemies teamed up to bring him down."

"What do you mean?" Evelyn asked.

Lily smiled crookedly. "It's my turn to ask a question, remember?"

Evelyn huffed and gestured for the woman to ask.

"Do you hate me?" Lily asked.

Evelyn thought about it. "No."

"Why," Lily scrutinized.

"Because I choose not to," Evelyn replied sincerely. "Now, tell me what happened to Maxwell, and why there are the bones of five people in my basement."

25

PARTY OF FIVE

"Human bones?" Lily asked with a horrified expression.

"You don't know about them?" Evelyn asked.

"No, I… that can't be true," Lily said.

"It is." Evelyn replied. *I talked to the victims.* "The killing stopped after Maxwell vanished."

"It wasn't just the killings that ceased," Lily replied. "Maxwell stopped visiting me too."

Evelyn pinched the bridge of her nose. She glanced up the painted mountain vista on the wall and then at her mother. "Maxwell visited you after your separation?"

Lily set her glass aside and rubbed her eye. "He did. Once a year."

"Do you remember the dates?" Evelyn asked.

Lily opened a lap stand drawer and withdrew a small notepad. She flipped through pages of notes and doodles. "I like to keep track of things, otherwise I might forget." After a few moments, Lily found the page and handed the notebook to Evelyn. The visitation days took place between 1998-2002. Wide-eyed, Evelyn scoured her own notes.

"No way," Evelyn said.

"What is it?" Lily asked.

"The murders all took place during the days he visited you."

"That means he couldn't have murdered those people," Lily thought aloud.

"Maxwell's innocent," Evelyn declared. "I can't believe it."

The phantoms were right. It was a setup. Someone planted the bodies in the basement. Someone who knew the house and its secret passages. "You said new and old enemies worked together to bring Maxwell down. How did that happen?"

"Rumor says there was a break-in, but you won't find that in the news. The people who attacked Maxwell acted quickly and efficiently, making sure there was nothing left of him."

"Who are these men? I need names."

"I have none to give," Lily replied. "I've been out of Adders for too long to keep track of the movers and shakers. They had enough clout to bury the violent nature of Max's disappearance, so that says something about the social standing."

"One of the men who attacked Maxwell could be the real killer. He may have directed the attention onto Maxwell for the perfect getaway. After all, the majority of the town still believe Maxwell killed those people and is attacking again. We need to prove it to them that Maxwell is innocent by finding the real killer."

"You speak as if Maxwell is still alive," Lily said.

"That's because he is."

Lily's leathery face turned pale.

"I saw him," Evelyn admitted. "He stopped the man who was trying to kill me."

"All these years..." Lily's voice trailed off. Her eyes glossed over.

Evelyn leaned forward in her seat. "That's why I came

here, Lily. With the hope that you could help me find him, and, in light of this new revelation, save him from the false accusations. Can you help me?"

Lily gingerly approached Evelyn. "I want to. More than anything, but what can I do?"

Evelyn stood up. "I don't know, but there must be something."

Lily looked at Evelyn with a sad smile. "You're tall like him, you know that? You have his gusto, too. Evelyn, you aren't the woman I imagined you to be."

Evelyn listened to Lily speak.

"You're much better than that. Much better than me. I can't give you anything you don't already have."

"Come home with me. We'll finish this. Together," Evelyn declared.

Lily looked around the room, the painting on the wall, the spiraling birds painted on the ceiling. "This is my home now. I'm sorry, Evelyn. But I'll only weigh you down."

"Mom," Evelyn's voice cracked.

Lily wrapped her arms around her daughter. Evelyn returned the embrace. "I said I forgave you. Return with me. I'll let you meet my husband. I can take you to my crappy apartment in Detroit. For the first time in our lives, we can be a family."

Lily pulled away from Evelyn. "I broke your father. I won't break you, too."

"You think I'm still that fragile infant?" Evelyn chuckled with frustration.

"I'm your mother," Lily said firmly. "To me, you'll always be that fragile infant."

She could see in her mother's tired blue eyes that her mind was set. Evelyn cracked a smile. "At least I can tell Terrence where I got my stubbornness."

"That's his name?" Lily asked.

"It is."

"Is he a good man?"

Evelyn nodded.

Lily stopped herself from crying too much. She hugged her daughter a final time. Evelyn said her goodbyes and walked out the trailer. Her mother watched her from the doorway with her arms crossed over her jean jacket and her eyes wet with tears. As Evelyn escaped down the dirt and wooden road, she saw her mother close the door to her trailer and Evelyn's life.

During the drive back, Evelyn listened to the clacking of her tires on the road. She thought about Lily's story and the timeline. Dr. Gregory, the man that had paid Terrence's medical expenses, had been kind to Evelyn since their first meeting. Was he really Lily's husband? She didn't know what to think of it. Another clue from Lily's recollection came to mind as well. Dr. Waxen, the gray-haired skeletal practitioner who questioned if Evelyn was the killer. By the way he licked his thin lips, he was hoping she was, and for some other reason than turning her in.

Evelyn shuddered. She focused on the road. It would be another long two-hour ride to Adders.

It was dark as she rumbled down the red brick path to Quenby House. It would be a night of strategizing, she knew. With Lily unable to help her with Maxwell, all of her hopes for finding him were up in the air. Worse, there had been no news of nine-year-old Bella Day. The phantoms were convinced that her vanishing was connected to the killer, but without any more bodies or missing people showing up, Evelyn wasn't quite sure. Moreover, the killer was patient, only killing once a year and only on the days Maxwell was away. Evelyn might be in this for the long haul. *I sure hope not.*

Quenby House cast its glow from its rectangular

windows and stood as a beacon in the darkness. She guessed that Terrence was nervous when he was alone and left all the lights on. It was kind of a sweet thought.

But that was when Evelyn noticed something was wrong.

Five cars were parked out front of the mansion, forming the edges of the brick circle. Going from left to right, there was a new Lexus the color of champagne, a red sports car, a BMW convertible, and two cruisers owned by the sheriff's department. Evelyn parked in the center of them and stepped out. A breeze howled in the night. The tall trees beside Quenby swayed. Their branches clawed at the air. An unseen owl screeched. A cloud drifted over the near-full moon.

Five figures stood silhouetted on the second-floor exterior balcony, in the same place where Terrence had waved her goodbye.

"Mrs. Carr!" A familiar voice shouted. "Glad you could join us!"

"Sheriff?" Evelyn called out to the silhouettes. "What are you doing here?"

Another voice said, "We decided to stop on by and enjoy a meal. Welcome you to Adders, officially."

Evelyn tried to recognize the voice. "Mayor Timberland?"

"Indeed," the shadowy figure replied. "I know we got off on the wrong foot the last time we spoke. I thought I'd make amends. Ordered y'all the best barbecue Adders has to offer."

Evelyn locked her car. She felt her skin crawl. "Where's Terrence?"

"He's inside," Timberland said. "Come on in. He's been waiting for you all night."

"I appreciate getting invited into my own home," Evelyn said sarcastically.

"You're funny and cute!" Deputy Painter shouted. He had the strongest twang out of all the men on the balcony. "Come on in and get yourself something to eat. That BBQ will have you carnivorous."

Evelyn remembered how the deputy had checked her out at the station and insulted her while she was looking into Bella Day's disappearance. She wondered what other predators lay in wait for her. "Tell me who else is up there."

"You'll see when you get inside."

Evelyn set her jaw. She felt her pulse quicken as she headed for the front door. It was moments like this that made her wish Maxwell hadn't taken her weapons.

She stepped into the foyer. The chandelier lights were turned on low, giving the room and its red carpeted floors a dim glow. Oil paintings of Quenby lands hung on the walls. Soft blues music drifted through the house. The acoustics in the place drowned out the singer's words. With a loud thud, the door shut behind Evelyn. Guest chatter sounded on the walkway overhead. The outside balcony door must've been open.

Evelyn followed the music, masking her footsteps in silence. She approached the dining room. Light spilled from the ajar door. Evelyn stretched her arm out and wrapped her fingers around the glass doorknob. Holding her breath, she stepped into the room. A three-arm candlestick stood at the middle of the covered twelve-person table. More flame-shaped lightbulbs illuminated the room from candles lining both walls. Oil paintings of great forests, farmlands, valleys, and rivers hung nearby them.

Back to Evelyn, Terrence slouched forward in a chair. He wore a baby blue button-up spotted with tic-tac sized violins. A blob of light reflected off the back of his shaven head. Lying on the table in front of him were aluminum tubs of steaming BBQ. It didn't look like Terrence was breathing.

Evelyn loomed over her husband's back. "Terrence?"

Quickly, he turned back to her. His hazel eyes were bloodshot. He had a new phone in his hand. "Eve."

Evelyn let herself breathe. "What's going on here?"

"I'm putting my old contacts into my phone," he flashed the replacement, a cheap-looking flip phone.

"Why didn't you tell me you had guests?"

"They just showed up. I don't know. I was about to--"

Voices and laughter echoed through the halls. Terrence straightened his posture. He and Evelyn turned back to the door.

"Be careful, darling." a woman's voice said.

Evelyn and Terrence glanced at Alannah Gimmerson. The curvaceous woman had blood pouring from her neck into her revealing glossy green dress. Zoey, clad in black, was there along with star player Peter Calhoon, old James Barker, and naked and seething Winslow.

The houseguests neared.

Terrence's lips parted nervously as he anticipated the meeting of the party of the dead and party of the living. "Go away," he whispered to the phantoms.

Evelyn directed her attention on Alannah. "What do you mean *be careful?*"

"Evelyn," Sheriff Yates stated as he stepped inside the dining room.

Evelyn quickly turned to him.

The sheriff bounced his gaze between them. "You look like you've seen a ghost."

Evelyn quickly glanced behind her. The phantoms had vanished.

Deputy Painter, mid-thirties, steel-colored five o'clock shadow, shark eyes, and wearing a green uniform topped by a black felt hat, entered behind him. He stank of cigarettes. He smirked at Evelyn and wouldn't even look at Terrence.

Mayor Timberland had clear skin, dark brown hair,

squinted eyes, and a rectangular head. He wore a three-piece suit with golden, diamond-studded cufflinks that he fiddled with every few minutes. "The last time I came here, Maxwell Quenby tried to blackmail me. Funny how times change."

"I wouldn't know," Evelyn replied. "I never met the man."

Mr. Calhoon, a middle-aged version of his son with the same dimpled chin, dashing looks, and silky hair, followed the mayor. "I was telling Terrence that I had no clue you were Maxwell's girl."

"It didn't pertain to your son's case," Evelyn replied.

By the way Mr. Calhoon's face suddenly sank, it was obvious he didn't believe her.

The final guest was Dr. Vincent Gregory. He was a tall man with a handsome face and brown hair striped with white. With a guilty expression, he humbly nodded to Evelyn. "I apology for the spontaneity of this visit, but you'll be glad we came."

"I'm famished," Mayor Timberland said and took a seat near the head of the table.

He gestured for Terrence to sit at the end seat.

"I couldn't," Terrence replied.

"As mayor, I say you do as you're told."

"In that case." Smiling, Terrence claimed the end seat. Evelyn sat next him, opposite of Timberland and Sheriff Yates. Dr. Gregory sat down beside Evelyn and, with great disappointment, Deputy Painter sat next to Gregory.

"Let's eat," Sheriff Yates said, setting his coffee thermos next to his plate.

Evelyn and Terrence traded looks and then dug in. The barbecue was tender that it nearly melted in her mouth. Evelyn, of course, didn't take a bite until the rest of the guests had. Calhoon and Terrence talked football. The sheriff and the deputy talked about the women in their life. Evelyn ate quietly with Gregory, the man that beat her mother.

"Why did you come here?" Evelyn asked him, not doing well to hide her hostility.

Gregory lowered his fork. "It's a surprise."

"I don't like surprises," Evelyn replied.

"Neither do I," Gregory took a bite.

Evelyn whispered. "I'm going to ask you this, because you've been nothing but kind to me since I arrived. Why did you beat Lily Copperdoe?"

Gregory stopped his fork from going into his mouth. He gently put it back on his tray, but Evelyn could see something had scared him. "That's a ridiculous accusation."

Evelyn glared at him. "I heard it from Lily's own mouth. Now answer my question."

Gregory looked at the sauce-slathered pulled pork on his plate. "I was not a pleasant young man, Evelyn. Not that it's an excuse, but I had a lot of pent-up stress from college, my parents, and the idea of a lifelong commitment to one woman. I needed to feel in control again. I saw Lily for the woman I wanted to her to be, not the woman she was. It was a...challenging thing to overcome."

"Hitting women?" Evelyn berated.

Gregory turned to her. His handsome eyes were soft and vulnerable. "That was over thirty years ago. I'm fifty-nine and a lot smarter and a lot less impulsive. Nothing I say will make you believe I sincerely regret what I did to your mother, so I hope that my actions will speak for a penitent heart."

"How long have you known I was her daughter?" Evelyn asked.

"The moment I heard your last name. Maxwell had only ever been with one woman," Gregory said. "You turned out beautifully, if I might say. Wherever Maxwell is, I'm sure he would be proud."

Lily said that Gregory wore two faces. The friendly face

while outside and the abuser behind closed doors. Had he earnestly changed or was this the same charm he used to seduce her mother?

"Hey," Sheriff Yates said with a mouthful. He addressed Terrence and Evelyn. "There was a big breakthrough in the Doyle case."

Terrence and Evelyn exchanged a look.

Terrence smiled back at the sheriff. "Really? What's that?"

Yates cleared his throat. He was still in uniform and perhaps still on the clock. "A few hunters--local good ol' boys--were in that woods, the ones a few miles behind her property, and happened upon a cabin."

"Oh," Terrence said, getting sweaty. "Out there?"

Evelyn pursed her lips. *Terrence, you're such a bad liar.*

Yates and Painter nodded in unison. "Found a few of the Doyles' things and what appeared to be skull fragmentation and brain matter. Bloody business."

Deputy Painter leaned in. "We think someone or something got them."

Evelyn heart fluttered. "Who?"

Yates stopped mid-chew. After a moment, he said. "Don't know. The two of you are okay. That's what matters."

Something about the way Yates said it made Evelyn suspicious. She could tell Terrence was thinking the same thing.

"Any developments on who killed my son?" Mr. Calhoon asked.

"I'm sorry, no," Evelyn replied.

"Looking into a serial killer?" Mayor Timberland asked. "That sounds like dangerous work for a private investigator."

"Someone has to do it," Evelyn replied. "It's usually not the first person you guess. My father Maxwell picked up some heat during the preliminary investigation a decade ago, even though the evidence didn't point at him."

The air seemed to leave the room.

Mr. Calhoon spoke up. "I think the discovery of bones in his basement makes it pretty clear how involved in the murders he was. With evidence like that, it almost makes me wonder why you're looking into this case."

"I want to help people find closure."

"Oh, so that's it?" Calhoon asked with sarcasm.

"Hey, chill out," Terrence told him. "We're after the same thing you are: the truth. We don't want misconstrued evidence to fit our idea of the killer. We want a concrete testimony. Something to close this case for good."

Evelyn patted his knee. *Well said.*

"You know," Mayor Timberland said, dipping the tips of his napkin into his water glass and wiping his jowls. "I always loved this house. It's Adders' private castle. Seventeen rooms, not counting the attic or basement, the place is a palace. Maybe even the last surviving one in Georgia."

The change of topic caught them all off guard, it seemed.

Evelyn smiled falsely at the mayor, not forgetting how he kicked her out of the town hall for simply being Maxwell's daughter. His friendly facade was not fooling anyone. Evelyn glanced around the rest of the table. Yates, Painter, Timberland, Gregory, and Calhoon. Evelyn realized that she trusted none of these men, and even less so when they were together. They were similar ages, but what drew them together? A lifelong friendship, a similar goal, or a common enemy? She glanced at Terrence. Even he was acting odd tonight. Why?

Mayor Timberland pushed his polished plate away. "I suppose it's time to tell you the nature of our visit, Evelyn."

The men nodded in agreement. Even Calhoon, though he was still visibly angry.

Evelyn familiarized herself with the door in case anything unexpected happened. Alannah's words replayed in her mind. *Be careful. Be careful. Be careful.*

"And what's that, Mayor?" Evelyn asked as politely as she could, though it still came out scrutinizing.

"The Quenby House has been here back when this town was nothing but a trade post, a creek, and couple of lousy cattle pastures," Timberland started. "Now your family hung on to this place like a root on a cliff. Never letting go. Scared to. After your father's passing, the Quenby plantation has been in purgatory, so to say. Speaking on behalf of all of your guests tonight, we would like to change that."

"What are you suggesting?" Evelyn asked.

"We want to buy the property."

Evelyn wasn't expecting that. "Why? It's not finished."

Dr. Gregory smiled at her. "That won't be an issue."

"I work in the carpentry business," Mr. Calhoon said. "I have people that can correct the damages for a fraction of what you would be spending."

Terrence looked at Evelyn. There was excitement in his eyes.

Mr. Calhoon pulled out his checkbook from his suit jacket's inner pocket. "The others and I have pooled our money together. We can write the check right now, and you'll have the money in your account by the time you get home. To Detroit, if I've heard correctly."

Evelyn opened her mouth to speak but Terrence cut her off. "How much are you offering?"

"For the house, the land, and everything in between," Mayor Timberland locked eyes with Evelyn. He bounced a pen on his checkbook. "Two point five million dollars, right here, right now, but you both leave tonight."

26

THE BUYERS

Evelyn couldn't believe it. She stared at the blank check and thought about the posh houses in Birmington, outside of Detroit. The timing to start her family never seemed right. That money, even after the IRS knocked them down a few pegs, would give them more than enough breathing room. The ghosts. The murders. All the BS she'd dealt with since she arrived in Adders would be nothing but a bad memory. Maybe the house and the items within were worth more than the two and a half million dollars combined, but this money was sitting in front of her.

Seated at the head of the table, Terrence covered his mouth. By how his face contorted, he was hiding a huge smile.

Evelyn studied the men around the table. They watched her anxiously.

"Why?" Evelyn asked.

The mayor looked confused.

"Why do you want the house?" Evelyn asked.

Mayor Timberland bounced his eyes between his business partners. "Adders needs to expand. Expansion comes from publicity. Publicity comes from tourism. We're going to restore Quenby to its former glory and make it into our very own Biltmore. Families, children, foreigners from all over the world will come to our Podunk town to witness the life of an Antebellum-era plantation owner. Workers in the cotton field. Balls in the foyer. Costumes. Gift shops. A wholly unique experience in my backyard. Some might find the whole recreation offensive, but all history is."

Sheriff Yates set aside his coffee thermos. "Your family name, Evelyn, will be immortalized. Quenby House will be advertised on every billboard in the surrounding hundred miles. How cool is that?"

"Frankly," Deputy Painter said, clicking his tongue on the roof of his mouth. "I think we're paying you too much for it, but after ten years of sitting on our thumbs, we want to make some profit off this ruin, and we're willing to pay to do so."

Evelyn glared at them. "If it's only about the money, then why the hell do you need me and my husband out of here? Tonight?"

Mr. Calhoon spoke up. "Because you're a problem."

"Excuse me?"

"Yeah," Calhoon continued. "You've stirred up more trouble in this town since you arrived that we haven't seen since--big surprise--your father was around."

"I'm doing everything in my power to help you, Mr. Calhoon," Evelyn objected. "To help your son find rest."

"My son is dead and gone, thanks to your father," Calhoon retorted. "The only way you can help Peter is by getting the hell out of Adders and never coming back."

Evelyn thought of the other phantoms in her house. Their wounds. Their families. Evelyn wasn't the problem. She was their salvation.

"My father is innocent," Evelyn said to the men.

"This really isn't about your father," Dr. Gregory said calmly.

Evelyn boiled. "It has everything to do with my father, and if any of you think I'll just take your money and forget about the lives that were lost and broken, you don't know anything about me."

Terrence slowly stood up. "Eve, babe, can we discuss this. Privately. Please."

Evelyn turned to her rational husband and forced herself to calm down. After everything she'd put him though, she needed to hear him out even if she had no intention of listening. Without a word, she followed Terrence out of the room.

He turned back to the men. "I'm sorry, gentlemen. It's been a rough couple of day, but, um, don't write us off yet."

Leaving the door cracked, he stopped in the stubby hallway that connected to the back of the foyer and rubbed both hands up his sweaty bald head. "Evelyn. I love you, but… holy crap. You may have just cost us the biggest payday of our lives."

"Listen to me, Terrence. The same night my mother confirmed that Maxwell is innocent and was attacked in his home by his enemies is the same night that these five men decide to show up and buy our mansion. Doesn't that seem a little off to you?"

Terrence nodded a few times. "Yeah. Yes. It does, but-- Evelyn, do their motives really matter when it comes to that type of money? This is the moment we've been waiting for since we came down here."

"What about the phantoms? We just condemn them to this mansion until the end of time?"

Terrence grabbed her upper arms gently. "We didn't do anything to them. Your father didn't do anything to them. Our hands are clean, Evelyn. Alannah, Zoey, hell, even Bella

Day are not our responsibility. They were never our responsibility."

Evelyn glared at him. "Then who will help them?"

Terrence shrugged. "I don't know. God? We aren't the liaison for the dead. We're two normal, married people who want to start a family. Isn't that what you want?"

Evelyn cast down her eyes. "I do, Terrence, but…"

"No buts," Terrence said. "If you really, truly want that, then let's take the money and run while that's still an option."

He brushed his hand down her cheek. "I've been your wingman since we came down here. Largely because I know how much learning about your father and helping people means to you. Let me have a chance to take the lead."

"So we leave?" Evelyn asked rhetorically. "And everything we've done down here means nothing?"

Terrence pointed to the cracked open door. "That check is not nothing. That's the end of all of our problems. Unlike Mary Sullivan and the others who made us sleepwalk, crashed our van, forced you to see how they died, have done nothing to aid our investigation, and overall made our lives a living hell. In the nicest way possible, I say screw 'em. If they're that desperate to go home, they can find a new champion."

Evelyn glanced over and saw Alannah, Zoey, Peter, Barker, and Winslow standing in the hall a few feet away.

Terrence's eyes went wide, and he slowly turned to them. He gulped as they stared at him with lifeless eyes.

Barker puffed on his pipe. Thick blood leaked from his lip like sap. "He's right."

"You can't possibly believe that?" Alannah said with shock. "How else will we get out?"

Barker took another puff. "I don't know, but it might be time to explore our options elsewhere."

Peter's glance bounced between Evelyn and Terrence.

"Mary was the strongest out of all of us. She kept the two of you bound to this place. Now that she's gone, nothing is stopping you from walking away. It's not something we want, but it's your lives."

Winslow muttered something and sniffled.

Evelyn looked to Zoey. The fifteen-year-old goth girl crossed her arms. "I thought you were different. I thought you actually cared. I guess I was wrong. What a stupid girl I am."

Terrence took a deep breath. For the first time, he didn't look intimidated by the dead. "Evelyn. We helped who we could. Let's go home."

Evelyn stood still. She looked at Zoey and let the cogs in her mind spin.

"An opportunity like this might never come up again," Terrence replied.

"Terrence," Evelyn said and looked to her husband with a sad smile. "I can't just walk away."

"You can," Terrence begged.

Evelyn forced herself to say the next few words. "I'm the sole inheritor. It's my decision."

Dread sank Terrence's face. "Evelyn, please don't do this. I'm asking you as your husband."

Evelyn took a deep breath. She turned around and entered the dining room. The men stopped their quiet chatter and directed their attention to Evelyn. Terrence lingered in the doorway behind her.

"Well, Mrs. Carr?" Timberland asked and held the pen over the blank check. "Have you come to your senses?"

"At this time, I will not be selling Quenby House," Evelyn said.

Terrence covered his face with his palm.

Silence lingered in the room. The candlelight on the table flickered. One of the wicks burnt out, leaving behind a tiny wisp of smoke. Mayor Timberland looked disappointed and angry, Mr. Calhoon's face was red with rage, Deputy Painter shook his head, Sheriff Yates appeared unfazed, and Dr. Gregory, with glassed-over eyes, had a small, disappointed smile on his face.

Mayor Timberland closed his checkbook and put it back into his suit jacket. Chair legs screeching against the floor, he stood up and straightened out his clothes. He locked eyes with Evelyn. "Enjoy your evening, Mrs. Carr. We won't be seeing each other again."

He turned to the door and gave Terrence a nod. "Mr. Carr."

The other men followed the mayor's lead. Deputy Painter mumbled a few curses under his breath. The rest didn't say anything. Evelyn followed behind them, watching them back out their vehicles and, one by one, vanish down the red brick road.

Evelyn stood outside and hugged herself, listening to the soft breeze, rustling of leaves, and chirping crickets. Maybe it was the wrong decision? Maybe she was a mad woman for not accepting? She'd questioned her own sanity from time to time and wouldn't be surprised if she'd finally lost it completely. *It was your estate, your choice.* Her internal justifications meant nothing. Evelyn slumped her shoulders and returned inside. She closed and locked the front door behind her. The plastic sealing the nearest window flapped in the wind, reminding her just how vulnerable her house was.

Zoey approached her under the dim chandelier light. It cast its odd multi-tier shadow over the goth in blobs. "You've managed to piss off the mayor, sheriff, and your doctor all in the same night. Impressive."

With apathetic eyes, Evelyn looked at the goth teenager. "You don't need to remind me."

Zoey opened her mouth but struggled to say the words. "I

know what you did wasn't easy, but all of us are grateful for it. You really are making a difference."

"Tell my husband that," Evelyn replied, heading for the light switch.

"I mean it," Zoey followed her up the curving stairs. "No one will ever know what you did for us, but I have a feeling that when we pass onto the other side, we'll remember the sacrifice you made."

"Goodnight, Zoey." Evelyn said, effectively ending the conversation. She didn't want to be reminded of the millions of dollars and the marriage she just flushed down the toilet. Toggling off every light switch she came across, Evelyn eventually made it to the master bedroom. Terrence sat at the edge of the king-sized canopy bed, staring intensely at his open hands. The nearest window was open and allowed the cold wind to flow into the room.

Evelyn closed the door and began to disrobe for her evening shower.

Terrence didn't bat an eye.

Stopping in the bathroom's doorway, Evelyn turned to him. She didn't know what to say. An apology would be disingenuous. A verbal reaffirming would further draw a wedge between them. Asking if he was alright would be futile, seeing that she knew the answer. She felt like she needed to say something.

The breeze gave her goose bumps.

"What can I do to make this up to you?" Evelyn asked him.

Terrence broke his stare but didn't looked at Evelyn. He spoke softly. "Tomorrow… I'm going to go through the catalogs we made when we first got here and see if I can't get a few buyers."

"What about the case?" Evelyn asked, rubbing her upper arm.

"That's your baby," Terrence replied. "I'll be more useful doing work here. Our month stay is almost over, and if we're going to start paying for electricity and water here, we're going to need some money. A lot of it. The antiques are our solution."

Evelyn bit the inside of her cheek. She breathed in through her nose and didn't let it out until the bathroom door was closed behind her. She climbed into the bathtub and turned on the showerhead. Jets of hot water punched her skin. She felt the deep grooves in her back, remembering her car "crash."

It was years ago. She hadn't been sleeping, or eating for that matter. The case was getting to her. A kidnapping of a fourteen-year-old screw-up. No one cared the girl was gone. No one cared what her piggish abductor was doing to her as he slowly turned her from a lost girl to a streetwalker.

The case wasn't going anywhere. Worse, the pimp knew that someone was after him. Evelyn went to his hideout: a nine-story tenement built on vices. She curled her white knuckles around her baton's grip. Her plan was already in motion. The message she sent had been received by the girl, or so said the big-hearted streetwalker that Evelyn had befriended during the investigation. Evelyn just hoped the girl was packed and ready to go the moment the apartment door swung open. There would be no police this time. Not when they were making money off the pimp's trade. With the balled point of the baton, she knocked on the matte-gray and chipped door. No response.

Evelyn waited, feeling her heart rate quicken. She pulled out her lock-picking tools and started to work on the lock. Within moments, she was inside. The place reeked. Trash and old food littered nearly every surface. Evelyn waded through the ankle-deep garbage. Just the idea that a human being could live here had her queasy. Keeping her baton out and moving quietly, she navigated the apartment. Evelyn approached the bedroom door. She pushed it open and found the girl lying on the bed. Two large, hand-shaped bruises ringed around the fourteen-year-old's neck. Peeking out of her purple lips was a folded piece of paper about the size of that found in a fortune cookie. Hesitant, Evelyn approached the girl's cold cadaver. A piece of Evelyn died when she withdrew the paper.

"Hope is on the way," it read in Evelyn's handwriting. The word *hope* was crossed out and replaced with *death.*

Evelyn balled it up and put it in her pocket. Carefully and without disturbing anything else, she walked out of the apartment, down the emergency flight of stairs, and vomited her lunch on the alleyway's floor. She wiped her red eyes and hopped into her crappy sedan. When she looked in the rearview mirror, she saw the dead girl. Completely unwanted and wasting away in an apartment full of trash. Evelyn stomped the accelerator and raced down the dark, wet road. As the RPM climbed, the semi-truck's high beams grew brighter. Right as it was about to pass by her, Evelyn made a split-second decision and swerved in front of it.

Metal and bone crunched.

Lights out.

Marinated in twisted metal and her own blood, Evelyn was shocked to see she was alive. Even more shocked, someone had gotten her out of the car and had taken her hand.

"Help is on the way," the dark-skinned stranger said. "Hold on."

He kept her awake until the paramedics arrived.

"You should be dead," they told her.

Evelyn didn't reply. She knew they were right. The man, Terrence, visited her during the recovery process. He was the only one who did, and Evelyn knew she wanted to spend the rest of her life with him.

Evelyn found herself standing under a cool shower. She must've used up all the hot water. She stepped out and dried off with a towel. The mirror was too fogged up to look at her reflection. Perhaps that was a good thing.

She walked into the master bedroom. Terrence was not there. Keeping her towel wrapped around her, she walked through the room and peered into the hallway. The lights were off.

"Terrence?" She stepped out and turned into the closest bedroom. Snoring softly, Terrence slept on a twin bed. Evelyn shut the door and retired, alone, on the master bedroom's king-sized mattress.

Evelyn watched the sun come up. Its beams grew over her face, causing her to squint.

Bella Day had been missing four days now.

Getting dressed, Evelyn headed down the hallway. She saw Terrence doing what he said he would: reviewing the pictures they had taken of various antiques and comparing them to similar items online. He glanced up at Evelyn.

"I'm heading out," Evelyn told him.

"Be careful," Terrence replied.

"Thanks. I love you."

Evelyn turned to walk away.

"Evelyn," Terrence called out.

Evelyn twisted back quickly.

"I love you, too," Terrence replied.

Evelyn climbed into the minivan. She took a deep breath and deliberated which of the men she would follow first. It didn't seem like a coincidence those specific five men wanted her gone. Were they all part of her father's disappearance or was it just one of them? Perhaps one of them had ties to the killer? The faster she found that person, the faster the phantoms would go away. As much as she'd like to dedicate her time in searching for her father, there was too much land to cover and not enough hints. Also, since he was innocent, that meant that he didn't have Bella Day. If there was a priority, it was her safe recovery. A dangerous amount of time had passed since her disappearance. Evelyn would much rather save a living girl than avenge a spirit.

Out of all the men, the easiest man to track would be Mr. Calhoon. Evelyn parked a block from his house. He marched out of the front door and kissed his wife goodbye, but it seemed out of habit than passion. His collared shirt was slightly disheveled and his hair was hastily combed. Evelyn trailed him to the biggest strip mall in Adders.

Evelyn watched from across the street as Calhoon went from store to store collecting money from the managers. *He must be the property owner,* Evelyn surmised. Judging by Calhoon's face to face approach at collecting dues, he didn't mind doing the heavy lifting.

Even checked her clock. Following them one by one would take too long. Evelyn regretted not bringing her tracking equipment back in Detroit. She didn't expect to work this vacation, and tracking someone was illegal, not that it stopped her before. She had to improvise.

She headed to a local supermarket, picked up a few pre-paid burner phones, magnets, small plastic boxes, and glue. She pulled off to the side of the road, activated the phones with a fake name, turned them on, downloaded the proper location app, and sealed them inside the plastic containers. She then glued magnets to the tops of the containers. She stuck the first one in the wheel well of Calhoon's Lexus.

She headed to the hospital next and spotted Dr. Gregory's BMW. She snuck back to the employee lot by crawling under the fence. Black cap and sunglasses on, she sped-walked to his vehicle and stuck the magnetized box containing the phone in the wheel well. Wasting no time and not looking up at the camera, she scurried under the fence and raced back to her minivan.

Knowing there was no way to get one of the makeshift trackers on the sheriff's and deputy's squad cars, she headed to the town hall. Wiping sweat from her forehead, Evelyn put her shades back on and scanned the quiet streets of Adders' tiny Main Street. It was past lunchtime. The streets were relatively devoid of witnesses. She rolled around the back of the town hall building, glancing up at the multiple cameras mounted on arms on the colonial style-brick building's side. As long as Evelyn didn't make any mistakes, they'd have no reason to review video footage and look up her dingy minivan's license plate. Evelyn pulled up to the guard post at the employee lot. The elderly guard with droopy ears and a pot belly read a Lionel train magazine. He gave Evelyn a suspicious look as she rolled down her window.

"I took a wrong turn," Evelyn said with a sweet smile. "You mind if I make a U-turn back here?"

The old guard paused. Without a word, he gestured for Evelyn to go ahead and then went back to reading. Evelyn pulled into the packed employee lot and spotted the red sports car. Evelyn's breath quickened. She kept a hard face and stopped next to it. She popped her hood.

She walked around the car and looked at the engine and the guard staring back at them both. Evelyn smiled nervously. "Could you give me hand?"

Grumbling, the man put aside his magazine.

While he was standing up and setting the magazine aside, Evelyn unplugged her corroded battery and then pretended to look confused.

The guard approached her. "Heck of a place to break down."

"Tell me about it," Evelyn said, rubbing her forehead. "It's usually my husband who takes care of the car stuff. We're in a little bit of a rough patch right now."

The man nodded slowly. He looked over the engine and pointed. "Your battery."

"Oh, let me tell my husband," Evelyn reached her hand into her purse and "accidentally" dropped her lipstick as she reached for her phone. It rolled to the red sports car wheel. "God, I'm such a mess. Can you fix it?"

The man nodded. He leaned over the engine and began plugging in the battery. Evelyn knelt beside the sports car. Back to the guard, she pulled the magnetized box out of her purse and slipped it into the wheel well. She snatched up the red lipstick and returned to him.

He eyed her. "You should be okay now."

"Oh, thank you," Evelyn said with relief. "You saved my life."

"I don't know about that, ma'am. Double check your battery before you head out. If it's not tightly secure--"

"Thank you," Evelyn said and climbed into the van. She waved him goodbye and drove away.

Evelyn's next destination was the mom-and-pop restaurant a block away from the sheriff's department. She requested a window seat and ordered a cheap dinner. She watched the department and sipped her Diet Coke. Yates wouldn't be off work for another hour. She pulled out her tablet and reviewed her tracking app. She input phone numbers she had synced up with the phones and was able to see the various men's cars on the GPS. They were all still at work.

After Evelyn finished her slice of pie, she saw Sheriff Yates pull out of the department. She followed behind his cruiser to a small but well-kept house with a garden gnome out front. After he pulled into the driveway, Evelyn drove on, memorizing his address. She wouldn't be able to track

Deputy Painter today. She had enough on her plate already. Dr. Gregory was the first to go home but also the farthest to drive. Evelyn floored the accelerator and arrived at his two-story brick home with an attached two-car garage. There were four skinny pillars on the front porch. A cobblestone path led to his front porch stairs where a lantern was hanging on a black hook. Using her binoculars, she saw him cooking in the kitchen. It looked like he was in for a quiet night.

Evelyn headed to the mayor's house. It was a beautiful McMansion with a horse pen.

Evelyn's phone rang. Terrence.

"Hey," Evelyn answered softly as she watched Mayor Timberland yell at his twenty-something-year-old daughter in the living room.

"I need you to come home right now."

"What happened?"

Evelyn raced back to the Quenby House as fast as she could. Between two vine-wrapped colonnades, Terrence stood outside of Quenby House. The window to the left side of the door had plastic sheeting on it. The window on the right was shattered.

"What the hell happened?" Evelyn asked as she stepped out of her van.

Terrence gestured for her to enter.

On the foyer's red-carpet floor sat a brick amidst the shattered window glass.

"I was upstairs when it happened. I couldn't see the culprit."

Evelyn knelt down beside the brick.

"I haven't touched it. Should we call the cops?" Terrence asked.

"Probably," Evelyn replied. Putting on a plastic glove, she

picked up the brick and flipped it over. There was a note taped to the back.

Terrence leaned in and his eyes widened.

Evelyn read the hastily written note.

"Child Killer."

27

BARNSTORMER

Hands on their hips, Officers Davis and Bailey surrounded the brick. With chewing tobacco packed behind his lower lip, Davis, in his 30s, was a short and stout man with a buzz cut and angry mug. He bounced his intense eyes between the brick and the shattered window.

Bailey, a similarly aged granite-faced woman with fiery red hair and Georgia twang, seemed more concerned with Evelyn and Terrence. Even from a few feet away, one could smell the officer's taco dinner.

"Is there anything you can do?" Terrence asked. He had on white shorts and a teal button-up.

"Y'all said you saw no suspect," Bailey said suspiciously. "There really ain't much we can do without a lead."

The wind flapped the long crimson curtains flanking the inner window. Evelyn warmed her hands on the front pockets of her black double-breasted raincoat. She was still clad in black from her long day of surveillance. "I'm sure you know that my family are not the most well-liked people in this town, but this is unacceptable."

Davis picked up the note. He mouthed the words as he read it. He glanced up at them. "Maybe you should spend a few days away." Tobacco muffled his voice. Little black leaves stuck onto and in between his yellow teeth.

"Not gonna happen," Evelyn said, sick of running. Having turned down over two million dollars to keep the house, she wasn't going risk having a stranger burn it down while she cowered in a cheap hotel room.

Davis glared at her and put the note into a Ziploc baggie. "Then I suggest you buy a gun."

Terrence gawked at him. "That's it? There's nothing at all you can do for us?"

Davis turned his angry mug toward him. "There's over twenty thousand people in Adders. We can't stop everything because some teenager decided to toss a brick at your window, so either get armed or get out. That's the Adders way."

"I wish someone told us that when we moved here. Would've saved us a lot of trouble," said Terrence.

"You have any advice?" Evelyn asked Officer Bailey.

"Y'all are in a precarious position: outsiders veiled in mystery and at the heart of the town's most brutal murders. People don't know what to think of you. It's no surprise some want you gone. If you stay, listen to Davis. Buy a weapon and stake claim to what belongs to you," Bailey warned.

Evelyn eyed the woman. "What do you think of us? Are we really that much of a threat?"

Bailey and Davis traded looks. Bailey replied. "You don't cause trouble, I don't see a reason why you can't stay."

"You're the first ones to say that to us," Terrence admitted.

"Davis and I aren't as traditional as most Adders folk."

Officer Davis nodded in agreement.

Bailey handed Evelyn her card. "Can't promise I'll pick up, but there's my number."

Evelyn stuck it in her wallet. The officers left soon after. Evelyn grabbed the broom and dustbin and started cleaning up the glass. Terrence returned with a roll of plastic sheeting they had used when they were painting the walls. He cut out the proper rectangular shape and taped it around the window. When he finished, he looked at the other plastic cover window. "Well, now they match."

Terrence turned to march up the stairs. Evelyn called out to him.

Hand on the railing and foot on the second step, he turned back.

"If it wasn't for this ordeal with my father and the murders, I would've sold this place in a heartbeat," Evelyn said.

"What's done is done," Terrence said with a sunken face. "No use dwelling on it."

"It's okay to be mad at me," Evelyn felt like she had to say.

"That's the thing, Evelyn. I don't want to be mad at you." Hand sliding up the smooth rail, Terrence hiked the curved stairs.

Evelyn stood in the massive foyer. She looked at the broken windows, wondering how much damage this old house could take before it fell in. She marched down the hall where she had painted Mary's mural and entered into the red velvet lounge. Bookshelves, a brick fireplace, and various large portraits lined the walls. Without warning, the blackened wood burst into flame and all the lights flickered on.

"You look dreadful, darling," Alannah said, lounging on the lover's seat with one arm stretched above her head.

"I just sold my chance at a family to help you," Evelyn replied coldly. Apart from Andrew, the five victims occupied various sections and chairs in the room. "The least you can do is tell me who threw the brick."

Peter Calhoon stepped forward. He wore his number thirteen purple and yellow varsity jacket and rubbed his right wrist, right under the bloody stump. With guilt, he said. "My dad threw it."

By the looks on the others' faces, they had seen him too.

Infuriated, Evelyn marched out of the room, grabbed the brick, and fished out her car keys. Slamming the minivan door behind her, she raced to the Calhoon house. *He must've done it when I was watching one of the others.* Evelyn's fingers tightened around the steering wheel until her knuckles turned white. She could feel herself reaching her long overdue breaking point. You could only get shot at, see someone have their head explode, and deal with estranged family for so long before you needed to smash something.

Her brakes screeched to a stop out of the Calhoon residence. Their house was large and modern, probably constructed in the last twenty or thirty years. Upon Evelyn's first visit here, before Calhoon knew about the bones in her basement, he and Terrence were hitting it off by talking about football. Both Mr. and Mrs. Calhoon were very supportive of Evelyn's investigation. That had changed.

Though it was 10:38 p.m. and the lights were off apart for the upstairs bedroom TV, Evelyn punched her finger against the doorbell multiple times and then hammered her fist against the door's face. She could hear Mr. Calhoon swearing as he neared the opposite side of the door.

Hair disheveled and wearing pajamas, Mr. Calhoon yanked open the door. With tired eyes and a pissed-off face, he loomed over Evelyn. "Do you have any idea what time it is?"

"You left something at my house." Evelyn presented the brick.

Mr. Calhoon fumed. "Leave, or I swear--"

"So you're admitting that you vandalized my home?" Evelyn replied with fire in her voice.

"I don't know what you're talking about," Mr. Calhoon denied. The man was a good liar.

"I've done nothing but try to help you," Evelyn said. "And yet this is how you treat me. Why? Because of my father?"

"The one who killed my son?" Mr. Calhoon asked rhetorically and took an angry step toward Evelyn. She held her ground and looked directly into his eyes. Her fingernails dug into the brick in her lowered hand.

"Maxwell's innocent. I have proof," Evelyn said firmly.

"Liar," the man barked.

"He was with my mother the days of the murders," Evelyn explained.

"His lover, you mean? Someone who would lie to protect him. What a testimony!"

"You don't want to believe me, fine," Evelyn said. "But stay away from my house."

"I didn't throw that brick," Calhoon seethed.

"That's not what your son said," Evelyn replied, her blood pressure rising.

Calhoon grabbed her by the scruff of her coat. "What did you say?"

"Peter. Your son. His apparition saw everything," Evelyn said.

Mr. Calhoon's lip quivered. "You're a psychopath, just like your father."

With a powerful shove, he pushed Evelyn onto the front lawn. She landed on her bottom and glared at him as he slammed the door. Clenching the brick, she guessed it wouldn't be hard to break the window from here. *What are you doing, Evelyn?* an internal voice asked her. She forced herself up, quickly brushed off the dirt, and then returned to her minivan before she did something stupid.

She pulled into a gas station. Under the dim light over the awning, she rested her back against the minivan and pinched the bridge of her nose as the gas pump refilled her car. *You need to slow down,* she told herself. Eyes closed, she saw Stephen Doyle's head exploding and felt his warm blood cascading down her face. She had him at gunpoint. Her father, a shell of a man with a beard-covered face, pulled the trigger without hesitation. Was Lily covering for Maxwell this whole time? Was Evelyn trying to prove the innocence of a serial killer?

No, she had to trust her gut.

Currently, her gut told that her Calhoon was going to do something stupid. Evelyn needed to stop that, and the best way to do so would be to get people looking at him. If he knew the police were watching him, he wouldn't make a move, or, at the very least, he might hesitate.

Evelyn pulled out her phone and dialed Officer Bailey.

"*Yeah?*" the woman answered sleepily.

"It's Evelyn. I have an idea who threw that brick."

"*Who's that?*"

"It's Calhoon. We had a falling out recently. He may try to get back at me."

"*We'll talk to him tomorrow.*"

Evelyn thanked her and hung up. She pulled up Sheriff Yates's number. On a number of occasions, he'd claimed to be a friend of the Quenbys, praising their donations to the department. Nonetheless, Evelyn didn't trust any of the men who had attempted to bribe her out of town.

Pulling the pump out of her vehicle, Evelyn listened to the ringing. She was patched into the sheriff's office. Sunshine wasn't working this late. A different receptionist took her call.

"I need to speak to Yates,"

"He's not in right now."

"It's an emergency. Tell him it's Evelyn Carr."

With hesitation, the night worker put Evelyn on hold. By the time she was on the road, Sheriff Yates answered. *"I usually don't take calls this late. Consider yourself a lucky lady."*

Evelyn told him about the brick and Calhoon, ending with, "You said people would come after me because of what my father has done. Now, I'm asking for your help."

"You sure it was Calhoon?"

"I'm positive." Evelyn would've shown him the burner phone's GPS path, but the evidence would be inadmissible because of its illegal nature.

"Hmm," Yates said contemplatively. *"I have to say, Evelyn. Maybe this is a sign."*

"A what?"

"Maybe instead of going on a witch hunt, you and Terrence, you know, end your vacation early."

"You're saying I should run away?" Evelyn asked. "Why can't you talk to Calhoon? Tell him you have an eye on him. Scare him a little bit."

"Yeah, and then someone else who hates you will rise up and take his place. You want my two cents: contact Mayor Timberland. He'll probably offer you a fourth of the price for the property since you offended him, but take it anyway and skedaddle. There's nothing here for you."

"You said you were a friend of my family."

"I'm a friend of their money," the sheriff said honestly. *"And that well dried up a long time ago."*

"Wow," Evelyn replied, pulling off to the side of the road. "You're really something else, Sheriff."

"Hey now, don't blame me. I told you our community was a fragile thing, and clearly you don't fit in the bubble. I would say that it's only a suggestion that you leave but..."

"So that's it then? Because of my father's supposed crimes, I'm the one who suffers."

"You know it's more than that. You disturb the peace, and Adders wouldn't be Adders without its peace and quiet. Now rest up. I imagine you've got a lot to pack tomorrow."

"I'm not leaving until I prove my father's innocence," Evelyn stated. "Or until I find Bella Day. Remember her? The nine-year-old we're looking for. No, I guess she doesn't matter. It's only me and the breath in my lungs that disturbs the peace."

"Have a good night, Evelyn," the sheriff said coldly and hung up.

Evelyn rested her forehead on the steering wheel. Another burned bridge. After a moment to reflect on the conversation, Evelyn returned to Quenby House. She arrived after midnight and looked up at the mansion under the moon's glow. Drooping white flowers dangled from the vines that twisted around the mighty colonnades and suffocated the building's white paint. Letting out an exasperated sigh, she marched up the steps and went inside.

She knocked on Terrence's bedroom door.

"Come in," he said.

Evelyn found him seated in bed, resting his back on the backboard and a laptop on his outstretched legs. He wore a white t-shirt and boxers. "You look worried."

"Really?" Evelyn replied sarcastically. "The sheriff told us to buzz off. He's not going to help us find the culprit."

"Yates?" Terrence cursed. "He must've been upset we didn't sell."

"I'm sorry, Terrence," Evelyn apologized. "I was selfish and bullheaded. We should've taken the money."

Terrence looked like he was squirming to say something, but didn't. He asked, "What about the victims? Bella Day? Your father? Why are you having doubt now?"

"I'm chasing ghosts," Evelyn admitted. "Literally. Figuratively." Evelyn chuckled at the ridiculousness of the situation. "I'm giving this case my all, and my reward is a bus ticket the hell out of here."

Terrence set aside his computer. "The Evelyn I knew never worried about the payout. It's always been about helping others. Sticking up for the little man."

"I don't know, Terrence. I'm tired of all of it. It's like I'm running, but I'm not going anywhere."

Terrence gestured for her to come over.

Hesitant and guilt-ridden, she made her way to the side of the bed. Terrence squeezed her hand. "I haven't been completely honest with you."

Evelyn crinkled her brows.

"When those guys showed up last night, they told me about how they wanted to buy the house way before dinner. I was half-tempted to sign off there and then, but I knew your father gave this place to you. Heck, it was the only thing your father ever gave you. When you arrived, I needed to see your reaction to the men's offer. Your response wasn't what, um, I had hoped. Still isn't, but this land, it's yours, Evelyn. And though I don't agree with your choice, I respect it. Because at the end of the day, we're going to be the only ones in the world that knew what you did for the people downstairs, not for a reward or fame, but because it's the right thing to do."

"Thanks." Evelyn sat down next to him. He scooted over, giving her room to lay down beside him. Evelyn smiled at the situation, knowing that the twin bed was too small for the both of them.

"Yeah, I don't know how well this sleeping arrangement is going to work," Terrence said jokingly as he struggled to keep both legs on the bed.

"You could come back to my room."

"Nervous that Alannah's going to try to seduce me?"

"Should I be?" Evelyn asked with a small smile.

"She did say she liked my cowboy hat."

"That's it. I'm never letting you out of my sight again."

They snuggled on the tiny bed. Evelyn knew one thing: come hell or high water, they'd have each other.

Evelyn woke up hours before sunrise. She untangled herself from her husband and cringed as she stood up from the creaking bed. Seeing that Terrence was still fast asleep, she headed downstairs. With a pensive look, she studied the plastic sheeting on the two front windows. The killer didn't need to use a secret passageway; he could simply step inside. That was not a jolly thought. She headed to the kitchen and poured a glass of orange juice. By the tightness in her gut, she remembered how little she ate yesterday. That reminded her...

She found her purse and pulled out her tablet. With the light still off, she sat in the study on a cracked leather office chair. Yawning, she loaded up her tracking app. *That's odd,* she thought. Calhoon's vehicle was parked in a field a dozen miles from his house. Evelyn checked the clock. 5:01 a.m. She checked on Mayor Timberland's car. He was parked in the same field. Quickly, Evelyn cycled to Dr. Gregory. They were all in the same location. Deputy Painter and Sheriff Yates were the only ones she wasn't sure about, because she never got a chance to put trackers on them.

Unsure how much time she had, Evelyn rushed out of the study, threw on some dark clothes, put her blonde hair into a ponytail, and grabbed her extendable baton. She thought about waking Terrence but didn't want to wait for the men's meet to adjourn. Groaning, Evelyn left her husband to his sleep and sped down the road.

Inky blackness shrouded Adders. Outside of her head-light beams, she could barely make out the silhouettes of trees and farmlands. The moon was almost full, and the universe painted the dark sky. Evelyn drove past the mayor's property. She turned into a dirt road that had a metal guard blocking the path. Evelyn got out of her car. There was a chain, but the gate wasn't locked. Quietly, Evelyn put her hands on the metal bar and pushed it open. When she had enough for her van to fit through, she climbed back into her vehicle and continued onward.

A thin line of skinny trees flanked either side of the road. Behind them, cattle pastures sprawled into the darkness. Evelyn turned off her headlight and quietly rolled her van forward.

She saw the barn appear as she rounded the road's bend. It was a big red building with an A-frame tin roof and massive double doors. Rays of light burst from the thin gaps of the tall vertical slats that made up the walls. Metal mesh fence with chipped posts bordered the barn from three sides.

Timberland's red sports car, Calhoon's Lexus, Gregory's BMW, and two sheriff cruisers were parked outside. *The whole gang.* Evelyn reversed her minivan and parked it on the other side of the bend to make sure that if the men walked out of the barn, they wouldn't immediately spot her vehicle. Under the cover of night, Evelyn scurried over to the barn. She weaved through the parked cars and slowed in front of the structure. Calming herself, she peeked through the gap between the double doors. The light inside reflected on her blue iris.

The interior consisted of two rows of cattle pens, one on the right wall and one on the left. They had closed wooden gates but currently held no livestock. Packed dirt and straw made up the path between them. It led to a small table near the back where the five men sat. Evelyn could hear their voices, but she was too far to decipher the words. A loft formed a U above. The bottom--the widest portion and full of haystacks--hovered over the table. One ladder could access it from the inside.

Evelyn pulled away from the gap and snuck around the side of the barn. There was a chicken coop attached to the side of the building and a stack of pallets nearby. Carefully, Evelyn climbed the pallets, feeling them wobble beneath her feet. When she found her balance, she pulled herself up onto the chicken coop. The tin roof bent in for a moment and then popped back into place. Evelyn froze, waiting to see if any one of the men had heard it. It didn't seem like it. She'd need to be quieter. Putting the ball of her hands against the roof's edge, she pulled up, sliding her torso onto the roof's edge. With slow and controlled steps, she walked the incline to the place where the loft jutted out of the rest of the room. There was a window on the left and right side. Evelyn approached the nearest one. One of the four glass panes had been knocked out. The others remained. Evelyn heard the voices clearer, but not clear enough. She needed to get inside. Using a point of her pocketknife, she loosened another pane. She threw it like a Frisbee into a bush and did the same to the other panels. When she cleared out the glass, she pulled out the window plus-shaped pane divider and crawled inside.

Using hay bales as steps, she walked down to the loft's floor. She pulled out her cell phone, got on her knees and elbows, and filmed through a crack in the floor.

Deputy Painter leaned back in a rusty metal chair with his boots on the cracked circular table. His felt hat rested beside his feet on the table. He said, "Let me take care of her personally."

Sheriff Yates, sitting beside him, pushed the deputy's feet off the table. Painter almost flipped backward. He caught himself and glared at the sheriff.

"There are much cleaner ways of handling things," Yates

told him. "I brought in this meth head the other day. It wouldn't be hard to plant some of his product in her possession."

"But that's only temporary," Painter argued.

Mayor Timberland sat on the chair opposite of him. "I agree. She is dangerously close to learning the truth and needs to be dealt with permanently."

"Yeah, and now Maxwell's killing again," Painter added. "Maybe with her help."

Standing away from others, Dr. Gregory shook his head. "Evelyn isn't the problem. It's Maxwell. He's back. We all know it."

"One girl goes missing and now it's Maxwell," Timberland said with doubt.

"I'm a man of certainties, Joshua," Gregory stated. "Maxwell is our killer. We knew it then and we know it now."

"Be that as it may, you can't deny that Evelyn's a threat," Timberland said.

Gregory pursed his lips.

Mr. Calhoon, seated at the table, lifted his face from his hands. "I wish we dealt with Max when we had the chance. Put a bullet in his brain."

"What he knew mattered too much," Timberland replied.

Deputy Painter scoffed. "It was a lack of commitment that allowed the snake to escape us."

"We should've just burned down the whole plantation," Mr. Calhoon said. "Toasted him in those passageways he adored so much."

"I'm glad we didn't," Timberland said. "Because all the blackmail he has could still be inside. I don't care what the bastard said. There's no way he'd destroy his family's work."

Yates sniffed his coffee, seemingly getting rid of all his stress. "Instead of going around in circles for another two hours, we just need to decide what we want to do about

Evelyn. Eventually, she'll figure out what we did to her father. Worse, finds out he's alive, and then we're really screwed."

Painter leaned back, arms behind his head, and looked up at the crack on the floor and directly at Evelyn.

28

THE WOODS

Evelyn pulled her face away from the crack. Her heart raced. Painter got out of his chair, keeping an eye on the loft above his head. The other men looked at him inquisitively. Evelyn slowly stood. The floor creaked beneath her feet. All of the men turned their eyes to the loft.

"Is there someone up there?" one of them asked the others.

Silent as death, Deputy Painter climbed the ladder. The rungs groaned under every step.

Evelyn's stomach dropped.

Sticking her phone in her pocket, she dashed for the window.

Painter quickened his pace.

Evelyn slid down the inclined tin roof.

Footsteps stomped through the loft behind her.

When Evelyn reached the end of the roof, she jumped off. The ground came up much quicker than she would've liked. It was a twelve-foot drop. She got a few bruises, but nothing felt broken. Evelyn pushed her body off the dewy grass. The sky was turning from black to indigo. Evelyn raced around the front of the barn as Painter peered out of the broken window.

Shouts sounded in the barn.

Evelyn weaved back through the cars. The barn door opened as Evelyn rounded the bend on the dirt path. She unlocked her car with the clicker and clambered inside. She turned the ignition and floored the gas petal. Kicking up dust and pebbles, the minivan skidded down the dirt path and onto the main road.

Evelyn constantly glanced back in the rearview mirror as she got farther and farther away. It didn't look like she was being followed. Nonetheless, Evelyn couldn't tell herself to slow down. When the barn was miles behind, Evelyn reached for her cell phone and the incriminating evidence inside.

She felt her coat pockets. It wasn't there. *I thought...* she tried her front and back jean pockets. Wallet, but no cell phone. She lifted her bottom a few inches off the chair and felt around beneath her. Nothing. She checked the cubby at her feet. Nope.

Dread flooded over Evelyn. She tried to remember where she could've lost it. It had to have been when she was sliding down the roof or when she jumped. *I have to go back.* Evelyn pulled into the parking lot of a restaurant. She withdrew her tablet from her purse and tracked the men's cars. They were dispersing. Two were coming her way and one going the other, with no way of knowing about Painter or Yates.

Evelyn turned off her minivan and stayed parked in front of the restaurant as Timberland's red sports car raced by. Soon after, one of the sheriff's cruisers zipped down the street. Evelyn watched them vanish. She restarted her van and returned to the main road. Looking both ways, Evelyn went back the way she came down the field-flanked road

Driving the speed limit and trying to appear inconspicuous, Evelyn returned to the dirt road. The sun cast its golden rays. Evelyn parked in front of the gate to the dirt road. The chain locked it to a metal post. Evelyn would have to walk in.

She ducked under the rail and jogged down the dirt path. She was out of breath by the time she arrived at the vacant barn. Pacing across the place where the cars had been parked, she searched the ground for her cell. After a few minutes and no results, she wondered around the side of the barn. It seemed like the most logical conclusion. Evelyn slowly walked back and forth in the grass. No luck. She climbed up to the coop and peeked at the roof. No sign of it. She returned to the loft. Hay bales, loose straw, still no cell phone.

Evelyn ran her hand up her scalp. *This is bad. Very bad.*

Winded, she arrived back at the minivan empty-handed. She pulled out her tracker app, wondering if she still had her own phone's data on there. She did. Evelyn followed the blip down the opposite side of the road where she came from. Before she could overlay and see which man's car it was in, her phone blip disappeared.

"Oh come on!" She tried restarting her tablet and walked around, searching for a signal. She got a bar, but her blip wouldn't return. The revelation hit her. *They broke my SIM card.*

Evelyn didn't know why they broke it, but they wouldn't have done so unless they knew she was filming. She had assumed that any or all of them now knew she was spying on them. Evelyn chewed on her nail and rushed home.

She didn't waste time closing her van's door. She sprinted inside and upstairs to the guest bedroom. She burst through the door. Terrence shot out of bed with an alarmed look on his face.

"Dang, Eve!" Terrence yelled. "You nearly scared me half to death!"

"Terrence, I messed up," Evelyn said breathlessly. She told him what happened back at the barn.

Terrence covered his mouth and averted his eyes. After a long while, he pulled his hand away from his face. "Yeah, that's not good. Do we have any idea who took it?"

"It doesn't matter. They could've told the others. We need to assume the worst."

"Let's get a hold of Officer Bailey," Terrence said, trying to think up a game plan. "She can… you can tell her your testimony."

"I suppose, but I don't expect her to buy it," Evelyn replied.

"It's that or run," said Terrence, putting on his pants.

"Make the call," Evelyn pulled out the policewoman's card.

Upon hearing what they were talking about, Bailey shut them up. *"Don't say any more over the phone. Come to the station. We'll talk in private."*

Not wasting time on a shower or to change her clothes, Evelyn headed to the police station. Terrence drove, giving Evelyn a little time to recover. It seemed like she hadn't breathed normally since she left the barn.

The police station was a little bigger than the sheriff's department, but not by much. It was still a single-story rectangular building, but just had a little more to it. It had a large flagpole outside the front of the building. Two flags flapped in the wind: the American one and the Georgia State flag.

Keeping as calm as they could, Terrence and Evelyn walked side by side through the double doors with the police department's decal over it. The bullpen was relatively compact, with only a few officers manning desks. There was a receiving desk manned by a male officer with glasses whose frames looked like orange slices. His hair was a malt gray color, and his stern expression made Evelyn miss pretty desk girl Sunshine back at the sheriff's department.

As Terrence was about to speak to him, Office Bailey approached and gestured for them to follow her. Her frizzy red hair was in a tight bun on the back of her head. Officer Davis hunched over a desk, with his eyes locked on the outdated, box-shaped computer monitor. When he saw them pass, he stopped clicking on the keyboard and followed them into the unused interrogation room.

Bailey told Davis to check the observation room and make sure this meeting wasn't recorded. None of them said a word until Davis returned. Though there was a table and chairs, no one sat.

"Mr. Calhoon, Mayor Timberland, Dr. Gregory, Sheriff Yates, and Deputy Painter. Those are the men," Evelyn explained.

"You sure?" Bailey asked.

"I had them on video before the footage was destroyed." Evelyn gestured to herself. "Look at me. You think I would've come out here covered in dirt if I wasn't serious?"

Davis traded looks with Bailey and then locked eyes with Evelyn. "You saw the Mayor and Sheriff Yates, in the same room, plotting your murder and conversing about how they killed your father?"

"In a sense, sure." Evelyn crossed her hands over her chest and chewed her thumbnails.

"Ah," the officers said condescendingly.

"Hey, we wouldn't lie about this," Terrence declared.

"It's just as far as tall tales go, this one takes the cake," Bailey said.

Her partner seemed to agree. "And your convicting video record was conveniently destroyed so you have no evidence to support these claims."

Terrence twisted around and rubbed his hands up his bald head.

Evelyn took a breath. “What do we need to do to convince you?”

The duo of officers thought for a moment. Bailey spoke up. “You say your father is alive. Bring him in. Let us hear his testimony, and you may have a case. Otherwise, there’s nothing we can do.”

The drive back to Quenby didn’t inspire confidence. Evelyn propped her head against the window and watched the world blur by.

Terrence put his hand on her thigh. “We’ll find a way.”

Evelyn kept her mouth closed. It felt like some invisible force was pushing down on her, seconds away from crushing her scarred body.

Quenby House came into view. Horrified, Terrence leaned over the steering wheel as the van came to a stop. Evelyn straightened her posture and saw what terrified her husband.

Blood.

Thick and dark red, it splattered on the steps leading to the mansion and splashed across the front door, as if someone had slung gallons of crimson paint on the porch and door. Evelyn quickly exited the car. Terrence followed. With cautious steps, they hiked the steps and avoided the dripping blood. By the looks of it, someone had splashed it here within the hour.

They reached the front door. Painted in the blood and lopsided, the word “LEAVE” looked directly at Terrence and Evelyn. Nearby, a black bird cawed. The breeze ruffled Evelyn’s blonde hair. There must’ve been at least two gallons of blood.

“Is it real?” Terrence asked soberly.

Evelyn outstretched her bony finger and dipped into the

letter L. She brought back her red fingertip to her nose and sniffed. She turned to Terrence and nodded.

Terrence cursed softly and then loudly. He turned back to the red brick path flanked by old oaks and at the single lane road beyond.

Evelyn dialed 9-1-1.

Screaming sirens were followed by two squad cars. The first car hailed from the police department. The other ventured from the sheriff's office.

Officers Bailey and Davis stepped out of their car while Deputy Painter and Sheriff Yates stepped out of his.

With his eyes, Davis traced the messy trail of blood to the front door. He spat dip spit into a bottle.

Bailey directed her attention on Yates. "What are you doing here, Sheriff?"

Yates took a sip from a fat thermos. By his joyous expression, it seemed like he was drinking the manna from heaven. "I promised the Carrs that I'd look after them if anything happened. A sheriff keeps his promises."

"That's fine and dandy, but Davis and I got this covered," Bailey argued.

With lust, Deputy Painter observed Bailey's body that looked very blocky in her uniform. "We won't be long, sweetheart."

Yates hiked up the steps, careful not to get his polished boots bloody. He looked at the door and took another gulp. "Looks like cow blood."

"How do you know?" Evelyn replied, keeping her expression hard.

Yates smiled at her. "Just a guess."

"Probably should've sold the house," Painter added, his left boot slight stepping in the blood. Red partial boot prints followed his trek through the double colonnades and to the front door. Officers Bailey and Davis eyed him suspiciously.

Bailey studied the word "leave" written in blood. "I ain't ever seen anything like this before."

Yates nodded. "Bad omen. Mrs. Carr, I know of a few motels you might be interested in staying at for a number of days. I know money is a little tight for you at the moment. So, on behalf of the sheriff's department, I am offering to cover the expenses."

"You know," Evelyn said and wrapped her arm around Terrence's lower back. "I think my husband and I are fine right here."

Terrence glared at her. "Evelyn," he nudged. "They're offering to cover our expenses. Maybe we should listen to them."

Bailey read the word again and shook her head. With a pitying look, she said to Evelyn, "I have to agree with Sheriff Yates. I don't believe this place is safe anymore. Tell us your motel and room number when you make a decision and we'll provide the necessary protection."

Painter agreed. "Yep, we'll make sure you're taken care of. There are some real creeps out here. You never know who might show up."

Evelyn cast her eyes down to the cow's blood, just imagining the figure pouring it from a bucket as he walked backwards up the stairs. She glanced at her watch. It was almost eleven in the morning.

"You want us to drive you over to the motel now?" Yates asked politely. "We can wait here until you pack your things."

Officer Bailey smiled falsely at the sheriff. "We'll take her. Y'all got work to do."

"Every one of you can leave," Evelyn said. "Terrence and I need to clean this mess up."

"We need to wait for Forensics to get samples first," said officer Davis.

"The sheriff is probably right," Evelyn said. "It's likely just cow blood. I should clean it before it ruins the hardwood."

"While we're waiting, you can pack," Yates suggested.

"Good idea," Terrence said, obviously wanting to get away from the blood.

Evelyn nodded at the officers. With Terrence, Evelyn left the officers, deputy, and sheriff behind. Her walk turned into a jog as she rounded the bend of the massive house. Running between the vine-covered left wall and the line of tall trees, she reached the side door to the kitchen and hustled inside. Once Terrence entered, Evelyn closed the door, locked it, and pressed her back against it.

"We need to leave, Terrence," Evelyn said as directly as she could.

"I think that's a brilliant idea," her husband replied, using a rag lying on the stove handle to pat down his sweaty face. "You're not thinking about going to the motel though, right? I only went along with it to play village idiot. It really sounds like a trap."

"Probably because it is," Evelyn paced. "Within six hours of learning of their conspiracy, they're already making their moves. I underestimated them. Big time."

"You think they'll try to kill us?" Terrence asked awkwardly, as if he didn't believe the words.

"I don't know, but they're royally pissed. After Forensics comes and does their thing, we'll grab anything that can fit into our minivan and get out of town."

"What about the victims?" Terrence asked. Evelyn could tell he was more concerned with Evelyn than helping the ghosts. "We turned down millions of dollars to help them."

"I don't know. Maybe we can come back later," Evelyn hated saying it. It felt like she was going against everything that defined her by leaving the job unfinished. Nonetheless, she couldn't deny her fear any longer. These men that tried to kill her father were nearly untouchable, and now they had Evelyn in their crosshairs. They could wait until Bailey and Davis left and put a bullet in Evelyn and Terrence's heads, hide the bodies, and get rid of the minivan. To the world, it would look like the Carrs had left town. There wouldn't be any need to warrant an investigation. That was the worst-case scenario, of course, but Evelyn would be an idiot if she didn't recognize the possibility of such a thing.

"I'm going to call Mayor Timberland," Terrence said. "See if he's still willing to buy the place. Is that alright with you?"

Feeling her heart twisting inside, Evelyn gestured for him to proceed. *You're not a bad person,* Evelyn told herself. *You're doing what you can to survive. The dead aren't going anywhere. You can come back when the situation has mellowed out.* As much as the internal dialogue gave her some justification for her actions, she knew that the moment she left Adders behind, she would never be able to bring herself to return. Too many bad memories. Too many possibilities for things to go wrong. While she was here, there was a sense of urgency, one that pulled on her like a strong wind. She felt it now, stronger than ever. *Hurry up and make the call, Terrence, before I put us any more at risk.*

"*Timberland speaking,*" a voice said on the other end of the phone.

Terrence put the phone on speaker and placed it on the large kitchen island. "Hey, Mayor Timberland. This is Terrence Carr. I was hoping you'd have a moment to talk about the Quenby property."

"*What's there to talk about?*" the man said gruffly. "*Your wife turned down the money.*"

"Yeah, uh, that's why I'm calling," Terrence said with a nervous chuckle. "We've had some time to reconsider your proposal and would like to sell the property. Right now, if you wish."

The line went quiet on Timberland's end.

"Hello?" Terrence asked. "You still there?"

"Tell your wife that she has made her decision," Timberland said spitefully. *"We don't want the property anymore."*

Evelyn spoke into the phone. "A million dollars, it's yours and we leave right now. Forever."

"No." The mayor's voice thundered through the large, empty kitchen. *"You made your bed, Mrs. Carr. Lie in it."*

The line went dead.

Evelyn and Terrence stood in silence for a long moment.

Terrence put his phone away. "Well, it's not exactly how I thought our vacation would turn out."

The forensics team from the state arrived and took the necessary blood samples and photographs. Evelyn and Terrence watched them leave.

"Last call," Sheriff Yates said. "I can take you to the best motel in town."

"Thanks for the offer, Sheriff," Terrence said, shaking the man's hand. "We'll find our own."

The sheriff smiled at them, though the motive behind it couldn't be interpreted. Was it spiteful? Disappointed? Happy?

He and Deputy Painter ducked into their squad car and left Quenby. Officers Bailey and Davis followed, but not before saying, "You bring us solid proof, we'll make the case for you, but we need your father."

Terrence waved them goodbye. Evelyn didn't say anything. She stood under the shadow of the mansion, wondering if it was even worth it to clean up the blood. Probably not. She returned inside.

The phantoms waited in the foyer, standing just under the interior balcony.

"We're going," Evelyn told them, already thinking about all the sleep she'd get back in her small Detroit flat.

"Without the money?" Barker exclaimed. He wiped away the blood on his lip with the top of his hand.

Evelyn took a deep breath and nodded. "It didn't work out. Hell, you can have the place if you want it."

Zoey scoffed and shook her head. "After all that you've done, you're leaving?"

Evelyn felt her blood pressure rising. "Maybe you haven't noticed the blood on our door or the brick dashed through our window?"

The victims looked at her with pursed lips and bleeding wounds.

Evelyn continued. "I did everything I could to help you. I risked my life. I turned down the fortune I needed to start a family of my own. I'm sorry, but I can't offer anything else."

"But you're so close, darling," Alannah said with her normal sultry tone.

"To what?" Evelyn asked. "Solving your murder? Finding the killer? Saving Bella? There's only one person who might be able to help us, and we have no means of finding him."

Terrence took a step forward and spoke to the phantoms. "We tried, but it's time to move on."

Zoey gnashed her teeth. She fidgeted as Evelyn and Terrence started up the stairs. "Wait!" Zoey called out.

Evelyn let go of the curved stairs handrail and looked at the goth.

"Let's do what Mary Sullivan did," Zoey declared.

Everyone in the room gave her their attention.

The fifteen-year-old girl clad in black continued speaking. "She was able to…guide you."

"Possess us," Evelyn clarified. "While we slept and while we were awake. How will that help?"

"It will allow us to leave this house. To see the outside world," said Zoey.

Barker puffed smoke from his pipe. "That's a possibility. Seven pairs of eyes are better than two."

"If we even have the strength to do it," Peter said. The young football player put his one good hand on a nearby vase stand. "Something about Mary made her stronger than us."

"I don't believe that to be true," Alannah said. She glanced at Terrence on the stairs. "We've never realized our full potential because we never had a chance to."

Evelyn looked at them with doubt. "We're still marching out into miles of woods. How will you know where to find Maxwell?"

Barker lowered his pipe to his chest. "I know you living folk look different than us. When you're nearby, we can always sense you."

Terrence shuddered. "That's a terrifying revelation."

"Tell me about it," Barker replied. "If it works the same out there, we could potentially know if Maxwell or someone else is nearby even if we don't see them."

Evelyn contemplated what the phantoms were asking.

Terrence shook his head in disbelief. "Yeah, I'd rather not have anyone possessing me."

Evelyn locked eyes with Zoey. "How can you guarantee we'll be free after it's all said and done?"

"Because we want to get home as much as you do," Zoey said. "If we can't find Maxwell, then you and Terrence are free to leave."

"We were always free to leave," Terrence replied. "Right?"

Zoey glared at him. "Leave guilt free."

"Evelyn," Terrence said. "This is a stupid idea."

Evelyn walked back through the foyer floor. She glanced up at the angels in the door above, hoping that somewhere, a higher power was looking down on her. "If this fails and we come home tonight to the five men that tried to kill my father, I need you to promise me that you will put a stop to them if necessary."

"We can certainly try," Barker said.

Winslow nodded rapidly in agreement.

Terrence walked to his wife and put his hands on her shoulders. "Eve, let's go upstairs and pack before it's too late."

Evelyn gave Terrence a soft smile and looked into his tired, handsome dark eyes. "Our life has been a whirlwind since the first day we showed up. This is our chance to finally get some answers. To find my father."

Terrence glanced up the phantoms standing shoulder-to-shoulder in a line and then back to Evelyn. "I'll only do this under one condition."

"Name it."

"We leave all this risk-taking behind and start a quiet little family."

"I'd like that." Evelyn smiled at him. They let go of one another and turned to the five bloodied individuals before them. "How will this work?"

The ghosts approached them. Their movements were in sync with one another. They formed a circle around Evelyn and Terrence directly below the chandelier.

"Hold still," Zoey said.

Evelyn blinked. She felt the ground moved beneath her feet. Suddenly, she saw double of Zoey and the other ghosts. Their doppelgangers overlapped one another as they walked in a circle. Terrence wobbled in place. He hunched over and dry heaved. Evelyn felt something punch her chest, sucking the breath out of her lungs. She dropped to a kneeling position. Candlelight illuminated the foyer around her. She heard piano music but couldn't recognize the song.

Men in tops hats and jackets with long coat tails strolled by, with their arms locked with women in long dresses. Their faces were distorted, but they tracked Evelyn as they walked through the party that was now under way. Evelyn smelled cigarette and strong perfume. She blinked and the foyer was empty and dim, just how it was before she spoke to the phantoms. No music. No laughter. No odd smells. No people. Something pulled at her. It was Zoey. The girl clasped Evelyn's hand in her own and led her out the front door, like how a child pulled at her mother.

Walking through the splattered cow's blood, Evelyn looked out from behind the towering colonnade in front of her and at the bright sun. Terrence was moving ahead of her, being pulled by Alannah. They bounced down the few porch steps and onto the circular brick landing.

In an instant, blurred-face figures in fancy 19th and 20th-century attire filled the brick road in wonderfully-crafted, horse-drawn buggies. One of the horses passed by Evelyn and breathed her nostrils at her face. Evelyn smelled the wretched odor and stared into the horse's eyes. They were a spiraling black hole.

Evelyn pulled her gaze away, and the afternoon returned to normal. Her feet took her beside the house. From the first floor to the attic, figures were silhouetted in the windows of Quenby House.

Evelyn shut her eyes and reopened them to the cotton field. Slaves in loose white shirts and brown pants plucked at the thorny crop while turning their distorted faces to Evelyn. There were seven in all, and each at a different distance. Evelyn tried to talk to one of them, but could not. She heard Zoey's voice in her mind. "Leave them be. They're nothing but memories of their former lives. Fragments, if that makes more sense, left behind when their living counterpart cast off of this plane. I don't know if they're good or bad, or why they stayed, but they're always around."

"How do you know this?" Evelyn asked.

"I can't say. I just… do."

The woods came into view, meaning Evelyn had blacked out for at least six acres' worth of land. Terrence stayed ahead, Alannah still pulling him by the hand. Peter walked a few feet away, but there seemed to be some white cord connecting him to Terrence's body. The farther Peter walked away, the farther the cord stretched. It looked like it didn't have a limit.

A pack of deer darted past. Their beautiful brown and white skin was mutilated by bullets. One had an exposed portion on its ribs. The breeze swayed the flap of skin hanging in front. All the animals had eyes like spiraling black holes that seemed to drain Evelyn's will the more she looked at them. Tattered-skinned squirrels scurried up trees. Decaying birds took flight across the indigo sky. In one second, the sun was high above. In the next, it was falling away.

Evelyn glanced around the unfamiliar forest as tall trees cast large shadows over the endless underbrush. The usual animal cries and screeches filled the woodlands, but there were other, alien sounds too; things that Evelyn had never heard before. Sounds that she could never hope to imitate. Shadowy quadrupedal beings lumbered just out of view, some of them three times the size of a human being. Somehow, Evelyn knew they were ancient or otherworldly. The only one Evelyn saw had a face like a black vortex, endlessly spinning. Instinct caused Evelyn to turn away her gaze. She saw a few of her hairs fall from her own head and turn gray as they hit the dirt.

Clouds raced and morphed overhead like in a time lapse video.

Sweat covered Evelyn's body, but she suffered no fatigue. Though she walked on uneven ground and overfilled trees, she felt like she was floating across a flat plain. Like a speck in the woods, Winslow strolled. Evelyn traced the glowing cord snaking from his chest to the center of her own. A second cord grew out of her in the opposite direction, connecting her to Barker, who was five hundred feet to her right. Zoey continued pulling her along. Up ahead, Alannah did the same for Terrence with Peter tethered to him.

Instantly, it was night.

The woods seemed much more active now. New, terrifying cries and twisted shadows ruled the woodlands. Evelyn could only really see the glowing cords coming out of her and Terrence. Dozens of circular red dots spotted the darkness far up ahead. Zoey turned Evelyn in a different direction. Evelyn swore the teenage whispered the word, "eyes."

"What is this place?" Evelyn finally mustered the courage to ask.

"The woods," the girl in black replied. "You're seeing it for what it really is."

Evelyn thought her heart rate would quicken at the statement, but it stayed at the same steady pace it had been since they left the mansion. She blinked again and all the stars were out, more than she'd ever seen before, and the moon was white and full, seemingly quadruple the size of what it should be.

Suddenly, Terrence took off into a sprint. He and Alannah ran out of sight.

"What's happening?" Evelyn asked.

"They found something," Zoey replied and started running. Evelyn couldn't let go of the girl even if she tried. Her feet crushed felled leaves and twigs. She hurdled over a jagged tree stump and ran through a bush, blocking her face with the arm Zoey wasn't pulling. A dirt path came into view. It appeared to be too wide to be a game trail.

At the end of it was a small cabin. Yellow light bled from its windows. A skinny tower of smoke leaked from its tiny chimney.

Zoey let go of Evelyn's hand and turned back to her, finally giving Evelyn a view that wasn't a bloody head wound.

With wide eyes, the teenage said, "That's Maxwell's home."

29

THE FREE MAN

Zoey, Winslow, and Barker vanished. Evelyn collapsed in the middle of the trail. Her muscles ached. Her head screamed in pain. Tears blurred her vision. Up ahead, Terrence wobbled and caught himself on the trunk of a crooked tree. His cheeks were gaunt and his eyes sunken. A gray stripe painted the left side of his small chin beard.

Under a normal-sized moon and black sky, he staggered over to Evelyn and dropped on his knees.

"I am never doing that again," he said as he helped lift Evelyn up. "You saw those creatures out there, right? Or was that just me?"

Evelyn shook her head. "It wasn't just you," she said weakly. Her stomach grumbled. She felt like she had aged twenty years. The moment she stood, she wanted to fall back down again. "Do I look as bad as you?" she asked Terrence.

He brushed aside strands of greasy blonde hair spit-glued to the corner of Evelyn's mouth. "It's what's on the inside that counts," he teased with a froggy voice.

Leaning on one another, the couple shambled toward the solitary cabin.

Sporting wooden walls and a pointed frame roof, the cabin stood in a small clearing that consisted of a tree stump scarred by an axe head, a tanning rack, a table with fat logs for chairs, a garden surrounded by a crooked wooden fence, and a red water pump with chipped paint. The building didn't have a porch, and all the windows had wooden blinds preventing anyone from seeing within. The light inside flickered, hinting at an active fireplace and candles. There was a rusty 1950s Ford truck parked nearby. Heaven only knew if it still ran.

"I wonder how far they took us?" Terrence asked as they neared the cabin's front.

Evelyn struggled. She was too exhausted to speak. Her once-steady heart rate was wonky, slow one moment and then fast the next. All she wanted to do was sleep for a week. "What time is it?"

Wincing, Terrence fished out his cell phone from his jeans' tight pocket. He held down the power button but it didn't boot up.

"Dead," he said hopelessly. "Let's hope your father doesn't chase us out of here. Otherwise we're screwed."

"Don't joke like that," Evelyn said as they stopped at the front door. She took inventory of her wrinkled and sweat-soaked shirt and pulled a twig from her hair. "Hi, Dad, it's me, Evelyn. Yes, I am doing very well for myself."

Evelyn knocked on the door.

"You think he'll like me?" Terrence asked.

"I don't know."

"Thanks for the vote of confidence," Terrence replied.

"Just being realistic," Evelyn said plainly. "Try to impress him. I don't want to walk home."

Terrence chuckled. "If my parents could see me now.

Voluntarily possessed, hallucinating, and about to meet the guy who blew off someone's head in front of my wife. My pops would probably disown me. My ma would lock me in the church house."

"I won't tell them," Evelyn replied.

It was official. They were both delirious.

Evelyn knocked again.

No response.

"Hello?" Her voice cracked as she called out.

Evelyn tried the knob. Her brows rose.

"Unlocked," she whispered.

Evelyn pushed the door open and stepped into the one-room cabin. It had a kitchen area, fireplace, homemade table, and a ladder that climbed into a loft without a railing. From the front door, Evelyn saw the corners of a cot up there.

"Maxwell?" she called out, feeling some déjà vu to Stephen Doyle's trap. Only this time, Evelyn and Terrence had no firearms to defend themselves. If not for the spontaneity of the whole situation, Evelyn would've prepared more.

"There's no place to hide in here," Terrence said, stretching out his palms in front of the active fireplace. Wood cracked under the small orange flame.

Evelyn glanced around the kitchen. In place of a refrigerator was an old plastic beer cooler. Evelyn opened it, revealing fresh slabs of meat. She closed it and checked the cupboards. Hard0carved mugs and bowls sat within. In one of the drawers, she found rusty knives of all different varieties. Evelyn guessed they had been lost by hunters and found by her father. In another drawer, she found nonfiction history books and survival guides with pages torn out alongside various magazines pertaining to firearms and muscle cars. These, Evelyn assumed, were lost by hunters as well.

"Should we go through all his stuff?" Terrence asked.

Evelyn handed him a knife with black serrated edge and an olive-green handle. "Keep this on you. Just in case."

Hesitant, he accepted the blade and put it in the back of his jeans. Evelyn did the same.

After, she climbed into the loft. It had a bed made of towels and tattered covers. As she climbed back down, the front door slung open.

A tall man stood in the threshold. He wore faded camouflage pants and a jacket. His black boots had turned the color of wet ash. The toes of the right one peeled back, revealing a black sock with a hole on the big toe. Parted down the middle, thick, ash-colored hair ran down the man's back and shoulders. A shaggy beard covered seventy percent of his skeletal face and flowed down his chest. Deep wrinkles etched his tan forehead, and out and around his eyes. In his skinny hands, he held a shotgun. The eye of the barrel was aimed directly at Terrence.

Slowly, Terrence put his hands up. "We don't want any trouble."

The man walked inside and used his foot to shut the door behind him. His shaggy mustache concealed his mouth, and his dark eyes made it hard to read his emotions.

Making no sudden movements, Evelyn climbed down the ladder and stood next to Terrence. There was an awkward pause. Evelyn felt her throat go dry and her palms become sweaty. *Is this man really him?* Evelyn didn't voice her doubts, she just pointed at herself. "It's me. Evelyn."

The man said nothing.

His unreadable gaze and the shotgun he held by his skinny hip didn't make the encounter any easier.

"This is my husband, Terrence." Evelyn said, struggling to keep a strong demeanor. "Please lower the weapon."

Without clicking on the safety, the man rested the shotgun against his shoulder, the barrel pointed to the roof.

Able to breathe again, Evelyn took a step toward him, but something about the man's look gave her pause.

"You are Maxwell, right?" Evelyn asked, unsure what to make of the wild man.

The man opened his mouth, but no words came out.

Terrence gently took Evelyn's hand. "I don't think he's--"

Evelyn cut him off by talking to the stranger. "Max, you saved my life. Don't you remember? Say something. Please."

The man spoke with a gravelly tone. "Why did you come here?"

It sounded like it was the first words he'd spoken in a decade.

"I needed to find you," Evelyn explained. "We know you are innocent."

The man walked forward. Evelyn and Terrence took a step back. The man eyed them and put the shotgun on the table.

"You are Maxwell Quenby?" Evelyn asked.

The man locked his dark eyes with her. "Maxwell's dead."

Evelyn's heart sank. Her eyes watered.

Terrence squeezed Evelyn's hand by his side. "Then who are you?"

"No one," the man replied. He stood, his back to the table and within arm's reach of the loaded shotgun. "Maxwell died in that house ten years ago. He'd like to stay dead."

"We didn't come all this way to play mind games," Evelyn said. "We need your help."

"Then you wasted your time," the man said.

If Terrence had hair, he'd be pulling it out. "Do you have any idea what we went through to find you? What Evelyn and I had to give up?"

Evelyn stood and planted her feet. "We aren't taking no for an answer."

The man set his jaw. "This is about the murders."

"That's one facet of it," Evelyn replied. "We also know the men who tried to kill you."

"Tried?" The man glared at her. "Did."

Evelyn felt herself becoming red. "You ran away. There's a huge difference. Now, I have two officers back in town who are ready and willing to take down your testimony. We can put the men who did this to you behind bars. At least for a few years."

The man sat against the edge of the table. "That night. When they came into the house. I could've run anywhere I wanted."

"Why didn't you?" Evelyn asked.

"I wanted to be free," the man said.

"You could've been free anywhere in the world," Evelyn said, not understanding.

"Free of people," the man elaborated. "Free of society. Free of my failures. Out here, there's no Maxwell Quenby. There's just me. Another beast in nature."

"Lily said you were dramatic," Evelyn replied.

The man tensed up at the name.

"I saw her," Evelyn said, off his expression. "We talked about you, her, and me."

The man's eyes glossed over.

"I forgave her," Evelyn said. "I'm willing to forgive you, but I need you to come home."

"You don't really mean that," the man replied.

Evelyn didn't know how she pictured this encounter before coming here, but it certainly wasn't like this. "I thought you'd be more excited. Wasn't the whole reason you took Mary Sullivan and Zoey Pinkerton under your wing was to have a daughter of your own? I'm far from perfect, Maxwell, but I'm here."

Maxwell studied his tattered gloves. "I gave up the right to call you daughter."

"Lily forced your hand. You didn't have a choice."

Maxwell glared at her. "There is always a choice."

"Make one now: come back with me and right your wrongs, or stay here and let us clean up your mess. After all, the men who were after you are now after me."

Maxwell tensed up. His hand involuntarily landed on the shotgun. His guilt and fear hung in the air like a cloud. "They're..."

Terrence nodded.

"Evelyn, run away." Maxwell implored. "Those men will not be trifled with and cannot be stopped."

Terrence locked his fingers with Evelyn. "Trust me, we've been thinking about it."

"You don't understand," Maxwell hissed.

Evelyn let go of Terrence and put her hand in her pockets. "I know what I'm dealing with, and I know the solution to the problem: your testimony."

"I won't give it," Maxwell said defiantly.

"You're going to cower for another ten years?" Evelyn lashed out.

"No, I won't give it because I'll be dead!"

Silence filled the stuffy cabin.

Calming down, Maxwell elaborated, "One of those men who came after me is responsible for the killings. He won't hesitate to do the same to us, especially if he knows you're going to expose him."

"Who is it?" Terrence asked anxiously. "Timberland, Yates, Calhoon?"

Maxwell shook his head. "I don't know. I followed the missing persons' trail myself. One of the men got wind of it, pinned the murders on me, and used that to rally the rest. I didn't have any idea who it was until I saw the five of them burst into my private study and pull me out. I was able to slip out of their grasp and escape through the tunnel, but not without taking a hit."

He unzipped the top of his camouflage jacket and pulled down the neck of his shirt, revealing a deep slash running down his chest. "It cut from there to my belly. Adrenaline kept me going. I was able to clean it out with maggots when I got out into the woods."

"Oh," Terrence said, looking queasy.

"Were you aware of the bodies stored in your basement?" Evelyn asked suspiciously.

Maxwell stared at her like he didn't understand the words she just said.

Evelyn elaborated. "Zoey Pinkerton, Winslow Darvey, James Barker, Peter Calhoon, and Alannah Gimmerson. I found their remains in a secret basement compartment. I know Lily vouched that you were with her during the murders, but how did the bodies go undiscovered, and which of the men would've known how to access the body dump?"

Maxwell rubbed his hand over his chapped lips. "To answer your first question, I knew something was amiss. I could smell it. The mix of decay and strong perfume. However, I couldn't find the source. After all these years, it finally makes sense."

"You know Quenby House better than anyone, how could you not know?" Evelyn asked.

"The mansion has secrets even I'm only faintly aware of," Maxwell explained. "You can choose not to believe me, but I'm telling the truth."

Evelyn studied the rugged man. Was Lily really covering for him? Evelyn didn't know. He was a hard person to read.

"As for who would've known of the passageways, I cannot

say," Maxwell continued. "None of them should've had that knowledge."

Evelyn processed the information for a moment before saying, "The killer's identity won't matter as much if we can put all five men behind bars, so let me ask you again, Maxwell: are you coming us?"

"My advice for the two of you is to leave Adders."

"That's a no, then?" Evelyn asked, irritated.

"There's nothing I can do that will change the past. Dead is dead." He noticed Evelyn's heavy frown. "I'm sorry to disappoint you."

"Zoey," Evelyn called out into the room. "Show yourself."

Stepping out of the far corner of the room, the goth girl made herself known. She sheepishly hid her hands in her black hoodie's pocket and averted her eyes from Maxwell. "Hey."

Face turning pale, Maxwell staggered back, wobbling against the table. He grabbed the shotgun. With shaking hands, he held the weapon at his hip with the barrel pointed at Zoey.

"It won't do anything," Zoey replied. She turned the back of her head to him, revealing the red gash.

Maxwell bounced his dark eyes between Evelyn, Terrence, and the specter. He tried to speak.

"I know," Zoey said. "I didn't expect to be around this long either."

Maxwell's eyes went wet.

"Maxwell," Evelyn said softly. "This is why it matters that you help. If not for my sake, for theirs."

Suddenly, the cabin was swarmed with all five of the specters. Maxwell's spine hit the closed door. The victims made a semicircle in the room. Evelyn and Terrence stayed still and calm, watching Maxwell's reaction and recalling their own first encounter with the supernatural. Barker puffed his pipe, Alannah put her hands on her shapely hips, Winslow "smiled," and Peter folded his arms behind his back to hide his stump.

"Don't be terrified, darling," Alannah said. "We know you quite well."

Barker smiled to himself. "Yeah, telling him about all those nights you watched him sleep will really calm him down."

Peter took a step forward. Maxwell pressed himself closer against the door. "We would've revealed ourselves years ago, but we never knew how or when."

Maxwell gulped and turned to Evelyn. "Why are they…"

"They can't leave unless their killer is brought to justice," Evelyn explained. "I didn't know it for sure, but after Catherine and Stephen Doyle were taken out, Mary Sullivan was able to pass into the next life."

"Mary was killed at Quenby House?" Maxwell asked.

Zoey smiled sympathetically. "We need your help, Max."

Maxwell lowered the gun. One step at a time, he walked to Zoey, put the weapon on the table, removed his glove, and reached out to touch her face. Zoey didn't move. Maxwell's hand phased through the teenager's cheek. He quickly pulled back his hands a few inches and tried again, and hovered it on her cheek. "I've missed you."

"Me too," Zoey replied. Suddenly, she hugged him. Maxwell stepped back at the unexpected weight. He returned the hug, this time not passing through her ethereal body.

"I'm sorry," he whispered.

After a moment, Maxwell released her and turned back to Evelyn. "Alright."

"You'll come back with us?" Terrence asked.

"Yeah," Maxwell said, seemingly not believing his own voice, "Let me grab my things."

Evelyn sighed deeply. "We'll get you back home and clean you up. Does that truck still run?"

"We're about to find out," Maxwell said.

It took a few minutes, but they got the old Ford running. The phantoms may have vanished from their sight, but Evelyn knew they were stored up inside of her and Terrence. Knowing the way back, Maxwell drove. The rusty truck bounced on uneven ground until it reached a dirt road. Terrence held the shotguns in the backseat. He looked out the window at the dark woods and shuddered.

Evelyn kept her eyes ahead. She knew she had million questions for Maxwell, but at the moment, she didn't know where to start. Though Maxwell was her father, it didn't feel like it. He still seemed like a bearded stranger. *I wonder what he thinks of me?* Evelyn didn't know if she wanted to know the answer.

Apart from the rumble of the engine block, their ride home was quiet and tense. Maxwell scarcely looked at her. Evelyn couldn't fault him because she did the same. In the inky black sky above, the moon was finally full.

They rolled onto Quenby Avenue and turned onto the brick road, passing by the wooden sign that read "The Path." Mossy oaks flanked either side of them and reached their branches overhead. It was a sight that Evelyn had grown accustomed to. Parking beside the minivan, Evelyn and Terrence got out and each clenched a shotgun. Maxwell followed behind him. He stopped in front of Quenby House, eyeing it from base to roof. A million stars backed the light-less, vine-dressed mansion.

"I never thought I'd come back here," he confessed.

Evelyn unlocked the front door. "Welcome home."

Keeping their weapons aimed, Evelyn and Terrence fanned out through the foyer. Maxwell flipped the light switches, watching the chandelier glow to life. He smirked at the trumpeting angels on the domed ceiling.

He examined the oil paintings on the wall and peeked into the hall of portraits. "What happened in there?"

Still aiming her weapon, Evelyn hiked up the left set of stairs in the foyer. "Long story."

Evelyn explored the upstairs hall, opening every door she came across, checking bedrooms and bathrooms for any uninvited guests while Terrence surveyed the downstairs. After a few minutes, they reconvened at the balcony.

"It's all clear," Terrence said.

Evelyn clicked on the weapon's safety and peered down at Maxwell, who seemed to be studying the various paintings. "You can use the master bathroom to shower and shave. Terrence needs to charge his phone anyway before we can get ahold of the cops."

"You aren't going to get some sleep first?" Maxwell asked.

"No," Evelyn replied. "This ends tonight. Don't worry. Terrence and I will keep guard."

Without a word, he walked up the stairs past them and headed into the master bedroom. Evelyn lowered the gun and rubbed her fingers up her hair.

"What a day," Terrence said.

"Tell me about it."

"I don't think Maxwell's fully adapted yet," Terrence said.

"He just saw ghosts. Speaking of which. Zoey, Barker, Winslow. Come out." Evelyn felt a tightening in her chest.

Terrence must've too, because he grimaced and clenched his pecs. The crushing feeling grew stronger and then instantly subsided. Thought they didn't see the phantoms, they knew they had left them.

Evelyn felt even more exhausted than before. Terrence leaned against the railing. "You sure you don't want to wait for tomorrow? As soon as Maxwell gives his confession, it's going to be an all-night affair."

"I know," Evelyn grumbled. "But the longer we wait, the higher the possibility that we are attacked. We need to be ready."

Terrence closed his tired eyes and smiled. "I have to say, it's been an interesting trip if nothing else. We should write a book about couples' therapy."

"We had our rough patches, that's for sure," Evelyn admitted. "Especially with you and Alannah."

"Okay, that's the last time we bring that up," Terrence replied jokingly.

Evelyn cracked a smile and joined him by the railing. "I love you, you know that."

"I know," Terrence replied and grinned at her. "Go wash up. I'll keep guard."

"You sure?" Evelyn asked nervously.

"I got this," Terrence replied confidently and cocked the shotgun, discharging the already loaded bullet out of the chamber. It shot out over the railing. "Oops."

"Nice," Evelyn said sarcastically. "Don't shoot yourself."

"No promises."

Evelyn kissed him on his scruffy cheek, tasting sweaty salt and dirt.

"Ew," she replied and headed for the guest bedroom.

"Ew? *Ew?* Come on now, that's not fair," Terrence said as Evelyn turned into the room, keeping her shotgun with her and smiling to herself. She turned and closed the bathroom door, knowing that their odd sense of humor was the only thing keeping them sane. Or it was adding to their insanity. Evelyn couldn't tell. She stripped down and climbed into the bathtub. Standing, the showerhead sputtered down on her and took a few seconds to warm up. She was grateful for that. The cold water woke her up.

Keeping her eyes closed, she let the water wash away all of the small twigs and crunched leaves from her blonde hair. She wanted to stand here forever, but forced herself to turn the dial off. She lifted one foot over the rim of the bathtub before noticing the man staring at her.

He wore all black and had a featureless white mask. Evelyn's heart skipped a beat. She covered her parts with her hands. "Andrew? What are you doing in here?"

The specter stared at her through his button-sized eye holes. He took a step toward her and then another.

"Back off," Evelyn growled.

Andrew paused, glared at her, and then vanished.

Evelyn waited for a moment before hastily grabbing a towel and drying off. She still felt like he was watching her. Wearing her towel like a dress, Evelyn cracked open the door and peered into the hallway.

"Terrence, can you get me some clothes?" Evelyn glanced at the interior balcony but saw no sign of her husband. "Terrence?"

She turned her gaze to the open master bedroom at the other end of the hall. The door was ajar and lamp light spilled out of it across the hardwood. Apart from the wind battering the windows, Quenby House was deathly quiet. Leaving behind her clump of dirty clothes, Evelyn exited the guest bedroom.

Silently, she held the shotgun and jogged to the master bedroom. The bathroom door was open and the light was off.

"Maxwell?" she called out.

No reply.

Evelyn felt her skin crawl. Instinct told her to look at the peephole in the wallpaper. Without a sound, she approached it. It was pitch black inside. Breath quickening, she slowly leaned in and pressed her face against the wall. Faintly, she could make out the tight corridor and bent nails within. She swiftly pulled away and turned back, expecting to see someone.

Evelyn was the only one in the room.

Closing the door, she quickly threw on some ashen shorts and a black t-shirt, leaving the wet towel on the white hardwood floor.

Clenching the weapon tightly, Evelyn moved through the hall and onto the interior balcony. The foyer was quiet and empty, the front door was closed, and the plastic sheets on the two adjacent windows were intact. That was a relief. "Terrence? Maxwell?"

Evelyn's voice seemed to bounce off the high walls. She hiked down the stairs, keeping the stock of the shotgun against her shoulder. She reached the bottom of the stairs and heard some talking, but their voices were muffled. She followed the sound to the dining room. The door was open an inch. Keeping the gun up high, she pushed it open with her foot.

Terrence sat at the right of the head of the table. Maxwell sat at the head. His gray hair was in a ponytail. His face was clean-shaven, revealing his gaunt cheeks and chapped lips. He wore a blue business suit, white button-up, and no tie. Though rugged, he wasn't a bad-looking man.

Evelyn lowered her gun and glared at Terrence. "What's going on?"

"I'm heating up some barbecue for Maxwell," Terrence explained. "It was only gonna take five minutes and then I was going back up there."

"This is not the time to act stupid," Evelyn reminded him sternly.

Terrence didn't reply.

"When was the last time you ate something?" Maxwell asked.

Evelyn didn't remember. She had felt famished since before she arrived at the cabin. "We shouldn't waste any more time."

"Ten minutes," Maxwell bargained. "I can't remember when I had something other than squirrel and deer."

The microwave dinged.

"Well, now you get to eat more meat," Terrence joked.

Evelyn sighed and sat down. She kept the shotgun propped against the table. "Ten minutes."

Maxwell nodded in affirmation while Terrence got the leftovers.

Similar to the car ride, silence fell over them.

"How long have you known about Zoey and the others?" Maxwell asked, searching for a conversation.

"There were signs since we moved in, but we didn't actually see them until a week or two ago."

"That's something else," Maxwell replied. "To have them here this whole time and never notice them. I must've been so blind."

"Maybe they didn't want to be noticed. It was Mary who reached out to Terrence and me. Through blackouts at first."

"Mary," Maxwell said, grieved by just saying the name. "Nice girl. I should've sought after you instead of treating her as a daughter, and she might still be alive."

Evelyn pursed her lips.

Maxwell leaned in, a red rim about his tired eyes. "I apologize for what happened in the woods during our first encounter," Maxwell said. "When I saw that man and the axe, something came over me. I couldn't stand by."

Evelyn remembered Stephen's head explode with the shotgun blast. It was a memory she did not want to revisit, especially before dinner.

"You must think I'm a madman," Maxwell said

"I believe we're all a little crazy," Evelyn replied.

Maxwell cracked a smile. It was the first time Evelyn had seen it. It was gentle and fatherly, if you could look past the yellow teeth.

Terrence returned with three plates of barbecue, two on one arm and one in his other hand. He served Maxwell, then Evelyn, and then himself. He plopped into his seat and let out a sigh of relief. Without saying a word, they started eating. Awkwardness lingered at first but by the time they cleared their plates, the feeling had lessened. Still, Evelyn didn't know what to make of the "stranger" in her home. *It's not your home. It's his,* she reminded herself.

Maxwell lowered his fork. "I'm proud of both of you."

Terrence and Evelyn glanced at each and then him.

"I don't know anybody who would stick around after all that's happened and all that you've seen."

"It's not always been pleasant," Evelyn replied.

Chewing and staring endlessly, Terrence nodded.

"What's the plan now? Terrence said you live in Detroit. Do you plan to go back?"

"I don't know," Evelyn said honestly. "Wherever I go, it needs to be relaxing."

Maxwell leaned back in his seat. "As a kid, I used to be so proud of this house and its secret hideaways. Then I learned the truth about my parents. That pride quickly turned to shame. You've had a similar experience, no doubt."

Evelyn opened her mouth to speak.

That's when the power cut out.

30

FATHER

One moment, Evelyn could see the dining room, her husband, and her father, and then next it was nothing but blackness. The Quenby House instantly became much more dangerous, ominous and mysterious than it ever had before.

Evelyn waited for her eyes to adjust and reached carefully for her shotgun, making sure to not accidentally pull the trigger. When she got ahold of the firearm, she snuggled it against her shoulder and kept her finger off the trigger.

"Who do you think it is?" Terrence whispered. Evelyn heard him clamber out of his chair.

Maxwell's chair scooted out.

"Where are you going?" Evelyn asked.

"Have you moved anything around since you got here?" Maxwell replied.

"For the most part, no."

Evelyn heard his footsteps go to the side of the room. A drawer opened. Suddenly, a match was lit and illuminated Maxwell's skeletal face and the dark circles under his nearly black eyes. He suddenly froze, and fear caked his hardened expression.

Evelyn turned back, seeing the five phantoms behind her. In the darkness, their leaking blood looked black.

"He's here," Barker whispered.

"Who?" Terrence asked, standing behind his chair.

Zoey replied. "Our killer."

Evelyn tightened her grip around the pump action shotgun. "You've got to stop him," Evelyn told Zoey.

"We can't," the goth replied dreadfully. "Every time we look at him, it feels like we're dying. We can't even see his face."

The others nodded in agreement.

Evelyn gnashed her teeth, frustrated with their response. She bounced her eyes to Terrence. "Where's your phone?"

"Charging in the foyer."

The match died out. Darkness enveloped the room.

Maxwell struck another match. The match top burst to life. The phantoms had vanished, leaving the three of them alone in the large dining room.

"We get the phone, call the cops, and then get to the van," Evelyn stated.

"Simple enough," Maxwell said. "Give me your gun."

The command sent a chill down Evelyn's spine. *He plans to go after the killer.*

"I've been hunting for the last decade," Maxwell explained sternly, his hand still outstretched. "I won't miss."

Reluctant, Evelyn handed him the shotgun in exchange for the matchbox. She glanced back at Terrence.

"I got your back," he said, keeping the gun.

Maxwell stepped ahead of her and opened the door into the stubby hall that linked with the back of the foyer. If not for the phone, Evelyn would've suggested they cut through the kitchen and out the back. Nonetheless, their chances of survival would be much better with a cell phone and the police on their side.

Evelyn followed close behind Maxwell while Terrence walked backwards, keeping the shotgun pointed at their rear flank. The walls had oil paintings of Antebellum-era plantations, cotton fields, and mountain vistas.

Thump.

Evelyn held up her finger and listened. Terrence and Maxwell glanced about the hallway.

Thump.

"It's coming from the walls," Evelyn said quietly.

Fire bit her finger. She shook out the flame that ate away the matchstick.

No one moving, they heard creaking within the wall nearby.

With hands trembling, Evelyn struck another match. It didn't take.

Something clicked nearby.

Evelyn tried the match again.

It lit.

About seven feet away, a three-foot portion of the wall was open like a door. The "door" part was on Evelyn's side, preventing them from seeing into the corridor.

Evelyn's heart pumped rapidly. Terrence's breath quickened.

Gun up and seemingly without fear, Maxwell approached the opening. He slid his back against the opposite wall. In the match light, the sweat on his wrinkled brow reflected in the fire. When he reached the opening in the wall ahead, his finger slid on the trigger.

Evelyn tensed, knowing that if he went into the corridor, he may not come out.

Keeping both hands on the shotgun, Maxwell walked around the "door" and vanished from Evelyn's sight. With Terrence's back against her own, she approached the opening. The floorboards groaned beneath her feet, giving her pause. Her throat dried up. The killer probably could see the match light, but any noise she made still caused her to shudder.

Following Maxwell's trajectory, Evelyn pressed her shoulder against the opposite wall and started around the "door." Standing away from the opening, Evelyn held the match out, trying to illuminate the corridor. The walls within were unpainted wood with a vertical beam flush against the inner walls. The sharp points of dozens of black nails jutted from the walls, but most had been hammered down to prevent anyone from catching on them. Like white hair, clumps of cobwebs dangling from the ceiling. The corridor branched left and right. Evelyn saw no sign of Maxwell.

Footsteps neared down the right side. Terrence swiftly maneuvered in front of Evelyn and took aim with the shotgun. His finger hovered over the trigger. His body quaked.

The footsteps neared, getting closer and closer and closer.

The hairs on Evelyn's neck stood.

A figure rounded the corner. Maxwell.

Terrence released his breath and lowered his firearm as Maxwell stepped out of the tight corridor. His suit and soot-colored hair were covered with dust and cobwebs. His line-etched face was drenched with sweat. "There's no one back there."

The match burnt out.

Evelyn stuck another one, longing for a flashlight or oil lamp. Anything that wouldn't die every twelve seconds.

The little dancing flame came to life, illuminating

Maxwell's face and the tall man, clad in black, wearing a featureless white mask, looming behind him.

"What?" Maxwell asked off Evelyn's and Terrence's disturbed look.

"Andrew," Evelyn said shakily.

As Maxwell went to turn back, the phantom swiftly wrapped his arms around Maxwell's torso and sucked him into the corridor.

"Dad!" Evelyn screamed.

Suddenly, the "door" slammed shut in her face. Her father's muffled scream raced down the hall at sixty miles per hour, and then Quenby House was silent again.

The match quaked in Evelyn's hand. After a second of shock, she rushed to the wall and felt it with her free hand. There was no lever, button, or hidden switch. It seemed it only opened from the other side.

"What the hell was that?" Terrence asked soberly. "I thought Andrew was on our side."

"I don't know, Terrence," Evelyn replied quickly. "But we need to get in there."

"Eve, we stick to the plan."

Evelyn twisted back to him, seeing the terror on her husband's face. "Without my father, there is no plan."

Terrence didn't deny it. "Then let us at least call the cops first. The killer is still in here, remember?"

Evelyn chewed her lip nervously. She nodded in agreement, silently praying the other phantoms would deal with Andrew Doyle.

With one gun and a few matches, they reached the foyer. The windows gave the room a little more light than the inky black hall, but Evelyn still had to rely on the matches for guidance. There were flashlights upstairs and maybe one in the kitchen, but Evelyn didn't want to risk the journey. The phone had a weak light anyway.

Keep the gun stock against his shoulder, Terrence stepped out from under the balcony and aimed upward, keeping an eye out for anyone lurking above. He bounced the barrel between the front door, hall of portraits, and the opposite hall with Evelyn's mural. "Clear," he whispered.

Evelyn stepped out of the shadows and dashed for the sideboard near the right curving stairway. With Terrence pacing about the foyer, constantly aiming the weapon at the many entrances, Evelyn pulled the flip phone from the charger and held down the power button. Terrence's smart phone had fried when the Doyles attacked, and his replacement left something to be desired.

The phone company logo flickered and the phone fully booted up. Evelyn dialed 9-1-1 and held the phone close to her ear.

"*Evelyn,*" a cheery, familiar voice said on the other end of the line.

Terrence glanced back at her. His lips were parted and his eyes were wide. He heard the voice too.

"*Deputy Painter and I decided to direct your calls to us personally. What seems to be the emergency?*" Sheriff Yates asked. "*You aren't still in town, are you? Don't answer that. We're on our way now.*"

Evelyn swiftly hung up. She patted down her short pockets in search of her wallet containing Officer Bailey's personal number. *No no no!* She locked eyes with Terrence. "It's in my jeans upstairs."

"Check the recent calls."

Evelyn did. "It's not saved. Terrence, this phone sucks."

Dread sank Terrence's face.

Evelyn hated herself for not emptying her pockets before leaving the shower. That meant… "The car keys!" Evelyn exclaimed. She darted up the stairs.

"Evelyn!" Terrence shouted as loud as one could when whispering. He chased after his wife.

Using the railing to guide her, Evelyn reached the top of the interior balcony and headed for the nearest bathroom. Her sprint slowed when she noticed the figure silhouetted in the bedroom doorway. The moonlight leaking into the room behind him glistened on the abnormally long and skinny barreled pistol in his hand. Evelyn dropped prone as the pistol made a *pint* sound.

"Terrence, stay back!" Evelyn shouted and rolled to the bathroom as the silhouetted figure slid another lengthy, feather-tailed dart into the pistol's chamber.

Evelyn clambered into the bathroom just as the needle-nose dart punched the bathroom's door frame.

Terrence pressed his back against the wall near the hallway. "Back off or I will shoot you!" he shouted.

Inside the bathroom, Evelyn got on her knees and tossed aside the day's shirt still damp with sweat and grabbed her dirty jeans. She shoved her hands into the pockets. Both back pockets were empty. She tried the front ones. She mouthed a curse and felt her chest tighten, like someone was clenching her heart in a vise grip. *It's not here. Why isn't it here?*

"Make the call, Evelyn!" Terrence shouted.

She desperately crawled around the floor, checking under the sink counter and beneath the door.

Boom!

The shotgun's thunderous boom echoed through the house and deep into Evelyn's ears.

With shaking hands, she quickly lit a match. Everything in the room was as she had left it, unless... *Andrew!*

"Why are you doing this?" Evelyn mumbled, her eyes getting wet. "I've done nothing but help you."

Terrence's shotgun cocked. Evelyn peered out the doorway, no longer seeing the figure silhouetted in the master bedroom. Buckshot peppered the front end of the canopied bed's mattress.

Terrence carefully stepped into the hall.

He examined the long, feather-tailed dart stuck into the railing and then returned his attention to the master bedroom. He proceeded forward.

"Terrence," Evelyn called out from the bathroom. "It's not here. Andrew must've..."

"We stop him ourselves," Terrence said, equally determined and terrified.

He passed by Evelyn, keeping an eye on the various closed doors on either side of the hall. The hardwood groaned beneath his feet. Evelyn stepped out and followed behind him. As they neared the threshold to the bedroom, another scream sounded through the walls.

Evelyn turned to the sealed billiard room door, remembering the passageway through the arcade game cabinet. She had to make a choice. Go after the killer or go after her father. Both options were deadly.

Evelyn grabbed Terrence's sleeve. He stopped walking but didn't turn to face her.

"Maxwell," she whispered into his ear.

Terrence frowned at Evelyn. Evelyn could tell he wanted to try stopping the killer.

Maxwell screamed again.

Terrence's brave facade weakened. He glanced at the billiard room and then back to the door.

"Whatever we do, we do it together," Evelyn said.

Locking his jaw, Terrence headed for the billiard room. They closed the door behind them and opened the arcade cabinet. Evelyn went first, pushing aside a tangle of multicolored wires overhead. She crawled into the uncomfortable wooden floor that brushed her knees. She stood up in the tight passageway, catching the sleeve of her shirt against the point of a small, rusty nail. It tore a small hole when she took a few steps forward into the musty corridor and lit a match. Terrence followed her inside. The shotgun wouldn't function well in the three-foot-wide tunnel.

"Which way?" Terrence asked.

If they went straight, the corridor would take them to the master bedroom. If they went back, it would take her to the two-way mirror bathroom and to the ladder downstairs.

Evelyn pointed ahead and whispered, "We try the bedroom and then double back."

Terrence nodded. "You're in front. You take the gun."

He slid the weapon barrel under her arm far enough for her to take it. If anything came behind her, they would be screwed. Terrence took the matches and illuminated the path ahead. Surefooted, Evelyn moved through the corridor. She gulped down a mouthful of dust and kept her lips closed to prevent from coughing too loudly. They turned a corner and saw the peephole to the bedroom. Evelyn leaned in and squinted through it. The only light in the room streamed from the full moon outside. There was no sign of the killer. Evelyn continued to the dead end.

Maxwell wasn't here. He must be downstairs.

Evelyn and Terrence traded the shotgun and matches. There were about twenty or so matchsticks left. It wouldn't last long. They moved back to the way they came. It seemed to get hotter and dustier the longer they stayed in. After the long hike today, Evelyn felt like she was walking on spikes. The long hours hit Terrence. With slumped shoulders and heavy breathing, he held the shotgun near his waist. His eyelids shut like lazy garage doors. Evelyn punched him. He straightened up, but within moments, he was slumping again.

A match burnt out.

Evelyn lit another. The small glow only gave them roughly four feet of vision before the tunnel seemed to plunge into eternal blackness. They glanced into the small cubby with the double-sided bathroom mirror. Evelyn saw the figure within and grabbed Terrence's shoulder, signaling for him to stop. The killer wore a black form-fitting turtleneck to match his black pants and black leather gloves. A ski mask concealed his identity. By the looks of him, he was in great shape with a stiff posture. He pulled aside the shower curtain and aimed the long dart pistol inside. He glanced at the mirror.

Evelyn felt her heart skip a beat.

Suddenly, the killer punched the glass, sending a spiderweb crack across the mirror.

Terrence and Evelyn covered their mouths, muting their gasps.

The man studied the crack with acute fixation.

Perspiration dampened Evelyn's forehead and trickled down her cheek.

Just when she thought the man was leaving, he turned back to the mirror, made a finger gun with the finger and thumb of his free hand, and pointed at the glass.

He mouthed "pew" and popped the finger gun upward to signify recoil. The mouth of his mask curved upward, hinting at a smile. Without warning, the killer bolted out of the room and then turned to the billiard room.

Evelyn didn't need to say anything. Terrence was already moving swiftly in the opposite direction.

They navigated the tunnel and found the drop-off to the first floor. It was a tight shaft with a few ladder rungs. Another match seared Evelyn's fingers. She winced and shook it out. The wood and dust in the corridor made every match a risky endeavor. Old houses like these were prone to fire and if something started in the tunnel, the smoke would suffocate Evelyn and Terrence if the fire didn't reach them first.

Far behind them, they heard footsteps.

"It's him," Terrence whispered dreadfully.

"Get down there." Evelyn commanded. "Hurry."

Without time to swap out the gun for the matches, Terrence descended into the dark pit. He held the weapon between his thighs, pointing the barrel up high as his shoulders scraped against the sides of the shaft. Evelyn stared out into the blackness before her, expected to take a dart to the eye. Her pessimistic attitude wasn't doing her any favors.

Wood snapped behind her, followed by Terrence's brief shout and then the defining boom of a shotgun.

Evelyn felt the wind break by her head as buckshot blow through the ceiling. She ducked low as wood splinters and dust rained down upon her. The noise ricocheted through the tight corridor and deafened Evelyn to everything but a sharp ringing deep in her ear canal. The lit match fell from her hand and hit the floor, starting a small fire between her feet.

Still trying to process what just happened, Evelyn stomped the fire with her bare foot. She felt the flaming tongues lick her soul, but she suffered through the pain until the small inferno was extinguished. Teary-eyed, she glanced at the corridor ahead of her.

No sign of the killer. No yet. But he was coming, and Evelyn wouldn't be able to hear his footsteps.

She glanced back down the shaft. "Terrence?" she called out. Her own voice sound like it was covered with a tin can.

Her husband mumbled something back, but Evelyn didn't understand it. Feeling the walls were pressing in on her, she started down the shaft.

Terrence kept speaking, but it was like listening to someone talking under underwater.

Evelyn's aching foot found the rung that had snapped away. She extended her leg down farther to the next rung and continued her swift descent. She reached the bottom and bumped into Terrence.

"Evelyn," he said. "Are...okay?"

Evelyn found the match and struck it, casting a light on Terrence's horrified expression. He put both his hands on her cheeks and locked her watery eyes with his own.

"Shi… I… Sorry, Eve…"

"Shut up," Evelyn barked. "We need to keep moving."

Terrence nodded and picked up his shotgun. He hastily started forward. Evelyn lagged behind. It still felt like she was stepping on fire. The pain worsened. She bounced from one wall to the next, like a pinball machine. An unbent nail scraped against the side of her chin, taking off a bit of her skin.

In the darkness up ahead, Evelyn saw a disembodied, featureless white mask.

"Andr… Doyl..," Terrence said.

The ringing in Evelyn's ears grew louder.

Something big flung through the darkness.

Terrence backed up a step, bumping into Evelyn as Maxwell's limp body crashed down before them. He lay face down, with his arm twisted behind his back and no shotgun to speak of.

Evelyn did not have time to mourn.

Andrew Doyle approached.

Terrence aimed the gun.

"It won't do anything," Evelyn told him.

"I kno…" Terrence shouted back, but couldn't bring himself to lower the gun.

Doom crushed Evelyn's spirit knowing that the killer

would be flanking them within moments. Evelyn pressed close to her husband. The match was dying. She had to choose: the condemned phantom or the killer at the rear.

Andrew's walk gained momentum. It seemed like his mask was floating, but Evelyn could feel his stomping rattle the floor.

Together, Evelyn and Terrence watched their death sprinting to them. *Wake up.* Evelyn told herself. *It's all a bad dream.* Deep down though, she knew it was very real.

Andrew was only a few yards away. He stretched out both hands. Terrence backed up into Evelyn. She could feel his every rapid breath. He could feel her. They'd be a couple to the end.

In a blink, Peter Calhoon appeared between the Carrs and Andrew.

"I told you…stay away from her!" Peter shouted and charged the masked phantom. They clashed, locking one another in place as the other four phantoms phased through walls and took ahold of Andrew from all directions. He tried to break free but failed. The phantoms pulled at him continuously. Andrew let out the most horrific scream, one that shook Evelyn to the core, as he was torn apart.

Instantly, the corridor was clear and quiet, apart from the dripping crimson smear splattering the floor, walls, and ceiling where the masked phantom once stood.

Terrence turned back to Evelyn, using his hand to wipe red from his face. Despite the blood, Evelyn would've kissed him. Nonetheless, the killer at their tail seemed to be the more pressing issue.

"Help me get Maxwell up," Evelyn told him.

Terrence handed her back the shotgun and lifted her father's limp body, propping it against his own.

"He's breathing," Terrence said with relief.

Evelyn felt her hearing starting to clear up. She gestured

for Terrence to move forward while she watched the rear flank. *He should be here by now,* Evelyn thought as they stepped over the hot blood spattered and moved farther and farther away from the shaft.

They reached the place where the tunnel branched into the foyer and lounge.

A door opened.

Terrence took a few steps ahead, allowing Evelyn room into a cubby beneath the left set of curving stairs. Shaking the fire off her match, she peered through the peephole, seeing Deputy Painter and Sheriff Yates enter the house. The two plastic sheet windows bowed in at the will of the heavy wind.

"Evelyn!" Yates yelled out, keeping his pistol clasped in both hands and pointed at the floor. "It's the sheriff. Come on out!"

Painter tried the light switch. "Must've blown a fuse."

"Keep your theories to yourself," Yates said. "She's expecting us."

"Ohh, I'm real scared," Painter said sarcastically as he lit up a cigarette. The lighter's flame reflected in his shark-like eyes.

"It never ends," Terrence mumbled.

Evelyn followed him around to a better vantage point of the foyer that allowed her to see the curving sets of stairs, balcony, and a little bit of the domed ceiling.

The deputy and sheriff started toward the stairs.

"Hello, boys," Alannah said from the balcony railing.

Painter and Yates stopped in their tracks and aimed their pistols.

Painter cursed loudly.

Yates raised both brows.

"Her neck!" Painter shouted, jabbing his pistol at her. "Look at her neck!"

"Oh, this?" Alannah said and raised up her chin, giving them a clear view of the slash that yawned with the ounce of blood it pumped down her chest. "It's really nothing, darling."

Painter scurried back and fell to his bottom. Cussing up a storm, he scrambled to his feet and ran for the door. Winslow appeared in front of him and "smiled."

Painter shrieked and dove through the plastic sheeting, vanishing down the road.

Yates didn't move. He bounced his eyes between Alannah and Winslow. "You, uh, Evelyn's friends?"

"Much more than that, darling," Alannah said, going down the stairs with her hips swaying and her fingers walking down the railing.

Winslow nodded many times.

"You might be able to scare my dimwitted partner with your… whatever you call this getup, but I'm the sheriff of this town and I'm going to have to ask you to leave." Yates aimed his gun at Alannah. "Right now."

Alannah clicked her tongue. "Oh, darling. You're way out of your league."

Alannah vanished mid step and appeared inches from Sheriff Yates. His face went stark white as Alannah kissed him on the lips.

After his hands phased through her, Yates took a few steps back, twisted around, and bumped into naked Winslow. Yates stumbled. He looked at the two phantoms, blinked a few times, and then ran out of the door without saying another word.

Evelyn smiled at the victory.

Terrence suddenly grabbed her wrist. Evelyn twisted back and saw the silhouetted figure at the end of the corridor. He aimed the dart pistol.

Terrence opened his mouth to say something when the

dart pistol made a *pint* sound and a feather dart punched Terrence's chest. He gasped and collapsed to the ground, taking Maxwell with him.

Evelyn leveled the shotgun and squeezed the trigger. The muzzle flash revealed the man's ski mask as he dropped a phone. The scattershot blew over his head and punched a hole into a downstairs room. Evelyn readied the pump action when she felt a sharp, stinging sensation in her throat. She glanced down, seeing the long feather dart jutting from her neck. *One shot. All I need.* Her mind told her finger to pull the trigger, but instead her arms dropped the gun. The corridor grew ever darker as the masked man approached. Evelyn's shoulder hit the wall beside her and she slid to her bottom. She fought to keep her arms open, but they disobeyed her. Like curtains, her eyelids shut and the world slid into an abyss.

EVELYN DIDN'T DREAM.

She awoke, strapped in a chair in a cold, square room devoid of any doors and windows. She recognized the brick walls and candle sconces. Little flames danced on a wick standing in a pond of wet wax. White tears dripped down the candlestick. Evelyn knew the room at once: the killer's body dump.

She faced two other chairs, forming a triangle around the dip in the floor. With his head slack on his neck, Maxwell sat to her right. To the left was Terrence in a similar state. Like Evelyn, their wrists and ankles were tied to their chair's arms and legs.

Evelyn heard whistling behind her and metal clanging. She tried to look back but couldn't extend her neck far enough to see the source. A thick orange cable ran down from the corpse chute in the ceiling and ended somewhere behind. It appeared to be an extension cord.

"I used to do this in the hay field out back," the familiar voice said, taking a break from his whistling. "I was honestly a little nervous to kill inside Quenby House. A little stupid now that I think about it. Heck, I was already storing the bodies here, why not kill two birds with one stone? Maybe I didn't want to test fate. Max coming home during the act was a legitimate fear of mine."

"A little part of me knew it was you," Evelyn said. "Why not bring your friends along and make this a public lynching?"

The man paused to think about it. "It didn't work out so well when we tried it on Maxwell. Besides, I wanted spend a little more time with you."

Evelyn pursed her lips. She tried to pull out of her binds. It was very tight rope, coiled around a half-dozen times.

"This is the part where you beg for your life and the lives of your family," the man said, still fiddling with something.

"I'm a realist," Evelyn said. "Groveling is not going to get me anywhere."

The man chuckled softy. "It might. Everyone at work says I'm a softie."

"I'd rather not give you the pleasure," Evelyn said.

Footsteps neared. The man leaned in next to her ear. "You already are."

He pulled back and walked away. "It took me many years to find my method. I'm still searching in some ways, but chasing you through those tunnels… that felt so right. If you could feel my heart right now, you'd know."

If it was anything like her own, Evelyn didn't need to feel it.

Terrence groaned and lifted his head. His groggy eyes met

Evelyn, and suddenly a burst of adrenaline snapped him awake. He tried to pull out of his binds. His chair teeter-tottered. The wood moaned but didn't give. After his burst of strength, he mellowed out. He glanced up at the killer behind him. "Out of all the possibilities, you were the only one I liked."

Dr. Gregory walked around Evelyn and stopped before Terrence. "You weren't a bad guy yourself. Now, let's wake up the father."

With the back of his hand, Dr. Gregory slapped Maxwell's face. He didn't wake. Gregory tried again. This time, Maxwell sat up, grimacing. He took in the situation, and Evelyn saw true fear turn to rage.

"I said that if you ever came back to this house, I'd kill you," Maxwell said and spit on Gregory's black boot.

Gregory smiled at him. "That's what I love about this whole situation. I've been killing here, right under your nose."

"Because I took away Lily?" Maxwell asked.

"Yep," the doctor replied. "Plus you were an easy target. And the house, good lord, I've loved it ever since you showed me the passageways when we were children. I'd sneak in sometimes when you and your parents were asleep and find new nooks and crannies myself. I believe I know it better than you."

"All those years, you could've just killed me," Maxwell said.

"Sure," Gregory said. "But this felt better, knowing you'd be the perfect scapegoat. Rallying the others was so easy. I never needed to show them the bodies to convince them. They already hated you."

"The one you want is me. It's always been me." Maxwell said. "Let them go."

"Come on, man. There has to be some way we can work this out," Terrence begged.

Gregory gave Evelyn an I-told-you-so smile. Strong jawed and with hazel eyes, he was devilishly handsome with silver stripes in his rich brown hair.

He headed back to whatever he was working on.

"Don't walk away from me!" Maxwell said through his teeth and leaned forward in his chair.

"Don't worry, Max. I'm going to kill you first."

Evelyn looked around, waiting for the phantoms to come and rescue them, but Quenby House was quiet. She knew she was on her own. She needed a plan. Something in this room must be able to help her. *Think, Evelyn. Think.*

Her thought was interrupted by a metallic scream behind her.

"Oh," Terrence said, wide eyes on whatever Dr. Gregory held.

Evelyn twisted back to see it but failed.

She heard footsteps and the cord dragging behind her. Gregory stopped in the middle of them and showed off the modified circular saw without a safety guard. Its blade had polished teeth.

"It's the first time I've used one of these." He walked around Maxwell. "I'm going to open the back of your skull with it."

Gregory pressed the power tool's trigger. The blade screamed and blurred as it rotated. "I'm sorry, Evelyn," Maxwell yelled over the noise. "I failed as a father, but I love you."

"I love you too, Dad." Evelyn said, feeling tears trickling down her pale cheeks. She didn't know if her words were truth, but it felt real at the moment.

Gregory hovered the whirling blade an inch from Maxwell's skull. His face sank with a frown and he let go of the trigger. The spinning blade died down.

"Thank God," Terrence mumbled.

Gregory glared at Evelyn. “You know what’s funny? He may not actually be your father. It may be me. I’ll test your DNA after this.”

“You’ll kill me without knowing?” Evelyn taunted. “I thought you were a man of certainties.”

Gregory glared at her for a moment, as if he was a parent thinking up some punishment for his child. “For that snide comment, I’ll kill Terrence first.”

He turned the blade back on and marched to Terrence’s chair.

“No!” Evelyn shouted. “No!!!”

Terrence pulled back his bald head as far as he could from the spinning blade.

“Zoey! Alannah! Barker!” Evelyn yelled up at the corpse chute. “Do something!”

The blade neared Terrence’s skull. “Evelyn!” he shouted.

Evelyn stood up, chair and all, and dived at Gregory. The spinning blade nicked the side of Terrence’s head as Evelyn took Gregory down.

Gregory rose up with the circular saw, readying to bring it down on Evelyn, when Barker appeared. Standing over his head, the seventy-year-old in a sweater vest vomited blood on Gregory’s face. Eyes closed, Gregory swung the blade through Barker’s legs. The deadly power tool phased through the phantom.

“What are you!?” the doctor screamed desperately, being showered by Barker’s blood.

Evelyn rolled over, breaking the back leg of the chair. She saw Zoey. The goth clenched the back of her head with her face screwed up in pain. She knelt down and untied Evelyn’s hand.

“I can’t--it hurts too bad,” Zoey yelled and vanished. With one hand free, Evelyn loosened her other hand. By the time she got her ankles out, Barker had vanished.

Gregory wiped away the blood and saw Evelyn standing before him. He looked down the barrel of the shotgun. He let go of the tool.

"Please," Gregory begged and whimpered. "What's happening?"

"You'll confess to everything or they'll tear you apart." Evelyn said coldly. Behind her, Winslow, Zoey, Peter, Alannah, and Barker stood, keeping the reins on their pain. Gregory stared at them with pure horror. His lip quivered.

"Y-yes," Gregory said, tears streaming down his face. "Anything you want."

The phantoms vanished.

With a hardened expression, Evelyn slammed the shotgun stock into his nose. Unconscious, the doctor toppled over.

Evelyn set the gun aside and rushed to Terrence. She turned his chin up to her face. There was a slash on the side of his head about three inches long and a centimeter deep. "Terrence."

Wincing, he looked her in the eyes. "You're perfect, you know that?"

Evelyn kissed him more passionately than ever before.

After a moment, Maxwell cleared his throat.

Evelyn realized he and Terrence were still bound. Swiftly, she freed the two of them before searching Gregory's body and retrieving her wallet. She pulled out Officer Bailey's number. No service.

Evelyn set her jaw. She turned back to the men. "I need to make a call."

"I was feeling a little stuffy anyway," Terrence said, looking green.

Maxwell nodded in agreement.

Evelyn pressed the right brick, and a five-foot section of the wall opened into a dirt tunnel, reminiscent of a mine.

Leaning on one another, Evelyn, Terrence, and Maxwell shambled down the dirt tunnel.

They reached the busted trap door at the other end and ascended into the shed. Outside, the sun rose, casting scarlet rays over dewy fields and the mighty Quenby House. Birds chirped. The morning breeze blew over them.

"Home sweet home," Maxwell said weakly.

"It's like we never left," Evelyn replied.

Evelyn kept the phone call brief, making sure that Bailey sent someone to search Gregory's home. Good thing, too. The police found nine-year-old Bella Day an hour away from starving to death. The press called her the Adders Trooper, as she had survived five days in Gregory's basement without food.

Dr. Gregory kept his word, confessing to plotting Maxwell Quenby's murder and admitting to killing nearly two dozen people. When he wasn't talking to the police, he was speaking to himself. "I thought I killed you... you did... no... then how am I talking?" Evelyn didn't know if he was possessed or crazy.

As for the rest of them, Maxwell opened a case against Mayor Timberland and Mr. Calhoon. Calhoon apologized to him privately, but Timberland denied everything. It would be a jury who would decide his fate. Deputy Painter was found across the country, drunk in a dive bar and spouting nonsense about sexy ghosts. Yates returned to the sheriff station and locked himself in the holding cell. When questioned why, his only response was "I'm guilty."

After a few days of rest and revival (paid for by the hospital staff in apology for Gregory's actions), Evelyn, Terrence, and Maxwell returned to Quenby House. They paused in the mansion's shadow, taking in its grandeur before stepping into the foyer.

In a line, naked Winslow, sexy Alannah, athletic Peter,

witty Barker, and goth Zoey watched them enter. They stood under the interior balcony and smiled at Evelyn.

"I thought you'd be gone by now," Evelyn said.

"We were waiting for you," Zoey replied.

Barker smiled at what he was about to say. "If Peter had both hands, he would've baked you a cake."

"That's messed up," Peter replied.

"Too soon?" Barker replied and puffed on his pipe.

Alannah looked Terrence up and down. "Darling, may I have one kiss before we part ways?"

Terrence looked at Evelyn and then back at the curvaceous woman. "I'm a married man. Sorry."

Evelyn smiled to herself.

"You're a tease, that's what you are," Alannah replied with her sultry voice.

Winslow revealed the vase of wildflowers he'd been hiding behind his back. He approached and handed it to Evelyn. She accepted. "Thank you."

Winslow nodded and stepped back with the others.

"I guess this is really goodbye," Zoey said sadly.

"It's better this way," Maxwell replied. "You'll get to be with your mother."

Zoey scoffed.

"Give her a chance," Maxwell said. "A lot can change in ten years."

Zoey didn't reply, but everyone knew she'd follow his advice.

Evelyn opened up the front door and stepped aside.

One by one, the phantoms exited. Barker nodded at them. Peter smiled with dimpled cheeks. Alannah blew a kiss. Winslow "smiled," and Zoey waved them goodbye. Hand in hand, they walked down the red brick path. Once they passed by the second oak tree, they faded into dust that the wind swept away.

The flowers in the vase withered. A sense of peace lingered in the house.

Evelyn blinked away her tears and turned to Maxwell. She pulled out the old, rust-spotted key. "This belongs to you."

Maxwell didn't accept it. "You can have it."

"If you're giving it out of guilt--"

"No, it's a present," Maxwell said with a small smile. "Adders has been dead to me a long time ago."

Evelyn pocketed the key.

A Harley Davison motorcycle rumbled up the brick road.

It parked, and Lily got off. She wore a jean jacket with a crooked smile on her face. After a brief moment, Maxwell and her rushed to one another and kissed. When it ended, they held each other's hands and locked eyes. Fluffy clouds surfed over blue skies. Wind ruffled their gray hair.

Lily spoke up, "I wanted to say--"

"There's no need," Maxwell replied. "We're together now. That's all that matters."

Standing between the colonnades, Evelyn and Terrence watched the couple and intertwined their fingers.

"That's sweet," Terrence said.

Evelyn rested her hand on Terrence's broad shoulder. "I can get used to sweet."

"What now?"

"We go home," Evelyn said.

"Detroit?"

"Maybe, or someplace else, but if I have to spend another second in this plantation, I'm going to need to shoot somebody."

Terrence chuckled. "Let me get my cowboy hat."

He kissed Evelyn's temple and rushed inside.

Evelyn grinned and shook her head.

After they packed up the van, the four of them caravanned away from the vine-covered Quenby House. As the van drove by the real estate sign picketed near the front of the red brick path, a figure watched from the mansion's upstairs window. Clad in black, he wore a featureless white mask with crude eye holes the size of buttons.

The End

Made in the USA
Middletown, DE
28 March 2024

52234427R00236